Comanche Sundown

A NOVEL

Also by Jan Reid

The Improbable Rise of Redneck Rock
Deerinwater
Vain Glory
Close Calls
The Bullet Meant for Me
The Hammer: Tom DeLay (with Lou Dubose)
Rio Grande
Layla and Other Assorted Love Songs
Texas Tornado: The Times and Music of Doug Sahm
(with Shawn Sahm)

Comanche Sundown

A NOVEL

by JAN REID

TCU Press / *Fort Worth, Texas*

Copyright © 2010 by Jan Reid
Library of Congress Cataloging-in-Publication Data

Reid, Jan.
Comanche sundown : a novel / Jan Reid.
p. cm.
ISBN 978-0-87565-422-5 (cloth : alk. paper)
ISBN 978-0-87565-427-0 ePub
ISBN 978-0-87565-428-7 Mobi
1. Comanche Indians–Fiction. 2. Freedmen–Fiction.
I. Title.
PS3568.E47655C66 2010
813'.54–dc22

2010004004

TCU Press
P. O. Box 298300
Fort Worth, Texas 76129
817.257.7822
http://www.prs.tcu.edu

To order books: 800.826.8911

Designed by Barbara Mathews Whitehead

For
Bill Hauptman
&
David McCormick
&
Tom Zigal

Contents

>≶<

If the Texans had kept out of my country,
there might have been peace.
But that which you now say we must live on is too small.
The Texans have taken away the places where
the grass grew thickest and the timber was the best.
Had we kept that, we might have done the things you ask.
But it is too late.
The whites have the country that we loved,
and we only wish to wander on the prairie until we die.

Comanche Chief Ten Bears
Medicine Lodge, Kansas, 1867

Prologue

COUP
1869

THE HORSE WAS A TWO-YEAR-OLD dark palomino, sixteen hands tall. Bose Ikard had picked him out first thing in the picket corral, his neck slung way up over the others in the milling and the dust. His eyes were wild but interested in all these creatures yelling, whistling, assaulting them with coils of rope. There weren't many broncs of such promise in the Palo Pinto country, and the peelers wasted no time moving these through. They just concentrated on getting Garland Shelton's herd broken second saddle—ridden twice, terms of the contract—and driven hard to the army buyers at Camp Wichita. Otherwise, they'd next be seen at a high lope in south Kansas.

Knowing better than to ask the price of the palomino, Bose decided to deliver him broken fit for a colonel. Unlike the others, all of whom were white boys in their teens and early twenties, and one of them his half-brother, Bose had reason to value the efforts and institution of the United States Army. The white boys were disenfranchised by what their papas called the War of Northern Aggression. Bose, on the other hand, had been set free by that distant thunder. He had gone up the drovers' trail to New Mexico Territory three times with Oliver Loving, now dead from a Comanche arrow and the gangrene that set in, and his partner Charles Goodnight. Bose was waiting on Goodnight to finish signing powers of attorney for another large herd, and off they'd go again. In the meantime Bose peeled broncs.

He kept up his quota of the lesser stock, of which there were a hundred forty head; the corral behind the Sheltons' house was a dawn-to-dusk frenzy of horse abuse. Two boys would grab and twist the ears of a roped horse and ear him down motionless, jaws clenched and groaning, until a bronc rig could be cinched on him and a rider climbed aboard. The rodeo commenced from there, the first ride of the contracted pair. But Bose took his time with the palomino. The horse spent the better part of two days flopping on his side, roped by the forelegs, and lying with his wind knocked out. Then, with the rope around one fetlock, he decided it was less wear and tear on him to stand still while the human crooned to him and touched his nose and rubbed him all over with a rough gunny sack. Then, with the rope tied to a hind foot and hitched in a loop around his neck, suffered it as the man pulled on, twisted, and put scissors and comb to his cream-colored tail. Until finally the horse was halter-broke and unafraid of the light tarp popped close to his ear in likeness of a windblown slicker. Bose was so patient and steady that by the time he stood up in the stirrup, swung his leg across the cantle, and took a seat, the palomino just trembled. He never even jumped.

Bose didn't use the rough bronc rig they put on the others. He broke this one to the nicely tooled Fort Worth saddle Doctor Milton Ikard had given him, along with peso-studded bridle and saddlebags, which contained his freedom papers. A lot of slave-owners chose to do it that way, once it was apparent the war was lost. It was a point of pride with them; also they desired to get their affairs in order. The younger Milt Ikard, the doctor's acknowledged son, had grown up playing and running with Bose, and Milt thought sure that one day he'd inherit him. Milt sulked over his papa's act for nearly two months. It almost ruined their friendship, Bose thought with a bitter little smile. But Milt got over it, and he was among the youths who peered through the pickets and sat on the crossties with the dew still thick on the grass and the sun just up over the trees. Holstered

2

pistols and a few shotguns were arrayed with their meal bags and canteens along the fence, in case need of them arose. There was a good deal of drawn-out coffee drinking. They were all beat up and bone-sore.

The palomino stood reasonably still as Bose laid the pad snug against his withers and saddled him the second time. The two-year-old stepped around more when Bose put the hackamore on him; the heavy strap leather reins were borrowed from a plowman's harness. "What are you going to do with those reins, Bose?" Elbert Doss called as he got on. "Ride skids behind him, comes a blizzard? Tie him way up in a tree and let him tread water, case it floods?"

Elbert was a slender youth with a shock of auburn hair, long-lashed green eyes, and a dimpled chin—in great demand at dances, his mama's pride and joy. His dad was the Parker County judge, and Elbert aimed to become a lawyer and a politician in his own right, if that were still allowed in the rejoined country. There was talk of him moving back East and going to a college, so the war's bitter reckonings wouldn't set him back so much. Bose guided the horse away from the boys in a leftward circle, then in answer to Elbert whirled the reins like a lariat, close upon the horse's ears and far out in front of his eyes. The palomino shied very little. Bose turned him in a circle, back the other way, and stopped him. He slipped his boots out of the stirrups, drew up his knees, hooked a heel on one of the riggings, knelt with the other leg, and slowly stood up.

"Whoa, now, easy. That's right," he said, playing out the reins and taking light backward steps until finally he stood on the horse's croup.

The palomino cast curious glances and swished his tail but didn't seem to mind. Bose clicked his tongue and the horse took three steps forward. The others turned up the jeering, but he stood quiet and just turned his ears back and forth. Bose took two light steps forward and balanced again on the saddle.

"Almost finished horse," he boasted. "Can you do this, Elbert?"

3

"I can't think of any reason why I would," he answered.

"He wants to go join the circus," Milt Ikard said.

Behind the ranch house clearing was a brushy cliff that leveled off in pasture toward the west. A couple of buzzards lazed out over the valley below. Under some elm trees on the edge of the cliff, half a dozen young Comanches admired the size of the herd, if not its overall quality, and watched the trickster's exhibition on the honey-colored horse. They couldn't do anything about the horses; the sun was too far up, and close by, other raiders in the party were resting and watering another rancher's herd that they had run off during the night. Quanah, the leader of the raid, was tall and long-legged for a Comanche. He wore moccasins, deer-hide leggings, a breechclout, a red bandanna around his throat, and a blood-stained U. S. Army tunic with master sergeant stripes. It was a warm spring day. The wool bluecoat was hot and scratchy, but it was Quanah's signature, his mark of tuibitsi, swaggering youth. The cliff was about a quarter of a mile from the corral, and at that distance Quanah didn't recognize Bose. Quanah just said, "I want the tuh-tahvoa." The dirty whiteass, the nigger.

Quanah could do anything he pleased, as long as he held the others' confidence. A fellow member of the Quohada band named Cold Hawk voiced his concerns politely. "I count nine of them, and we need to get those horses across some rivers."

"You couldn't hit him anyway," said Toes Grown Together. "Too far."

Quanah looked at his best friend and grinned.

"Two geldings and a mule?" he said.

"Done," Toes accepted the wager.

Cold Hawk's misgivings simmered in his eyes.

Quanah stepped quickly to the horses and came back with his .44 Henry repeater. He lay down and, using a rock, first squared the sight on the tuh-tahvoa's shoulders, raised it a couple of inches higher for the distance, and waited for the horse to turn him around broadside again.

"Wind coming up," Toes ragged him.

"Which geldings?" retorted Quanah.

⊱⊰

Bose felt the whispering shock of the first shot well before its crack echoed through the valley. It passed under his chin, two inches from his throat. The second one came in low, bucked by a shoulder annoyed by the miss and rushing to get another bullet off. Bose thought certain he was hit because his feet were thrown out from under him and when he landed on his hip, there was a sharp jag of pain and his right leg went numb. For an instant the others froze in crouches and perched on the fence like crows, then they began to clamber and jump, in the odd way of people trying to will themselves smaller. They picked up speed and dove for cover.

From the dirt where he was sprawled, across the corral Bose watched the young horse stagger hard and pull up limping. He'd stepped on the long reins and hurt himself. The saddle was askew. Bose rolled toward the fence and lay there until he thought there wouldn't be any more shooting, then got to his feet and with much swearing and a limp of his own backed the palomino against the fence. With a lunge he caught one of the reins. Bose talked him down to where he just shuddered, but the eyes were wide and yellow and their expressions were way back in his skull—all the trust was gone.

"You all right?" called Sam Newberry.

"Yeah, but look at my saddle," said Bose.

The bullet had hit just below the horn, ruining good leather and splintering the fork. "Somebody come hold him," he said.

"What are you doing?" said Will Gray.

"He's hurt, I've gotta get the saddle off him."

5

"Fuck that horse!"

They calmed down and milled in an angry circle, ramming bullets in pistols and strapping on holsters. "Indian sons of bitches," fumed Milt Ikard.

"Now," drawled Elbert Doss, the would-be lawyer, "let's don't have any unreasoned massacres. Mighta been stray shots. Or somebody hunting."

"Stray shots!" said Bose. "Five feet and ten seconds apart? Hunting me!"

"Shut up and listen," said Milt.

The wind carried a sound of horses running. Or being run.

Gladiolia Shelton came hurtling from the ranch house, where the dogs were in an uproar. Her husband Garland had taken a wagon to Weatherford that morning. She wore the dungarees and long shirt of a man; during the raid seasons all the women on the farms and ranches did that when their husbands were away, trying to fool any savages who might be close by, watching. Mrs. Shelton threw back her head, turned red, and puffed up like a toad at the least excitement, and she looked explosive now. "We heard the shooting," she said. "Is anybody hurt?"

"No, ma'am," answered Milt. "There might be a damaged horse."

"Me and Emma was out front," she said, trying to catch her breath. "Cleon Hallsey had just rode off. He said there was Comanches all around here last night. They ran off a bunch of horses over on Sanchez Creek. Tried to grab a little girl off one of them Swede farms, but she got away."

"There's your evidence, your honor," Milt said to Elbert.

"Somebody's gonna pay for that saddle," swore Bose.

Quanah didn't actually try to steal that little girl. Due to his family history his attitudes toward that practice were complicated. And he didn't want to have to hang on to the child, share his food with her, watch her at night, and drive horses hard three days, too. They never would have seen her if she hadn't panicked and run out of the brush near a privy where she was hiding with a calico cat. In a cloud of blinking fireflies she took off running one way, the whitish cat bounding and scampering another, her nightshirt and braided blonde hair luminescent in the moonlight. Quanah just rode her down and leaned over to touch the back of her head. He was counting coup lightly.

The act had nothing to do with fighting, but some part of her spirit was lifted nonetheless. When they got back to the Quohada camp on the plains, there would be a dance celebrating their success and enrichment of the band in horses, and Quanah was already rehearsing his half-joking speech conveying the great beauty of this sight and swearing to the powers that the deed was his. "I now give this gift to my brother, Toes Grown Together," he would say. And his friend would have to reply with the same formality. "I now take this deed. Sun, Father, Moon above, and Earth, Mother, witness that it's mine."

Making it harder for Toes to gloat over the wagered geldings and mule and Quanah's inability to kill that nigger.

The Comanches pushed the horses west through sandstone and granite canyons, certain they were being chased and spoiling to be overtaken. Their spare horses were trained to keep the stolen ones bunched close and moving until the herding instinct took over, which freed the raiders to send relays of sentries out in crisscrossing loops, maintaining a watch to the rear. Has No Teeth saw the Texans crossing a creek, some grabbing their saddle horns as the horses drove hard to get up over a loose bank. One of them, the raider saw, was the dirty whiteass, now riding a gray. The Quohada would either lure them into a blind curve of a high-banked creek, or else get them running out in the open till their horses played out. They were riding hard, in search of their own deaths.

Has No Teeth got his name from a boyhood horse race in what

proved to be a prairie dog town.He was thrown head first and tried to eat a rock. His riding skill was no better than fair, and now as he reined his bay around to gallop off and inform the others of their good fortune, horse medicine failed him again. Almost stepped upon, a rattlesnake coiled up and rose out of the grass whirring loud and shrill. The bay horse reared up and bolted, bringing the rider, before he could duck, flush into a low post oak branch. Has No Teeth sat on the ground for a moment, holding his broken nose and watching blood drip through his fingers. Knowing how hard it would be to walk down that particular horse, he got to his feet, wiped his hands on his leggings, raised his war club, and took vengeance on the snake.

Because of that, the youth riding lookout behind the herd failed to see or hear the Texans coming. Consequently Quanah's raiders were the ones surprised. They were coming out of woods in a bluestem meadow when he heard the first gun go off. Coming from two sides, the Texans rammed their horses right through the herd. The sound they made in a fight chilled and rattled Quanah like no Ute or Tonkawa cry. It was an ongoing talking, snarling scream—as hateful and unhinged as the jabber of a rabid wolf. Quanah heard two bullets sing past him. He kicked his blue roan horse in a circle, analyzing the situation with a quick count of the hats. His gaze froze on the black horse-breaker. Quanah recognized him now; he should have killed him the first time he saw him, that day on the Pecos with the drovers and the Leopard Coat Man.

The tuh-tahvoa drove his gray into the side of Toes Grown Together's spotted horse and jarred them hard. Nearly unhorsed, Toes waved backhand at him with his war club and missed clumsily. As he regained his seat and balance and drew back his arm for a better swing, the black cowboy spurred again, leaned in from his saddle with a pistol, and shot Toes in the chest from less than an arm's length. Quanah knew his friend was in mortal trouble from the way he flopped off the horse.

Quanah saw two Texans bearing down on him. With some fast

8

dodging through the mesquites and a fair amount of shame, he got away. Horses were squalling, escaping into the trees; it was a running fight now. Quanah stopped the horse and watched the stampede. They were going to lose half the herd. He counted at least five of the raiders' horses running free—and not one of the saddled Texas horses was running without a rider, that he could see. Ducking branches, he circled his horse back through the trees until he found his friend sitting in the tall grass. Toes' belly, breechclout, and leggings were soaked with blood. He groaned when Quanah tried to help him up. "Just let me sit," he said. "It hurts too much." Then he lay back. His color was all wrong, and his eyes were cloudy.

"Stole those horses," he said.

"Sure did," said Quanah. "Toes, I'm sorry. It's my fault."

"You mean you shot me?" he said, trying to joke.

"We were gone. I never should have made us stop."

"Quanah, someday you're going to be a man with four thousand horses. Pick of wives. Famous war chief, like that other." He referred to Quanah's late father, Nocona.

"I hung us up," Quanah despaired. "We should have been riding. Crossing rivers."

"Reason more to kill that nigger."

"Have his ugly hair."

The little clearing was a soft and pretty place, abloom with spring's blanket of blue and white buffalo clover. There was a nice breeze. "Quanah?" said Toes, after a time.

"Say it."

"Give my mother the geldings," he said. "Brother Runs Far, the mule."

And then his spirit left.

⋙⋘

The disquietude of shooting that Indian had not gone away. Bose had often fantasized the act. But this gun kick still tingled in

9

the bones of his arm; the boom echoed in his mind. What stayed with him most was the dull, conceding change of expression that had come over the Indian's face as he saw there was nothing to be done. It was the broad, flat, unlined face of a boy no older than himself. Without a blink of hesitation Bose shot to kill him. In a heartbeat his sensations went from anger and fright to elation and gloom. Killing wasn't how he was raised, and the odd mix of the aftertaste was not something to be desired, just now. Bullets hissed and rifles cracked all around them. Bose rode his tiring gray horse beside a skinny mare that galloped and wheezed with an arrow in her neck.

The peelers were being herded with the stolen horses they ran among. None of them were down, as far as Bose could see, but they were outnumbered two to one. Outside the range of their shotguns and revolvers, the Indians raced along both sides of the herd, yelling insults and performing stunts. For a time one sat backward on a running paint, thoughtfully firing shots from a lever-action rifle. But the big one with the army tunic and blue roan horse was the one who had their attention. The blood stains and the sergeant stripes afforded the coat a very personal quality. The peelers got these close looks at him because Quanah rode a fast and strong horse, and he looped back and then rode among them as they twisted in their saddles, trying to keep him in sight, and fired off wild blind shots. They were in serious danger of shooting themselves, trying to hit him. His war club was a carpenter's claw hammer: Bose remembered how he'd swung that thing around, the first time he saw him. When Quanah passed a rider he reached out and whopped him on the back or shoulder, then he weaved back through the herd and rejoined the others, who cheered him wildly. Courage medicine.

The third time Bose had a sense that the bluecoat was coming after him personally. Bose slowed his horse a little and reined him tighter. He looked back and saw the Comanche's expression and knew this time he wasn't planning any love tap. Bose decided he had more faith in a riding quirt than his bouncing aim with a pistol.

The bluecoat closed in kneeing his horse left and right, trying to stay in the blind spot. Bose guessed right. As the bluecoat came around on the right, preparing to brain him with that hammer, Bose lashed out with the quirt and got him good across the chest.

Just then three guns went off one right after another, and Bose's horse jumped a little gully, and it was all he could do just to stay on and absorb the gonad hurt. When he got his wits back, the bluecoat was nowhere around.

"Bose!" yelled Milt Ikard, reining his horse alongside.

"What!"

"You see that son of a bitch?"

"Yeah, I see him! Stop shooting at him, if you can't hit him!"

The colors of the grasses and wildflowers went by in a blur, but in fact the horses were slowing almost to a trot. Every breath of wind came out a grunt, and their mouths were smeared with foam.

"We've got to find a place to stop," said Milt.

"Is everybody still with us?"

"Yeah. But the horses are give out."

Bose grabbed his bullet-wrecked saddle horn and pulled himself up in the stirrups, so he could see farther. They were nearing the mouth of a short narrowing canyon that he knew from running mustangs. At the end were successive ledges and boulders with an immense bank of prickly pear. "Quarter mile back in that canyon," he called, "let's get up in the cactus. They can shoot through it, but it'll be hard to see us, and they're not gonna want to come in after us. They've got those horses. I think they'll go on."

The plan moved back through shout and gesture. The Comanches tried to head them off, but the horse breakers discouraged it with pistol fire and kicked the last run out of their horses. When they reached the rocks they jumped off their horses and ran with guns and canteens and bags of cartridge boxes. Bose was seated with his back to a sandstone slab, pulling cactus spines out of his elbow and feeling somewhat hopeful, when Will Gray said, "Oh, no."

A hundred fifty yards from the cactus bank, Elbert Doss had gotten cut off. His horse was overheated or shot, for it walked around unsteadily. Elbert sat stunned as the crowd of Indians grew, all aiming rifles at him. He held his pistol like it was a toy. He had lost his hat, and he looked about thirteen years old. "God damn it, Elbert, ride!" yelled his friend Sam Newberry. "Spur him! Get on through there!"

All around Bose the bronc peelers started laying out all the fire they had. Sidearms, shotguns, hysterical and useless. Several raiders walked around Elbert now, yelling taunts at the ones in the rocks and prickly pear. Nobody had to say anything; finally the shooting just petered out.

A Comanche rode up behind Elbert swinging a lariat and tossed the loop over him. He dragged Elbert off his horse and rode around a bit, tumbling him through stickers and rocks. Then with pokes of arrows, the ones on the ground made him get up. The roper kept his horse backing and sidestepping so that Elbert had to work to stay on his feet. The others would fall dead silent, then with a screech one would lope past him and slice him with the edge of an arrow— his shoulders, his arms, his chest, the backs of his thighs and neck. The arrows must have been stropped like razors, for soon he was drenched red and crying out over and over the only prayer he knew. "Lead us not into temptation," he went on and on, "but deliver us from evil."

This must have gone on ten or fifteen minutes. Through it all, the bluecoat sat on his roan horse well off to the side. Having none of it, Bose thought, but doing nothing to stop it, nor hurry it up. Once when Elbert fell, the roper let him lie still for a minute. Almost gently, the roper backed up his horse and brought Elbert to his feet.

Suddenly the bluecoat kicked his horse into a gallop and bore down on Elbert from behind. His bowstring was pulled back so far that when he let go, the arrow went all the way through Elbert and skittered across the ground. Elbert arched his back and looked down, vaguely moving his hands, like he was trying to button a shirt. The bluecoat let out a whoop and rode on past him, leaning down from his horse to retrieve the arrow. Elbert tottered and wobbled and finally fell.

The Texas boys laid out another sheet of fire when the bluecoat slipped off his horse and walked to Elbert, who was making sounds of dying. The big Comanche stood looking at the cactus bank, ignoring the skip ricochets. He produced a knife and showed it to them. Then he grabbed a fistful of Elbert's auburn hair and raised his head. He made one quick circular slash, then put a heel on Elbert's chest. With both hands and a hard yank, before their eyes that savage scalped him.

The Comanches had been gone about two hours when a ranger party found the bronc peelers. None but Elbert had suffered more than bruises and scrapes. The fight was recorded in the Palo Pinto country as a considerable defeat of the hostile Indians, as a testament to the bravery of the youth in those frontier communities, and, as time went by, as the first confirmed local sighting of the one who came to be known as Quanah Parker. Bose cast it in a different light. It was easy enough to get over killing that Indian. But he dwelled for years on the mother's cries when they rode up in the yard of the biggest house in Weatherford late that day and Sam Newberry had to show her Elbert's body. "Horses!" she shrieked. "You got this done to him over a bunch of horses!"

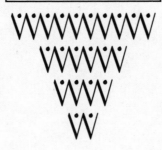

PART I

Dirt Luck

1860-1868

1

I f Bose Ikard had to labor another life, he hoped to be relieved of doctors. At fourteen he was the property of a physician who had given him his name in Noxubee County, Mississippi, while living along a stream called the Tombigbee—all those places as foreign to Bose's ears as the Bight of Biafra, which was where his people probably came from, his owner once told him with a chuckle. Doctor Milton Ikard heard all the talk about the noble rights of Southerners and the cowardly radicals up North but put all the distance he could between himself and that growing trouble; also he disliked a damp climate. He did not give much thought to the family he dragged along. After stops in Shreveport, Louisiana, and Paris, Texas, the doctor trundled his itemized possessions due west in six-mule wagons to the dry skirt of the Comanche plain. Among them was "the orphan Negro Bose." The value he attached to the boy, $1,500, was a damn lie. That was the going rate for prime field hands, and Bose never was that.

The mix of post oak forest and bunchgrass prairie called the Palo Pinto country began with a thickening of the savannah thirty miles west of Fort Worth. It was the far reach of the settled frontier. Nothing lay beyond but six hundred miles of fear, bloodshed, and grief, and it had been that way for a hundred fifty years. Giving up their claim, the Spaniards gave the plains and canyonlands a name in grudging honor of the nomads, Comanchería. Soon after the Ikards' arrival in the Palo Pinto country, a Comanche war axe laid open the chest of Ikard's nine-year-old daughter like a pullet prepared for a frying pan. A single rider, who must have gotten separated from his raiding party, came along wearing black face paint and a cap of wooly buffalo topknot and horns and killed that little girl out in the yard just because he took a mind to. It's a wonder he didn't kill them all. The doctor who ought to have been the child's protector was nowhere around. After that, seeking strength in numbers and patients for his practice, he moved them into the little town of Weatherford.

Bose had the barest memory of coffee-colored arms and a smell perhaps of milk-giving breasts, but the doctor and his wife, a fragile creature Bose was required to call Lady Isabella, told him nothing about his mother except that she died in that place where he was born. Gave him not even a name. Bose was light-skinned, and the older and taller he got, the more obvious it became that he was the son of the man who owned him. The doctor could joke about his ancestors but he didn't feel obliged to say one word to him about that. Not one, not ever. The son of a bitch.

That little girl, his half-sister, was named Euphrasia, after a plant and flower that was a parasite of grass, of which there was a great wealth in the Palo Pinto country. Eyebright, the plant was also called. Dust those scales and crush me some eyebright, boy. Yes sir, right to it. Doctor Ikard believed his Euphrasia tea would, in the most careful and minute dilution, cure cataracts and most all kinds of visual impairment caused by airborne miasma. Bose's father was not observed to shed one tear for his dead child Euphrasia or question his decision to transport his family to the most dangerous place on that portion of the earth. He complicated the life of one of Bose's half-brothers by naming him William Susan. Boy named Sue. He knew his mind and slept like a baby.

The kind of medicine he practiced was a craze in those years. Doctor Ikard was little more than a horse lineament salesman, but people in that town honored him as a man of great learning. He might have had it chiseled on his tombstone, for he said it so often: "Always remember, the enemy is the morbid derangement of the organism." He was talking about illness, not Comanches.

While Bose's half-brother, Milt the younger, roamed the country with a gang of pals on horses that they ran near to death for the devil of it, in those years Bose got no closer to the back of a moving horse than the seat of a buggy. Doctor Ikard made him a house slave and his medical assistant. Often abed, Lady Isabella would summon him with rings of a silver bell and calls of "Where is that nigger?" Better days were spent in the laboratory behind the little clinic on Main Street, where Bose made dust of the potions that would leave minute suggestive traces in carefully boiled water. There were virtues to that kind of bondage. He picked no cotton and bore no scars of a whip. He slept in a feather bed, he learned to read and do the figuring required by the doctor's concoctions, and he took to it. He was Lady Isabella's kitchen help, her cook, and in her gayer states of mind she taught him a few keys and chords of a piano. But Bose's hands were calloused and his arms and shoulders were hard from all the work with a shovel. The homeopath was just another sawbones, when it came down to it. Bose cleaned up after enough amputations, threw enough sawdust on the clinic's blood-soaked floor, buried enough arms and legs to muster an army of cripples. Sometimes the amputees in his dreams had no heads.

Bose:

IN THOSE LAST WEEKS of 1860, white folks in Weatherford decided their most urgent concern was not the election of Abraham Lincoln as president. A party of Comanches and Kiowas led by the dreaded chief Nocona set fire to another outlying town just north of us, Jacksboro, and left bodies and ashes on almost every ranch and farm as they swept south and west through the Palo Pinto country. People huddled in misery beside the walls of the little army fort on the Brazos River, Camp Cooper, whose dragoons were suspect because most of them were Irish, and it was rumored that all the forts built for settlers' protection from the Indians would soon be closed. If it could happen to Jacksboro, it could happen to us. And out in the countryside, the danger was much worse.

Elihu and Martha Sherman were known but not treasured by the community because they were Anabaptists. Pacifists, they ploughed their fields with oxen, figuring that horses or mules just incited the Indians. The Shermans had no guns at all; they trapped what meat they had to eat. When the war party showed up on their farm, Mrs. Sherman was eight months pregnant. With smiles and gestures to hurry along, the Indians put the settlers walking, with Mr. Sherman smoking a pipe and two little children holding on his hands. Raiders then ganged Mrs. Sherman, yanked her drawers down, took turns raping her, shot arrows into her belly, and scalped her. Nocona jammed a war lance in her when they finally stood away. Mrs. Sherman lived on for two days in Doctor Ikard's clinic, screaming in labor and telling her story with no god's mercy or rest. Her baby was born dead, and then she died. I dug both of their graves—Mr. Sherman had some Anabaptist objection to their being buried together.

A hard rain had set in before the Indians were through killing, and because of all the stolen horses the volunteer rangers had no difficulty tracking them far up on the plains. But they were too outnumbered to attack, so they turned back, bitter that the soldiers at Camp Cooper hadn't saddled up to help. It was the worst Christmas Weatherford had known. Men stood out on Main Street preaching. The one who scared me most wasn't properly a preacher. John Baylor was the publisher of the only newspaper on the Texas frontier. He called it *The White Man* and wrote all its stories to suit that label. Baylor had wild eyes, a bald head, and a long black beard. I came out of the clinic's alley entrance one dreary day and heard the man bellowing out in the street. I peeked between the clapboard buildings and observed Baylor flinging one hand about, an open Bible in the other. Rain poured off his head, and hanging limp from buildings behind him were black flags flown in protest of Lincoln's election. "Nahum the Elkoshite," he roared, "begins his Old Testament prophecy with a cry for vengeance against Nineveh. 'The Lord is slow to anger, and great in power, and will not at all acquit the wicked; the Lord hath his way in the whirlwind and in the storm, and the clouds are the dust of his feet. The mountains quake at him, and the hills melt, and the earth is burned at his presence, yea, the world, and all that dwell therein.'"

People in the Palo Pinto country were hot to get even, all right, but they were also at a loss to explain. The Comanches and Kiowas raided in the warm months, almost never in the winter, and they had never come in such numbers. At Camp Cooper the army's Tonkawa scouts, who hated Comanches above all human beings and studied them intently, said it was a vengeance raid, for certain. What were they avenging? All you had to do was read the paper.

To the privy out behind the clinic I happened to carry sheets of *The White Man* that John Baylor had published in November, weeks before the raid. The biggest story was the one he made up about Old Hicks the Texas Ranger and his serial search for Cynthia Ann Parker, the white girl who had been carried off as a child a quarter of a century ago, and then when she was near forgotten, army explorers and traders came back from the plains with the story that she had married and borne babies of the evil Comanche Nocona. No, that can't be true! Speak up, Old Hicks, you Indian killer.

Here's how he imagined rescuing the princess of the plains and routing the coward Indians. "When we reached the other shore and obtained our footing on the rocks, we turned again to see them. We pointed our pistols, and they dipped under the water, and held their white shields above their heads. We renewed our retreat, and were very quickly out of reach of their arrows, and answered their demon howls with jeers of laughter. The Indians stood in the stream and on the bank, watching for some moments, while we deliberately loaded our rifles and plucked out the arrows they had shot into our clothes and limbs. These we threw back toward them with scornful gestures; when we again raised our rifles, they dived like a flock of chicks when a hawk swoops into their midst.

"We could distinguish traces of the woman's flight for some distance up the ravine. I could not help observing the delicate smallness of the wet foot marks she left upon the stones. Poor creature!

Her naked feet had been cut in the rapid flight by those cruel stones. When we overtook them, she held quite a large round pebble in her small hand, which was upraised above her head, as if in the act of hurling it in our faces. I could see an expression of unutterable defiance in the flashing of her black eyes, and in the compression of her thin, delicate lips. I saw at once, from the fairness of her complexion, not only that she was not an Indian, but felt this must be the face which had so possessed my imagination. She was a clear brunette, and evidently a foreigner. I signed as eloquently as I could, for I knew how to express friendliness and good will by gestures. She paid no attention to that but sharply asked me, 'Qui êtes-vous?'

"I speak French very lamely, and answered, as best I could, 'Texans, Americans, et amis.' She smiled brightly, threw away her pebble, and came bounding down the rocks to join us. That night her small, graceful head lay upon my shoulder, while the long and silken hair streamed in a raven cloud to my feet. She was very lightly clothed, since the only garment of civilization her captors had left her was something like a chemise of fine linen, which left her breast exposed and her arms naked; she, however, had thrown over her shoulders, as a cape, the brightly rosetted skin of an ocelot, but this had now fallen off. From an instinct of delicacy that does not desert even rude backwoods men, I swept her long hair as the most appropriate veil over her bosom. It was sacred to me!"

Texas Ranger that could speak French! John Baylor must have had to take a walk, he got himself so aroused. Elsewhere in the paper, he praised the lynching of a suspected abolitionist and swore that slaves were sneaking off at night and poisoning wells. Then he turned to his column "Late Indian News."

"We learn from a gentleman just in from Camp Cooper, who belongs to Captain Barry's Company of Rangers, that on the 1st, while some ten or twelve of the Company were on scout at or about the head of the Pease River, they discovered a party of Indians, some twenty in number, and immediately gave them chase, and overwhelming them, killed and scalped four, and wounded several others. Two of the white men were wounded in the fight, but not badly. One of the men, a citizen of Weatherford, was shot in the neck with an arrow. We say, three cheers for Captain Barry and his brave Company. We wish them success and hope them many more scalps."

Gentlemen must have scalped the wrong ones.

When two companies of rangers and the two platoons of cavalry came back from their punishment raid of a camp on the Pease River, a young captain named Sul Ross bragged to anyone who'd listen that he had personally killed Nocona, and with them was a dirty and melancholy woman and a dark-haired little girl who was about two years old. The winners of that battle kept it secret as long as they could. Few people in Weatherford had any idea they were Cynthia Ann Parker and her daughter.

Parker County, where they were now captive, was named for one of the patriarchs of her Texas family—a prominent politician in his day, a friend of Sam Houston, the governor. She had some siblings, one of them a brother who'd been a captive and after his ransom had chosen to lose himself in Mexico. But both parents were dead. Rumors blew through Weatherford like northers; one had it that Nocona was much alive and terribly angry. Some who knew about the pair began to grumble that the Parker clan was taking its sweet time getting that killer's wife and daughter out of a badly shaken and endangered town. The rangers soon lost interest in standing guard over them, and the soldiers retreated to Camp Cooper. What were people to do? Why, call the doctor.

Doctor Ikard's clinic didn't have any rooms with locks on the doors, so they took the woman and her baby to his house on Main Street—to the distress of Lady Isabella. She'd be shrieking behind one door, the white Comanche was throwing herself against the woodwork behind another, and Bose was caught between them in the hall.

Bose's father gave up trying to examine the squaw or her baby. The woman took one look at his stethoscope and believed he either wanted to strangle her or steal the heartbeat of her child. "They appear to be in good health, considering," the doctor said. It fell to some women from the Parker County Baptist Church to get the squaw changed from greasy deerskin into a loose-fitting dress, but Bose gathered from the whispers that she'd have nothing to do with undergarments. Proper shoes hurt her feet; they had to let her keep her moccasins. Bose was jailer and manservant to the most famous woman in all of Texas. She didn't know how to use a chamber pot.

Governor Sam Houston himself sent up a senior ranger from Austin. A quiet man with a long nose and even-tempered eyes, Major Byrne knew the plains sign language and spoke a fair amount of Comanche. But he approached his task warily. With the old politician Isaac Parker in the doctor's parlor were three of his kinfolks, one of them a woman. There were also eight local men—the Parker County judge, a banker, a lawyer, and the Baptist preacher—and their wives. Doctor Ikard motioned at Bose to come along as they crowded upstairs for the interrogation. "God knows what we're in for," the doctor muttered to him. "Strokes, heart attacks. People jumping out windows. I need somebody in there with me who won't just gawk."

They had the look of a mob inside that small bedroom—the woman's eyes started walling. The ranger placed himself on a chair facing Cynthia Ann and made signs and talked a long while before she said anything. She just rocked in her chair and clutched her baby. Finally she spoke so haltingly and quietly that Byrne had to turn his head and lean closer to make it out. The ranger listened through it all then sat there staring at her with his hands clasped on his knees.

"Good God, man, what is it?" said the patriarch, Isaac Parker.

The man drew breath and let it out. "She remembers when she was carried off by the Indians. She has a clear recollection of her ma and pa and brother. Her pa was the first one killed. Her mother told her to take her brother and run. But everything else about that day is just a blank."

"God is merciful," said the Parker woman.

"She says she's sorry for what the Comanches did, but they must have had a reason. She says they're good people who took her in and raised her, and she's one of them now. The way they live is all she's ever known. She says she's got a husband and two sons—"

"That there's wrong, she ain't got no husband," snapped one of the Parkers. "Sul Ross done seen to that."

The ranger looked him over. "I wouldn't know about that, sir. I'm just telling you what she told me. She says her boys need her. She's begging you to let her go."

⧓

After the interview Cynthia Ann and her baby continued to be locked in the house where Bose was a slave. Word had to get out now who she was and where she was, and when it did, Bose took on another job—zookeeper. People stood out in the street yelling for a look at her. Doctor Ikard retired to the clinic every day. Lady Isabella went on raving. Milt Junior just cleared out. Bose was the only one available to go to the door when John Baylor and *The White Man* came calling.

The newspaperman's eyes blazed like a furnace. Baylor had been a U.S. Indian agent on the Brazos when reservation Comanches were made to live out there, before they were all evicted to the Indian Territory. He was fired, Bose heard his father say, under suspicion of stealing way more than was commonly allowed. See the man coming, you eased across the street.

Bose had no such option now, but as ordered, he kept the door chain locked. "Boy, get your master," Baylor said. "I am here to interview Cynthia Ann Parker."

"The doctor's not here, sir. You'll find him at his clinic, I believe."

"Well, where is she?"

"Who's that, sir?"

"Cynthia Ann Parker."

Bose tried to look confused. "Don't know if I know her, sir."

Baylor glared. "Boy, it is common knowledge that a white woman stolen as a child by the Comanches is lodged in this house. And I aim to announce that news to the world. The public demands it."

"Ohhh, you mean that woman they brought back from the Indian scrap."

Baylor's lip curled. "I asked you where she is."

"Locked up in a room, sir, with her little girl."

"Bring me the missus of the house."

"Lady's in her room, sir. Feeling poorly."

It wasn't fair of Doctor Ikard, doing this to him.

"Their son, then," said Baylor.

"He's gone, too. I wouldn't know where."

The man was so amazed that he gripped his pistol. "You're the only one here seeing that no harm comes to the lady of this house?"

"None of 'em been gone long," Bose said in haste.

"Open that door."

"No, sir. I can't do it."

"Nigger," he bellowed.

"Please, sir. I'd do it if it was up to me—but Doctor Ikard gave me orders not to let anyone see her, unless he's here. Please go see him at the clinic. Shouldn't be no trouble at all."

John Baylor cursed him roundly and stomped off. Bose closed the door and put his head against it. In a moment the clock in the parlor chimed, and in weariness he trudged toward the kitchen. The only food he'd been able to get the captive woman to taste was chicken and dumplings. In the stove Bose stirred the coals of the breakfast fire, added a log, and warmed up a pot of the dumplings he'd made two days before.

He spooned the doughy mess into a bowl, picked out bones and gristle, and put it on a tray with a spoon, a wedge of cornbread, a cup of sweet milk, and the key to the bedroom door.

Bose always knocked before he put the key in the lock. Stone silence was always the reply. He opened it and found the woman sitting in the hardwood chair. The little girl was lying on her back on the bed, staring at the ceiling and chewing on a corner of the sheet. The air in the room was thick, rank, and ammoniac; there was nothing Bose could do about it—just wait for their kin to come for them, then open the windows and scrub it all down. Burn the bedclothes, most likely.

"Hello, again," said Bose. "Brought you something to eat."

They said the Parker woman was about thirty-five, but she looked older. She had a lot of gray in her hair, her skin was lined from all the sun, and back in her mouth you could see gaps of a few missing teeth. The first day her eyes had been wild with terror, and at first they seemed to light on Bose with particular contempt. Wasn't going to hurt his feelings, nor win her favors either. Since then her gaze had registered curiosity and a pathetic kind of grasping. You favored the hand that treated you best.

"Your family's coming," Bose told her. "Gonna take you and that child home where you belong. Heard Doctor Ikard say so this morning." She didn't understand a word he said, of course—only recognized the tone of his voice.

Trying not to spill the milk, Bose had neglected to put the key and its ring in his pocket. As he set the tray on the bed, her hand shot out and snatched the key. She didn't try to go anywhere—just sat there holding it. That interested him. Bose had never used it on this side of the door, and he doubted they had many locks and keys in Comanche tipis.

Was it a memory stirring, or did she just think it through?

"Now what are you gonna do with that?" he said. "Except get me in trouble."

She raised on him a look of pleading. Bose strode to the window, gestured at the street below, and tried to make her understand. "You think you're just gonna walk down the stairs and out the door? Say hidy to the crowd? Steal the first horse? How you gonna keep that baby warm? They took your buffalo robe away. It's fifteen degrees out there."

Lady, they ain't ever going to turn you loose.

At last she gave him back the key. He sat on the bed and played with the foot of her baby. It stared at him and laughed. "Yeah, I'm a funny one. They all say that." The woman wiped her face with her sleeve and said something to him in Comanche. Bose picked up the bowl of dumplings and offered it to her. She held the bowl close to her chin and scooped dough and chicken to her mouth.

Bose touched her on the arm. "Wait, ma'am. Look here. Somebody's gonna make you learn this anyway."

He showed her the utensil and how you held it. Then dipped it in the dumplings and persuaded her to let him give her that bite. The touch of metal to her teeth startled her. Then he got her to try it. Cynthia Ann Parker, remembering how to eat with a spoon.

Downstairs the front door opened; men clomped their boots, muddying a rug and knocking off snow. "Bose?" Doctor Ikard called.

"Up here, sir," he answered, quickly on his feet.

The woman stared at him, frightened again. He waved his hands, trying to reassure her, but as the boots ascended the stairs, she dumped the bowl and the dumplings on the floor and grabbed her child. The door opened, and Bose's owner looked in with a worried frown.

Pencil and tablet at the ready, *The White Man's* publisher marched in the room with Isaac Parker's son Jacob. Cynthia Ann took one look at John Baylor, who was aghast at the stink, and she knocked over the chair, hissed him like a cat.

2

THE HOME GUARD RANGERS STYLED themselves "the Frontier Regiment" and "Minute Men," that last one encouraged by the legislature. About a hundred fifty plainsmen, cowboys, bail jumpers, Bible thumpers, a few Tonkawas, and two cavalry platoons had gone out on that punitive expedition. But it was no good sign that the riders from the Palo Pinto country answered to three different commands. Cornering a bunch of Comanches required discipline, and this bunch had none. Charlie Goodnight, then twenty-four, was an outrider and scout. Way this one was going, it would be a miracle, he thought, if very many of them made it home alive.

Still, he wanted to push the matter. Goodnight was a banty rooster in an ocelot skin vest. He wanted Indians to remember and fear him, by God. His legs were so short and his feet so small that he had to pay premium money to keep saddled and shod. Not that Charlie needed much stirrup—he had learned to ride bareback and near to being a man had won fair wages as an eighty-four-pound jockey. A good tracker, he noticed things like bugs that scratched and wormed up a hoof print only at night—narrowing the time in which the horse could have laid the track. Horses, he'd learned, never would stray and graze more than a mile from a source of water. If you found some horses that looked about half-Indian, half-stolen, then you knew an Indian camp was close by, and like as not, their outriders already knew about you. Charlie's disposition was to keep going, just one more ridge or river, at the point others lost their nerve and turned back. It was the only way to catch Indians like this new firebrand Nocona. The Comanches who laid waste to the Brazos River valley would run to the end of the earth if they didn't like the looks of a fight. But God help you if you blundered in one where they knew all the advantages lay with them.

Like most of the riders who lived in the Palo Pinto country, Goodnight answered to a crusty fellow named Jack Cureton, who had settled along Keechi Creek after going bust in the California gold rush. Sent out by no less than Governor Sam Houston was a ranging company led by another captain, a thin and feisty braggart named Sul Ross. Then there was Sergeant Spangler, in command of the troopers. With all the talk of secession, Charlie couldn't much blame the soldiers for wanting to stay close to their barracks and bunks. He rather wished these had. Spangler kept the Texans' nerves on edge by leading the dragoons in frequent Irish glees. The three separate commands pitched camp where they chose, rose and rode out at different hours, and cut back and forth across each other's trails. And all of them ignored the silence of the Tonkawa guides, who were terrified to be this deep in Comanche country.

Goodnight had worked up a pretty good case of worry himself. Their horses were weak from drinking the gyp water that ran in every stream, and the four pyramid hills that rose up to the north filled him with an eerie and uncommon dread. Charlie was weak and sick himself. A case of measles had laid him low enough to call out Dr. Milton Ikard, who assured him it wasn't smallpox but warned him to expect some loss of hearing. Charlie's face was just scabbing and scaling over from the welts.

Mexicans called these plains tierra de no entrada. Land of no entry. A strong north wind was whipping grass all around, and Charlie's eyes fell on something small, curious, and black. He kicked his boots out of the stirrups, raised his right leg, and scooted, landing poised, reins in his hand. Some folks were impressed when they saw him do his jockey's trick; others thought he was a showy little fart. He moved the mare around and raised a Bible from the grass. Charlie stared at the woods, wary of letting them go unwatched for an instant, but with the grain heads beating against his pants he opened the book and read the first page.

This Holy Bible
Was Presented to
Martha May Sherman
By Her Loving Husband
Elihu Will Sherman
On April 27, 1852

And on through the Family Record of parents born, married, and passed away, and two children born, with pages for their marriages and grandchildren she'd never know. The last pages, blank, just said Deaths.

Goodnight stood for a moment watching the windswept grass. Maintaining sight contact between Cureton and him was a Parker County stockman named Bill Mosely. He rode up as Charlie put his hands on the horn and cantle and gave a small hop to get his boot to the stirrup. When Charlie was astride the horse he handed Mosely the Bible.

Mosely studied it in bafflement. "I've seen five or six books thrown out on the ground. They trying to learn how to read?"

"They use the pages to pack their shields. Pack 'em in and they'll stop or deflect a bullet, they claim. But look there what it says on the gift page. Read that, then go show it to Captain Jack. Tell him to pass it round."

⟩⟨

They were advancing with care and quiet when Sul Ross's column jumped up a deer, and the sudden thrash and movement sent them all into the bottom at a pell-mell gallop. Ducking branches, Charlie heard curses and cracks of limb all around him; some rider got knocked off and dragged. The first he saw of the camp was a wood rack hung with dark strips of drying meat. Then they were into the tipis amid spooked horses, snarling dogs, Comanche women screaming at their young, rangers and dragoons yowling strings of words that made no sense at all, a babel of tongues percussed by the blunt pops of the long handguns.

The rangers later blamed any excess on the soldiers, but everybody got a piece of them. Charlie saw horses collide and men reach around another to get a blind shot in. Half-grown boys, squaws, babies, and a very old man who lurched toward them shouting were just piled up in a heap.

Charlie came around a lodge on his mare and a woman jumped out cursing him in Spanish. He saw enough of her to think she was good-looking, but then she jammed a skinning knife deep in his horse's throat. Charlie cursed and shot her in the chest. Her moccasins flew up and she flopped on her back in the ash of a cooking fire. Her mouth hung slack and worked for air but her eyes stayed on him.

That killing haunted him the rest of his days. She was a Mexican woman who'd taken up their ways, no older than he was. The .44 slug had gone through her. He heard a hiss and sizzle of her blood against the coals. "Lo siento," he apologized. The wife that Nocona called Ruins a Travois closed her eyes, and he put a bullet through her head.

Charlie's hand was shaking so violently he could barely get his Colt holstered. He pulled out the knife and flung it. Since he had little voice in the matter, and it was a quick way to find out if she was hurt badly and he was soon to be afoot, Charlie let the mare run. Beyond the camp he steered her into the chase of Indians who had gotten to their horses and were whipping them and splashing up the winding creek, trying to reach hills above the camp.

Among them were a man of fighting age who had a lance and a little boy who rode behind him with arms tight around his waist. The Comanche saw that he was being overtaken. He swept an arm back, pried the boy loose, and threw him. With a yelp the boy bounced, rolled, and came up on his hands and knees, pondering horses that were running straight at him. Somehow he wasn't trampled. Several Colts boomed then, and Charlie saw that the Comanche was down. He was shot just above the shoulder blade, and the slug had come out through his chest. As the rangers circled him, he jabbed at them with the lance and started warbling a tune that gave Charlie gooseflesh—he'd never heard a death song before. The lance identified him as someone of rank. His name was No-bah. He disliked hunting because a buffalo bull had once turned a horse upside down with him sitting on it. But he was respected on the raids, so he was a sub-chief in charge of the hunting camp. He turned away from the rangers and clung to a mesquite.

"What's he doing?" Sul Ross asked.

"Likely praying," Charlie replied.

"Does he understand Spanish?" said Ross.

"They say most do."

"Tell him to surrender. He doesn't have to die." The captain saw in him a prize. A captured chief!

"Man's bleeding to death, it looks like," observed Charlie, with a shrug, but he relayed the message to the Comanche. No-bah listened and answered, then turned back to the tree and went on with his singing. Charlie reported, "He says he'll surrender when he dies, and it won't be to you."

"Well, somebody shoot him," a ranger shouted.

"You got a trigger," another replied.

"For the love of god," Sul Ross said, and spurred forward to do it himself. He raised his pistol theatrically and brought the barrel down. Quick as a cat the Comanche grabbed a quirt hanging from his arm and gave it a yank; Ross flew off and dug a mouthful of river bottom sand. He jumped to his feet spitting and blinded, and he'd lost his hold on his gun.

Charlie and the other rangers stopped their horses and sat back to watch. Ross was a lithe and slender man with a stylish mustache. He seemed to fancy himself as a pugilist, for he stepped about the

Indian with his hands and forearms raised. The Comanche's singing had begun to gargle. Ross gave a shoulder feint inward but hung back, eyes on that ugly lance. The head of it was two feet long.

"Kick him, Sul," someone recommended.

"Offer him tobacco."

"Throw me a gun!" cried the harried captain.

Someone did, and the pitched Colt went through his hands.

Charlie would grow to despise Sul Ross when he ran for governor of Texas as a great Indian fighter and won the election, but Ross proved his mettle that day. With a shout of temper Ross drove under the lance, and they went spinning and tripping through the sand, the chief singing all the while. Ross got him down, pinned him with a knee, and wrestled the lance away from him. He gripped it with both hands, hesitated, and then plunged it deep in the Indian's chest.

His audience offered quiet whistles of respect. Sul stood up panting and rested with his hands on his knees. He looked like he was about to puke. "Killed him," he said.

"All but the foot," came the wisecrack. The right one quivered still.

"My horse," said Ross. The rangers exchanged glances, and then one came forward leading the horse and offered the captain his reins. Ross found his hat, which he stuck on his head, then a long gun, which he inspected and jammed in his holster. Another ranger dismounted and searched the kicked-about sand for the Colt he had tossed into the fray. All the shooting had died down. The Battle of the Pease River appeared to be over. But then Ross raised a victor's cry and put more spurs to his horse.

Goodnight:

UPSTREAM WE HEARD BRUSH CRACKING, and off we tore in chase of one huddled in a buffalo robe. The Comanche rode a fast gray gelding with no halter or bridle. With nothing but knees and a fistful of mane, that Indian steered it down through the riverbed, weaving from sand to the water, giving anyone close a cold spray. Damn, those devils could ride. One of our fellows went sailing over the head of his horse, arms flailing. A ranger named Tom Kelliher got close enough to the rider to fling off a shot, then a vine grabbed his arm and like to tore his shoulder out of the socket. Kelliher groaned and swayed in the saddle, hanging on the horn.

The Indian threw back looks as the gray horse tired. I was close behind Ross when they went up a steep rise and found the way blocked by a bramble of saplings and vine. Seeing Ross was about to shoot, the rider yanked the gray's head around and hoisted a bundle from the buffalo robe.

"Americano! Americano! Americano!" the Comanche screamed.

The bareback rider was a woman. And the bundle was a baby.

With our jaws hanging loose, Ross and I jogged our horses around the gray. The woman was stocky and filthy with dried buffalo blood and gore. I started trying to calm her down. At a loss for anything else to offer, I held out my canteen. She stared at my face and started shrieking, holding the child far away.

Finally it dawned on me that she thought my measle scabs were smallpox. I was waving my hands like a fool. "No, no, I'm not infectious. It's not the pox! The doctor said so."

I felt ridiculous and hideous. Because the gray didn't have a halter, we were having a hard time bringing it still. In the swirl I got a close look at her. For just a second our gazes met and held.

"My god, Ross," I said. "This woman's white."

He circled around her until he saw her eyes, too. About that time Tom Kelliher caught up; his shoulder was on fire, and neither he nor his horse were used to that rough and tumble a ride. He wrestled his Colt free of his belt and prepared to be done with her. Ross yelled: "Tom, this is a captive white woman! Indians don't have blue eyes!"

"Hell, no!" Kelliher yelled back. "Hell, no! Damn that squaw! If I have to worry with her anymore, I'm going to shoot her."

The hesitation gave me a chance to get a lariat over the gray's head. Tom reined close to the woman and yanked the buffalo robe off her shoulders. Her hair was cut short in grieving for someone, and where it was hacked off we could see the blond. "Is she armed?" Tom yelled.

"With a cradleboard, you idiot," I yelled back.

"Enough of that, both of you," snapped Ross.

We jogged back through the bottom and riverbed to the camp, where bodies were flung all about. Ross rode his horse right over them. We all did. Feeling my mare shudder, I pulled the gray along. I saw that woman I'd shot lying dead on the campfire. The coals had burned off the back of her buckskin dress. I wasn't fond of that smell at all.

The rangers and dragoons had circled up a group of women, children, and old-timers, who raised a terrible wail. Whites and Tonks were on the ground scalping. The Indian dogs dashed in this chaos snarling, so the guns continued to pop. Two rangers argued over the scalp of No-bah. The woman observed all of this and held a little girl close against her chest. Ross ordered a couple of rangers to get her off the horse. She came off the gray in an agile leap and spun away from them, holding the baby up and away like they meant to eat it. She grieved over the chief, No-bah, then fell to her knees at the sight of the Mexican woman Charlie had shot. She wiped her face and screamed at them. "Nokoni!" In her heartbreak she swept her arm at the dead and seemed to point at the scalped chief. "Uakatz Nokoni!" The dead were all Nokoni, the band to which her children were born.

Ross suddenly spurred his horse in a joyous circle. "Hear that, boys? Hear that? The one I killed is the son of a bitch *Nocona*."

He gave a whoop and shook a fist in celebration. Meanwhile, the Tonk scouts were cutting off hands, intending to cook a fine pot of enemy soup. Charlie and Cureton bellowed at them to get to scouting. Expressions sullen, they rode out at a wary trot. Ross's chest was swelled up so much he all but floated from the saddle. He had gone from recovering a white captive to certainty he had killed the most hated Comanche of them all. What a glorious report he would have to write to Sam Houston!

Charlie reined up beside him and said, "Captain, we'd better not dally round and tarry."

Ross didn't want anyone spoiling his moment. "You and Captain Cureton run ahead," he said darkly. "Prepare for us a homecoming."

"You're a damn fool, Ross. There's Comanches all around here."

"If you were in my command I'd have you flogged for insubordination. You just go on, like I said."

The Tonks soon came back at a high lope, their expressions grim. In urgent signs and pidgin Tonkawa, English, and Spanish they indicated that in close proximity there were about five hundred well-armed Comanches. The Texans herded the women and children away from the camp and spent the rest of that day longing for nightfall in a brushy canyon of the Pease.

Charlie kept pacing, staring at the squaw. They tied her against a tree to keep her from running off, and then put her child back in her arms. The white squaw cried and beat her head against the bark like all life on earth was lost. Men crowded around her and the girl, speaking English. Her eyes looked like her skull was about to explode. One man said, "What's that woman's name they carry on about all the time in *The White Man?*"

"I use that paper to wipe my ass," another ranger snorted.

A third one scoffed, "Why, that massacre was twenty-odd years ago."

When night came they let all the Indians go except the woman and her baby. Though Sul Ross had taken charge of her, on Cureton's orders Charlie stayed close and helped guard her. At Camp Cooper, the major in command looked at the pair and shook his head. This was all he needed. Some officers' wives and a slave woman took the squaw into a tent and tried to get her dressed in decent clothing. In a moment she shot through the flap throwing camisole and petticoat in the air and at a trot struggled back into her filthy smock, a slave woman running after her.

The soldier listened again to the story about some farmers on the Navasota River who left the gate of their stockade open when they went out to work their fields. One of the rangers said that Isaac Parker, a member of that clan, now lived over at Birdville, near Fort Worth. Parker County was named for him, and he had been elected to the legislature until he got tired of the privilege. The major sent a courier asking him to come.

The old man told the rider that he hadn't been at the compound during the raid on the Navasota, but he was indeed a member of the Parker family. He said he had close kin who lost their lives at Fort Parker. The old man asked a relative to accompany him; the man answered that no man in his right mind would go out in that Indian country. Bring that pair over to Birdville, where they were safe, if they were so important. So Isaac Parker arrived at Camp Cooper with just the neighbor.

Charlie watched the interrogation. The soldiers and Texans were getting nowhere; when the Tonks were brought in the room, she and the scouts flung insults at each other, sneering. She clung to her child and shook like some demon was trying to escape her.

"I just don't see how it could be," Parker said.

"Say the name," Charlie suggested.

The old man looked at him, then to his neighbor. "If this is my niece, God help us, her name is Cynthia Ann."

The woman shot to her feet. She beat her breast with two hard thumps, and a wild cry escaped her. "Me, Cyntee Ann! Me, Cyntee Ann!"

3

N OCONA AND HIS SONS Quanah and Peanut had been up in canyons of the Little Red River hunting when the Texans raged through their camp. All the fighting men were. In prime coat the buffalo were moving south, driven by the cold weather, and the hunters were waiting for them in gullies and ravines as they came bucking and skidding down their ancestral trails off the flat and treeless grassland, the llano. The Texans didn't even hit the Nokoni's main camp, which they'd moved near a spring on the Iron River, the Wichita. They'd left lodges in sight of the Medicine Mounds in preparation of the butchering and hide-preparing of the women. By the time the Texans rode out to avenge Nocona's great raid of the cabins and settlements in the valley of the Brazos, it was a camp full of women, children, and old people. Those rangers had no reason to be so proud.

The Medicine Mounds are four cone-shaped hills that rise from the plains north of the river the Comanche bands called Acunacup Neovit, the Buffalo Tongue. The Texans named it the Pease, in honor of a governor. On a sunny day the hills stood out as blue and vivid as pine-forest peaks. That was the first sign of the Medicine Mounds' power—they grew with distance, looked bigger than they were. They played tricks on the eyes. In the long ago, the story went, a medicine man had a beautiful daughter dying of a fever. He tried to suck worms and evil spirits out of her. He chanted and smoked but could tell she was slipping away. But then the spirts told him to climb up on the flat cap rock summit of the northernmost hill, the Big Mound. He prayed and fasted, and one day up there he thought he heard her singing in his lodge. The father rushed down from the Mound, splashed across the river, and he found her sleeping. He thought she'd died; that was the reason he heard her. But when he put his hand on her face, it was cool—the spirits had broken the fever.

Though the sheltered bend of the river overlooked by the Medicine Mounds was their favorite place on earth, after the massacre the Nokoni never camped there again. They lost belief in the Medicine Mounds. All across the plains the horse tribes had whiteasses on the run. The Texans' line of settlement reeled back a whole day's ride to the outskirts of their big town Fort Worth. Yet the Nokoni, who for a time had been the people's most feared band, played no part in those triumphs. Warriors drifted off in disgust and joined more virile bands.

The Nokoni went north, fearing more raids by the rangers, and more than most years, that winter was the Time When Babies Cry for Food. All at once Peanut got so weak he had to be helped on his horse. The burning in him was hot to the hand; he cried out from his dreams and soaked his robes with floods of sweat. An old man named Jaybird Pesters was the band's puhakut, the shaman. He filled Nocona's lodge with smoke of otter fur and red berry cedar, put powdered sneezeweed up Peanut's nose and made him drink teas of water iris and prairie root, the vomit medicine. Nothing helped. The boy lay under the robes gasping, his teeth chattering, and could barely raise his head. He couldn't keep any food down. His eyes fluttered, and he didn't seem to recognize his father or his brother. The shaman peered at the boy's mouth, and with his thumbs suddenly pried it open. "Tásia!" the old man shrieked, and he ran away. Horses squalled and dogs yapped in the confusion and haste. The whole band fled.

The people had an expression: dirt luck. On one winter day Nocona's number one wife and baby daughter disappeared from the hunting camp, and his number two wife was killed by a Texan in the slaughter. Months later his younger son died from smallpox. In mourning he killed half his two thousand horses—made Quanah help him—and gave the rest away. The people expected to provide for those like him in their devastation and grief, but likewise expected them, at some point, to rise up and start their lives over. Nocona never did. The rage and love of war that had driven him throughout his grown life was used up, spent. He grew distracted, reflective, and some would say lazy—he wouldn't even hunt for himself. Quanah had to bring him his meat. He put on a paunch.

Quanah:

THE UTES, A MEAN mountain people we mostly stayed away from, were the ones who started everybody calling us Comanches. Their word meant Anybody Who Wants to Fight Me All the Time. A Ute later told me that it used to mean all their enemies, not just us. But that slur was fair enough—we had warred against just about every people we came across, even our friends the Kiowas. The real name of our many roving bands was Numina, Our People. But I never could be entirely one of us. I was half-white, half-Texan, and everyone knew it. The band of my rearing was the Nokoni, Those Who Move Often and Turn Back. We moved so often and far that people thought we were very numerous. Our lodges were strewn all over the plains, canyons, and rock hills that we hunted, and we knew many places where the earth leaked hot springs. I would soak in them until I looked like a raisin. I was trying to boil my blood clean.

People put sounds to my father's name many ways, especially our enemies. It meant He Who Travels Alone and Returns. He's gone from us now, and in the belief of Our People I'm not supposed to say his name—or that of anyone else of ours who has passed on from this world. But I believe that's a lonely burden to inflict on your life. Nocona was a hard man to please; to him I was always a Boy of His Mother. Her name was Naduah, Keeps Warm with Us, though the Texans inflicted her with another one. I was her firstborn, come to being at the foot of the small, pretty range of mountains that were Our People's when we desired them but were honored by the Kiowas as their ancients' birthplace, and they were named for the Wichitas. The Wichita Mountains were a fearsome place, too, especially for children. Somewhere back in their many caves, our mothers told us, lurked the worst of all creatures, the Big Cannibal Owl. He ate bad children at night.

Mother said my birth lodge was put up over a hummock of yellow spring flowers that smelled like spiced honey, and she tried to concentrate on them as she clung to the birthing frame and I hunched my way to a soft landing, with the help of the midwives. She named me Quanah, Fragrant. That's just how she was. She named my little brother Peanut, for an orb that grew on roots and that she remembered from her childhood as a tasty snack. I wouldn't know; when I got the chance I could never make myself eat one. Later she named our sister Topsannah, Prairie Flower. Dad pestered me to think of a more manly name, something about eagles. But, shit, Our People had about as many eagle names as we had bears. I stuck to Quanah, I guess to irritate him. But you can imagine how it was for me. Boys were jealous of me for having a father whose name put the assholes of Texans in an angry and frightened clench. At the same time those boys scorned me for having white blood. They would pelt me with rocks and sing, "Fraagrant, Fraagrant, your blood stinks!"

I couldn't help but turn out a fighter.

Dad's younger wife was named Ruins a Travois. Chore wife, we called ones like her, but he sure enjoyed the nighttime part of the chores. She was a Mexican he had carried back from some raid across the Río Grande. She was good-looking and also hot-blooded, judging from the cries coming out of her lodge when he joined her. Ruins a Travois was more like an older sister to me than a stepmother. She taught me my good Spanish, a useful thing to know. Mother was the opposite way. Despite her fondness for trifles like peanuts, she didn't want us to know a word of the ugly tongue spoken by her onetime Texas kin. She must have feared what it might set off in her.

One spring before Dad brought back Ruins a Travois from the raid in the Sierra Madres, we were on our way to Santa Fe. Mother was so pregnant with Peanut that Dad and I had to put our hands on her butt and shove her up on her horse. Yet she rode for days without complaint. We saw a train of wagons accompanied by soldiers. Some of them rode over to give us a look. Mother went rigid as bois d'arc, she was so scared, and Dad braced for a fight if they recognized her as a white woman. The soldiers waved their hands around in signs that made no sense to anybody, and they left us a cloth sack filled with white powder. The sack split when the soldier dumped it on the ground. Mother yelled at me to stay away. "Poison!" But before she could grab me I jabbed my finger at the powder and put it in my mouth. Pasinapihnab—my first taste of sugar. It was my first notion that whiteasses could do something right.

Then we were up in high cool air and rode through a mountain pass into Santa Fe. In the long ago we'd made a treaty with those Mexicans in the mountains of the upper Río Grande. It didn't apply to all the other Mexicans we raided and plundered every summer. The only treaty we had with Texans was with odd farmers who spent their lives dragging up rocks to build short fences and called themselves Germans. Mother waddled through the Santa Fe markets trading wolf and bobcat skins for bunches of tobacco leaves, peppers of many colors, and kinds of fruit I'd never seen before. We camped outside town, and one day Dad rode back carrying a big green gourd. He handed it down to me from his horse, and it went right through my hands, it was so heavy. I started bawling. For once Dad just laughed and put his arm around my shoulders. The gourd was split in a couple of places. He tapped it on the ground, and with a ripping sound broke it open. The flesh inside was bright red, my first watermelon. A couple of mornings later, Mother walked away from our camp toward some other lodges, and when she came back she was carrying my little brother Peanut. That was the happiest time of my life.

⊱⊰

Quanah was growing into the tallest man in the Nokoni band, and he was putting on the chest and shoulders to go with his height. But he had never counted coup, never made the fabled ride to Mexico, never put an arrow or bullet in a man. And he knew he had no medicine. All he'd done was steal a few horses from a hungry band of Navajos. It got boring, just killing buffalo.

But he and his dad talked like they never had before. In some ways Quanah liked him more. One summer afternoon the band was camped along the Canadian River, trailing the herd north. When the sun was low Quanah and Nocona went off with gunnysacks to harvest some plums, especially ripe and tasty along that river. In the bottom they ate the red fruit until their hands and chests were so sticky from juice that they had to go bathe in the river. They reclined on the hard sand bed, letting the shallow stream run past their chins.

"Dad," said Quanah.

"Jaa."

"Tell me about my mother."

Nocona gave him a sidelong glance.

"When she was young. Before we were born."

"Well, you know she was white."

"All white?"

Nocona chuckled. "Didn't you ever look at her?"

"Well, sure. But I thought, you know, somewhere back in the line . . ."

"Near enough to count for your gray eyes."

"Whose gray eyes?" Quanah said quickly.

Nocona rolled and put his face down, blew bubbles in his mirth. "Oh, son," he said when he surfaced. "Never even looked in a mirror."

"Yeah, I do. Have. They don't look gray to me." Quanah felt this strangeness rush through him. "How did she get to be one of us?"

"I stole her."

"Twice you married someone you stole?"

"Sure, I did. Warrior's right." Nocona's eyes brimmed with tears at the thought of his other captive who made a wife, Ruins a Travois. After a moment he went on about the one called Naduah. "I was about your age. We were way off east, almost to the pines. I've heard it said the Texans claim we were looking for just anybody to raid. That's not how it happened. We were after one man in particular. Caddos who live around there had been helping us steal horses from the Texans. One of the men in the fort had been paying us for the horses, and he gave us money that was inked to look right but was no good. We rode up to those people with a white flag, telling them to bring that one out. Another fellow started talking us down, throwing us looks. The big talker got killed, one thing led to another. I saw this little girl running. She had on a blue dress, and she had the prettiest yellow hair." Nocona shrugged. "So I gave her a ride on my horse."

"How come I never knew that?"

"Your mother. She just didn't want to talk about it. And people respected that. I carried her to the peace chief, and he gave her to some people who weren't able to have children. They adopted her, loved her. Later on she married me, and when people realized how she felt, they didn't talk about it either. The Texans offered a big ransom for her. Whiteass traders and bluecoats used to come around, suspicious she was the one all those Texans were looking for. One time a couple of traders and their scouts almost got themselves killed, trying to buy her. Know what they offered for her? Twelve mules and some cooking pots. Her parents told the peace chief they'd die before they gave her up. People were all stirred up, and the peace chief told those traders they'd better get moving. Last time it happened, we were on this same river, but way out west. You were a little boy, and the next one was just born. Peace chief got me to let her talk to some soldiers and traders. One of them asked her if she wasn't tired of being a *slave*. She let them get way far gone before she told me that. Your mother was always the first one wanting to move—be as far away from whites as she could."

Quanah rested on his elbows and watched the current move his breechclout. "Why can't we find them?"

"Son," he cried out, "don't you think I've tried? I went to the bluecoats' Fort Cobb and found the translator who was there when the Texans captured and carried them off. He turned white as a wagon tarp, thought I was there to kill him. I told him, 'No, no, I'm just asking for your help. She never made war on anybody.' But no one knows where they are. Those people named Parker have swallowed them up."

Quanah said, "Didn't she have a brother?"

"Why? You think *he* could find them?"

Quanah flinched but almost welcomed the flash of his old temper. "No, that's not what I mean. I'm just curious about him."

"Mexico," Nocona said, after a moment. "That was his name, Mexico. We carried him off that same raid. He was younger than she was, and he got traded around some, to Kiowa Apaches, then Kotsoteka. The Kotsoteka took the ransom money because they hadn't seen his promise, and some Delawares carried him back to his Texan family. Hated being back there, of course. When he was getting near grown, his white mother sent him out here to try to talk his sister into coming back. Rode all that way alone, and he found us. She and I were married by then, couldn't get enough of each other. So he just got down off his horse and stayed.

"Mexico made a mean little son of a bitch, and he liked it so much down there, somebody just named him that. He was along that time I stole the one who made the other wife. Mexico stole one, too, but she wasn't no little girl. Hoo! That one was a full-grown looker. But on the way back he started getting sick. Just like your brother. Chills, throwing up, so sore he could hardly ride. Then his face broke out, and the tongue spots showed up. Scared us all to death. There wasn't anything to do but leave him. We did let him

46

keep the looker. Mexico always held that against us, and I'm sorry. But he would have done the same thing.

"About three years after that, he and the looker just rode up one day, come to see his sister. Scared us and shamed us all over again. He was pocked up pretty bad, but other than that, he was fine. We put on a dance for them. Asked him what happened, he said he was given back his life by some Kickapoo that live down there. Mexico said they put him in a whiteass bathtub and pissed on him. Called people all around, women even, to get enough bladders, pissed it full, and then built a fire under him. Then they broke up some little pepper pods in the piss that stung like he'd fallen in a log of scorpions. But he got well! Talk about medicine."

Watching his father tell that story, Quanah thought he might make it to the council of elders and smoke lodge after all.

"Do you know where he is?"

"Probably still down there," said Nocona. "Still married to that Mexican looker. There's a place at the foot of the sierras where the Kickapoo and some black Indians called Seminoles live. It's close to a town called Múzquiz. I bet you'd find Mexico and that wife living close to them. Be careful if you go looking, though. Our People been known to raid down there. Some people might get it in their minds to kill you."

Eventually they got around to picking some more plums. Quanah lost interest first and wandered back toward the lodges, shouldering his sack. When the sun went down he wanted to be with his sweetheart, Weckeah. Nocona approved of that pairing, if Quanah could get up enough horses to make her father a fair offer. Weckeah was the daughter of Nocona's best friend, Yellow Bear. In the riverbed Nocona watched his son silhouetted against the coral dusk and thought, I bet those girls get him off and wallow him good. A covey of quail whistled nearby in the grass, then the nighthawks piped up, and a big growing moon jumped up over the sand. The loveliness of that sight filled Nocona with such nostalgia and sadness that he had to cry a little. Turned into an old woman, he sniffed. Getting where you enjoy it.

4

Nocona sat in the Canadian bottom until the moon was high. He'd missed his supper: a woman in the camp had offered, but he had little appetite these days. As he started back a sound of bulk erupted from a cottonwood, and a Great-Horned Owl, dark as charcoal in the light, beat its heavy wings to stay aloft and crossed the river right in front of him—gave him a terrible fright. Owl could be many things. Then he heard the footsteps behind him. He walked faster, and the footsteps broke into a trot.

"Oh, no," said Nocona. Turn around, he told himself. Confront it. But the courage that could save him was a dry well in his heart. He dropped the sack of plums and started running. Overtaken easily, he raised his arms, lurched and staggered from the clouts upside his head. They fell like the war club of a Ute.

In the camp Quanah had given his plums to Weckeah's mother, Nice Enough to Eat. She asked him to join them for a supper of marrow and mesquite bean mush. "How's your dad?" Yellow Bear inquired after his friend's health.

"Seems better," said Quanah.

He stayed until it grew awkward then announced he had to go check on his horses—he owned all of two head. Every time Quanah started to build a herd, his dad renewed his mourning and gave them away. Weckeah dawdled until what she was doing was also apparent, then walked to a sand bar around the river's bend. They were sitting on the sand watching the moon and kissing when they saw his father stooped and wading upstream.

Quanah reached him first, then jumped back like he'd stepped on a snake. Nocona's hands were gnarled, an elbow was pressed hard against his hip, and his neck and jaws were wrenched far around. He was drooling.

Weckeah gasped and said, "Twisted face!"

Quanah picked him up on his shoulder while she ran for help. In the lodge Nocona lay on his back, breathing all right, but unable to stand or speak; a nervous and morbid crowd had gathered outside. Yellow Bear brought in a torch so they could see—it was not a pretty sight. Nocona's face was drawn from his right hairline to his left jaw. Water poured from eyelids that were stretched blood red. He raised his hand like the glare bothered him. The puhakut Jaybird Pesters walked in carrying a protective fan of crow feathers. "Bedeyai," he quickly diagnosed.

Ghost done it.

You had to be an Indian to suffer the dread disease twisted face, or ghost sickness. Time would come when white folk tried to convince Quanah it was just something they called a stroke. Quanah knew better, and all the rest of his days, he worried and wondered if he could get it.

Some people had mild cases. They hated what it did to their looks, how it beat their hands into useless claws, but after a while the ghost let go, and they got back almost normal. But Quanah could tell that Nocona was in bad trouble. Parts of him were useless, and all at once the people seemed to believe that if they didn't break camp right that minute, they'd never see another buffalo. Quanah was having to father his own dad. But a woman who'd known Nocona all his life was supposed to hire the medicine man. Every woman in the band who fit the description turned him down—even Nice Enough to Eat.

"Will you do it?" Quanah asked Weckeah.

"*Can* I?" she said, rattled.

"I guess he'll tell you if you can't."

"What do I say? I'm scared of that old man."

"Just ask him if he'll treat my father. Tell him I'll pay what I can."

"Which is what?"

"Well, everything we have. I've got to have a horse to ride, and so does Dad, if he lives. That leaves one mare and a mule."

Jaybird Pesters consented to treat the fallen warrior. When the shaman came, Quanah had a pipe of tobacco waiting. He offered it first to his dad, who was supposed to sit up and smoke. Nocona eyed the pipe with an agitated sigh. Quanah couldn't bear to look at him. He smoked four times in his father's behalf, then handed the pipe to Jaybird Pesters. The puhakut drew his four puffs thoughtfully. "I don't believe it's sorcery."

"Good," said Quanah.

"It'd be better if he could tell me his troubles. He may have brought this on himself. He thinks too much of the dead. You hear comment."

"Well, lately he's had too much dead."

The old man gave him a quick hard look. "First you bathe him. Do it west of camp, in the river. I'll be back in the morning."

"He's clean. He was just bathed today."

Anger and offense glinted in the bloodshot eyes. "Do it."

Quanah wasn't trying to be insolent; he just had trouble believing that was going to help. He laid his dad on a travois and pulled it gently along. Nocona kicked and twitched in a frail rage.

Jaybird Pesters tried. The first morning he made Nocona choke down buttons of peyote, which made him sick but left him dreamy of gaze, the pain relieved. The shaman came three times a day. He hung crow feathers from the tent flap and fanned Nocona with cedar and pecan smoke to chase off ghosts. He brewed more peyote tea, filled his mouth with it, spilled it into his hands, and bathed Nocona's rigid and tormented face. Another time he walked around the patient and spat the tea on him in fine sprays. The puhakut prayed

50

till his hands shook then chewed up grayroot and rained that on him, too. It made a mess, and Quanah could tell that Nocona didn't appreciate it. Quanah sat with his dad, sometimes with Weckeah. "Why don't you talk to him?" she said one night.

"Why don't you?" he snapped at her. She ducked her eyes, hurt.

"I don't know what to say," Quanah answered. "I can't just carry on. I hear him hearing it. Embarrassed by it. Feeling sorry for it. He was a proud man."

Nocona wasn't doing any better, but out of respect the old man kept coming back, brewing and spewing his peyote tea. He made a thick paint out of water, buffalo tallow, and powdered red clay. He coated Nocona's face, arms, and legs with it and said wearily, "Leave it on two days."

Late that night, lying beside Nocona in the lodge, Quanah could feel him trying to speak, but there was only the vexed sound of his breathing. It came to Quanah that they might have had their last conversation. He had been mourning a man who was still pulling air. He reached out for his dad's hand—something he hadn't done in years—and from the claw there was a slight answering squeeze. Quanah at last fell asleep, and when a horse woke him at sunrise he looked over and saw that under the cracked red plaster, Nocona's face was relaxed again. Close to a smile. Quanah sat up and almost gave a shout of celebration and relief. But it was no miracle. His dad was gone.

They put him down in the Antelope Hills. Such days had become the fixture of the Nokoni's lives: a last horseback ride for the bound and parted one, women riding beside and holding it upright, family and friends coming along behind, until they reached the burial cave and pile of rocks and brush. Draped over the body's binding was the elaborate feathered bonnet possessed only by the main war chiefs. But only a few people joined Nocona's procession, and when Quanah and Weckeah returned, they found that the band had broken camp—left the tipis of Quanah and his dad standing in the rubble.

Quanah just left them there. He didn't have a pack animal to drag a travois, if he had felt like tearing them down. Paying Jaybird Pesters had taken all but the horse he rode, and honoring the tradition, he shot his father's horses after they put him down. Quanah trailed after the Nokoni, not knowing what else to do, and overtook them the next day. A few walked out to meet his horse. Weckeah's mother gripped his hand and filled his sack with fresh pemmican. But no one offered him shelter or asked him to come to their fires.

At a distance from the camp Weckeah sat beside him, arms around her legs, as he scorched a marmot. He hadn't skinned it thoroughly, and the pieces of hide stunk. Stronger than that was the air of general upset. He heard it in the pitch of voices and saw it in the way that people walked.

"What's going on?" he asked her.

"The council is meeting."

"Making your dad war chief?"

"He seems to think they will."

Quanah nodded to keep from shrugging. "He deserves it."

The council also debated whether to change the name of the band. Nokoni sounded too much like Nocona—saying a dead man's name aloud violated a taboo. So they talked about calling themselves Detsanawyeka. Why, that was an insult name. Other bands called them that. Stragglers Who Make Bad Camps.

And Yellow Bear came out of the council stunned and humiliated. The elders passed over him and named Horse Back war chief, though he was a man of mediocre reputation and much talk of peace.

Whatever road these people were on, they made it clear to Quanah that he was bad medicine to them now. He had hoped they would include him when they returned to the warring trails. But there were no warring trails, and they didn't even ask him to join the hunts; even Yellow Bear fell quiet and wary when Quanah came around. One day Quanah walked out in the prairie with a bow and short arrows and flushed a wild turkey. It stuck out its neck like a pecker grown hard and flew across a ravine with a lot of commotion but not much speed. He made a good shot with his arrow and walked back to camp holding the turkey by its feet. Two teams of girls were playing shinny, chasing and batting a deerskin ball with crook sticks. A crowd had gathered, and he stopped to watch. The boys heckling the girls were the age Peanut would have been—Quanah knew a couple of them as his brother's friends. One called out a taunt. "Whiteass!"

"Come here," he called, though they were too young to fight.

"Couldn't stand the stink," came the jeering reply. They all laughed.

Quanah had grown almost to a man conditioned by one set of assumptions and circumstances. Then the ground fell out from under his feet. He had been the son of his people's most ferocious war chief. Now he was dispossessed by a band in cowed retreat. Finally he bridled and inspected the hooves of the dun gelding he had stolen from the Navajos and then started rolling up and binding what few possessions he had. As he packed, the horse perked its ears, fluttered its nostrils, and moved around. Carrying a rifle, Yellow Bear led toward them a brown mule cinched with a packsaddle. "I want you to have these," Weckeah's father said gruffly. "You'll need them."

It was an old, long, and heavy rifle, a single-shot Mexican army breechloader, but appeared in good repair. Lashed to the mule's pack frame was a full pouch of cartridges. The mule looked strong. "Thank you," said Quanah.

Yellow Bear grasped a wrist behind his back and gazed at the horizon. "You need to understand. It's not you."

Quanah laughed in his face. "Who else could it be?"

Yellow Bear nodded, respecting his bitterness, for it was warrior's fuel. He turned his gaze toward the hills and reflected. "Ought not to be no distinction between the blood-born and captives who've won and deserve the honor. It's devotion to the ways that make people Our People. But these ones here, they're looking for reasons why so much bad has happened to them. If it wasn't you and your family's misfortune, they'd find something else. And Quanah, this happens to men all the time. That one you miss, who was my friend, he changed bands three or four times, and I've done it twice. Way things are going here, I may well do it again. Man stays his whole life with the band that raised him, he'll wind up like that mule there— beat down from carrying too much load."

Trailing the mule behind his dun, Quanah rode out through a meadow pungent with skunk cabbage. The wind was blowing hard from the west, and the air was filled with grit. He and the animals had reached the third ridge when Weckeah caught up. She rode a spotted horse bareback, skirts high and comely on her legs, but she reined around him in a fury.

"You're going to just leave?" she assailed him. "The last I see is the tail of the worm?" She had chopped her hair off in mourning for his father.

"I was urged not to put this off."

"You couldn't even talk to me?"

"I'm no good for you—or good enough for you. Ask your dad."

She gaped at him. "What did he say to you?"

"He said these people feel a great need to keep their blood pure."

She flinched and raised her hand to her face.

"Come with me," he said.

"You know I can't."

"Don't you see then? That's why I tried to just go on. All that's what I didn't want said."

He left her crying and rode due west, coming up through a small red canyon cut by a creek of the Red River. He killed and ate prairie dogs and saw no one close up, only a band of Kiowa hunters who gave him a look and waved him past. As he rode on, the land flattened out and trees grew scarce. Everywhere he looked, fumes wavered and rose from the lakes of mirage. He saw plenty of pronghorn antelope but fewer and fewer buffalo. One day he saw a floating object that became a white man's wagon. It was loaded with something large, dark, and jagged. Years would pass before Quanah knew it for what it was—a teamster's rick of buffalo hides.

He rested his horse and mule in the heat of the day. They were into the llano now—an endless brown pan lidded by a bowl of sky. Buzzards drifted in the wind. At night tongues of distant lightning flicked, but there was no water. At last Quanah saw some mustangs and gave a sigh of relief. Wild horses ranged no more than half a day's walk from a source of water. He circled until he found a seeping spring muddy from their hooves.

Quanah pushed hard, hoping the Quohada were where Yellow Bear thought they'd be. He was almost to the Cimarron when the spiral of buzzards thickened, and then he saw the flocks of crows. There were blood smears on the grass from a buffalo skinning.

On a ridge he saw hunters. The Quohada followed the buffalo, but they were called Antelopes. Like the pronghorns they knew the secrets of the llano, where to find the water. They were standoffish people baked dark brown by the constant sun; they sewed squares of hide to the shoulders of their shirts and wore the flaps as hoods on hot summer days. They were the wildest bunch of all.

One man rode out to meet Quanah. He was thick of chest and girth and had a nose that looked like a chunk of tree root. Parra-o-coom, whose name meant He Bear, was war chief of the Quohada, and he had been a friend of Nocona. Quanah had sat with them around winter fires on the Washita laughing at wild stories of their adventures together. As Quanah approached, Parra-o-coom called out to him and laid his hood back, grinning. "You've grown too tall to sit down good on a horse," he said. "Seen you coming, I thought that horse had a second neck."

"Parra-o-coom, I'm hungry."

"So am I, now you mention it. And we got meat."

It was the safeguard of an innumerous and quarrelsome people. Quanah was no longer Nokoni. He had joined the Quohada band.

5

A FEW MILES NORTH OF FORT WORTH, in country that still lost some horses to the Indians but was largely secure from raiders, a newlywed man named Coho Smith drew wages as a dry goods store clerk in a hamlet called Azle. He got his name from the Spanish cojo, crippled or wobbly. Orphaned by a Dutch family, Smith had been adopted by Mexicans who brought him up in the village of Santa Rosa on the Río Sabinas, across the Río Grande. Comanches came raiding one June, and Smith got shot with an arrow in the knee, unhorsed, and captured. He expected to be killed, for he was past twenty, but instead the Indians roped him to an ill-broken horse, which beat him senseless in the daylong rides, and at night they tied his wrists to stakes in the ground. From the chaparral they tore soapbush leaves for his binding. The twisted green foliage was as tough as leather, and as it dried through the night, it shrank. His wrists still bore white ridges of scar from those nights.

His captors were Tenawa Comanches, the Downstream band, and finally he got up the nerve to ask why they hadn't killed him. The raider said they decided they had use for him. He spoke Spanish, which they could understand, and also spoke the language of the whites. The Tenawa wanted to know what was being said if they got their hands on a Texan who was more valuable than el cojo. They warned that if he ever lied to them or tried to escape, they would kill him with great pleasure. Intent on being useful, Coho set his mind to learning Comanche. He served an old man who was too frail to beat him severely—he had no sons, and all he really wanted from Coho was meat for him and his wives. Coho participated in the interrogation of some white captives. He traded mares, which the raiders disdained to ride, until he had a good fast one, and one day in the swirl and dust of a buffalo hunt, he put his heels to her and got away.

Coho married a young woman from Parker County. At the store in Azle he was making a hundred dollars a month selling bolt denim, linen, shoes, coffee, sugar, salt. Then the war between the states began, and the Yankee blockade cut off deliveries to Texas ports and merchants. People hauled looms out of dusty storage, wore homespun clothes, tried to make coffee out of okra, peanuts, or sweet potatoes. Then a man who claimed to be a Confederate official approached Coho and asked if he would smuggle Texas cotton across the Río Grande to the Mexican port of Matamoros. English ships gladly loaded the cargo under a trade agreement with Mexico; the Yanks, the Confederates said, were too frightened of English frigates cruising the Gulf to do anything about it. Coho was weighing the offer when a letter reached him that said: "Yr knowing of Spanish and Camanch is remark upon. If the name <u>Cynthia Ann Parker</u> means anything to you, it is in yr interest to come to this farm Sunday next. Here is how you come." There was a map. "In trust, Billy Parker."

Of course he knew who she was. He even knew her brother, John Parker. John Parker's ranch was in Coahuila, between a town called Múzquiz and the foot of the Sierra Madres. It was the Río Sabinas country where the Mexican couple had taken in Cojo as a Dutch orphan. John was a thin, dark-haired man who would have been handsome if not for all the pockmarks. In a pulquería they had gotten drunk and traded stories of their capivities. John never spoke of this cousin Billy. He talked like he wanted nothing more to do with Comanches, the Parker family, or with Texas.

Sure, Coho knew the story of the Parkers. And he knew about the league of land that the Texas legislature had awarded Cynthia Ann. He saddled his horse as soon as the dew dried that Sunday and reached Billy Parker's farm shortly before noon. The man wore threadbare overalls and supported himself with a cane he was still whittling, judging from the marks. He grasped Coho's hand and pumped it heartily, and his eyes lit up when he saw the way Coho swung his bad leg. Parker talked about the ball that got him at Shiloh and wanted to know the nature of Coho's misfortune; he seemed to hope it bound them in some way. Wanting no such bond, Coho said a horse fell on him.

"Well, I thank you for coming," he said. "That cousin of mine's a worker, but I don't think she's learned one word of English, and I don't know Spanish or Indian sign." They heard the echoed thocks of an axe. "There she is," said Parker, setting off with his cane. "You'll usually find her moping in the woods."

In a clearing a tree lay partly sawed into a stack of corral posts. The woman was turning the trim into firewood, and there was nothing tentative about her swings of an axe. A sturdy figure, she wore an old sunbonnet and a shapeless cotton dress that was sweated through. "Cynthia Ann, dinner!" her cousin called.

When she saw Coho she threw him a glare that set him back on his heels, then she dropped her eyes. She fell in step behind them, dragging the axe, and Coho maneuvered slightly on the trail, keeping her in glancing view. "We get gawkers," Parker explained. "That's why she's so spiteful."

Cynthia Ann was not the beauty that newspaper illustrators and her legend made her out to be. A dark-skinned little girl ran behind her and hid when she saw Coho. Parker said it was her daughter, Topsannah. Parker's wife was gaunt and haggard, but she had made a fatback and roots stew and set a rough plank table. As Parker said a wordy grace Coho rested his forearms on the table and noted there were no knives on the table, just spoons. With his elbows bent, his sleeves naturally shortened and he noticed that Cynthia Ann was staring at the scars on his left wrist. When their gazes met, her cheeks dimpled in an odd, sweet smile.

"Now, sir," Billy Parker was saying. "We have pressing matters to discuss with our cousin. You are highly recommended, and I trust you are a man of honor and absolute discretion."

Coho watched Cynthia Ann. Ignoring the spoons, she got soup to the mouth of the daughter in her lap by sopping with the stale pone. Coho said the first thing in Comanche that came to him. "Tuepit tsihasuri." Hungry little girl.

The commotion nearly overturned the table. In a flash Cynthia Ann set her little girl on her feet; Prairie Flower looked about, startled, then toppled on her rump and began to cry; while her mother grabbed her skirt, swung her legs over the bench, and pitched to her knees beside Coho, throwing her arms around his waist. In a torrent of Comanche and Spanish, "I knew it, I knew from the mark of the bowstring. Oh, good. I want to go back to my boys, I want to go back to my people, and my cousin Billy wants to go with us. You can take us. You'll take us, won't you? Don't say no. Let's talk. Please, let's talk."

She thought the scars from the soapbush had been caused by a bowstring continually thrumming against his wrist. Coho gave Cynthia Ann's shoulder a couple of awkward pats and looked at the farmer. "*You* want to go to the Comanches?"

"Yes!" he shouted. "That's why I sent for you! To interpret. My wife is sick, very sick, and as you can see I'm crippled for life. All I want to do is go back to Illinois and make a home for us. The Confederates discharged me, sent me back here, but now they're going to conscript me again. I'll never fight against the Union, never again. My wife is fixed with everything she needs while we make our journey. The Comanches hate this damn Texas. If Cynthia Ann and I can reach them, they'll help me find my way back to Illinois."

Coho sat there blinking. "You've talked to him enough," she said in Spanish. "Talk to me." She touched his face. "You'll take us, won't you?"

He stalled, thinking of how his life would change if he could get title to that league of land. Ten square miles, six thousand acres — oh, he was foolish to dream of it. "Where are your people?"

"Maybe the Cimarron," she said. "Or the headwaters of the Arkansas."

"But you have no horse, and that mare of mine is not fit for such a ride."

"Horses! There are some first-rate horses around here. I see them every day licking a salt block out by the gate. If I get my hand in a horse's mane, it is mine. Don't think for a moment about horses. Please, my heart is crying for my sons."

"But I'm just married. I have a young wife."

"That's nothing. Take me there and they will give you as many wives as you want. Our People are not like white men. They take as many wives as they wish. They will give you anything you want. Ten wives, ten guns, ten horses."

Coho was getting agitated. "Why don't you just go? With your cousin?"

"Oh, Billy. He doesn't know anything about peoples. Kiowas, Cheyennes, Apaches, they'd take one look at Billy and kill him. I can't hunt game and care for a child and find the way. I would never get to see my boys and my people. Never, never, never."

"Now, look here," said the farmer. "I want to talk to you some myself. If my cousin wants to know what I'm saying, then you can tell her in Spanish or Indian. I hired you to interpret."

"You haven't hired me to do nothing."

Parker glared at his wife and told her to quiet the child. "I need you, what I meant to say. You're not compelled to live in Texas. You might not want to come back here at all. But you've seen this place. Eighty acres, all in good cultivation, and if you'll take us, I'll make you a deed to half of it tomorrow, and I'll furnish the horses, a good pack mule, and thirty dollars in gold pieces." He winked and said, "I'll show you my whiskey still directly." Parker produced a hemp sack and dropped it on the table with a thump. "We'll go on from the Comanches to Illinois, and sell this off by attorney. What do you say?"

"Your dinner's getting cold," Coho said.

"I have put my life in your hands," Parker said, his voice quaver-

61

ing. "If the people around here knew what I've told you, they'd hang me tomorrow."

Coho looked at Cynthia Ann. "My people will give you all the wives you want," she begged him. "All pretty and well-made."

"You're right," he told her in Spanish. "This man could get you and your girl killed. I can't take you to your people. You own a league of land. If I carried you out of Texas, I could never come here again."

The store clerk wasn't going anywhere near the Cimarron or Arkansas rivers. But he could have taken her to her brother across the Río Grande, or just gone to see John and tell him he'd better come get his sister and the little girl away from this fellow. Coho chose to say and do nothing, and it bothered him the rest of his life.

Naduah:

THE BLACK BOY who cooked us the bad food was the only one who showed us any real kindness. When they took us away from the house in that first town, the speed at which my life vanished made me cry out and moan. I knew the two men in the leather-smelling carriage were some kind of kin to me, but it made no difference. They were nervous white men smoking cheroots. Everywhere outside, the grassland was skinned away for ugly patches of bare earth, and streams of smoke poured from houses into the sky. It was the first time I realized how many white people there were. Nocona must have known this, yet he never told me.

That morning they took me into a world I couldn't have made up in a dream. Their town Fort Worth made no more sense to my eyes than the ruin of a tornado. On a bluff over a wide-bottomed river, endless lodges of timber and rock were piled against each other, people swarmed in and out like ants, poles of rock poured smoke into the sky, and the ground was covered with smooth rock that the horses' iron shoes rang like chimes.

The driver stopped the team and carriage before one of the

lodges, and the men hustled us inside. It was a store with wood floors and bins of tools, cloth, and dry food. I had once seen a store like it in Santa Fe. The two men who were my kin made me sit in a chair, and they tied rope around me. I rocked and soothed Prairie Flower as best I could. The white women had taken away my cradleboard, and Prairie Flower was a strong little girl. It was a struggle to keep her still. Then a noise arose outside the store—young voices, excited. A woman and another man led a bunch of white children inside. We were being shown off like we were dancing bears.

The women kept the children at a distance. Many hung back, scared. One little boy, a yellow-haired one, stepped out toward us and pretended to pull back a bowstring and shoot an arrow at us. The woman said strong words to him and swatted him on the back. I don't know what shocked me more—that boy's cruelty or the way the woman hit him. I burst into tears, and of course that got Prairie Flower started.

At last they took the children away. Then another man propped together what looked like small lodge poles. His clothes were black, he had a black box that he set up on top of the poles where they came together, and the hide of his strange tipi was not skin but more black cloth. The man ducked inside it as he and the ones who were my kin went on speaking that tongue. I thought I had Prairie Flower settled down, but she began to nuzzle at me, poking with her chin. She was hungry, and it's not easy to make a baby wait. I couldn't get up and walk her, so I opened that scratchy dress they made me wear. She favored my right breast, and I felt the sharp little teeth dig in. The looks on the faces of those men. You'd have thought I pulled up my skirt and emptied my bowels on their floor.

The one dressed in black swooped back under the cloak of his box. He stuck his arm out from under the black cloak, holding in his hand a tray that contained white powder. My captivity had begun to stir memories of the first time it happened to me. I remembered my little brother John hanging on our mother's hip at Fort Parker, and as she hoisted our infant sister on her hip she handed me a small cloth sack. "Cynthia Ann, hide the money, don't let them get the money," her words came back to me. I heard them now in Our People's way of speech but she had to have said it in her Americano talk. Then one of the riders leaned down at Mama and us and howled and shook something in his hand. I recognized it as Grandpa Parker's scalp.

Trying now to hold back more tears, I watched grains of the powder in the man's tray fall like snow to the floor. The man's box contained a glass eye; fixed on me and my swollen breast and suckling child, it looked as cold and merciless as a wolf's. Then the powder in the tray—white gunpowder, I guess—blew up in a blinding flash that made Topsannah forget all about her mother's milk. She about bit through my nipple. That was the medicine that let them make the pictures. They put that one of us in newspapers far and wide. They thought nursing a child was cause for shame.

Later they made us ride the iron monster train to their big town Austin. Prairie Flower took one look at it hulking and breathing smoke and was certain it was the Big Cannibal Owl I'd been telling her about. Some women kin came along to help with the child. One gave her a doll with red hair and pock marks sewn on the face. They took us inside the biggest lodge I'd ever seen, and waiting for us was that killer man they called Sul Ross. Making a speech to some old whiteasses, he stood beside us and put his hand on my shoulder! I could tell it was a council of elders. That was when they promised the land and money I never saw. The old men stood up baying and beating their hands together. I turned over chairs, trying to get away. I thought they were about to kill me.

6

PRAISE THE LORD AND Abraham Lincoln—Bose Ikard was a free man. Which at the moment inclined him to believe he was crazy. Would a sane man of his own choosing be naked in the saddle with the Pecos River a flooding brown froth before him, and a norther blowing in? Charles Goodnight sat beside Bose stuffing boots and pistol and that day's clothes in a rubber bag he claimed was waterproof. The runty trail boss looked ridiculous. Above his loin hair, hands so charred by sun they resembled gloves, a matching dark red neck, a thick-jawed beard, and otherwise pale gooseflesh, Mister Charlie wore his hat.

A blue norther was a handsome thing, at a distance. They had watched the front spread across the sky and mottled white sand all morning. Though they hadn't felt a drop of rain in weeks, storms in the mountains upstream had shoved a big rise down the Pecos. Eighteen hundred head of longhorns were being pushed toward the water by forty-odd drovers who shed clothes and loosened saddle cinches for the swim. Among them were a few Mexicans and a few more beaten Johnny Rebs who either couldn't settle down or had nothing to settle down to. But most were just ordinary white boys, too young for that war, on the run from dreary prospects in the Palo Pinto country. The trail boss was just thirty-one himself. The drovers knew this because a few nights earlier Goodnight obliged them to celebrate his birthday in a modest way; he did that wherever March the fifth might find him. He treasured his birthday more than most grown men because he came into the world, albeit in Illinois, three days after Texas declared its independence from Mexico. It was also about the time, Bose learned in his most stressful weeks as a house slave, that Comanches had sacked a little family fort on the Navasota River and carried off Cynthia Ann Parker, among others.

Not that there was any drinking, music-playing, or other levity on his cherished birthday. "It's too damn bad," Mister Charlie had grumbled as a bunch of cowboys who knew and cared nothing about politics mumbled yes, claro, that's right, "that the people who ran the republic had just enough business mind to drive it bankrupt. What did annexation get us but two killer wars in a dozen years?" The ranger companies had been disbanded and outlawed after the War of Northern Aggression, as it was called by most of the losers, and Goodnight was unwilling to scout for the army of occupation. Texas cattle growers had thought they were going to feed the Confederacy, but the orders and disbursements never came through; Mister Charlie said it was part of the fraud to get the legislature to approve secession. There was nothing to do with those longhorns in Texas but wait for the Comanches and Kiowas to steal them. So they drove them toward New Mexico Territory and Kansas and points beyond, where there were railheads now and Union troops and Mormons and gold miners and reservation Indians needing to be fed.

It was largely a new crew of drovers. Goodnight led and badgered them across desert they scarcely could have imagined, trying to stay west of the Comanches and Kiowas, which put them in danger now of Mescalero Apaches. The country along the Pecos was an alkaline waste of spines, thorns, and knife-edged rocks that crippled horses and pierced boot leather like paper. Bose wondered what all the rattlesnakes in that country could possibly find to eat. Goodnight ordered his men to quit shooting the snakes. Pop their damn heads off with a rope, if they had to kill them—it was a waste of ammunition. The drovers feared stampedes, of course. But they most dreaded a rain-swollen river.

Bose also feared losing his only material possessions. Doctor Ikard had given him a peso-studded bridle, a nicely tooled Fort

66

Worth saddle, and a pair of saddlebags that contained his freedman's papers, wrapped for safekeeping in waxed parchment. Damn sure the nicest thing he ever did for Bose. But it was a mistake, Bose thought, to attribute it to any sort of family feeling; a lot of slave owners chose to do it that way, once it became clear the war was lost. It was a point of pride with them, and they desired to put their affairs in legal order, in anticipation of the forthcoming duresses.

Bose had put his clothes inside his bedroll, in hopes they'd stay a little drier. His boots were tied by a short rope wrapped securely around the saddle horn. He looked back at the herd. "Think they're gonna follow?"

"Not if we give 'em the god damn vote," said Goodnight. The small man spat. The surprise of the flooded crossing had put him in a foul mood.

A few yards away, a section of the cut bank broke off, and the Pecos swallowed it one loud gulp. Their horses stepped around nervously, feeling the loose ground shift. Bose's day horse was a black-maned sorrel he called Plug. Bose leaned forward, gave Plug's jaw a pat, and slipped his ears out of the bridle's headstall; the horse turned his head and let the bit fall in his hand. He wrapped the bridle and reins around the horn and eyed the water, which ran the color of milked coffee. It was only a couple of hundred yards across, but just off the bank, tops of over-washed saplings lashed hard in the current.

"Damn, I hate this river," said Goodnight.

You're the one chose the way, thought Bose. "How come we got to cross the thing again?" he asked.

Goodnight set his gaze on the Guadalupe Mountains, to the west. For days the wooded peaks had moved closer and grown larger as they followed the river upstream. "There's eyes all up in there," he said. "We been making ten miles a day. Apaches can cover that in two hours. We need this rise between us and them."

Bose gave a sigh and nod and prepared to put Plug in the water.

He had offered to swim pilot and test the strength of the freshet, not because he cherished the bonus wage of one dollar; he was trying to make sure he was out of the way. If the current turned the cattle around and got them milling, horses and drovers caught among them were in for a hellish time. Plug remained calm in deep water as long as he wasn't crowded. Bose was looking out for his own hide. It was safer out front.

Bose looked at Goodnight and his horse and asked him what he meant to do. "Set in downstream," the boss replied, "and try to keep the first ones hazed, following you. They're bound to spread out some, but if we can keep the horns pointed all the same direction, semblance of a herd, we'll be all right."

"Other words, you're asking that fat horse to tread water."

"By God, I have swum rivers half a mile wide with trees floating down 'em while you was still carrying out afterbirth for that doctor!" Goodnight roared. "Now stop your tarrying or I'll find me someone else."

Bose raised his hands and let it go. "Gonna leave that bridle on?"

"Got to steer him some way."

Ain't the way to do it, thought Bose.

He put both hands around the horn, kicked Plug's sides, and in a spray of dislodged bank they hit the cold water. The horse grunted and floundered, trying to find footing. Bose felt him start to balk and roll over on his side. "Hyah, quit," he barked, and with his palm bailed a spray of water in the horse's face. Plug made another noise, stuck out his nose, and swam. A moment later there was a second large splash, followed by another Mister Charlie tirade. Bose looked back and had to laugh. The boss held his reins out of the water with one hand and tried to keep his hat on with the other. "What I want to know is," Bose called, "what was so wrong with Texas?"

"Hopeless country," the boss yelled back. "Plagues loose on the land. Got people slaughtering good beef for hide and tallow, feed the meat to hogs. It's gone to hell and the Indians. Yankee sons of bitches telling us what to do. And unionists! Damn thieves act like they won that war, when all they done was run off to Kansas."

"Look behind you," said Bose.

On the bank a line of naked drovers yelled and charged their horses forward at the first bunch of cattle and shooed them head-first and bawling off the slope. Muddy water shot up like a row of geysers. There was a great churning of confusion—horns fencing like sabers—then they got straightened out, raised their chins, and swam. Only humans are born without the instinct.

Goodnight wouldn't loosen the reins and let his horse have his head. The black was wild-eyed and breathing hard. He was strong, though, and he pulled within ten feet of Plug. But then the torrent jerked the horses around and sent them straight downstream. In a panic, Goodnight tried to wrench the black around with the reins. "You're gonna turn him over!" Bose shouted. He pulled on the horn and leaned far enough out to slug Plug's jaw. After a few hard clouts the horse gradually began to angle toward the bank. In the same way Goodnight managed to get his horse turned. Except for hoarse breathing and the odd gurgle and splash, the bitter Pecos swept them along with hardly a sound.

The bank was beginning to look achievable when a bobbing piece of driftwood jabbed Plug right in the eye. The horse threw back his head, dropped his hooves, and went under like a stone. Bose had just enough time to get one foot on the horse's neck and give himself a clearing shove. But he neglected to hold his breath and came up choking. Plug resurfaced, collided with the black, and turned him over. The trail boss vanished. For a moment Bose watched his hat and rubber bag go floating downstream. The bag twirled and wobbled as the weight of its contents pulled it under. Then Goodnight burst up flailing with his arms and yawping through his beard. "I can't swim!"

Who the hell could, in this? Near them the black horse caught a leg in the bridle reins and rolled over and over, thrashing and groaning. Where it drowned, the river boiled.

Bose made a splashing lunge, hoping his panicked boss didn't drown him. "Grab hold of this one's tail!"

Somehow the sorrel found the strength and heart to tow them both the last eighty yards. As Plug staggered in the shallows they let go and clambered with knees, elbows, and buttocks—broke off a wall of sand and were almost swept back in. Finally they lay on their backs, gulping and gasping. The horse stood in some willow saplings in a daze, saddle loose and drooping.

"Godalmighty," said Goodnight.

"Yeah."

They lay a while longer.

"I just killed a damn good horse."

Bose was quiet and sympathetic.

"What'll you take for that one there?" Mister Charlie said. Then he laughed.

They sat up and observed the disaster. They were so far down-stream now that the point of entry was hidden around the bend. Horses, men, and cattle were strewn far and wide, but they were swimming—the horns on the brown water looked like an armada of wishbones.

Hitched to a team of mules, the wagon cruised around the bend with floats of empty flour barrels lashed to the sides. The cook, Juan, was the only other black man on the drive. A border mongrel born of peasant girls, runaway slaves, and Seminole Indians, Juan had lost his right hand —to an axe, it was said—in summary judgment of theft in some Mexican placita. A blacksmith made him a glove claw of three pronged hooks that he strapped on his arm and managed quite well. He could hold and pour a coffeepot without scalding a fellow. The Mexicans called him demonio, and there was some-thing scary in his eyes, all right. But Goodnight liked his crisped marrow-gut and suet raisin pudding. Juan perched forlornly on the wagon seat with a blanket wrapped around him, waiting to capsize or sink. "Ahoy and call for biscuit, captain," Mister Charlie encour-aged him. "You got all my clothes, and all the money."

They drowned or otherwise lost about a hundred head of cattle on that Pecos crossing, several horses and mules, and one of the best-liked Mexican drovers. They couldn't even look for his body. It took them all afternoon to get the cattle pushed back into a herd. At the wagon Goodnight called together all the drovers he could spare. Most of them still wore the damp clothes they had stuffed in their saddlebags for the swim, but Goodnight dressed for the occasion, put on a dry white shirt and his ocelot skin vest. Having lost his own, he wore another man's hat. The boss wasn't a prayerful man, but he was thoughtful, and his store of preparations contained a sort of service. Bose had heard him say the words before. "Bible says, 'God is not unjust. He will not forget your work.' We commend him to you, Lord. Our friend and herder Cesar Vizcaya." Then he ducked his head.

Vaqueros were making signs of the cross when the norther hit; the lost soul was consigned to memory in a bluster of wind and sand. The drovers ate supper on their feet, reins of fretful horses wrapped around their elbows or thighs. The only solace was that the cattle were as tired as they were. Maybe they wouldn't run.

As the early spring storm came through, its thunder changed from muffled thumps to cannon shots. There were flashes of lightning, then forks that shot out and fused back then spread again above them, veins bleeding fire. Then the sky began to throw down bolts that hit the ground and just stood upright blazing. Bose's night horse tossed its head and trembled. The downpour came at them in gales and angles. Bose couldn't see through the waterfall off his hat. Another bolt lit up the sand and greasewood, close enough that both he and the horse jumped, and he thought for certain the stampede was on. For an instant he caught a glimpse of Goodnight on his saddle mule, Jenny. His slicker was parted over the white shirt and yellow spotted vest, and he sat back in his saddle with his face raised and his arms flung wide.

The drovers pressed against the herd and kept them moving—singing to them, pleading with them. At last the downpour slackened, but every dark gully crossed was now a drowning stream. The rain eventually quit. and through racing clouds a bright moon came out. But the herd was never going to bed down now. There was nothing to do but keep going. Normally they rode and slept in two-hour watches, but now they were all in the saddle. The riders circled the herd in relays and opposite directions, trying to keep them bunched. Some chewed tobacco and rubbed juice in their eyes to stay awake. Others clamped both hands tight on their saddle horns and gave it up—swayed and dozed in jerks and snorts. Goodnight came up beside Bose on the mule.

"Some day and night," Bose greeted him.

The boss yawned hugely through his beard. "Ain't near over."

Wind whistled and popped the skirts of their slickers. "Mister Charlie, don't mind my saying, how come you ain't married?"

"Too damn ugly, I suppose."

"You want to marry?"

"Oh, sure. Right time and place. I sort of got a woman in mind."

"Think when you made all this money you'll go back home?"

"Home?" Goodnight said darkly. "Where would that be?"

"I'm thinking the same way. Trying to put some plan in my life, now I got a say. Palo Pinto country, there ain't nothing there for me. Nor anybody. And I can't vision it being much different anyplace I go."

"You're sounding blue."

"I'm cold and wet."

The herd was spread out now. Moonlight shone on the spotted backs and ground. "Someday," Goodnight advised, "you're gonna need and want to be among numbers of your own kind."

"Not on no cotton farm in Parker County."

"I'd find myself a city."

Bose stared at him in astonishment.

"This here's a transcience," the boss said, nodding at the scene before them. "It'll be gone in the blink of an eye. Where in the hell was Babylon? In a forest? Was the countryside flat? Time goes by, nobody even thinks to ask. I'll die someplace where maybe some fellow will notice and dig me a hole in the ground. What lasts is numbers of people living close around. Banks and opera houses and schools. History don't look kindly on them that seek the grass."

He yawned. "Can't keep my eyes open, but you got me talking jabber. It's a rare gift you have, Bose, needlessness of sleep."

Goodnight banged his heels and jogged off on the mule. Bose carried in his saddlebag a mouth organ rolled in a scrap of canvas. He pulled it out and blew the harmonica softly, finding its reeds swollen from the swim. Cows seemed to find music soothing. He played and sang a piece rearranged to suit his own composing. A few voices joined in.

Drink that rotgut, drink that wine
Drink the river Jordan
Used to sport a white hat
Horse and buggy fine
Went round with a sometime girl
But always called her mine
Her love was like a rain shower
On a long hot summer day
Smelled just like a rose
But oh so far away

By dawn they had the frazzled cattle down or grazing, and most of the drovers were gathered around the wagon, smoking and comparing tales of the swim and the storm. Juan had scrabbled together a fire from greasewood and dried cowchips that he kept in sacks for emergency. Bose paid close attention to Juan and valued his company, though the Mexican half-breed spoke next to no English. Bose had learned to cook on Lady Isabella's kitchen woodstove, but doing it over a campfire required a different set of skills. Bose figured cooking was a useful knowledge to have, particularly when a man got tired and too old to stay on a horse. Juan made coffee just by pouring grounds in spouted pots and letting two gallons of water boil. Trying to raise their spirits, this morning he fried bacon and made the sweet called sucamagrowl. He made a syrup of water, sugar, flour, and vinegar, and when it was good and thick, seasoned it with nutmeg. Then he pulled off snatches of sourdough from the clamped bowl where it brewed and laid these in the hot syrup, where they swelled like dumplings. The drovers were standing in line with their cups and plates when someone groaned: "Aw, hell. Look at this."

Riding through the herd, as a drover on watch moved his horse before them, were Indians carrying rifles propped against their hips. A number of them wore black hats of buffalo scalp and horns. Bose, who was a fast and accurate counter, put their number at about fifty.

"What kind are they?" a drover asked.

"Comanches," Goodnight said.

Seated on a horse with a Union army brand, the leader had a thick waist and firm set of jaw. The trail boss stepped out to meet him. The Comanche tapped his finger on his breastbone and spoke Spanish. "Mi nombre es Parra-o-coom."

"Buenas Noches," Goodnight said, thumping his own chest.

"Son Tejanos?" the Indian asked.

Goodnight denied it. "No. This herd is from the Choctaw Nation, in the Territory."

He Bear stretched his mouth in disdain for the lie. "You're Texans," he said and looked about coldly. Through words and gesture, the Comanche said that they had no interest in taking their lives this morning. They were on their way to kill Navajos. "They steal and eat our horses."

Goodnight said he understood. Navajos had eaten one of his.

"Wohaw," the Comanche demanded tribute and beef. He rubbed his stomach. "We're hungry."

Goodnight scowled and raised two fingers. "Two," he bargained.

"Ten!" Parra-o-coom replied, holding up both hands and all fingers. The third one on the right was a nub. Lord God, thought Bose. Give them all they want. Among the Indians was a tall, broad-shouldered youth who had on a breechclout and antelope-skin leggings but rode shirtless in the cold. It was the first time Bose had seen Quanah. He reined his horse toward the fire and wagon, moving drovers out of his way. The Comanche youth leaned forward, peering at Bose and Juan. He said something in Comanche and several of his fellows laughed. He shifted his weight and raised a knee.

"Don't get down," Goodnight said sharply.

Ignoring him, the youth hit the ground lightly with a skinning knife in his hand. Bose could tell he was scared and excited by the way he pushed out his chest and strutted. Boy warrior trying to make a name for himself. He smiled and glowered and kept up a commentary that others found funny.

The youth sauntered to the wagon. He poked his blade through its canvas, then slowly carved a moon-shaped flap. Bose saw rifle stocks pulled against shoulders, and he heard pistols cocked. The youth vaulted over the wagon side and rummaged in the bed. He tossed out a stove lid and coil of lariat and with the whoop of a rare find dropped back to the ground holding a claw hammer. He advanced on Bose.

Quanah made a show of standing apart smelling him, then moved closer and said something else, provoking more laughter. Bose noticed that he had gray eyes. He put the knife in his belt and ate the bacon off Bose's plate. Then he picked up the sucamagrowl dumpling, devoured it off his meat-grimed palm, and licked the syrup off his fingers. Their eyes were constantly engaged. Bose's voice came out unsteady. "That's not why I'm about to kill you."

"Easy," Goodnight said.

Nearly a head taller than Goodnight, the youth swung the carpenter's hammer loosely and now walked a slow circle around him.

75

The boss watched him amiably and observed, "They're known to eat grubworms."

Suddenly Quanah peered at Goodnight's chest. He snatched the slicker's lapels apart. Then he drew back the hammer and screeched, "Tenahpua amacusó naboróyarohco! Tenahpua amacusó naboróyarohco!"

Leopard Coat Man! Leopard Coat Man!

With a look of astonishment, the Comanche He Bear was counting men and guns. He had come in this camp to fill his belly with meat, not to get himself killed. "Hunh uh," he cautioned the young one. Goodnight knew why his own gun was still holstered. Money. He didn't want to die knowing he was a rich man and had never gotten to enjoy it. All the drovers and Indians were doing fast counts and none of them liking what they came up with. But the Comanche kept pointing at and yelling about Mister Charlie's ocelot skin vest.

Something's got to give here, thought Bose. He put himself between the big young Comanche and Goodnight, raised his chin, and through the torrent of angry words he yelled right back. "You a crazy motherfucker, you know that? Craziest bastard I ever saw. You don't quit waving that hammer around, I'm gonna take it away from you and drive nails so far in your eyeballs they'll come out your ass."

Neither one had any idea what the other was saying. Any of them might have died before breakfast that day on the Pecos, but Juan the Seminole cook wore a rough wool poncho and knew the minds of Indians. He knew a few words of Comanche, among them tuhpaé, coffee, which they had a taste for. He raised his voice enough to be heard and gestured for them to gather around and have a cup, as if they were just standing around passing the time of day. The long sleeves of his poncho obscured both his good black hand and the iron one made for him by the Mexican blacksmith. Juan squatted on his heels beside the fire and with rapid movement began to stir the coals. He snatched one that was red and flaming, lofted and caught it in his palm, found it unsatisfactory, and dropped it back in the fire.

All around them was a sharp intake of Comanche breath. What kind of magic was this?

He gave the poncho a shake over his arm and moved the catch claw so fast that none could see it wasn't a bare hand. Juan gripped the iron handle of a two-gallon pot, and, speaking Spanish, raised the pot and offered them coffee. He tipped the spout and let boiling water pour on the coals, raising an explosion of steam. In the hiss and cloud of it Juan set down the coffeepot and again let the poncho conceal the ends of his arms.

Parra-o-coom drew back, frightened. Red-hot coals didn't burn this man? "Aiii, demonio," a vaquero took the cue. After Juan pulled his trick, it was all ponies stepping and Indians muttering. Quanah wore a look of confusion, dejection, lost face.

Bose:

THAT NIGHT THE CATTLE were settled down, lowing. Goodnight and I sat with our backs to the Seminole's wagon wheels, gazing at the fire. I thought the boss had gone to sleep when he snickered. "You must not have had no mother raising you. Using language like that. Mine woulda washed my mouth out with soap."

That was as close to thanking me as Goodnight ever came.

"Mister Charlie, what was that all about?"

"Oh, like you said. Some crazy Indian."

"No, sir. That boy was just styling around showing off, then all of a sudden he saw something and was all over you. You're what made him crazy. I'd just like to know what I'm fighting about, if I'm liable to get killed over it."

Mister Charlie sighed. "You remember all the ruckus about Cynthia Ann Parker?"

"I guess I do. I took care of her like a mama's good son."

"That boy back there is her son. His name is Quanah."

I had to reflect on that. "Wonder what it was he kept yelling at you."

Goodnight held out a flap of his ocelot hide vest. "Not the first time I've heard it. Suppose it's time to throw this damn thing away. They call me the Leopard Coat Man. Story's been spread by ones we rounded up on the Pease and then let go. It's gospel among 'em now that I'm the one who carried off the Parker woman—reason why she's lost to 'em to this day."

He stared off at the darkness and listened to the calls of the night birds. After a while he spoke again. "There's something else. I haven't ever told anybody what I'm about to tell you. When we were riding through that camp a Mexican captive woman jumped out from behind a tipi and jammed a long knife right in the throat of my horse. Scared the shit out of me, and with nary a thought I shot her in the chest. Killed her. She was a good-looking young thing. Those people we let go on the Pease still talk about her, too. Turns out she was Nocona's chore wife. Those Comanches say it's bullshit that Sul Ross killed Nocona. But now if the son of such a man loses his mother, little sister, and stepmother all in one day, you can't hardly blame the boy for taking that hard."

All that skirmish wound up costing Mister Charlie was a claw hammer, a wagon tarp, six heifers, a little bit of guilt, and a case of indigestion, but that boy he called Quanah left us with a look of sure promise in his eyes. He knew the face of the Leopard Coat Man, and I was the nigger doing his fighting for him. One day our medicines would have another test.

PART II

*Steal
the Fire*

1870-1873

7

FROM A TEAR-SHAPED window of limestone a cascade fell into a pool of clear water that broadened out with the infant Acunacup Neovit into a canyon of tall woods and deep marshy grass. Filled with bass and perch, the river coursed over the white rock and then back and forth on a broad sand bed. In the spring, blankets of burnt red and yellow firewheels stretched between prickly pear and shin oak, and the air streamed and danced with wisps of floating cottonwood. Just as a bend of the same river below Medicine Mounds had been a revered place of the Nokoni, the Valley of Tears was a favorite of the Quohada. In the spring it became a marketplace of horses, mules, blankets, flour, tobacco, bullets, scrap iron for arrowheads and lance. But it took its name from the sorrow and wails of captives being separated and sold to another band or tribe. Sometimes Texas families with money ransomed women and children to Santa Fe and then to farms and ranches that would never suit them again. The ransom brokers called themselves comanchieres—meaning something like They Want Comanches. Texans heard the word and made it an obscenity—comancheros.

The trade went on year-round, but comancheros came from the west every spring in carts and wagons pulled by burros, gaunt horses, and mules. Their leader was an illiterate sheepherder and bandit named José Tafoya. From his adobe on the sagebrush plain below Santa Fe, Tafoya came to the Valley of Tears often enough that he had built himself a mud hut along the headwater creek the Mexicans called Las Lenguas, the Tongues. With Tafoya's comancheros this year had come an agitated U. S. Indian agent sent to ransom the daughter of a Texas family of some means and political influence. In the Valley of Tears, the agent counted eighteen raiding parties going out. He estimated twenty thousand horses, six hundred mules, and at least a dozen herds of stolen Texas cattle. By their primitive lights, the agent thought, these were incredibly rich Indians.

Every morning, the day was called into being by one man singing loudly. "Ahaii . . . ahai . . . ahaii . . . ahaii . . ." and then a shout, "Yow!" Not that many people burst out of their lodges at dawn. The Comanche word for warrior, tekniwop, was the same one as hero, and in camp the fighting men took full advantage of their prestige; the volume of snoring in the tipis made wives and children step lightly until the sun was well into the afternoon sky. But in the springtime bursts of song rose from the camp day and night. As soon as bugs filled the air and the prairie flowers bloomed, young men got their best horses legged up for the war trail. Shields hung from lodges, absorbing strength from the sun. When the first warm moon rose, it occasioned a big dance; painted men whirled and young girls sang. The headman of a raiding party was chosen by warriors who came to his lodge, listened to his plans, smoked in consent, or in rejection handed on the pipe. Comanches did not have lordly elites and camp police like the Cheyennes' Dog Soldiers and the Kiowas' Koitsenko, the Real Dogs. But they had societies of men who helped organize the hunts, the butchering, and the skinning. They resolved disputes over kills, kept the lines of riders, herds, and dogs from stringing out too far when the bands were on the move, and when the new camps were pitched they negotiated placement of the lodges with an eye to clan, rank, grass, water, and old squabbles. The societies were called True Friends, and a True Friend counted as a blood brother any man who had fought beside him. The Quohada had societies called Black Knives, Crow Tassel Wearers, Little Horses, and Big Horses. Parra-o-coom was not only war chief of the Quohada; he was the whipman of both the Big Horses and the Little Horses. At dances he carried a bat affixed with leather thongs and carved with images of past enemies and victims. With stern or gentle lashes, the whipman ruled on the verity of a warrior's claims of having counted coup.

Quanah belonged to the Little Horses, and was clearly a favorite of Parra-o-coom. The path to many coups and a wealth of horses and mules had seemed all laid out before him. But then he'd fallen prey to arrogance and lack of judgment. Wearing the soldier's coat he had led Toes Grown Together and five others to their deaths in the valley of the Brazos. Instead of bringing back many horses and telling their stories of touching their enemies in battle and having Parra-o-coom confirm their coups, Quanah and the others had hacked off their braids and shaved the tails of their horses. He carved stick figure pictures of how a successful raid had turned into disgrace in the bark of pecan trees at an often-used crossing of the Little Wichita, burned the bluecoat tunic, and rode west until the twin peaks called Quitaque rose from the plains. He painted his face, ears, and tongue black in his shame, skulked at night into the Quohada camp in the Valley of Tears, and called on each of the dead ones' families, accepting the mothers' and sisters' shrieks of grief and blame. Any True Friend who led a bad raid would have done the same.

In the moons that followed, Parra-o-coom told him, "Quanah, you fought well. You shot an arrow all the way through a Texan and brought back his hair. Bury your brothers and honor them by getting ready to fight again." But how could he offer himself as headman again when he knew he had no medicine, no guardian spirit? His medicine had been stolen by that dirty whiteass in the running fight with the horse breakers along the Brazos.

A nigger whipman.

Quanah had little interest in most of the raids that went out the following spring. The headmen who invited him to their lodges and handed around the pipes were consumed with stealing Texas cattle. In the Valley of Tears the Quohada sold the walking meat to the comancheros for more horses than they could steal. Then the comancheros sold the cattle to the bluecoats at forts in New Mexico.

Greed and New Mexico trade were making a people of warriors into a bunch of cowherds. What was the thrill and glory in that?

As one raiding party after another left camp, Quanah brooded and stayed behind in the company of pariahs. Tree Covered with Vines had never been able to give birth to a child, so she and her husband had adopted the white girl brought back from a raid in Texas. They named the child Scissortail. Then the father died of a great pain in his heart, and none of his kinsmen chose to take in his wife and daughter. The little girl had rabbit's teeth and squinted at objects in the distance. But Scissortail was all that woman had, and now the Indian agent who had come with the comancheros wanted to take her away. Quanah took pity on them and led them to a ravine obscured by brush that became their hiding place, and he kept them supplied in meat until it would be safe for them to rejoin the band. Quanah skidded down the dirt wall to them one night, bringing meat from his fire, when he heard quiet sobbing, a child's tears. He found Scissortail lying on the ground outside their lodge, stroking and pushing at the hide wall. In the cool spring night the girl only had a buffalo calfskin for cover and warmth. "Tree Covered with Vines," he announced himself. "It's Quanah."

The woman untied the flap and peered out. He looked toward the murmured sounds behind the lodge. "Why is your daughter sleeping outside?"

Tree Covered with Vines burst out weeping. "The Big Horses came here and said that if I don't give her up . . . if I cost them their guns . . . we can't live among the Quohada anymore. 'Go eat lizards and snakes and die.' They said those are the very words of Parra-o-coom."

Quanah let his breath out slowly. "I don't believe that," he said. After a moment he again gestured at the girl. "But what's Scissortail doing out there?"

"She told me that she wants to go back to her parents in Texas," the widow cried. "I can't bear it."

"Tree Covered with Vines, don't do this. Have her beside you in your robes while you can. Your daughter loves you—listen to her. It's going to get cold tonight. Let her in."

But it was true about Quanah's hero and war chief. A runner came and told Quanah that Parra-o-coom wanted to see him in his lodge. Quanah walked through the lodges quickly, his heart racing. He announced himself, stooped through the flap, and found the thick-bodied chief seated on his robes, running his thumb along the gleaming breech of a new Spencer carbine. Laid out before him were two big Colt pistols. Parra-o-coom offered the rifle to Quanah, who handled it admiringly and put the stock to his shoulder. He preferred the heft and balance of the .44 Henry he already had. But there were never enough guns.

Parra-o-coom studied him. "All these people in our camp," he grumbled, "and the stinking cattle. Begone! This whiteass agent from Santa Fe, I'm tired of his snooping." The war chief raised the rifle stock to his shoulder and peered down the barrel at the sight. "We could always just kill him."

"Let me do it," said Quanah, too quickly. "What's he doing out in strange country where it's so easy to just get lost?"

The war chief gave Quanah a sudden look that let him know he'd been tricked into saying the wrong thing. "You took it on your own to make trouble for all of us by trying to hide that woman and the girl," He Bear said angrily. "Go get that white girl and bring her to me."

Red-faced and stricken, Quanah gave up Scissortail without a word of protest. Parra-o-coom didn't give a coyote's yip about José Tafoya's cattle, it turned out. Scissortail, known by her Texas kin as Becky May, safely arrived with the Indian agent in Santa Fe, and He Bear was paid a fine ransom of five hundred dollars. Quanah moved the tipi of Tree Covered with Vines back in the main camp. But she seldom came out of her lodge, and when she did, her hair was a rat's nest; in this place of favor and season of plenty she snatched crickets and grasshoppers and gobbled them off her palm. Nobody consoled her for her loss, and only Quanah went looking for her the day or night she just walked off in the breaks and vanished. She was poisá, crazy, the worst of medicines. Better that the women just pulled down her tipi and burned it. Better that she crawled back in some earthen cave and at night watched the animals' eyes and heard their breathing until at last she moved no more and they bared their teeth and came forward to make sure.

Quanah was stewing on a resentment he hadn't known since he left the Nokoni when a surge of excitement stirred the camp. New people were coming to join their band; they proved to be none other than Nokoni who had feuded with chief Horse Back over his taking the band to live on the whiteass reservation. Yellow Bear, Weckeah's father and Nocona's best friend, rode out front, leading a procession of warriors on stallions that were brushed out sleek, manes and tails well-trimmed, scalps and feathers dangling from their bridles as they tossed their heads. Women, children, and old folk came along behind on mares and geldings. Their hides, their lodges, other possessions, and a small mountain of fresh meat were lashed on travoises. They were admirably horsed, well over a thousand head pushed along behind them, maybe a third that many mules. The dogs of the newcomers ran out yapping and sniffing and brawling with curs that greeted them with stiff legs and hackles raised, defending their camp.

After the Nokoni warriors, Yellow Bear's four wives and his children had come. His number one wife, Nice Enough to Eat, had broadened in the winters since Quanah had seen her. Close behind her, on a lineback mare, was Weckeah. The girlish plumpness was gone. She wore beaded moccasins and a sand-colored doeskin skirt that was fringed and cut for riding, allowing her to cover her legs from the sun and gazes of men who would dearly love to see them. Allowing a glimpse of dark collarbones, her poncho was beaded with gemstones and shell and dyed the changing reds of a ripe plum. Her hair was unbraided and tied back with a purple silk scarf. She had rubbed her cheeks and ears with vermilion and shaded her eyelids gold. Many of the women rode with their eyes lowered, but Weck-eah carried her chin high and looked around smartly. The sight of her sent Quanah's hope and spirits soaring. Her gaze brushed past many staring men but he thought: *She's looking for me.*

Grinning and turned sideward on his saddle pad, one hand resting on the croup of his brown horse, Yellow Bear led them slowly toward the lodge and the ginger-colored horse of Parra-o-coom. They greeted each other mounted on their horses, then stood down to voice their greetings and present their gifts and then go in the host's lodge to eat and smoke.

It was important for Yellow Bear to formally present himself to Parra-a-coom as a True Friend and ally, not a rival. The Nokoni had come straight from a hunt, and the next day they honored the Quohada band and its leaders with the dance and feast of the Buffalo Tongue. The tongue was a delicacy and was cooked and eaten when its juices still had the taste of life. It was a feast of hunting prowess and eternal plenty, and Yellow Bear made an extravagant gesture; he offered to feed everyone in the valley. Nokoni women built the fires early in the morning and roasted the meat on slow coals. At midday, when the tongues smelled delightfully done, Yellow Bear and the warriors of rank who had followed him seated themselves around the fire with Parra-o-coom, the council of elders, and his war leaders. Mingling freely now, Quohada, Nokoni, Kiowas, and Kiowa Apaches pressed close around to watch the ceremony. Children were hushed, a few dogs kicked. Yellow Bear lighted his pipe, smoked and blew a stream toward the sun, then toward the earth, and then toward the four corners of the earth. He presented it to Parra-o-coom, who smoked in the same fashion then passed it on.

When all the ranking warriors had smoked, they looked toward the women who had cooked all morning. They stood in a tight group, some whispering nervously, then parted, and from the midst walked Weckeah, chosen by her father to offer the first tongue. She was dressed and painted as she had been on the incoming ride, except she wore a different shirt, this one blue. She carried a tray carved from a buffalo shoulder blade. Arranged on the whitened bone were roasted roots, fresh berries and plums from the valley's woods, and the basted and seasoned golden brown tongue.

In the ritual, any man who had shamed her in the past was enabled to cry out, "No! No!" Marked as an impure vessel of truth, she could be obliged to go back to the women and hand the first tongue to another. But that almost never happened. They were not a people who prized or even thought much about virginity, and it would take a mean, jealous, or very guilty man to punish an unmarried young woman that way. At the end of the ritual silence, Weckeah handed the buffalo scapula and tongue to Parra-o-coom, and the camp erupted in bawdy cheering. She cut flirting glances all around, and women who had cooked with her yelled, "Li! Li! Li! Li!" As if to say, "You wish! You wish!"

Quanah was too nervous to go forward and eat. On a slope above the creek he sat in a bed of firewheels and sweet-smelling grass and just watched. Yellow Bear and his warriors hustled between lodges of the Quohada. The women in Yellow Bear's party were busy unpacking the travoises, erecting and decorating the lodges, sweeping the dirt free of pebbles and the vicious goathead stickers. Weckeah had an older sister named Pasocopi. She was taller than Weckeah, pretty in her way, but she possessed a pinched and harried look. Quanah saw that she was pregnant, and two naked children toddled after and clung to her. Quanah let himself dream for a moment about rising to the morning song with Weckeah and such a brood. In that moment his want of her hit him so hard that he didn't know whether to roll over in the wildflowers or puke.

He crossed his arms around his shins and watched a young man saunter through the lodges. The Nokoni stooped and spoke to one of the naked children, then stood next to Pasacopi with his hand familiar on her ass. So that was the sister's husband. His name was Tannap, Grown Man. He was the son of Eckitoacup, a middling warrior who had a great wealth in horses and mules. After Naduah and Prairie Flower were carried off and Peanut and Nocona died, Tannap had been one of the Nokoni boys who mocked Quanah and yelled after him tibitzi tibitzi tibitzi tuhtzanayoit, very very very white. But they were all boys just trying to become men. Tannap and his father had left the Nokoni and joined the Quohada, just as Quanah had. They were now fellow warriors, sworn to carry on the fight. Let the grudges go. He thought he would go down in a while and welcome Tannap to the camp and compliment him on his handsome children.

Quanah bathed in the creek, washed his hair, and rebraided it. He dressed in his best deerskins and longest loincloth and stuck his eagle feather in one braid so that it extended smartly below his ear. And at dusk he swelled his chest and walked out to present himself to Weckeah. It was a new day.

But in the circle of Yellow Bear's lodges Quanah saw a gathering that sent that his bright day plunging into night. Yellow Bear, Eckitoacup, and Parra-o-coom stood together with arms crossed over their chests and paunches; the old warriors looked highly pleased with the events of the day. Pasacopi was outside with her mother Nice Enough to Eat and others of Yellow Bear's wives, but she was keeping the children out of her husband's way. Tannap was done up in his utmost finery, skins bleached almost white, and from his hair, loincloth, and shirt dangled pieces of mirror that glinted the colors of the sundown and the evening fires. He strutted about and blew on a bone flute; girls in the clan raised a merry cry, calling someone out to acknowledge her suitor. What a dandy he had become. He was playing love songs on his flute, and they were not for his wife.

With the shock of a thunderclap, Quanah understood these truths: Tannap had a rich man's herd because his father was Eckitoacup; Yellow Bear had a daughter who was ripe to marry; and because

Tannap was the husband of Weckeah's older sister, he had first right to marry her as well. With these songs and dances Tannap was showing he meant to make good his claim.

Quanah spied and sulked until at last he saw Weckeah hauling paunches of water back from the creek. He stepped out from some tall cane and seized her bare arm—so cool and firm to his touch. "Quanah!" she gasped, sloshing the water. "You scared me."

He ducked his head. "I'm sorry. I've been seeing you. I didn't want to make trouble. I just had to talk to you."

She looked toward the creek and the lodges then stepped back with him into the canebrake. She said, "I knew you were here. Of course."

"Are you going to marry Tannap?" he blurted.

She colored at being questioned like this. "What if I am?"

"Please, Weckeah, you can't. I . . . I want you to marry me."

In exasperation she slung the water bags around. "Well, that just fixes everything, doesn't it?"

The mockery in her voice sparked his temper. "So all it takes is to sing you a song. Tenicuaró. A *crooner*."

"What are my choices, Quanah? You? How long has it been since we've even seen each other?"

"Guess I need some *mirrors* in my hair . . ."

In a burst of anger she poured water on his moccasins, filled them up. "Go away, Quanah. If this is how you tell a girl you love and want her, your head is full of rocks. Leave me alone. I'm not going to marry any man I don't want to marry. And that means you."

8

AND SO IT WAS THAT Quanah smoked the pipe of a Kiowa offering to be headman of the raid. Dohasan had skin the rich dark color of a bay horse. His cheekbones and brow had little room for his eyes; he had a permanent squint. Some said Dohasan's name meant Little Mountain—others, Top of the Cliff. In his lodge that night he wore a tangled mess of earrings and necklaces, a shirt decorated with pelts of ermine and strips of Navajo scalp, and an elk-skin sash dyed red. The red sash marked him as a member of the Koitsenko, the Real Dogs. His election to the elite camp and war police at such a young age was a great honor. But his uncle Dohasan, whose name this one claimed, had been the greatest of all Kiowa chiefs. The first Dohasan had been a friend of Nocona. Quanah remembered his father taking him to see the chief's lodge. Chief Dohasan was a famous painter; on the hide walls of his lodge were scenes that told all the history of the Kiowa people. Quanah thought this nephew was a pretender. When they smoked that night, Dohasan swore by the powers of the Sun Dance that his tales were true. He leaped up and pranced around shaking a lance with a bunch of feathers attached to one end that looked like the doll of a white child. The doll, he sang, was Tai-Me, the Kiowas' medicine god. One of his friends was beating frantically on the lodge pole, another pounding on a drum. "When Tai-Me's power is with us," Dohasan howled, "the bullets and arrows of our enemies are turned aside!" Dohasan brought the fetish down like a tomahawk, and with one resounding thump the drummers quit.

The Kiowas were so allied with the Antelopes that their southern band was called Gwa-halego, a name adapted from the way the Kiowas heard and pronounced Quohada. But Quanah's people also derided their Kiowa friends as Long Tongues. Kiowas had an uncommon gift for bullshit. But after the calamity with Weckeah Quanah didn't want to be in the Valley of Tears one more night, and unlike all the brave parties of Quohada going off to steal Texas cattle, Dohasan at least proposed to go down the long trail to Mexico.

Two Quohada joined Quanah smoking Dohasan's pipe. Dog Hates Thunder and Breaks Something had both followed Quanah on his raid of the Brazos. They also had lost friends and face and slunk back to the Quohada camp with their braids shorn. They said they bore no grudges, but he knew he would have to prove himself plenty before anyone rode behind him again. Though Quanah had little regard for Dohasan, he knew and respected some of the Kiowas committed to his raiding party—Timber Wolf, Woman's Heart, Big Blond. Quanah had gambled and hunted with them all when the peoples wintered together in the windbreaks of the Washita. Big Blond had been carried off as a boy from the farmers called Norsemen. When he rode out on summer days he wore a white woman's sun bonnet, a ridiculous sight—the bonnet looked like a mushroom sprouted on his brawny back and shoulders—but his ears and lips and nose were fair and always scabbing up with skin cancers. Big Blond said with a shrug that the bonnet was the only kind of hat that would both shade him from the blistering sun and that he could keep tied on in the gusty plains wind. Whatever he wore on his head, Big Blond was no one to trifle with. Once in the market fair at Taos, Quanah had seen him turn over a teamster's wagon with bare hands when his rile boiled over. The insulting teamster backed right off.

Dohasan spoke Comanche leavened with Spanish, Kiowa, and the language of signs. "The moon is halfway full and growing," he declared, holding the pipe aloft and savoring the fresh tobacco brought by the comancheros. "The days are at their longest. We can take our time making the ride, and the moon will be coming round again when we haunt the hearts of the Mexicanos." He went on, "We'll all ride mules, and take no horses. That way we'll bring back more."

Quanah exchanged glances with Dog Hates Thunder and Breaks Something. Dohasan smoked and handed out his pipe to start the circle anew. No one else spoke up. Quanah said politely, "Every man likes a good mule. But you know we like to trail our war horses behind. Keep them fresh, so we can catch up with any enemies we come across." Or outrun them to get away.

Dohasan responded with a cocksure shake of his head. "No. This time, just mules. We'll go down there unburdened by our riches, and that will free us to take all the more horses and mules and scalps and captives. I have seen it in my vision."

Among Kiowas, mules had a peculiar stature. Mules set the Kiowa price for blankets, tobacco, tools, pots and pans. Quanah had no idea why that was, but he admired the beasts himself and owned three that were able under saddle and pack. They were surer of foot than horses in broken country and could range twice as far without water. Mules were valuable, affectionate, and crazy. His favorite was a plump gelded strawberry roan he called Rose Hips. The mule would throw fits about blowing bits of weed and birds of bright color, and pity the man who tried to keep him from taking a roll in the dirt as soon as a blanket and saddle came off. If you touched his ears he would look for a chance to kick your ribs in. But Rose Hips was the steadiest walker Quanah had ever ridden. He hit a rhythm and just rolled his shoulders and strode. That smooth gait turned into a rockslide, though, if he broke a trot or the mule version of a gallop. The reason to ride a mule on a raid was to have your horse well-rested and ready. Two hops on the ground and you could be on the horse and gone. On hearing this plan, Quanah almost walked out. But he stayed where he was and smoked the man's choice leaf. If he didn't get away from Weckeah and the Valley of Tears right away he was going to start bawling himself.

Six Kiowas and three Quohada rode out from the headwaters of the Pease. The Comanche Trace was a system of trails that crisscrossed and zig-zagged down the llano and the even more harsh desert it became. To the south, the llano's clay and caliche turned to loose sand; the Kiowas and Quohada were three days slogging across that to the Pecos. They found Horsehead Crossing to be an eerie and oddly pretty spot, the water running clear and emerald over the sand, but its floods were known to be murderous, and a long dry spell or the flush of the wrong soils upstream could turn it poison overnight. It had killed more than one herd of thirst-crazed horses driven out of Mexico, and riders who used the ford had built on that tradition by hanging skulls to bleach in the willows. Horses, mules, coyotes, antelope, skunks, humans.

A dozen wellsprings were scattered between Red River and the Río Grande, and Quanah had to respect Dohasan for knowing how to find them. A day's ride south of the Pecos they arrived at a bubbling fount and pool of clear, cold, excellent water; other tribes named it Comanche Springs. There they found parties of Kotsoteka, Yamparika, and Kiowa raiders who were restoring themselves beside the rock-walled spring. The festive camp and gambling ground made Quanah wonder if there was enough plunder in Mexico to accommodate them all. Their nine napped and swam and continued onward two mornings later. The ground grew harder and the snakes and thorns longer, and mountains rose up blue and gray against the horizon. They came to a range that formed amid juniper and piñon and pillars of stone. At the foot of the mountains was a fort that the army had quit during those years the bluecoats disappeared. Nothing was left of Fort Davis but rock walls. Mescalero Apaches had burned it as soon as the soldiers were gone.

From the abandoned fort, Dohasan led them up a canyon where they found deep grass and a brook flowing from several springs. They stayed four days and nights in those mountains, letting the mules graze. The small range that Texans called the Davis Mountains was the handsomest country Quanah had ever seen. The sky was so clear that your eyes played tricks on you—its blue looked closer than the puffs of cloud. They loafed in cool shade, ate pemmican and small game, and told lies late into the night. Beside a creek one day they found some Apache middens. No one had cooked there for many weeks, judging from the dried horse manure, but the midden still smelled of the Mescaleros' char and grease: the odor prickled the hair on the back of Quanah's neck. "Apaches," he said, looking around with a turned-up nose. "They've been our enemies for ages of grandfathers. Up on the plains of many blizzards, before the gift of the horse."

"Your grandfathers fought like grandmothers," scoffed Dohasan, "and they wore petticoats." It was a brazen, insulting reference to Quanah's mixed blood and white mother. The other raiders saw from the flush of his face and throat that the Kiowa had gone too far. "Anyway," said Dohasan, who read the same looks, "we're fighting alongside Mescaleros now, not against them. We all come seeking the gifts of Mexico. And you know them Apaches," he said with a grin and wink, "they got some mighty fine-looking women."

They set out again, and high desert closed around them. Herds of pronghorn antelope stared at their approach, stamped their hooves, and raced off, flashing their ivory butts. Mountains rose up around them, arranged in shades of blue like piles of hatchet blades, but the only green they saw now were bushes and cottonwoods along creeks that were bone-dry. Immense whirlwinds roamed about. The riders uneasily watched the towers of dirt and cringed when one came stinging through them—the Quohada believed the whirlwinds were ghosts. The mules plugged on. Quanah could tell Rose Hips was in a good humor by the way he flopped his ears, one forward, one back, in the rhythm of his stride. They came on grassland bristling with cactus and cut with deep arroyos, and after a while they crested a ridge. Curving along the horizon was a massif of brown and gray cliffs, and below them was a broad valley and a thin winding line of golds and greens intermingled in the afternoon light. There at last was Ocuebi. The Río Grande.

Their mules jogged and clopped down to the bottom of cottonwoods, willows, mesquites, and cane. The way to the ford was scoured deep and the boulders hoof-marked by many comings and goings. In the river a couple of willow saplings were rooted to a sand bar angling through the bed. The stream ran clear and riffled over small rocks. Keeping his hand near the sleeve of his rifle, Quanah raised a leg over Rose Hip's neck and slid off. The raiders' crossing was an inviting place for ambush by bluecoats or Mexicans, he thought, peering around. But the river was warm and ran as deep as his thighs, and the sucking and long muscular swallowing of the mule was a sound of well-being to Quanah. He bent over and let the water fill his hands, then drank his fill of sweet water. He washed his face and chest and stared upriver at rock cliffs and hills that were the red of dried blood. Quanah had never seen so much solid rock.

"This same river runs cold as ice coming out of mountains way up north," he mused. "Cross Ocuebi up there you'd better look out, because you're in the country of the Utes. People seem to just naturally line themselves up with rivers. Is that how it is with Texans and Mexicans?"

"Who knows?" Timber Wolf said with a shrug.

"Soldiers and Texans," Woman's Heart put in. "You hate them the same, but they're as different as coyotes and wolves, deer and elk."

At this all the Long Tongues expounded, but Dohasan wanted nobody's voice heard but his own. "Off in that country," he said, waving his arm to the southwest, "are Seminoles, as wooly-haired and black as the buffalo soldiers they got wearing the bluecoats now, and Kickapoo. Mexicanos pay Kickapoo to fight us and the Apaches, but Kickapoo raid the Texans, too. While we're coming at them from the north, they're coming at them from the south."

Listening to the Long Tongues, Quanah wondered if it would ever be possible to bring these warrior peoples into an alliance that could challenge the whiteass numbers. Elders spoke of a great Penateka war chief called Buffalo Hump who assembled enough warriors to chase Texans off in boats, into the Big Salt Water, their Gulf of Mexico. But the Texans shot them to pieces at a place called Plum Creek. Quanah's father had led enough Comanches, Kiowas, and Kiowa Apaches to come ever so close to ridding the Brazos River valley of whiteass settlers and reclaiming its rich grass and choice buffalo range, but then Nocona lost heart and died young. Quanah ignored the Long Tongue jabber and imagined a day when *he* called the tribes into council and *he* led the alliance that turned the Texan settlements into charred logs and buzzard roosts. But then he found himself hearing his father's words again: how if he could find the Seminoles and Kickapoo, they might show him the way to his uncle called Mexico, and he was the kind of man who could help.

In half a day the mule riders were looking back from the mountains at the river narrowing to a thread in the woodland bottom. They crossed more bitter desert, but all the while climbing, the air growing cooler and fragrant with piñons and then spruce and firs. The canyons they came upon echoed the caws of magpies, crows, and jays. Like they'd just seen demons, a flock of bright green parrots burst out of tall trees and fled with long tails, squawks of panic, and flashes of yellow under their hard-beating wings.

At a distance the raiders saw multiple plumes of smoke. The raiders spoke with excitement, filling in the blanks with sign. They rode a while farther, into a large grove of trees and out into a meadow, but before they reached the ridge, Dohasan pulled his mule to a circling halt. "Here," he said. "We'll put our saddles and panniers in the trees, so the bears and skunks can't get them. We'll mark the trees so we can find them and we'll hobble the mules." He nodded at the wisdom of his planning. "They'll have plenty of grazing."

"Hobble the mules here?" said Quanah.

The Kiowa gave him an amused stare. "You'd rather stay with them?"

"No, I'd rather ride mine. I don't like walking. Or feeding a good animal to wolves and bears."

The Kiowas and Quohada looked at their squabbling leader and raider. Everyone knew this was not good medicine. As others followed Dohasan's orders and clambered up the trunks of trees to build a cache, Quanah finished hobbling his mule and stood for a moment rubbing Rose Hips' neck. The roan mule again pushed at his leg with his muzzle, then thoughtfully raised his hooves, set them down, then went hopping off like an insect or a frog. Quanah knew he'd never see his mule again.

When they set out, Dohasan sent parties up the slopes to maintain a watch while he led others along a rushing creek. Across Quanah's chest and back was strapped a coil of lariat. He carried his rifle, and the white man's carpenter's hammer was looped in his belt, bumping against his hip. The Kiowa made a game of stepping rock to rock beside the creek, while the ones on the hillsides scrambled to keep up. As they panted and shoved through the conifers, Quanah looked down at Dohasan and then his friend Breaks Something, who had a quiver and bow. "Why don't you put an arrow in him?" Quanah said.

They began to see patches of ground that had been burned, rooted out, and planted in corn. From a cliff they gaped at a waterfall that crashed on rocks where women were washing clothes. Young girls were bathing. "Which one do you want?" Breaks Something whispered.

"Any one of them. All of them," Quanah replied.

They thought the Mexicans were unprepared for their coming, that the raid would be easy. But a large number of Mexicans inhabited that valley. They lived in thatched-roof jacales with chickens, pigs, and dogs, and even the smallest of these villages had an adobe common, a thick-walled presidio that generations of the campesinos had put up for protection when the raiders came. The roofs were made of adobe as well—they couldn't be set on fire—and the only windows were narrow slits for their rifles. They kept stores of food and water in the presidios, and if their dogs raised a clamor, they dropped their hoes and swept up their infants and ran inside the presidio, barring with a steel pole a door too thick to be battered down. Then they climbed to their stations, gun barrels poking out like they were standing on each others' heads.

When the moon was up, the raiders from the plains filtered through more trees and looked upon the town. It had dirt streets, a church, a plaza, and a thick wall that curved along one end. Ignoring the hour, a rooster crowed over and over, and goats walked around bleating, tinkling their bells. Guitars rang, and men were singing. Quanah was filled with a loneliness and melancholy. He didn't want to kill those people. He wished he could join them.

Though the moon was bright and high above the trees, Dohasan led them onward to the town. When they reached the presidio wall, they gasped and stepped back. Though the fortification was unmanned, the terrible evidence of a raid gone wrong hung from poles sticking outward from the adobe. They had been Apaches, judging from cloth headbands that weather had not yet loosened and worn away. The heads were tied to the poles by their hair, and had been there long enough that the eyes and mouths had yielded to carrion birds and the faces collapsed into withered sacks. The lipless bared teeth mocked them, grinning.

A dog burst out of the darkness snarling. Big Blond put an arrow in its chest but didn't kill it, and it ran off with a howl that cost them all the element of surprise. A bugle sounded inside the presidio, people dashed from jacales into its walls, and in moments the alarm echoed from other villages, up and down the canyon. Afoot, the hunters had just become the hunted.

They ran up in the sierra, found caves, and hid out during the days, coming down at night near other clusters of jacales, walking the leather off their moccasins. They were exhausted, humiliated, and hungry. At last Woman's Heart ran down a bony calf, which raised an awful cry. Dohasan flopped on its head and clamped an arm around its jaws. Quanah's gaze was engaged by one wild white eye before they cut its throat and opened its chest and belly. Hungry as he was, he had never much liked raw meat. He watched them tearing out the calf's heart, lungs, and glands, and he envisioned a flock of buzzards. Dohasan sent a scout up a short ridge, yammered, and decided to risk building a fire. It was still several hours till dark, and the sky was gray. Smoke would be hard to see. They partly skinned the heifer and pitched it on the burning logs, rolling the carcass by its hooves as the meat charred and sizzled.

Then, damn if they didn't hear horses, a bunch of them, coming up the mountainside straight toward them. They listened for a moment, and with the tock and slide of hooves on rock the wind carried voices of men, speaking Spanish. In a frenzy of whispered curses they jumped to action, one yanking the calf out of the fire and dragging it back into a cedar brake, the others kicking burning logs apart and pitching dirt with their hands. They got the fire put out, though any fool could see what it was, and ran, chambering shells and notching arrows and, all in all, preparing to die. Before the Mexican rurales reached the fire they reined off along another draw. The Quohada and Kiowas listened to the voices receding, the laughter. After a while they came out of the trees; Quanah considered the calf, seeping with blood and crusted with char, dirt, and nettles of juniper. The meat was ruined, though they carved off what mouthfuls they could. The routed warriors sat on their heels, disgusted.

The next day they were on the edge of a long meadow when Big Blond signaled them quiet with a fling of his hand. As the raiders eased rifles and bows to hand and peered at the woods' mottled color and shade, the only sound was the crows. Quanah saw the buck. Carrying a bright and gleaming new rack of antlers, the deer nosed its head forward and back and took slow, delicate steps, its tail flapping like a pennant in the breeze. In time Quanah made out the hunter moving just as carefully. An Indian carried a very old rifle. He wore leather boots, leggings, a loincloth, and vest. He was thick of chest and waist and had a very large head. His hair was unbraided, tied back from his ears by a rag. Despite his bulk he moved lightly, trying to find clearance for his shot. He slowly raised the rifle and put his cheek to the stock.

Any gunshot might bring the rurales on them. Timber Wolf cleared his throat loudly. With a snort and weaving ducking stride the buck plunged across the clearing and crashed through brush and saplings and was gone. Rifles, arrows, and bows trained on the hunter, who pointed back with his antique gun.

"Buenas tardes," Dohasan called to the hunter. "Habla español?"

"Sí. Buenas tardes."

"Who are you?"

"I'm Kickapoo."

"Ahh," several men said at once. He fights us for the Mexicans. Kill him.

"Wait," Quanah barked. The Kiowas looked from their gunsights and bows to him and Dohasan and back. The Kickapoo raised his head from the musket but kept the stock against his shoulder. Quanah called, "Hunter, where are your horses?"

"Back there," the Kickapoo said. "There's just one."

"How were you going to get that deer back to your lodge?"

"Carry it."

"You hunt these mountains without a pack animal?"

The Kickapoo gave a nod and fidgeted, anxious to either fight or be on his way. "I have to kill four deer to baptize my son and give him his name."

"That's your tradition?" said Dohasan.

Another nod. "My beliefs."

Dohasan challenged him. "We are Kiowas and Comanches. You help the Mexicans fight us. Tell us why we shouldn't kill you."

"What difference would it make what I say?" the young man replied wearily. "We fight who we have to fight. Especially Mescaleros, because they come so often against us. The Mexicans are our neighbors. We have uncles and sisters among them; they pay us in food and horses to help them in fights we would have to fight anyway."

"Come smoke with us," Dohasan said. "Maybe we won't kill you."

"I have to name my son." He turned his back and took off after the deer in a long square-shouldered stride. Bows followed him with arrows aimed and strings far back. "Kickapoo, wait!" Quanah called after him. "Do you know a place called Múzquiz?"

The man paused. "Yes. It's a Mexican town."

"A river called Las Sabinas?"

The hunter looked back, ignoring the guns and arrows. He was clearly not afraid of the raiders, and it saved his life. "We just call it River."

"Do you know a white man called John Parker? He has lived around there many years. He grows cattle and has a Mexican wife."

"Yes, I know him. He's our neighbor."

"If I carry your deer for you, will you take me to his lodge?"

"So you can kill John Parker?"

"No, so I can honor him. He's my uncle."

Dohasan raised his beak nose and snorted. "You come to Mexico to *honor* a white man?" Quanah ignored him. No one could say he hadn't done it right. If you lost confidence in the leader of a raid, you didn't try to replace or undermine him; you just quit the raid and went off by yourself. As Quanah prepared to depart with the Kickapoo, Dog Hates Thunder and Breaks Something said they would see him back on the buffalo plains in a moon or two, though it wasn't clear how any of them would get there without any horses or mules.

⋈

The Kickapoo was a powerful walker. Quanah limped along sore of leg and foot, trying to keep up. He asked the hunter his name. "You couldn't get your tongue and teeth around the Kickapoo way of saying," the man replied. "It means Bramble of Blackberries Grows across the Ground. Just call me what the Mexicanos call me. José."

He was at first a man of considerable silences. They walked a good way, then he said, "And what are you called?"

"Quanah."

José nodded. "Does it have a meaning?"

"Fragrant," Quanah said defensively. "It's not my name of power. Story is, my mother—"

"It's a good name, I like it," the Kickapoo cut him off. "Comanches are said to be great buffalo hunters. We see buffalo only when we go to see kin in Kansas. They're faster than they look, and they're hard to kill. They must be sacred to you."

"Sagrado," Quanah repeated. "I don't think we have a word like that."

José looked at him in surprise then walked on. "Deer are sacred to Kickapoo. They were put here on earth for us. That's why we're great deer hunters. They love us. Of course, in that moment, no prey really wants to die."

José said, "Can I see your gun?" The men exchanged an ancient muzzle loader and a Henry repeater, murmured and stroked the stocks, raised the other's guns to their shoulders and followed the sweep of a cruising brown eagle. "Mine belonged to a dead Frenchman," said the Kickapoo.

"A dead what?"

"Frenchman. They're a kind of white man. They were the first ones we ever saw, in a country far to the north. They said, 'My, you

103

have some mighty fine deer hides. Could we trade you for some of these?' They came back again after the snowmelt and said, 'My, this is mighty fine forest you live in. Do you mind if we find just a small place to sleep?'" He looked at Quanah and smiled. "We once sieged a place called Detroit."

Quanah said, "In the long ago, we also lived in the north. We were one with the Shoshones, but there was some feud; old men still talk about it in our smoke lodges. Leaving them behind, the grandfathers hunted their way south, where they did find something magic—the horse." He yawned. "I'm glad the grandfathers went the way they did. I don't like being cold."

They came to the meadow where José had hidden his cache and hobbled a bony gelding of sickly color, like clabbered milk. But the Kickapoo swelled up and grinned at the sight of him, like a man who owned them by the thousands. The Kickapoo called the gelding by a Spanish word, Flaco, skinny, and the name fit. But Quanah of course complimented the man on his horse, and helped him saddle it. He grunted at the heavy weight of the saddle he flung on the horse's back. "Do you want to ride him?" offered the Kickapoo.

"What?" said Quanah, stunned. Why, he could just bump the nag with his heels and be gone, off to find the man called Mexico and steal better horses. Or he could just vanish down here, which he thought about more and more. "No, thanks. It's your horse."

José grinned. "But you're tired. And imagine, a Comanche without a horse." His gaze took the measure of Quanah's long legs. "I don't mind. I'll set the stirrups."

"No," Quanah insisted. "It will be a pleasure to ride him, but later. You have a deer to kill."

José put his foot in the stirrup, hopped twice, then swung his bulk up. The horse farted and sagged under the weight. Quanah handed José the Frenchman's musket, re-shouldered his gear, and they walked on. José rummaged in a sack and gnawed on some jerked venison, then tore him off a piece. Quanah went after it eagerly. José said, "This man John Parker, you called him your uncle . . ."

"Yes, he's my mother's brother."

José nodded thoughtfully. "He's white. Or looks it."

"He and my mother were freed from Texans when they were children," Quanah said. "Her name is Naduah. My father was a war chief. I can't say his name, because he's dead, it's our tradition."

The Kickapoo nodded. "And John Parker?"

"He used to ride with us," Quanah said. "But one raid down here he caught the tásia and, who knows what happened then— maybe he lost his nerve, maybe he found the right woman. I'm told he just keeps cattle now."

"What did he catch?"

Quanah found in his memory the Spanish word for smallpox. "Viruela."

José said with a sigh, "You're lucky to have him, your uncle."

"Story told," said Quanah, "is that a bunch of Kickapoo pissed on him in a bathtub, and that's what cured him."

The squat man smiled. "I know my people have liked that man John Parker since way before my time. So do they call you Quanah Parker?"

Quanah stumbled. "*What*? Who call me that? Never!"

José clicked his tongue at the sad horse and went on nodding. "That's your power name. Quanah Parker. Can't you hear it? Let me tell you about my uncles . . ."

9

S HOT IN THE THROAT as it nosed into a clearing at first light, the mule deer had grown heavy and rank on Quanah's shoulders as he followed José and his clabber-colored horse through mesquite and huisache. The country at the foot of the mountains was flat, the air dusty and stifling, and the deer was just gutted, legs and meat still in the skin, so it was heavy; but Quanah insisted on honoring the bargain. At last they came to a fork of hoof-worn trails. José pulled back on the reins and shoved with his boots at the stirrups, and the thin horse stopped gladly. He pointed down the path to the right and said, "Keep veering right, and you'll walk to your uncle's house. Watch for a dry creek and keep it on your right. If you cross the creek, you'll end up in a rattlesnake den."

José reached down, grabbed hold of the carcass, and pulled it up over his shoulders like a shawl. "Thank you for bringing me here," said Quanah.

"Be careful down here, amigo," said José. "Mexicans, they got bounties on raiders from the north."

"Good luck, Kickapoo," said Quanah.

"And you, Comanche."

José booted the horse, which sighed, fluttered his lips, and plugged on. Quanah watched the buck's head and rack of antlers bob as if the deer were the horse's rider, then the thick brush closed around them.

Following the path, Quanah found a small pool of stagnant water in the creek. His hands and arms were grimy and itching from the carcass, and he didn't like the way he smelled. The creek water was not too slimy, so he washed himself with one hand. He carried his Henry rifle and the bag containing his sleeping pad and fire kit slung across the other arm. As he walked on he saw bony-hipped black cattle that edged away from him or just stared, chewing their cud. Above the creek rose a bluff of gray rock ledges studded with yucca and sotol crowned with spikes and blooms, and thick banks of pink-leaved ocuebocopi. He had never seen pink prickly pear before. It seemed much too hot and bright for rattlesnakes to be moving around during the day, but he kept an eye out for them anyway. The big doves thick in this brush carried on their owl-like hooting, and he got a scolding by a jay with a head that was bright green. He began to see old burns of trash scattered through the brush. The trail came out of the thorn forest, revealing a low-roofed ramshackle house and an expanse of corrals put up willy-nilly with crooked posts of mesquite and ocotillo. Buzzards rode the breezes in the sky.

"Hola!" he yelled first. "Hola!"

In the ways of Comanche kinship, a youth called his father and uncle who were true brothers "Ap." They were supposed to be equals, friends, and rescuers if the other got in more fight and trouble than he could handle. If the boy wanted to borrow something of his uncle's, he just went and got it. So Quanah hollered, "Ap! Ap!"

A brindle dog limped out from the house, barking fiercely. Its right foreleg had been cut off at the knee. As the dog snarled and hobbled, Quanah kept calling; he was easing through the corrals, looking not to get dog bit, when he distinctly heard a hammer cock. "Stand where you are," a man ordered him in Spanish. "One more step and I'll kill you."

Quanah raised his hands, showing that he carried the rifle loosely, with no hostile intent. To the side he made out a thin man with black hair, a scarred face, and dark glaring eyes. He wore a soiled long john shirt and suspenders that were turned down over his britches and hips. The glare was fixed over a big bore shotgun. Quanah blurted, "John Parker?"

"Sí. Quien es? You with the hair and boots of a Comanche."

"I am Quohada," he answered quickly. "I'm called Quanah. Quanah Parker." It was the first time he'd ever said that—in his nervousness and fright it just leaped from his tongue. "Soy el hijo de Naduah."

The older man snapped at the dog and hollered it away. He lowered the shotgun a bit. "Are you now. Son of my sister. Who's your father, then?"

"I can't say his name."

"Yes, you can. You'd better."

The man was jabbing the barrel at his chest, making it easier to violate the taboo. "They called him Nocona."

John Parker stepped around and relieved him of the Henry. Looking for Quanah's knife, he saw the claw hammer hung in his belt and grunted. "What do you do with that? Build houses?"

"Makes a war club."

"Where's the rest of them?" his rude kinsman asked.

"There aren't any more. I'm alone." He could see John Parker was not too impressed by his claim or his story; he tried to say enough to convince him. "The Texans ransomed you. You rode back out to see the Nokoni once, to see my mother, and she wouldn't go back to the Texans, so you stayed with them, the Nokoni, and rode with them again. They talk about you still. They called you Mexico."

The pockmarked man stared at Quanah, then said with a sudden jerk of his head. "You come all this way to find me."

"I came some of it with a raiding party of Quohada and Kiowas. A Kickapoo neighbor of yours called José brought me to your road."

"Where are your horses?"

Quanah lagged his head, didn't want to go into it. "They got stolen."

John Parker barked a laugh and yelled toward the house, telling someone it was all right. A Mexican woman appeared in the doorway of the house. She had a rifle, too. Watching them, she raised a hand to shade her eyes from the sun. She looked tall for a Mexican woman. She wore a dress with a long skirt, and her hair was tied behind her ears. "Who is it?" she called.

"Come have a look," said John Parker. "This gray-eyed boy, this unhorsed Comanche, claims he's my sister's long lost baby."

The woman stayed where she was. "Do you believe him?"

"Guess I do," said the man, tilting his head. "What's your name again?"

"Quanah."

The man sorted and after a moment found the recollection in his mind. "Man called Fragrant?" Quanah sighed and shrugged. "Well, Quanah Parker, there is my wife, Doña Juanita. You can tell how pleased she is to meet you."

Quanah gave her a nod, and she nodded back. The Mexican looker. Even with the thickness of waist and hips and the gray in her hair, he could see how they would have called her that.

The man grinned and gave his head another vigorous shake. It seemed to be a trait. "What do you want from me?"

In the tongue of his people he began, "Ne tzaré tziareyia-jumiar."

John Parker understood and acknowledged him, because at once he sneered in Spanish, "Well, of course you're hungry! Great horseman that you are, and in this mean country somehow a man on foot. Some brave raiders in your party didn't run off and *leave* you, did they?"

Without knowing him, Quanah afforded his mother's brother great respect. Quanah lowered his eyes and shook his head, sorry that bitterness still festered in him.

"Mi amor," the man said to his wife, "can you fry up something for my nephew to eat? You may not know these Comanches believe in hospitality. All that people have got to do is ask for food and drink and some ground beside the fire, and the next thing you know they'll be piled up in robes sleeping all day, like kin you can't run out."

His wife shot back, "We're not Comanche."

The dog bobbed after her as she turned back toward the house.

But the next thing they heard was the banging of a skillet. Inside the low-roofed adobe, Quanah adjusted to the dimness and the musk of their longtime sharing of the same space. "Have you ever sat in a chair?" asked Doña Juanita.

"No, señora," Quanah answered.

"Well, please," she said, pointing at one set against a plank table. "It won't hurt you."

Perched stiffly on the chair, he watched as she chopped an onion and a handful of the small chili piquines that grew wild in swarms in the Mexican brush. She cut off a few slices of what he took to be cow meat, then dumped it all in a bowl and began to break chicken eggs over it, then stirred it all into yellow slop. Some people believed that eating birds' eggs diluted your medicine, but Quanah was not aware he had any medicine in the first place, and he was so hungry he would have swallowed the eggs raw. She broke kindling and laid a few short sticks on coals in a cook stove that raised a fire at once. Most of its smoke went up a pipe through the roof. She dumped the egg slop in the skillet and shook it as it cooked and congealed. She put it in a plate with two rounds of flat Indian cornbread and with a bang set the plate on the table before him.

Doña Juanita saw his awkwardness and hesitation, and for the first time smiled. She showed him how to grasp and scoop the food to his mouth with the tortilla. He murmured his thanks, then gasped at the fire instilled in the egg and meat mix by the chilis. Her husband got up and went outside, where he filled a pitcher of water with a hand pump, then walked back in and poured some for him to drink in a pewter cup. "Thirsty, too," he growled in the Comanche tongue.

Quanah had seen enough of the world to be impressed with some things the whites could do. He was born to a land that often had no water, but with no incantations this man could make it just belch out of the ground.

When he had wolfed down the spare but fiery meal and gulped

the rest of the water he licked his fingers and thumbs. He thanked his uncle and the señora, then began an oration he'd been rehearsing. "I'm glad I found you, Ap, and that we talked before something bad happened, as they do between Our People and Mexicanos. My father often told me of the adventures you had together on the warring trails and buffalo hunts." That was a lie offered as flattery— Nocona had spoken of his wife's brother just that one time on the Canadian, the day he got sick. "I found you because my spirit is determined, if not wise. You have lived in three worlds, and I've known just one. It left a great sadness in my father that he could never find and rescue my mother and sister, who were taken in a raid by the Texans. He believed they live among the Texans called Parker, but he didn't know where to look. I hope maybe you know those Texans. I ask you to help me find what's left of my family. I don't want to hurt anyone. Though I am what you see today, I'll pay those people who have them a fair ransom in horses and mules."

The pockmarked man gazed at his wife, and she looked sadly at both of them. In Comanche ways, Quanah's requesting this of an uncle he didn't know was hardly out of line. John Parker answered sadly and firmly, "I have to tell you that your mother and my sister, Naduah, who was born Cynthia Ann Parker, is dead. She passed away a few months ago, and her Texas kin grieved over her and buried her in their way. It was the same way with your sister, some years ago. I'm sorry."

Quanah reeled back in the chair. He saw the woman hesitate, then she removed his plate. "Who told you this?" Quanah cried.

"I pass back through that country now and then. I still have Parket kinfold there. I never saw your mother or sister after the Parkers took them back. But I see and hear sometimes from a cousin or two. Your sister came down with a terrible and fast illness called yellow fever. Your mother took her dying awfully hard, my cousin said. And after that"—he sighed and looked at his wife—"they say she just gave up. I don't know where the little girl died. Your mother is buried beside a churchyard in the forest part of Texas, where most of those Parker people live. A little stream runs past it called Indian Creek. She would have liked that, I guess."

Quanah banged his hand against the table. "How do you *know* this? I don't believe it. It's not true."

John Parker glanced at the looker, who shook her head and put her chin in her hand. He got up and walked to a contraption of wood that Quanah would come to know as a desk. He pulled out a drawer, picked up a sleeve of paper, and withdrew a folded piece of paper. He looked at it and thought for a moment over how to make it Spanish. "We heard about it first from one of my cousins. She wrote me, 'John, I regret to tell you that your brave sister Cynthia Ann passed away this winter into the hands of God. She is at peace now . . .'" He jerked his head again with a snort that did not quite come out a laugh. "Manos de dios," he said again.

The hammer in Quanah's belt gave the table a loud knock as he lurched up and stared at the ink-marked piece of paper. Something restrained him from snatching and tearing it up. "I don't hear these words! Can you hear anything?"

John Parker looked at his wife again, then sighed and raised the piece of paper. "They're here, Ap. Believe me. Even your mother learned how to read."

Quanah:

WITH THE THREE-LEGGED DOG at the heels of my worn-out moccasins, I wandered through my uncle's chaparral in a daze, staring above the layer of mesquites at the varied blue pyramids of the Sierra Madre and trying to calm down. "Maybe he'd like some time alone," the Mexican looker had said to my uncle. Alone! I was alone on the face of all the earth!

You need to understand how indifferent I was to the notion of cattle. When I was most alert to them, they were inferior creatures, as insignificant and offensive to me as flies. Ap's ugly black cross-breeds and skinny longhorns gave me a wary look and got out of the way, bawling in that brainless way they have. Mother cows put themselves between their calves and the weeping man and the crippled dog. I ignored them, talking to myself.

My Uncle John (I've since found I like the whiteass way of referring to him) had been trying to breed bulls for the strange sport that excites Mexicans and always winds up with the bull being stabbed to death. Ap hadn't been having much luck with that, he told me later. The young bull watching me was wall-eyed and worthless—one horn turned up, the other horn down. As I imagine the way it happened, the bull stood blinking in a grove of mesquite. He watched me a while longer, lowered his head to graze, and some knot in his brain changed his mind, for he was on top of me as fast as a spooked horse.

I heard the hooves and tried to spin out of the way, but the boulder of skull and horn whammed me in the back and launched me into a cenizo bush abloom in purple, I remember that flash of pretty color. The pain took my breath away, and the bull wasn't content with knocking me down. He breathed in angry rasping coughs, and he stomped around me, ramming his neck and head into me again and again, trying to gore me with those twisted horns. It's a good thing that wasn't the smartest bull. "Help!" I heard myself yelling. "Get him off me! Ayúdame!" I'd come all the way down the war trail for this. It had happened to everyone else in my family. Why not? It was my turn to die.

The barking dog saved me. I heard a man shouting and then in the same instant there was a shotgun blast and a spray of buckshot whacked the bull in the neck and jaw. The bull grunted and shuddered and lost all interest in me. He doused cenizo, huisache, and me with spray from a shocked bowel and crashed off in the brush. In my pain-wracked stupidity I thought someone had hit the bull trying to shoot me. "Carajo!" I heard my uncle swear. He chambered another shell, in case the bull came back, and kneeled beside me. "I've been meaning to kill that bull," he muttered. "Any calf that comes out of his seed would be just as sorry as he is."

He looked at me close and said, "How are you?"

"Hurts to breathe," I told him.

"Don't try to sit up yet," Ap advised, but I gripped his forearm and insisted on coming up that far. Should have listened to him. My vision went blurry for a minute, and he caught me and laid me back down. When I came back to myself Doña Juanita crouched beside us. "Go saddle us a horse," said my uncle. "The red mare."

"No," I put in. "I don't think I could get up on a horse. I'll walk."

I raised one arm over my uncle's shoulders, cried out when that turned out to be the latest in a run of bad decisions, and after some wobbling of my knees and fast help from the señora, I got to my feet. Sweat was pouring off the end of my nose. "I'm sorry I brought you all this trouble," I said.

"Oh, be quiet," said the señora, picking up the shotgun.

"What you get," John Parker teased me, "for trying to fight a bull. Cutznanojicuató."

"Wasn't no fight. I didn't know he was there until he had me." The dog hopped around us, then led the way toward the house. "How'd your dog lose his leg?" I gritted.

"Tried to fight a bear trap," said Uncle John.

"I have to hunt him a good piece of game when I'm well."

"Few weeks, you might."

By the time we reached the house, I wasn't inclined to argue when they laid me down on their bed. The señora pulled off my boots and leggings, then covered my legs and breechclout with a quilt. I drank some of the water she brought me. She set an empty jar on the floor within my reach. "You've got broken ribs and maybe worse," she told me. "You won't be feeling like going outside to pee." She laid her cool palm on my forehead, seeing if I had a fever.

I pitched into a sleep of exhaustion that didn't last long, and when I woke up I was so sore I cried out anytime I moved. Couldn't help it. There was a pungent odor in the house of burning juniper wood and sage—it took me back to old Jaybird Pesters trying to save my dad from the twisted face. The señora heard me stirring, and she walked in the bedroom carrying a small pan and a bundle of items in a black cloth tied with a leather thong. She put the pan on the floor, sat beside me on the bed, untied the thong, and removed from the bundle a tail feather of a golden eagle. She fanned the air above my face with it, then tapped me on my forehead, ears, chest, ribs, and thighs. With a smile of mischief she gave me a little tap on my breechclout as well. She put the feather away, picked up the pan, and stirred a grayish paste with her forefinger.

"What is it?" I asked.

"It's just milkweed plant. Hold your breath now. I have to put this on you." She smeared the paste on my breastbone and ribs, touching me as lightly as she could.

"Are you a medicine woman?" I asked.

Doña Juanita shrugged. "We don't call it that. I just know some plants and herbs to use."

She pulled from her kit a smaller folding of cloth and pulled from it round carvings of peyote, osidobeda. She set out four whole buttons on the quilt and poured water from a pitcher into a glass.

"I don't want that," I told her.

"Yes, you do. You hurt too much. Do you want that?"

The taste of peyote was putrid, bitter. My stomach roiled, but knowing how much it would hurt, I quelled the urge to vomit. I dozed again, this time longer. When I woke the señora came toward me with her hand extended, palm up. In her hand was a larger peyote button. It grew out of her arm, entwining her thumb and wrist like a vine grafted on a tree root. When I reached for her hand, she disappeared. We went through this several times. She was there, and then she was gone, and finally she let me hold the peyote. A tingling commenced in my hands and spread up my arms through my shoulders and filled up my chest. "It's just the medicine," she murmured. She was becoming the young woman of her voice and eyes and mouth. She wet her lips with her tongue. I almost reached up and touched her breast. More than anything in this world I wanted to make love to her. I reached for her arms but she was gone again. I looked at my hand. Nothing in it.

"Is this how you saved him?" I asked her once.

"Who?"

"Uncle John."

"I didn't save him. I just stayed with him."

"Were you ever tempted to run off?"

"Of course. I thought I was going to catch the viruela. I thought I'd die."

"Why didn't you do it?"

"And go where? Give it to someone else?"

Another time she was feeding me hot marrow broth with a spoon, which clicked against my teeth, a new sensation. I asked her, "Did you and Ap have children?"

"No. I think the illness scorched him. But it may have been me." She blew on a spoonful of soup and offered me more. "So get well, Quanah Parker. You're the last one in your line."

Another day or night a medicine eagle flew right inside the house. It did. I felt the air moved by its wings, heard the rustling, and when I opened my eyes and beheld it, the tingling the señora had imparted with her hands flushed all the way through me. It was a dark brown eagle, with just a flush of gold where the shoulders joined the neck. I was still in the bed, but there was no sky and no roof. My father was always trying to get me to change my name to some habit of an eagle. Now the eagle he wanted me to find hung there above me, barely a wingspan away, fixing me with that far-seeing glare. I began to shake, and when the eagle flew away the fever broke. I was drenched in sweat.

10

CHARLES GOODNIGHT'S new ranch in Colorado was the prairie floor of a canyon cut through foothills of the Greenhorn Mountains by twenty-five miles of Arkansas River. Cheyenne power that long dominated that country had been broken by the army that came with completion of the Union Pacific and Kansas Pacific railroads. Goodnight was always in search of netherworlds for his cattle growing, and this was an exceptional find. Blizzards howled across the tableland plains but left just traces of snow on the sheltered bunchgrass below. He kept about three thousand head of longhorns and a few hundred of the English breed Herefords grazing the main ranch, and he had trail foremen and drovers who were always pushing herds to Kansas and Nebraska, Wyoming and Montana, wherever free grass and new markets grew. He hired tradesmen out of Pueblo to build a new house out of adobe and log beams. He had an orchard of apple tree saplings bottom-wrapped in burlap and shipped to the stage depot in Pueblo. Impressed by market prices of corn and wheat, he hired men who knew how to farm. Eager to try out a thirsty forage called alfalfa that was brought from South America to California during the Gold Rush, he put crews to work trenching miles of irrigation ditches diverted from the Arkansas and its creeks. Mister Charlie was putting on airs of a gentleman planter, and he was not yet thirty-five.

The boss took on all these new things in addition to a bride named Mary. She was a sharp-chinned woman whose father had come to the Palo Pinto country from a busted law practice in Tennessee. Goodnight courted her all through his years scouting for the rangers and the drives of scavenged cattle up through the nowhere that came to be called the Goodnight-Loving Trail. She was in Kentucky living with relatives when he finally proposed that they marry. They journeyed by Mississippi steamer down to St. Louis and by train to Abilene, Kansas, then by stage down the Santa Fe Trail. The morning after their arrival in Pueblo, she looked out the window of their hotel and saw that two horse thieves hung lynched from the cross tie of a telegraph pole. "I don't think it hurt the pole," Mister Charlie said he joshed her, much to his regret. He made it up to her with a honeymoon at a hotel with a better view, of Pikes Peak.

Mary Goodnight was a handsome and genteel-sounding woman, but she was a Southerner with a large store of anger about the War of Northern Aggression, and she had no use for nigras, as she described black folk. Bose kept all the distance from her that he could. Denver had the only bank in the new state of Colorado, and Bose was always the one carrying the boss's money up there. Sooner or later on that road he was going to get shot over a horse or just some ignorant man's spite, if not the boss's satchels. Bose was greatly relieved one day when Mister Charlie said he was thinking about going in partners with some town fellows to start a bank in Pueblo. But later in that same conversation he said, "Bose, have you thought more about going back to Texas?"

They were riding beside a field of alfalfa when he made that remark, which startled him. The hay crop was green and pretty but smelled rank. "No, sir, I didn't give it any thought in the first place. I ain't lost one thing down there."

"But you've got nothing up here. You've got no one like you."

That was true but still a harsh thing to say. Bose leaned back in the saddle and in agitation extended his arm. "Mister Charlie, it's summertime, and the air's nice and cool. Look at those snowcaps. I like it here."

Goodnight's head was big for his small body. His shaggy haircut, beard, and chest hair were beginning to show some gray. "You're of an age now you ought to settle down," he lectured Bose. "I can speak from experience now—marrying is good for a man. You need to go back home and get you a farm. You'll find some girl that you've got fixed in your mind as a pickaninny has turned into a good-looking woman. There's nothing keeping you from it, now you're free."

"Nothing but Comanches and Kiowas," Bose testily rejoined.

Goodnight growled and leaned over his horse's neck to spit. "Those Indians got the same generals after them that brought down the Confederate States of America. You think they can't starve out and whip a bunch of feuding gut-eaters once they set their minds to it? All they've got to do is keep turning loose those outfits of buffalo hunters. Why, shit, how much of a hunt is it? Dumb beasts go right on grazing—take a little roll and dust themselves out—while they're getting knocked down right and left with forty-five and fifty caliber slugs. In Kansas they say they're thinning out that herd five thousand head a day. Myself, I hate to see the shaggies go. They'll hole up in canyons like this—where a man might give them a little protection, if he's a mind to—but the suns on the great herds will soon be set. It's not a piddling trade in coats and salted tongues no more. Some tanner found a way to make industrial leather of the hides. Buyers in England and Germany are lined up to get them. They're making hides into belts that keep wheels of cotton gins and textile mills turning. Explain that to those Indians. They're fixing to starve."

Bose thought Mister Charlie's melancholy might have steered the discourse to more comfortable ground, but Goodnight peered over and said, "A large amount of Indian country in Texas is prime farmland, just waiting for the plow. There's enough rain if you don't get too far west, and if soil will nourish prairie it ought to do as well with the right cash crop. State land's going for fifty cents an acre. You'd be smart to get your share of that before all the good parts are gone. I'd stake you, with a little mortgage."

Bose tried to keep the anger out of his voice. "Mister Charlie, it's not just buffalo finding shelter in this canyon. When winter blows there's no small number of maverick cattle that drift down in this canyon to get out of the wind. I help you brand the yearlings and calves. I was hoping you might let me rope a few of the poor ones next year and start building me a little herd, along with what I do here. I'd keep up my work and be out the way whenever you don't need me. Always have. I could make me a dugout and build me something better and permanent as time goes along. I don't need much."

But Goodnight was cool and distant, his mind made up. "Fair proposition," he said, "except you need to be among your own kind."

"You mean to say you're firing me? Who else is gonna carry your money to the bank?"

He'd never spoken to Goodnight in that tone of voice. The boss's eyebrows twitched but he said mildly, "No, firing's a different thing. But I am letting you go."

Later that day, Goodnight tossed him a heavily loaded Mexican game bag that Bose had hooked to his saddle when he was the boss's money courier and growled that he could have his pick of any horse and mule in the herd, except his own. Sitting under a cottonwood beside Hardscrabble Creek, Bose was shocked to find the bag contained four hundred dollars in gold. He got over his surprise, though, and from the remuda he cut out a trim paint gelding and a tall, burly black mule. The paint had chestnut spots on one hip and flags around three legs, but the color mark of value was on his head and neck. The bonnet broke the mane and covered his eyes, ears, and forehead like a sombrero's shade. Short or long distances, the gelding could run. And the brown patch over his eyes made him what the horse Indians called a Medicine Hat. Goodnight might think the plains tribes were finished, but Bose didn't share his optimism. Cheyennes in particular were said to believe a Medicine Hat was a near invincible horse. If Bose had to get across the plains on his own, he wanted all the bluff and magic he could get.

He named the horse Tricks, the big mule Juneteen, and despite the tension with the boss he took his time, riding them until they were legged up strong and knew him well. Bose left at sunrise on the first of April. He was tightening their cinches when Goodnight came out to the corral to say goodbye. An old stock saddle, another gift from the boss, was perched like a bellman's cap on the back of the black mule, which Bose would start out riding. The paint carried his good saddle and bags of clothes, gear, and food. It was an awkward moment for both men.

Goodnight handed Bose an envelope and said the letter of introduction might be of some assistance finding work down the trail. "You're a rare and fortunate man, knowing how to write a letter yourself. Send me one from time to time, if you don't mind." Then he shook Bose's hand like it was a dog's paw and ambled off to fix a gate. He was the most contradictory man Bose had ever known.

Bose was twenty-four years old. He didn't know where he was headed—just that he'd been told he had to go. Two days south of Pueblo he picked up the Mountain Branch of the Santa Fe Trail. The rocky and gully-washed switchbacks rose sharply amid piñon and ponderosa pines toward the Ratón Pass. The Mountain Branch of the trail was now a toll road. Some travelers still took their chances and choked the alkali dust of the shorter route over the plains, the Cimarron Cutoff, but the regularity of attacks by the Indians had driven most to the high road across a prong of the Sangre de Cristos. Bose and his mule and horse passed small groups of riders, some of whom threw him measuring and hostile looks. There were families with everything they owned jammed in tarpaulin-covered Conestogas, teamsters singing to strings of pack mules, and wagon masters of the Murphies cracking whips at six-mule teams that wheezed, groaned, and heaved at a dead weight of hoes and shovels, razor strops and thimbles, peppermint sticks and casks of wine. The Murphies were huge—a man could walk under the bed without stooping, and the back wheels had a seven-foot span. Strewn far below the trail were wrecks of wagons and bones of oxen and mules rotted in the traces.

Juneteen was a strong and sure-footed climber, but the grade up to Ratón Pass had him stopping and blowing and trailing strings of green slobber. Bose rode twisted in the saddle, keeping the lead rope tight and the paint horse coming. When they made the crest and started down he tied the rope in a hitch to the horn. They made good time coming off the mountain—he had to haul back on the reins and slow the mule down. As they neared the New Mexico Territory frontier Bose pulled his harmonica out of his pocket. He gave it a few slides across his mouth, playing softly. He put his voice to "Rye Whiskey," and Juneteen's ears turned around. No one else might like his singing, but he had an admirer in the mule.

> *I've no wife to quarrel, no babies to bawl*
> *The best way of living is no wife at all*
> *Way up on Clinch Mountain I wander alone*
> *I'm drunk as the devil, oh, leave me alone*

At the foot of Ratón Pass, across the line of the Territory, was a ramshackle trading post, Willow Springs. To the west rose the Sangre de Cristo range, their red rock bluffs and sunsets having inspired some priest to invoke the blood of Christ. Bose was three more days getting to Santa Fe. The trail as the town grew near was deeply rutted and lined with hummocks of trash—bottles and tins, sodden bedding, fractured wheels and axles, busted sacks of flour and corn, the horns and bones of an ox. The air soon filled up with popping whips and singsong growls to their mules. Out to the side were Mexican carts drawn by burros, herders of goats and geese, purveyors of apples, tortillas, crucifixes of twisted sticks.

The hills above Santa Fe were wooded in groves but spare of grass. The dust cast a pink tinge on the edges of the clouds and the angled light. The road crossed a bridge and a small clear running river. But the town was smudged and thick with odors of pine smoke and lard. There were a couple of big churches and a few houses with peaked and shingled roofs. Otherwise the town looked like a jumble of loose red adobe bricks.

The drivers of the big wagons harried the mules and oxen through cramped streets of adobes put up one wall right against another. Bose and his horse and mule arrived at the plaza that faced a structure with a covered walk along the front and a patio garden shaded by cottonwoods. Waving their arms and standing up in their seats, the caravanners circled past the Palace of the Governors with the crowd cheering. A band played. Comanches wandered through the market, handling bundles of fresh tobacco leaves. All across the plaza Bose saw their buffalo hats.

He found a livery where he could stable Tricks and Juneteen. There was a heavy steel box where he could lock up his Winchester and Colt and, for an extra six bits, he could bunk beside his animals in the straw. He watered and unsaddled them and began to brush them down. A skinny bucktoothed white boy, thirteen or so, who worked in the stable, watched him through boards of the stall. The boy's face had the aspect of a goat.

Billy the Kid:

NIGGER COME IN THERE like he owned the livery. You'd have thought that paint horse and mule had come off a Kentucky paddock with roses around their necks. And him about to sleep there in the shit-smelling straw. Occurred to me to take old McShan's straight razor and hamstring the paint, just to remind that nigger who he was.

He saw me watching him and said, "Go on, son."

Wasn't but in his early twenties himself. "Who you calling son?"

"Just a way of saying. What's your name?"

"Henry. Henry Bonney." School had me down as McCarty but I'd been trying out this one. Feller always needs a good line of names. Why that is, I don't know. You just know you're going to be one of those fellers.

"Stableman called you Kid, like it's your name."

"My step-pa's named Antrim. First man I recall with my ma was named McCarty, but my real pa's name was Bonney. Ma told me. He got killed in the war, fighting for Ulysses S. Grant. He's the president now."

"What I hear," the nigger said, giving me a look. People are always doing that. First like I'm nothing but a razor strop hung on some doorknob, then they get it in their sight that I'm holding the blade. I'm just talking here. There wasn't nothing going on between him and me. But I could see I made the nigger nervous. Suited me fine.

He went on brushing his horse and asked me, "Your ma all right?"

"She's got consumption."

"I'm sorry. So, Billy, you just lurk?"

"Told you it's Henry. Do I what?"

Nigger's the first one put that in my mind. Billy. I kind of liked Billy.

"Lurk," he said again. "Just stand there, don't do nothing. Never try and help."

"I'll help if you pay me. What do you want me to do?"

The gelding raised his tail and dropped manure. "Maybe later you can watch my horse and mule," nigger said. "Keep an eye on my things."

I was hanging onto a board above my head. I raised my feet and started swinging from it. "How much you pay me?" I asked.

"Depends on how well you do the work."

A scrawny gray tabby was poking around in the straw, flirting with me, rolling over on its side. The cat was a barn mouser but never had much luck. It meowed and scraped against a post, then bounded away a few hops when I made a move toward him. "Kitty," I said. "Come here, Kitty."

Nigger gathered up his saddlebags, bedding, and change of

clothes. He carried them to the end of the stall, sat down, and pulled his boots off. He gulped water from a canteen and gnawed on some jerky, then said, "Damn, I'm saddle sore. And this is a town where people got cook stoves and bread. Salt and pepper. Sugar for their coffee. Isn't that right, kid?"

Wasn't the sort of question I felt called to answer. I could see the nigger's money belt on him. He had it tied around his love handles and belly, beneath his shirt. Dumb son of a bitch would walk and clank.

He put the horse and mule between us, trying to make it where I couldn't see him good. He changed clothes and put his boots back on fast. Nigger locked his guns and saddlebags in McShan's strongbox with the locks provided and two of his own. Deal was, if it seemed worth the trouble you just carried off the strongbox, then worried about how to get into it. Or not. The guns might be worth something. But a nigger sleeping on the ground in a stable—he didn't have much money.

He came out pressing at wrinkles in his shirt, then he stuck his hand out, like that was a big thing, giving a boy like me a chance to shake it. "Tell you what, Henry or Billy or Whatever's Your Pleasure. My name is Bose, spell it b-o-s-e." After I consented to shake his hand he pointed at his saddle and blanket, which he'd set on a saw-horse to air. The bridle and reins were looped around the horn, his bags and bedding piled around. "I know they got you feeding horses and cleaning stalls here. Next to slave wages, I imagine. I'll give you two dollars gold to make sure none of this moves between now and the time I get back here tonight. Anybody comes in here, you start yelling for the stableman and me."

I knew a dice game that was missing me, but I said, "Sure."

"Be careful with the horse and mule," the nigger said, giving the big mule's flank a slap. "They don't like nobody walking up behind."

When he was walking out I gave him a social tip, just being agreeable. "Tonight's the first fandango of the spring."

He said, "Oh, it is?" Doubt he knew what a fandango was.

He'd find strolling musicians playing fiddles and guitars, waltzes and their lying brag songs, corridos. Time would come when they'd be making up corridos about me; I knew that, wasn't sure why. Anyway, he'd come on old women wearing the widows' black, mothers with babies in their arms, fancy little men wearing tailed black coats, flat-brimmed sombreros, high-heeled boots with tops that came up to their knees, and flimsy bright spurs that looked like damn ornaments on Christmas trees. And those Mexican girls I already had an eye for, with the bare throats and shoulders and a dust of blue powder around their eyes. None of them would give me the time of day yet, but I knew my time would come.

Until that night, I bet that nigger never had a thought his color could be anything but a wall to a girl who wasn't born on his side of it. She'd watch him coming and hold her cheroot between two fingers, blow a stream of smoke at him. "Guapo," she'd call out to him. "Ven aquí."

Nothing but a whore. But he'd know she called him handsome by the way she said the word.

Next morning I figured it had gone that way for him by the way he lay there in his bedroll. Smiling like a snake, and he had a hand down in there, probably picking crust off his pecker.

"Morning, Billy," he called out, like I was some old friend.

"Henry," I corrected him.

"I know. Just teasing you."

I was still trying to get that barn cat to come to me. "Kitty," I said, squatting on my heels and running my hand over the straw. "Kitty kitty."

Spells it b-o-s-e asked, "What you got there, Henry?"

"Mouse," I said, pushing the tin and small mound of hash toward the cat. "Caught it this morning. Bare hands."

"Good way to get yourself bit and infected. But that's nice. Cat'll like that."

The tabby minced closer, twitching its tail and sniffing. It tilted its head and began to eat. Bone popped between its jaws. And that's when I got it. I always had fast hands.

The cat was yowling and clawing; I had it by the nape of the neck but it twisted around and gouged my wrist good. Other hand, though, I got in six or seven stabs with my pocketknife before I had to let it go. Tabby flipped in the air and hit the ground running, turning somersaults, spouting blood. The paint horse squalled, reared up, and slammed his hooves down two feet from the nigger's love commodities. The mule was trying to kick down the barn—its hooves on the boards sounded like gunshots. And, best of it all, that cat ran right up the bedroll at the nigger. His hand speed wasn't bad.

"God damn you, boy!" he yelled when the cat was gone. He lurched around in there trying to grab the mule's halter but only grabbed him around the neck. That was a strong mule. It flung that nigger so hard against the wall his knees buckled—he was almost knocked out. "I'm gonna tan your hide!" he said when the fog cleared.

I was holding my sides, laughing so hard I tripped and took a seat in the straw. "No, you ain't," I gasped. "You gonna pay me my two dollars."

※※

The pleasant hours with the whore followed by the stunt of that lunatic urchin quenched Bose's thirst for Santa Fe. He rode east toward Las Vegas and Anton Chico, turning south with the Pecos River. A pretty river born in the mountains, it didn't take long to muddy up. In Bose's mind most of New Mexico Territory was dreary and cursed land, but it had strong appeal for men like Goodnight and his longtime friend and rival, Lucien Maxwell. Goodnight had urged Bose to call on Maxwell and show him his letter of recommendation, if he was not wise enough to take good advice and go claim a farm in Texas. All the mountain country between the Colorado border and Taos had once been the domain of Maxwell, who competed with Goodnight for army and Indian agency contracts. At Maxwell's first ranch along the Cimarron River, they would sit up late into the nights trading stories about their common boyhoods in Illinois and the paths that brought them to a juncture of the road. While Goodnight jockeyed racehorses in the Palo Pinto country, Maxwell had come along the upper Río Grande trapping beaver. He married a Mexican girl whose family held one of the Spanish land grants. When the Utes and Apaches threatened to kill him or burn him out, he hired the top mercenary in the West, Kit Carson, as his bodyguard. Maxwell and Carson went partners and pushed herds of sheep across the divide to Salt Lake and the coast of California; for a while Maxwell sprouted money no matter what he did. He always dressed in black whipcords and chewed a worn cheroot. He encouraged people to call him the Don. When his father-in-law died, it made him the biggest landowner in the entire country. Maxwell turned part of it into a goat ranch managed by Bill Cody, the huckster and hide hunter who came to be known as Buffalo Bill.

In the company of Goodnight, Bose had a few times been a guest at Maxwell's ranch on the Cimarron. It was the biggest house he'd ever seen. It had red carpets, silver candlesticks, grand pianos, billiard tables, a chapel, a "gentlemen's room" for brandy, whiskey, cigars, and poker. On the walls of that room angels played harps and sucked on bare women's tits in a mural flung across wallpaper of royal blue. Heavily armed Utes lolled and roamed around the hacienda. Their fathers had promised to roast Maxwell alive but now they were his private army. He must have had a thousand people working for him—Mexicans, Indians, Chinese. The dome ceiling of the house was gold. Genuine gold sheaves, Mister Charlie said.

Goodnight thought extravagance was a sign of Maxwell's weakness, and that was why he no longer ruled the Cimarron Valley. Adjacent to his ranch was a mountain where veins of copper and gold were discovered; Maxwell owned the mineral rights. The old man had a higher opinion of his four daughters than his son Pete, whom he called out in public as a wastrel and a drunk, but he made his son the superintendent of the mining company. It wasn't long until the prospectors and dreamers brought swarming by the gold motivated the Don to sell out in the Cimarron and move down the Pecos to the barren place called Bosque Redondo, where the Navajos had been forced to live on a reservation. After four miserable years, the federal government had let the starving Navajos go back to their homeland mesas and ravines, and the army shut down Fort Sumner because it was in the middle of nowhere on the Pecos. Maxwell let the Cimarron place go for a song, according to Goodnight, and bought the abandoned fort for five thousand dollars.

On arriving in the Don's new placita, Bose found adobe makers mixing bricks of mud and straw in a sluice off the river, but there was little timber for porches or cross supports. All the cottonwoods and willows had been cut down when the Navajos were there. The connecting walls between the officers' quarters sagged, buckled, and eroded. The same reddish dun color as the surrounding terrain, Maxwell's Fort Sumner had no zócalo or church and just one struggling peach orchard. Lean bawling cattle roamed through the town, looking for anything to eat. Fort Sumner had one saloon owned by Maxwell and run by his son Pete. Pouring drinks and wiping dust on the bar back and forth was a cross-eyed dolt called Beaver Smith, whose name was on the sign. The clientele was a crowd of white drifters, black cavalry on long patrol, and Mexicans who'd graduated from being sheepherders. The only commerce of Fort Sumner was livestock theft and the comanchero trade. From Sumner one of their routes crossed the llano estacado to the twin landmark Texas peaks called Quitaque. Nearby one found the notorious Valley of Tears.

Down the bar from Bose a plump and pretty brown-eyed girl hung on the arm of one of these scoundrels. The comanchero drew exaggerated laughter from the pistoleros around him. Bose was sipping a sotol and a beer when the Don himself lurched inside wearing a soiled nightshirt over his pants, boots, and a pair of spurs. He was only about fifty but didn't appear to be aging well. His hair was grimy and tangled, and he had about two weeks' beard on his jaws, throat, and chin. "Virginia, what did I tell you?" he yelled at the girl. Beaver Smith was dipping pulque out of a large jar filled with cloudy fluid and a coiled pickled rattlesnake. Bose had been noticing the girl—it was hard not to. She wore a blouse cut low, showing the crevice of nice young bosoms. When the Don jumped her out she cursed him back in Spanish. He tore across the room, grabbed her by her hair, and slung her wailing two times around and with a crash out through the swinging doors. A bone comb barrette skidded across the floor. In reflex Bose stepped over it like that snake had slithered right out of the jar.

"Pop, settle down," said Pete from a chair and hand at a keno table. Ignoring him, the Don looked with interest at the Mexican who'd been wooing the choice Virginia and seen her torn rudely from his arm. After a moment the pistolero shrugged, turned his back, and pushed his glass at Beaver Smith, who filled it with the diamondback pulque, then poured himself one as well. The Don stomped out, and the room breathed again.

Bose didn't believe he'd ask that man for work.

He had been having a casual word with a tall white man with thick black brows and mustaches drooping over his mouth. He wore pants that were cut too short for his legs, and to extend them down over his boots he had sewn on cylinders of bison hide. The Mexicans called him Juan Largo, Long John.

"Must be hard being that man's whore," Bose said.

The tall man snorted. "Harder yet being his daughter."

Contemplating that, Bose picked up the comb that had been flung from her hair. The tall man leaned toward him. "Do you know Lucien Maxwell?"

"Not much. I saw him some when he was living up on the Cimarron."

"Here's a man sitting on nearly two million acres clear title and a gold and copper mountain, and he sells out to some Englishmen and moves here. I believe Lucien Maxwell is dying, that or losing his mind. Did you see his color?"

"He doesn't look too good," Bose agreed. "Maybe he just doesn't like his daughter's choice of friends."

Another snort of contempt, "José Tafoya. 'King of the Comancheros.'"

"That's him? I'll be."

"Somebody needs to stretch that little man with a noose."

"You hear it said."

The man extended a long hand. "My name is Garrett. Pat Garrett."

He shook it and said, "Bose Ikard. Pleased to meet you."

"Your fame precedes you, Mister Ikard."

Bose gave him a wary look. "My fame?"

"Hard men, I must tell you, were talking about you as soon as you rode in town with that fine horse and mule. 'Look, there goes the nigger trail blazer.' You're one of the hardies of the cattle drives."

Bose shook his head. "I'm just a man looking for a job."

Garrett leaned close and murmured, "Why don't you come work for me?"

"Work for you? Doing what?"

"Surveying the Texas Panhandle, by God."

Bose gave him another look and waited.

"The General Land Office in Texas wants it done," Garrett said. "That country's going to be mapped and marked off in acres, leagues, roods. In no time at all the Staked Plains are going to be staked, all right—with fence and telegraph poles of railroads, specu-lators, universities. The Indians are finished."

Oh, yes, thought Bose. You and Charlie Goodnight are going to talk them into extinction. "You're a surveyor?" he said.

"Yes, and I could use a man like you to be my chain carrier. Of course, you don't survey by stepping out actual chains anymore. I'll teach you about azimuths, benchmarks, declination. Metes and bounds and the Searles Spiral."

Bose marked him as a hustler and blowhard. Garrett leaned closer yet. "Then there's hides."

"Hides?" Bose repeated.

"Yes, sir. Multiply your money. Buffalo hides are bringing three dollars and a quarter apiece at Fort Griffin, Texas. A good dry one does. A well-armed and accurate shooter can average a hundred and fifty dollars a day. Think of it, Ikard. Now I have lined up partners, skinners, a cook. Wagons full of slickers and hardtack, beans and bacon, dried peaches and bacon. Forty-four and fifty-caliber cartridges in thousand-round kegs. Corn for the horses and mules and, oh yes, some moon for the shine. But I'm leery of going off in country I don't know well. I'll pay you a handsome piece to be our guide and chain carrier, and you can have all the money for every hide you harvest."

"You want to go from here to the Clear Fork of the Brazos."

"Yes, sir. Taking down shaggies along the way. There'll be hunters from Dodge City nipping at the herd. But we'll be out in front of it, you see, getting all the best shots. I tell you, it'll be as easy as stepping on ants."

Bose considered it about five seconds. Hide hunters' wagons drew Comanches and Kiowas like a bad wound hatches blowflies and screwworms.

"Mister Garrett, I appreciate your offer and those things you said, but I can't help you. I don't know how to guide you from here to the headwaters of the Brazos. Some of these comancheros would. But I'd be careful. Those Indians don't know they're finished. You go off in those plains shooting loud guns and killing what they eat, you're liable to get yourself killed."

Garrett grinned and nipped his beer-dampened whiskers with his tongue. "Suit yourself, my friend. Care to play some cards?"

11

QUANAH WAS SHAMED by how much he moaned and groaned over the mauling by that bull—his ribs and breastbone healed with a rapidity that amazed him. In a week he could mount a horse, and in two he could ride one at a lope. One day when they were riding through the ranch's best grassland, John Parker asked him if he would consider staying on with them. "I've got some years on me, and I'm feeling them. The vaqueros I hire come and go with the seasons. I could teach you what I know of herding and selling cattle, and when my wife and I are gone, the ranch would be yours. It's not a bad way to live."

For a long moment cut only by chirruping birdsongs and the sound of hooves, Quanah considered it. Take on a completely new life of his choosing. "I can't do it, Ap. My people are always being warred upon, and it's getting worse. These aren't enemies who come raiding to take a few scalps and steal horses. These want to remove us from the face of the earth."

John Parker pulled a crumpled hat forward to his nose and nodded thoughtfully. "The people you call whiteasses had a great war among themselves. When it was starting up I got to feeling guilty and worried about my kin back in Texas. I hated to think of them being burned out and killed. So I went back up there and enlisted in the rebel army, the grays. Poisá!" he spat the Comanche word, crazy. "They didn't want me to defend anybody's home in Texas. They told us we were going somewhere way off in the east and fill the woods and creeks with dead Yankees. I told them that the west bank of the Sabine River was as far east as I was going with anybody. So they locked me in chains and stuck me in a cellar that rats and snakes crawled through. They said they were going to stand me up against a wall and shoot me. I believed them.

"I was trying to dig my way out of there with a spoon when the grays got it in their heads I knew all about Mexico and Indians. So they made me a scout. Our war chief, you'd call him, was crazy—man named John Baylor. He bluffed one little bunch of bluecoats in New Mexico into stampeding up the Río Grande, and then declared himself governor of all country west to the Pacific Ocean. Then he decided we were going to kill off all the Apaches in New Mexico and Arizona, and we'd chase them into Mexico to finish the job. And while we were at it, who could tell Apaches from Yaquis and Tarahumaras?

"One night John Baylor got to bragging about what a mighty Indian killer he'd been in Texas. Said he was known far and wide for putting out a newspaper called *The White Man*. Claimed he was the one who told the world how rangers rescued your mother from the Comanches at the Battle of the Pease River."

"It was no battle," said Quanah.

John Parker saw the storm of emotions in his nephew's face. "I know, Quanah. She was my sister. But it was also revenge for what your dad and his war party had done to them in the Brazos valley. Anyway, I came close to crawling back under the tent flap later that night and putting a knife in the throat of that white man. And I am a white man; all the time I rode with your people I never once forgot that. But I thought about the ways those grays could go about killing me. And all that got me thinking how much I wanted to be home in bed with my wife and raising cows in Coahuila instead of lying there in a rage about that man.

"So I didn't kill John Baylor. I scouted him and his troops into the place in New Mexico called Dead Man's March, then I left him to see if he could drink the sand while he was trying to find his way out."

That was the most Quanah ever heard his uncle say. "A man

chooses his wars," Parker went on. "I'm not going to argue against yours. But a man can choose not to fight them. None of them. Keep us in mind. That offer's always good."

When Quanah was making signs of leaving, his uncle asked him what he might need. Dried meat, Quanah said, and uiyá—all the lariat he could spare. Doña Juanita started filling parfleches with the best pemmican Quanah had ever tasted—no buffalo, but a mixture of jerked turkey, beef, venison, and marrow, sweet with honey, wild plums, piñon nuts, walnuts, pumpkin seeds, peaches, and pecans. Instead of the rawhide rope that Comanches favored, Quanah's uncle brought him coils of lariat made of maguey fiber. Quanah found that maguey rope was lighter and more pliant, easier to break in but still strong. At their table one evening Quanah was in a generous mood, saying he would never again make war on Mexicans. He went on that Mexicans had never done him any harm, and they never rode up on the plains looking for trouble with his people.

John Parker heard him out, then chortled. "So what are you going to do with all that rope?"

Quanah grinned. "Rounding up horses and mules is not war, Ap. It's just trade." The night before he left, a big moon lit up a clear sky. There was a time not far past when Quanah ridiculed spirit talk as the blather of old men and women, the wisdom of the smoke lodge. But growing up had come hard to him; he had gotten good men—among them his best friend—killed by his boyish arrogance. He honored rituals now.

In the tradition he coiled a rope in a large circle on the ground, out from under any trees. He took his deer-bone pipe out of his pouch and tamped it full of fresh tobacco. John Parker and Doña Juanita grew the tobacco in a garden they tended, right beside their peppers and beans, tomatoes and corn. Smoking husk-rolled cheroots, they watched him from rocking chairs on the porch of their adobe. From a buffalo horn he produced his fire kit, sprinkled some gunpowder on a scrap of cloth, and twirled a stick against the rag and an indented soapstone until the powder sparked and stick blazed.

When the pipe was well lit he laid his hand on the lariat on the ground and smoked then said the last of his prayer aloud. "Mother Moon, if it be your will, let this rope take many horses."

When that was done he coiled up the rope, pulled a knee against his chest, and smoked for pleasure. Without a word John Parker rose and walked off in the woods, the dog hobbling behind him. Quanah and Doña Juanita talked a while and she told him about a town in Chihuahua called Parral. It was her home until John Parker dragged her screaming from a house, yanked her up on his horse, and carried her away; she still had family there. John took her there to see them from time to time. Those relations had no idea that the scarface gringo she came to love and marry was one of the Comanches who cut the rope of the church's warning bell and captured the presidio, so that a whole town was caught off guard and sent running out through the brush and thorns with the chickens and goats. She said that people in Parral still told stories about that worst of all Comanche raids. But the kin asked no questions of Doña Juanita. Her disgrace at the hands of the Indians happened long ago. She lived through it, and whatever they did to her was a matter that should only be talked about with her priest. The scarface gringo, well, they figured a woman like her was lucky to have any man at all.

"I heard what you said the other night about Mexicans," she said, giving him a frank look. "Don't mistake manners for kindness. A lot of them would kill you in a minute and cut your head off. Just your scalp won't do. You've got to bring in a head to collect the bounty on Indians."

They fell quiet, watching a gauzy cloud that slipped across the moon. His uncle's dog could be heard carrying on a barking squabble with coyotes whose yips and yodels made them seem like they were all around—two or three could sound like twenty. His people knew and admired Coyote as a trickster. He was a troublemaker that made human lives hard, but often with humor and never with any particular malice. John Parker had been gone quite some time. "What's he doing?" Quanah fretted. "Where did he go?"

"He's poking around his cache," she said, smiling. "I'm not allowed to know where it is and what he has in it. You'd think I cared."

When John Parker returned he carried something under his arm. He walked up to Quanah and said, "I want you to have this."

The object was wrapped in a black wolf hide. Quanah stroked the fur and murmured his admiration, then unwrapped his present and gasped. It was John Parker's war shield. Like all Comanche shields it was made from the thick shoulder hide of a buffalo bull; days of steaming and drying and rubbing had cured it hard as stone. It was heavier than it looked, for packed in the buckskin-covered backing were pages torn from many books. Some raiders painted their shields with likenesses of bear teeth and bolts of lightning, but this one was plain. The only decorations were braids of horse hair, each cut from tails of a different color, that were woven into loops in the deer hide sewn as backing to the shield. In the moonlight he counted and stroked five dents and grooves in this one—five bullets that its crafting and medicine had deflected and ricocheted away. Quanah said that having the shield was a great honor. It was the best gift anyone had ever given him. "All that's finished," his uncle said gruffly, with an unsentimental shake of his head. "My name's not Mexico. I'm just John."

He handed Quanah another gift wrapped in a fur sleeve. It was a flat object of glass and steel that looked like the pocket watches whites used to keep track of time. Quanah had often seen watches, but when he put this kind to his ear and there was no ticking. He shook it, and still it made no noise.

John Parker and Doña Juanita laughed. The gadget was no timepiece; it was a navigating tool called a compass. He showed Quanah how to use it—no matter how you rolled it, one needle would dance but come back to the same place. That needle pointed north, always north, he swore. He said there were more complicated things you could do with it, but if you lined it up with landmarks on the horizon, you need never stray off course. Quanah had seen his uncle yank a pump handle up and down and command the earth to release good water. He figured there were things to learn from such people.

His uncle gave him a horse and two mules, and on his way out of Mexico he stole ten more horses and five more mules. Quanah took his time, avoided ridgelines, and studied a lot of habitations. When he saw several houses built close together he knew there would be a presidio and veered deeper in the woods. He ignored jacales of campesinos, who would likely have burros. But when he saw a lone adobe house he hobbled his animals and took off at dusk with his rifle and several short coils of rope. He listened for the sounds of their stock and read the manure. He could usually find them, and a good number of them let him walk up to them. He murmured to them and with the horses used a trick his uncle told him about. He stroked their foreheads then put their jaws between his hands and gently blew his breath into their nostrils. They might flutter their lips and shake their heads, but they had more knowing of him now. He slipped a lead rope over its head, and then coaxed and captured another. If the people had mules and he could catch them, he always did, no matter how scrawny. Horses followed the lead of mules in a herd, and when he was back home he could always trade the mules.

In this way Quanah gathered his first herd. On Apache and rurale trails he lost two horses getting around a massive pile of rock called the Pegris Mountains, but by the time he found the seam through the cordillera he was confident one of his gifts was horse and mule theft. As soon as he got the herd headed down through those stone mountains the sky and land opened out, and laid out below were the willows and cottonwoods of Ocuebi, the Río Grande. With whinnies, mule honk, and clatter and skid of hooves they all went galloping to get to the water. Quanah knew there was danger of bluecoat patrols and Texas bandits prowling the river, but as he viewed his animals lined up chest-deep and slaking their thirst, a distinctive long-winged shadow passed between him and the sun. He grinned and flung away the hat that Uncle John had said would disguise him at a distance as a Mexican. Quanah was not yet a proven warrior, but he was a good horse thief, and the medicine eagle had just given him another sign.

Watching for the army patrols that were especially thick around El Paso del Norte and the Santa Fe Trail's entry into Mexico, he started the fierce desert crossing of Texas and New Mexico Territory on his best mule. If he wandered just a bit he could wind up in White Sands or the nearby sink called Dead Man's March. By the end of the second day the mule's ears began to fall about—lopping ears were a sure sign he had to change mules. The exertion and the long ride had reignited the fire in his broken ribs. He circled and yelled and got them moving again. About midnight a thickening bank of clouds moved across the sky. The rest of the night he couldn't see the compass needle or the North Star. But dawn found them in foothills amid yucca and sotol and their spear-like flower stalks. He jerked awake in the saddle and saw the herd grazing.

The Sacramento Mountains were a considerable range and, Quanah hoped, an empty one. He just wanted to get this herd across the llano and find the Quohada camp before the fall hunt. Midday they were in higher ground; the air was cool and smelled of pine. He was leaning out of the saddle looking at the stones of an old cooking fire when the mule huffed and threw a balk. Surprised, Quanah cursed and pulled the mule's head around in two circles before he got him redirected. When he looked up from that, Apaches had stepped out of the piñons all around him. They wore long buckskin boots and shirts, their legs gaunt and bare between their knees and breechclouts. They had stony brows and bands of cloth tied around their unbraided hair. They cradled rifles in their arms like infants.

Then two men bellowed Quanah's name. He almost lost his seat on the mule, swinging stiffly around. It was Dog Hates Thunder and

Breaks Something, the two Quohada friends who had come down the trail with him and Dohasan's Kiowas. They wore big grins.

"How did you get here?" said Quanah, angry but greatly relieved.

"Same way you did," said Dog Hates Thunder. "Calm down. These are friends."

The Apaches strolled up to examine Quanah's herd. Quanah gradually got more accustomed to the idea of Mescaleros as friends. The number of them was persuasive. "Where did you get all these animals?" said Breaks Something.

"Stole them," Quanah said proudly.

"By yourself?"

"Of course." They noticed Quanah's wince as he slid to the ground. He said, "Did you find our mules?"

They laughed and jeered the likelihood of that. Breaks Something said, "The raid broke up right after you left. We were afraid we were going to have to stay down there and start being Mexicans. These people here took pity on us. We got out of that raid with nothing but our weapons and our asses."

><

An Apache ranchería was nothing like the adobes and corrals that John Parker called a ranch. It was just a place on high ground with grass and some water where the Apaches liked to camp. Quanah thought the lodges of these people were much inferior to the tall graceful tipis made of hide by peoples who followed the buffalo. They lived in squat wickiups supported by frames of arched saplings and patched and covered with brush. Quanah couldn't tell what kind of fighters these might be. They had a ferocious reputation, and the men were a scary-looking bunch, but Apaches had gotten to be a desert and mountain people because bands of Quanah's ancestors whipped and pushed them off the prairies.

The Mescaleros' favored country now was the Sacramento and

White mountain ranges of New Mexico and the green valley of the Río Bonito, but New Mexicans claimed the same country. They clustered their adobes in placitas and put sheep herds out to graze beneath the slopes of four mountains that were sacred to the Mescaleros. One of the bluecoat stockades reopened after the war, Fort Stanton was manned with buffalo soldiers who were supposed to protect the New Mexicans from the Mescaleros. As part of the bargain, the Apaches were supposed to stay where they were, though it wasn't officially a reservation. The ex-slaves were well-armed fighters, but they got their backs up if anyone tried to make them go into Mexico. The renegade band of Old Wolf would skip across the border and make war against the Mexicans and their protectors, the rurales. And then they'd be back again.

The ranchería of Old Wolf's band was now in a place in the Sacramentos called Dog Canyon. It looked west toward a stretch of tawny and rocky lowlands that became a strange furl of ghost blanket, White Sands. As the sun sank behind the dunes, they incandesced and appeared to rise from the earth. Raids on a stage and wagon road that cut between the Sacramentos and White Sands had long poured from Dog Canyon as if from a kicked-up anthill. Though the soldiers forbade it, on returning from the Mexican sierras Old Wolf's raiders had moved right back in the stronghold, taking their chances.

But Old Wolf's band had gotten careless during the past winter. In the next mountain range to the east, the Guadalupes, they had grown tired of shivering in their fortress highlands and moved their camp down beside a waterhole, Manzanillo Springs, at the warmer foot of the slopes. The Mescalero scouts were watching for patrols coming through the foothills and missed a hundred fifty buffalo soldiers who had gotten lost in the Guadalupes' canyons and happened on a crevice that let them out right behind the Apache ranchería. The surprised and outgunned Mescaleros scrambled to higher ground, carrying what they could. The bluecoat shooters killed and wounded several and shot down an avalanche of tumbling horses and mules. Then the buffalo soldiers and their chiefs made a huge blaze of the Mescalero wickiups, the stores of mescal and jerky they ate, and the robes and hides that kept them warm.

Quanah learned this from his Quohada friends and from Old Wolf himself. The band's chief was a sun-baked man who was beginning to be old but his eyes blazed wolf-like, for sure. He saw that Quanah had come across the desert at night and alone, riding a mule and managing a small herd of horses and mules. Old Wolf called him Criador de Caballos, Breeder of Horses. Apaches called many Comanches that, Quanah later found out, but it sounded like a generous compliment. Old Wolf's hospitality was calculated. The weather was warm now, but in a few months the snow and ice would return. The Mescaleros had to replace the buffalo robes burned up at Manzanillo Springs, and Old Wolf knew the terms would not be favorable or the delivery prompt if he had to go through the comancheros. It would be much better if he could trade directly with Comanches of stature and influence. He seemed to believe Quanah was one of those. Quanah saw no reason to correct his thinking.

Every few nights about thirty of them gathered for a meeting at sundown, and Old Wolf invited Quanah to join them. "Long it so has been," the Apache told him in Spanish, "since Killer-of-Enemies appeared to a chief in the White Mountains. Killer-of-Enemies revealed to him that Comanche raiders led by a fierce warrior were coming to attack our people and steal horses and mules. This warrior was so brave that sometimes he went on raids by himself. He had a quiver of mountain lion skin and rode a mule.

"There was a big fight, and the young Comanche used up all his arrows, but he fought on with his hatchet and lance. The Apaches respected him; he was the last one killed. After that, they held a meeting, and about midnight they heard someone moaning, then that Comanche crawled in the lodge. Everyone jumped back, thinking he was a ghost. Our leader said, 'People, sit down. He wouldn't come without a reason.'

"The young Comanche said, 'Though you stung me to death,

I've come to help you find what you need to know. Listen here, people. Seven more Comanches are coming to see you. In four days they'll arrive here for a proper peyote meeting. You are to give them back everything you've taken from me. Now I'm going to leave you. After I've taken seven steps outside I will stop and yell four times. Then I want you to start singing.'

"They didn't know what to sing, but as he prophesied, in four days seven Comanches appeared in the White Mountains. When they came to the ranchería they sat on the north side of the lodge, the Apaches on the south. They smoked tobacco, then they ate peyote. In this meeting there was a young woman. Suddenly the young woman spoke out to the Comanches, 'Relatives!' It shocked them that she knew their language—they were very surprised. The chief said to the girl, 'Tell them what they need to know.'

"She said, 'After we're through here, you are to take that young warrior's bow and mountain lion quiver, the peyote, and the songs, and go back home. From this time on, all the tribes to the north will use this peyote.'"

Old Wolf peered at Quanah. "There is more to this story, and in time I'll tell you, Criador de Caballos. The girl who spoke for our chief had been carried off from the Comanches as a child. That is why she knew both tongues. In all stories about the happening of peyote, a woman appears. Woman brings us all our knowledge of peyote. This happened a long time ago. I know it's true because I heard people talking about it."

At nightfall the men stooped through the entry of the wickiup one by one and took seats on a circular cushion of sagebrush with their backs to the walls. Lined up in front of a small fire were clay vessels with offerings of meat, fruit, corn, and water. The fire tender, Not Quite Enough, kept the ashes of a slow-burning fire arranged in a crescent. Behind the fire, more branches of sage were laid out the same way. Old Wolf told Quanah that the crescent shapes were tributes not to the moon, as one might suppose, but to the mountain in Mexico where Semayi, the Peyote Woman of legend, first discovered the herb.

Old Wolf was the band's war chief and, these nights, their road chief. He was naked but for mescal bean necklaces, his loincloth, and moccasins. He had no flab on him. He had painted the scalp under his part of his hair and ovals around his eyes yellow, with stripes of red across his forehead and down the middle of his chin. Old Wolf carried a gourd rattle and staff of hard wood in one hand, his medicine kit in the other. He sat behind the crescent of sage and pulled from his bag and arranged before him a fan made of eagle feathers, an eagle-bone whistle, a beaded drumstick, cheroots rolled in cornhusks, and a sack of juniper incense. On the altar of sage he positioned Father Peyote, a large, dry, gnarled bud of cactus dusted with yellow pollen. He said, "Beha'be sej'neki," inviting them to smoke in appreciation of the herb and its power, then put one of the corn-husked cigarettes in his mouth. He handed the others to Not Quite Enough, who distributed them around the circle.

After Quanah had scorched his throat and lungs smoking tobacco this way they snuffed the cheroots out in the ground around the horns of the altar. Old Wolf crushed some sage and rubbed his palms and the residue on his neck, shoulders, chest, and legs. The others grabbed handfuls of the sage and did the same. It was not a large wickiup; the air was hot, and they were crowded. Old Wolf sprinkled some cedar incense on the fire, which raised a shower of sparks. Soon after that, he passed around the peyote bag. On Old Wolf's advice Quanah started with four buds. In the midst of much spitting of the foul and woolly fibers, Old Wolf pitched more cedar dust on the flame and thrust his staff up and down while rattling his gourd. The drummer, Broken Foot, squeezed his thighs around a small drum and commenced banging with the road chief's beaded stick. Which brought Old Wolf to the first song. When he was through singing, long silences followed, then another man would abruptly start.

Quanah had no idea what they meant. Yet he began to understand the songs some way he couldn't fathom. He was giddy, elated. Everything he looked at jumped with clarity: tendrils of smoke coiling from a stick in the fire, bracelets dancing a jig on the drummer Broken Foot's wrist, a beetle that wandered and bumped along a timber of the wickiup, then swung off clumsily, caught itself and continued on its way upside down.

Just as quickly Quanah was exhausted. He had to bend forward to keep from lying down. Men stood up and lurched outside to puke. Quanah watched an Apache wave his arms and bellow some story, tears streaming down his face. Old Wolf smiled as the man sat down sobbing.

Then the colors came to Quanah. First there were green balls of every shade, bouncing in the air and then each one circling another. Then the lights paired off, green and yellow, orange and red, blue and green—he could call up any combination he desired. Then each thump of Broken Foot's drumstick began to spout geysers of fire. Quanah saw a field of yellow cup-shaped flowers, and as they swayed in a breeze they tipped and poured out cascades of purple. Old Wolf was blowing his eagle-bone whistle and making music of it. The air swirled with the sounds he made, each orb haloed in changing hues.

Then Quanah saw a tall Comanche coming. He was dressed smartly in new buckskins, ring hoops in his ears and an eagle feather in his hair. He realized he was gazing at himself. Father Peyote spoke to him. "Don't be afraid," he said. "The power has made you a leader. You didn't even know it. Look at how tall and easy you stand now." The man who was Quanah spread his arms and became the golden eagle who had come to him in the house of his uncle. The eagle's wingspan receded into a bank of clouds streaked outward by the sun. As the sun passed into the earth and its fire began to go out the eagle shrieked. Or was that Old Wolf's eagle-bone whistle?

Quanah hadn't seen the girl join them. Wearing a red shawl, she half-reclined with her legs folded beneath one hip. He watched her pull up branches of sage, making herself a pillow for her elbow and arm. Her hair was unbraided and parted to the side. She had raccoon eyes, hooded by thick eyebrows and lashes. She was the prettiest girl he had ever seen.

With a trace of smile she looked back to the fire. She kept quiet while the men sang. Quanah was shocked when one of the celebrants passed her the bag of cactus buttons—she picked out a couple and handed on the sack. She nibbled a peyote bud carefully and chewed for a time, then turned her shoulder and rid her mouth of the bristly fibers.

In a while Quanah became aware that Old Wolf was speaking to her, directing her in some way. Quanah could see the strange words tumbling from the Apache's mouth. Then to Quanah's utter astonishment she began to speak to him in Spanish. "That leader there is teaching you how the peyote meetings are held," she said. "Peyote says, 'Here on earth I do as I please because of my power. Pay attention to the roots of the grass. I am like the grass. My roots are my children. They increase with me.'"

The storytelling and prophesying resumed. As dawn began to break Old Wolf grabbed his eagle bone and whistled four times, cutting off the song of one of the men. The girl in the red shawl knelt beside the fire tender. Old Wolf sang another song, then passed a cheroot to the girl, who smoked it. The fire chief raised his water bucket and splashed some around the fire, then brought it with a dipper to the girl, and she drank. Then she picked up her blanket and the bucket and carried them out.

The men got to their feet and stiffly walked outside. Quanah was exceptionally weak in his knees. The girl had disappeared. Had his mind and the stories about the peyote woman made her up? Other women were serving a ritual breakfast of roasted corn, boiled yucca flowers, and fresh plums. Quanah gnawed the corn and stared out the mouth of Dog Canyon at White Sands, which looked like rolling fog. The fire tender Not Quite Enough stood beside him eating from his bowl. "That girl," Quanah said.

"Yes. What about her?"

"Was she ever carried off?"

"What?"

"Is she a Comanche?"

The Apache barked with laughter and amazement. "Of course not! Is she fat? That's To-ha-yea. Old Wolf's daughter."

12

OLD WOLF'S WIFE HAD DIED from some feverish malady that struck hard and fast, taking her in just three days. While still a child To-ha-yea cooked for her father, scraped and tanned deer hides, wove baskets. From her grandmother and other women in her clan she learned that the universe was composed of twelve black winds, that it was taboo to spill water on an eagle feather. And that she should say words of thanks to White Painted Woman whenever a child was born in good health and a lodge was put up. She followed her father's guidance down the peyote road, for he was a believer in its medicine—though many women in the clan gossiped that she was far too young to know anything of that.

When Old Wolf formed the renegade band she had come away with him, riding her own horse. The child in her still loved to play hoop and pole and listen to the yarns and fables of the storytellers. But Apaches believed it was necessary for a girl to come into marrying age a virgin. Without proper guidance To-ha-yea might give in to hot blood and impulse. In the peyote meeting he hadn't liked the way she looked at the big gray-eyed Comanche and how he gaped at her. Apache boys were more careful about where they went with their eyes. She was too good-looking for her own good.

Quanah used his bargaining with Old Wolf for the buffalo robes as an excuse to stay on with the Mescaleros. Every week he plunged deeper into this new medicine and tried to master and memorize the ritual of the peyote road. Before he was mauled by the Mexican bull he had seen the cactus buds used only for doctoring by shamans like old Jaybird Pesters. Quanah was confident that with this gift of power he could convince Parra-o-coom to be generous to these Apaches, but he let Old Wolf know that it would cost them plenty of horses and mules to trade for enough robes to warm all these people.

The stomachs and nerves of his Quohada friends Breaks Something and Dog Hates Thunder weren't suited for much peyote—they disliked throwing up—and they grew tired of watching Quanah parade around like he was a mighty war chief. They said their goodbyes to the Mescaleros and rode off without him. He knew he could have used their help with the horses, and the sudden rain in this country bothered him, too. From the long trail back into Dog Canyon, he could look past the ocotillo and saltbush to the hem of White Sands and see this was some of the driest country anywhere. But every afternoon the clouds began to build and push in from the west. Quanah liked the smell and coolness of the mountain rains, but had been sleeping beside his hobbled horses and mules. When the monsoons began, the woman called Lozen who talked about being a horse thief—she did know many of the tricks —offered him the leaky wickiup of a man who had died, and whose wife had been taken in by his brother. Which made Quanah's sleep fitful on the best nights. He had one reason to stay on with these Apaches: Old Wolf's daughter.

He liked it that the old-timers did not confine their storytelling to sweat lodges and their own ears. You would see the Apaches sitting and whittling under a tree beside a creek, and around them as they carried on would be boys and girls of all ages, the little ones rapt, the older ones listening for a while then drifting on. One day Not Quite Enough noticed Quanah standing apart with curiosity, and he called out to him in Spanish, waved him over. Resuming his oratory, the Apache widened his eyes and flapped his arms in exclamation, setting off a chorus of reaction among the little ones. Not Quite Enough told the story in Apache—Quanah understood none of it. His interest was not the tale anyway. On the edge of the crowd Old Wolf's daughter had seen him looking and for a moment tilted her head and held his gaze, then brushed her hair away from her eyes.

In a while she picked up a sling of rope around some firewood, pulled it up against the back of her shoulders, and sauntered along the creek toward the lodges. Quanah waited for a moment and then wandered after her. "Buenas días," he said when he came up beside her. "You speak Spanish?"

She gave him a wary look. "Buenas días. You've heard me."

"It means we can talk to each other. If you'd like that."

"Why would I want to talk to you?" she said.

"Because I'm such a fine young man."

She stretched her mouth but smiled a little and continued down the path. "Fine bunch of trouble."

"Please, is it all right if I just talk to you? I'm called Quanah."

"I know."

"You do?"

"Of course. My father calls you Breeder of Horses. They say you've been raiding in Mexico. So, caballero, how many raids have you been on?"

"Many!" Quanah couldn't help boasting; the habit of tuibitsi burst out. "Five or six—no, at least seven. And all of them long ones."

It was more than a polite and casual question. An Apache man had to have ridden on at least four raids to be eligible as a husband. She kept walking, and Quanah tried to keep her talking. "What's your name?"

"To-ha-yea."

"That man, the fire tender—can you tell me what he was saying?"

She pulled the ends of the lariat and hoisted the bundle of wood higher on her back. "Some day, maybe. I need to get back."

"Here, let me carry that for you."

She grinned at his persistence and steadied her balance, jutting a knee. Quanah reached quickly and took one end of the rope, then the other, and swung the bundle of firewood to his back. He veered from the trail along a division of the creek around a small sand bar island. She laughed as he got his feet tangled in tall switch grass and stumbled, dropping some of the wood. Quanah snatched at the ropes, and all the sticks clattered on the ground. He flung out his arms in mock dismay, flipped two branches end over end, and began to juggle them. He knelt and tossed up a third. Quanah was on fire, just looking at her. And he had her laughing, a good start.

To-ha-yea found ways and excuses to slip away and be with him. She told him places to meet her in the winding canyon, and she always came. One day he waited at the foot of a long bluff called the Elbow. Quanah had a sense he couldn't shake that he was being watched. Something made him swing around and look up. On a thick branch of the cottonwood a mountain lion watched him, a big paw lolling, its tail rising, falling. The panther laid back its ears and broke off staring with a hiss. It turned and paced out the limb, leaped to a boulder, and was gone.

Was this girl a witch? Had she called up that mountain lion?

After a morning-long climb, they sat on the edge of a clearing of pine saplings and stumps blackened some past year by a lightning strike and fire. As they talked he told her of the loveliness of the blond and rust prairie grasses blown in ripples by the wind, and the tremors in the ground and thunder in your ears amid a running herd of buffalo, and the wealth of turkey and deer when they wintered on the Washita. He told her about the waterfalls and immense stone canyons he had seen in Mexico and the folly of being saved from a bull by a three-legged dog. He made faces describing how the bull's horns twisted up and down—To-ha-yea giggled and bumped him with her shoulder.

The grass shared the ground with small flowers, purple and pink and white. He sifted strands of grass through his hand, then ducked his head and cried, "Look!" The clearing was full of small ripe strawberries. They crawled on hands and knees like children, eating their fill. Watching her bottom in the light skin dress, he got to his feet and grasped the points of her shoulders. She nestled the back of her head against his hip, and at the sound of his breathing she stood and turned around. He traced the ridge of her collarbones with a fingertip, and she raised her face to him. She made love to him with her mouth and tongue. The force and newness of that kiss drove him as wild as he thought her to be. They sank to their knees again, and then were rolling, his mouth full of her hair. He moved his palm over her stomach and cupped her breast, felt her nipple stiffen against his thumb. In a loincloth there was no concealing a hard-on. It swayed over flowers and grass.

Suddenly she began struggling to free herself. She struck his chest with her fists and forearms, hit him hard. "Stop!" she cried.

Quanah lay on his back, gasping. "Don't you want it?"

"You know I do."

He made a wordless sound of exasperation.

"I can't be like your women," she said. "Whores at Shakedown dances. Serenade you and then come crawling under your robes with four or five others when you go off to fight."

"Oh, is that how you hear it?" he replied. "Apache girls just make your balls hurt." He used the Comanche word, onóyo.

"Your people have ways that must be observed," she said. "So do mine. And one means I can't lie down with you. Even though being near you turns my táe into a fount." She shocked him; it was the Comanche word for her sex. "I could be thrown out, eating at dumps with coyotes and crows. There are whores among us now who lie down with bluecoat white eyes. Because they let their hearts run away with someone like you. Can you understand?"

To-ha-yea:

LOZEN WAS A MEDICINE WOMAN whose kin and clan were in the Warm Springs band. She had a brother named Victorio who was a firebrand while he was still a boy. But Lozen was honored with her own fighting name, Dextrous Horse Thief. She was the best we had at getting off unseen and unheard with other peoples' horses and mules. But our band wasn't doing any raiding that summer. Poor Quanah; he thought I wanted to run away from him. It was our most important time of the year. Six girls and I were being rubbed and perfumed. Because I had no mother, and no grandmothers had come with us in this way of living that the white eyes called renegade, Lozen had put her warring and divining skills aside and told Father she would sponsor me in the puberty ceremony and sew my buckskin dress.

She was a pretty woman, though her skin was turning hard. One day while she was brushing my hair I got up the nerve to ask, "Lozen, why have you never married? Because you're a shaman?"

"No," she answered, smiling. "That's no obstacle to loving a man. I have a hole in my heart that no one has ever been able to fill up. I don't look anymore for one who might. When I was your age a tall rider who was not one of us came through our canyons and stayed with us at Ojo Caliente. He rode the fastest horse we'd ever seen; none of our best would even try to race him. The warrior's hair was the color of ash. It slipped through your fingers like otter's fur." Lozen was quiet for a moment. "He would be here and gone, and then would find us, wherever we were, just reappear, bringing us horses and meat. People called him the Gray Ghost."

I moved my head away from the brush so I could see her. "But he wasn't really a spirit?"

She grinned. "He didn't feel like one."

"What was he? A Comanche? A Cheyenne?"

Lozen shrugged again and left that a mystery. "People said he shamed me. That's not true. I felt no shame at all. But he ruined me for being with anyone else. One time when we were on the trail to Riconada he came with a beautiful woman. It was the only time he didn't come alone. He had her riding in a wagon, shielding her pre-

153

cious white skin from the sun. I wanted to cut her throat," she said lightly. "I took one look and knew I'd never see him again."

I grasped Lozen's hand and held the palm to my cheek.

The Gray Ghost. I was thinking about Quanah's eyes.

In the very long ago a great war had been fought between birds and beasts, creatures of light and dark, and when it ended almost all but a few human beings were gone. White Painted Woman made love with the Sun and gave birth to many children, but each one was killed and eaten by a dragon, the last of its kind. She gave birth to a son called Slayer of Monsters and conceived another, Child of Water, while swimming in a cavern pool. She tried to hide them far back in the cavern, but the dragon smelled them, as it always did. It was not the firstborn warrior but the younger son who fought the dragon with bow and arrows and after a fierce struggle extinguished the winged serpent from the earth. White Painted Woman would never grow old, and she would teach all peoples how to live. Her son's reward was the name Apache.

A lodge pole of spruce was trimmed and dragged down from higher mountains, and around it grew a much larger wickiup than the ones we slept in. Plants of mescal thrived in Dog Canyon. Women gathered and cut them up while old men dug a pit, lined it with rocks, and built a cooking fire. The old men picked up slabs of the white roots and arranged them on the coals, just so. Then they spread dry grass across the mescal, rocks, and coals. They covered that with dirt, and then they pushed severed leaves down into the coals. They pulled out leaves from time to time to gauge the progress of the cooking. The women served the mescal on hard deerskin platters. Sprinkled with pumpkin seeds and piñon nuts and smeared across bread made from sunflower seeds, the mescal was hard to chew but extraordinarily tasty and sweet. To the feast the women added bowls of venison and rabbit stew and boiled pigweed greens, chokecherry and walnut relishes, and a mesquite bean pudding.

After the ritual feast the Mountain Spirit dancers came shuffling toward a blazing fire. They had the bellies and arms of aging men but wore deerskin boots and beaded and fringed skirts. Their faces were concealed by black hoods, and they wore crowns of tall painted spikes that jiggled with juniper berries, turkey and eagle feathers, and bits of wood and bone, hung from the spikes by mescal fiber. Their crowns looked like jagged lightning strikes and elk antlers armed with arrow points. Each dancer carried a rattle made from a deer hoof. They sang softly, with high voices, a call to the spirits. When they had circled the fire a few women came out and joined in the dance. Then with quiet singing they shuffled back into the darkness.

Finally one morning the other girls and I offered ourselves to the people blessing us. Each of us was now Changing Woman—White Painted Woman. Accompanied by our sponsors, the Mountain Spirit dancers, and a clown who jumped about wildly, we came toward the medicine lodge wearing beaded dresses of white buckskin tanned so fine they let through light, shawls of ermine and otter, necklaces of emeralds handed down from the days of a great lost mine. Our faces were dusted lightly with yellow pollen. Father was my sponsoring dancer. We came forward to the dancers, who kept up a rattling of their deer hooves. There was no movement of our feet—it was all hips and loins. I saw Quanah in the shadows looking astonished, just when the Mountain Spirits started singing.

> *I come to White Painted Woman*
> *By means of long life I come to her*
> *I come to her by means of her blessing*
> *I come to her by means of her good fortune*
> *I come to her by means of all her different fruits*
> *By means of the long life she bestows*
> *I come to her*

155

Two days after the ceremony, Quanah sat in Old Wolf's lodge and smoked tobacco with him. "I think your people are richer than mine," said Quanah, handing back the pipe.

The raider chief nodded and smiled at the compliment. "Not in horses, mules, and buffalo robes."

"I promise you'll have the robes. Long before you need them."

"I believe you."

"There's another reason I've come to see you," said Quanah.

"Yes?"

"I want to marry your daughter, Old Wolf, and I ask your blessings. I can give you six mules. I know she's fond of me. She'll never go hungry. Or be without honor. When we have children we'll bring them to see you."

After a time the Apache chief gave a sigh of consent. That was all there was to it. "You're a good trader, Comanche. I hope you're a better husband than I've been a father."

Quanah couldn't believe his good fortune. That night he and his bride sat with legs crossed in the wickiup on sleeping robes that Lozen had brought them. With his herd they would start across the plains in the morning. He knew To-ha-yea was sad to be leaving her father and her people, but she was eager to know more of the world beyond these mountains. He repositioned himself and reclined on a prop of his elbow. He touched her shin with his bare toe.

"I promised to tell you that story," she said.

"Now?"

She put her hands on his ankle and leaned forward, light from the small fire gleaming in her eyes. "Yes, listen. It's an old story that we grow up with. About the time Coyote went off to see the Wild Geese people."

She paused and then went on. "It was fall, and when the Wild Geese people started south, Coyote flew along. People started calling out below, 'Look at that rascal. Hey, Coyote! Throw us a bone!'

"Geese had warned him, 'Now don't look down,' but Coyote couldn't help it, and the instant he did, he started falling. He fell it seemed like forever and landed in a canyon among the Firefly people—the only people in all the world who had fire. They were sitting around admiring it. Coyote asked some of the Firefly children, 'Where's the road?'

"They answered, 'There is no road.'

"Coyote said, 'But there has to be some way out of here.'

"Firefly children said, 'We're not supposed to tell you.'

"Coyote took a necklace of shells off his neck and passed it back and forth through his hands. 'My, don't you think these are pretty? Here, try them on.'

"Coyote rolled around on the ground, playing with the Firefly children. Finally he got one to say, 'All right, here's what you do. Ask Juniper to bend over. Get up in the branches. He'll spring up and throw you way up on the road.'

"At sundown, the Firefly people had a big dance around the fire. Coyote tied some bark to his tail and joined right in. His tail was smoking, but they didn't think anything of it. Coyote's a good dancer—he's got them fooled.

"The next thing you know, Juniper bends over, snaps up, and throws Coyote over the cliff. Firefly people are furious. They chase him, but he's got them going crazy, putting out fires.

"Coyote gives it to the Buzzard, who gives it to the Whippoor-will, who gives it to the Swallow. Coyote's laughing, he don't care.

"The whole world would have burned up if it hadn't started to rain. Turtle got off with the last live coal. Lightning kept striking him, trying to get it away from him. That's why he's got all those yellow streaks on his shell. Rolled him over and over, but he wouldn't let go."

To-ha-yea performed the exquisite womanly trick of crossing her arms at her bracelets and lifting her garment until it cleared her shoulders, then dropped it with a toss of her hair. The loveliness of her took his breath away. She crawled toward him, one slow knee and then the palm of her hand, his eyes on the dark abundant tuft of love hair and the hang and sway of her breasts. She came to him, still not quite touching, then offered her mouth, nipped his teeth with her tongue. She gulped with her own desire and whispered, "And that's how Coyote stole the fire."

13

AGAINST HIS BETTER JUDGMENT, Bose had joined the buffalo soldiers. After the journey down through Santa Fe and Las Cruces, the Medicine Hat paint and mule had gotten him safely over the Pecos wasteland to the Palo Pinto country, where he found that Doctor Ikard, his father, was dead of a heart attack. It didn't matter to one soul that he had once fed soup to Cynthia Ann Parker, or that he'd gone up the cattle trails with Oliver Loving and Charles Goodnight, or that he had ridden off with bronc peelers and killed a Comanche in a fight with a band led by the one who turned out to be Cynthia Ann Parker's son. The half-breed killer was the one who fired up these people's conversation. He was believed to be everywhere at once, stealing every horse, leading every raid. Quanah Parker, Quanah Parker—it was like he was a fondly remembered nephew gone wrong.

Bose was bone-sore and tired of sleeping on the ground. He followed up on Goodnight's advice to approach the land office people at the courthouse in Jacksboro, rebuilt since the great Indian raid and the war but mostly a shambles of whorehouses and saloons. Certainly, those people told Bose—he could buy a little farmland from the state of Texas. Though of course it was none of their affair how he paid for the implements and seed. All that really mattered in Texas now was the darkness of his skin. With the government in Austin run by abolition Republicans and pompous black fools who couldn't read as well as he could—elected because those were the only groups allowed to vote—the hostility toward black people seemed more severe than it had been before the war. Freedmen who tried to farm cotton and compete with ignorant white sharecroppers were routinely burned out or lynched.

The first order of the Reconstructionists was to disband and outlaw the ranger companies. Men in the communities that were being raided could ride out at night and strike back in the unobserved plains as they had for a century, but if they got caught, they could go to jail and forfeit all they had. The army was supposed to do all the protecting now. Fort Richardson wasn't finished enough to merit the name, but because the short rolling hills between Texas settlement and the Indian Territory had become a no-man's land, it was on its way to having a garrison of over six hundred men, the biggest military post in the country.

Bose never would have taken the army's oath if he hadn't fallen under the spell of the one the Indians called Bad Hand, also the No-Finger Chief. Unlike Colonel Goodnight, who took the title because nobody in Pueblo, Colorado, could call him on it, Ranald Mackenzie was a real colonel, a graduate of West Point. Men who served under him out here learned that in the last three years of the war between the states, he fought in thirteen battles and got shot six times, one time most severely, in the lung. That wasn't counting the horse that got blown in half right under him in his very first action, leaving shrapnel in his knee.

Mackenzie was a slight man, clean-shaven except for reddish sideburns that grew past prominent ears and down his jaws. When he was thinking hard or trying to relax he had a habit of loudly cracking his knuckles, which drew attention to the fact that the right one was mangled by one of his battle wounds, missing the middle and third fingers, though he could waggle the stumps. The wound left him just enough control and steadiness of his hand to fire a gun, but it was an ugly thing. The colonel did not like to be saluted, for returning salutes drew attention to his hand; in formations and parades where it was required, he wore gloves. Bose never saw him with his clothes off, so he couldn't say precisely where all he had been hit.

He just saw the hand, the limp, and the spasms of pain. When they came on he coiled up sweating and cussing and grew clumsy.

Bose had drifted into Fort Richardson just to have a look. It was at a place called Lost Creek, in ugly mesquite woods and bunchgrass prairie. The soldiers had cut down all the cottonwoods, for the horse corrals; otherwise, they would have soon been cavalry afoot. At a distance the place looked more like a straggling ranch or nest of outlaws than an army fort. There was no stockade around the tents, corrals, and a lagging start on sandstone barracks. The army named it after a general for the North, killed in the war, who was called Israel Bush "Fighting Dick" Richardson. It was a bunch of name for them to live up to.

Bose was riding the black mule Juneteen and trailing the paint gelding Tricks when he arrived at what looked like the center of the tents. The air was full of rhythmic hollers and grunts, a strange singsong that had the animals snorting and stepping around. He quick-hitched the gelding's lead rope to the saddle horn and commanded the mule, "Whoa!" while hauling back firmly on both reins. Juneteen stood still, though his ears continued to move. Bose was starting to stand down and lead them to a hitching post when he saw the oddest thing: four lines of black men in army uniform were walking off into the dust and mesquite with rifles propped on their right shoulders. Another one stalked beside them, nagging them in a booming voice that carried all around, in that chant. Every once in a while they would, more or less together, move the rifles around and prop them on their left shoulders.

Suddenly a squat black man with chevrons on his sleeves and a silly billed cap on his head was on the ground beside Bose, saying welcome to Fort Richardson but in the same breath ordering, "Unhorse yourself."

"He's a mule," Bose observed, tempted to let Juneteen have a little rein and knock him down, or at least get him dancing. He never had liked men who started off conversations in a belligerent tone of voice.

"I know what the animal is," snapped the soldier. "I'm Sergeant Abner Hayes, special detachment, 11th Infantry, United States Army. Now stand down and identify yourself."

Bose unwrapped the paint's lead rope from the horn and slid down from the tall mule, but he and Sergeant Hayes were not off to a good start. "Bose Ikard," he introduced himself. He assumed the man would see they needed to walk to the hitching post before any chat could proceed, but evidently he did not. He blocked the way and stood with fists on his hips, looking Bose up and down. "What's infantry?" Bose taunted him.

With scorn for the question, Hayes pointed to the four lines of men walking off to nowhere, the man beside them really warbling now. "Best soldiers in this man's army," the sergeant said.

"Where are they going?" Bose asked.

"To find and kill the enemy."

Bose looked around at a distance of plain that stretched about twenty-five miles. "That's the most ignorant thing I've ever heard of."

Bose and Hayes got on each other's nerves sixty seconds into their first conversation, and it did not improve. Hayes' shouts had Juneteen and Tricks groaning and yanking their necks, backing up. "Fellow!" Bose yelled back. "If you run my animals off, I'm gonna whip you to the dust you're standing on!"

"At ease, sergeant!" another voice intervened. Bad Hand Mackenzie had seen and heard the clamor, and arriving at a brisk walk, he took command of the disturbance at once. "Can I help you with one of those?" he asked Bose.

"No, give me a minute and I'll get them tied up over there, if it's all right." Bose didn't call him sir because his ire was up, and at a glance he had only seen that the white soldier had no chevrons on his sleeves. When the horse and mule were tied up he recognized the insignia of Mackenzie's rank. Hayes had trailed them at a slight distance and he hovered close, mad as hell.

"Ranald Mackenzie," said the man, extending his hand. Bose felt there was something wrong with the hand the instant he gripped it. He told the colonel his name and apologized for causing them trouble. "Wasn't my intent," he said. He watched the battered hand, which Mackenzie was moving over the mule's hip in a knowing and practiced way—just letting Juneteen know where he was, and that he wasn't threatening. "Heard you bring the mule around," Mackenzie said with interest. "What did you say to him?"

"Just, you know, talking him down, which means more to mules than it does to horses."

"These are fine animals," said Mackenzie, moving on to the paint gelding. "They belong to you?"

"Yes, sir. Certainly. I'll show you the papers."

"What brings you to Fort Richardson, Mister Ikard?"

Bose looked around at the tents, corrals, and the scrub savanna beyond. "I can't say. I grew up around here. I'm looking for work."

"You mean to enlist?"

"Oh, I don't know about that, sir. I don't know nothing about the army, tell the truth. Otherwise I wouldn't have had words with your sergeant here."

Hayes didn't blink at the peace offer. "Infantry," he interjected. "Only openings we got, Colonel. Man wants to do it army way, he'll turn over his animals and weapons, just like everybody else. Won't be needing the animals anymore. Be issued a rifle, when he's earned it."

"I'll just be on my way," said Bose.

"Sergeant, you're dismissed, " said Mackenzie. Hayes stiffened and glowered—his elbows bowed out from his sides. "Dismissed," the colonel repeated, in a pointed tone.

The recruiting sergeant for the whole fort—Bose learned that later—pivoted on the heel of his right boot and stomped away. Amazing how easy it is to make enemies in the world.

"You were saying, Mister Ikard."

"Sir, I sure didn't mean to join no infantry. I heard that the army was building a new fort and might have jobs for some things. I can load and handle pack mules. Cook a little."

"Could be," Mackenzie said, nodding. "But I'm not sure that's how you best suit our needs. Indians call this one a Medicine Hat, don't they?" With the bad hand he stroked Tricks' neck and picked a burr out of his mane.

"Some do," said Bose.

"You say you've got papers? Some identification?"

"Yes, sir." He spoke to Juneteen and got the thin valise out of his saddlebag. It also contained his Colt and cartridge belt, his spare pistol, and the money belts with his gold. He had figured it was best not to go armed into an army post. Mackenzie just glanced at the freedom papers from Doctor Ikard and the transfer of title to the horse and the mule, but he read the letter vouching for Bose a couple of times, it looked like. "I'm not familiar with this man Goodnight."

"Well, he lived around here a long time. He's a respected man."

Mackenzie looked around thoughtfully. "When I made colonel and came out here, it was to command the 41st Infantry. Mississippi and Alabama field hands, most of them. Some would just as soon go without shoes, till they discovered the goathead stickers that grow around here. They made pretty good wagon and assault troops, by the time we got through with each other. When I took command of the 4th Cavalry, last winter, they were headquartered at Fort Concho. They were accustomed to sleeping till eight in the morning and keeping the mail routes flowing. We were there a month when I moved the command here, along with several infantry companies. That was six weeks ago. So I'm new to this country, you see."

With the bad hand Mackenzie raised the letter and extended it to Bose. "Can you read this?"

"Yes, sir."

"Do it."

"Sir?"

"Read it to me."

Bose turned the paper slightly to get a fix on the boss's crabbed script. "'Bose Ikard was in my employ on three drives of cows across Texas, New Mexico, and Colorado. He don't need much sleep, and he's not scared of Indians. He's honest. He saved my life once and expected no reward. Good man. Charles Goodnight.'"

Mackenzie handed him the pieces of paper, and Bose returned them to the valise and saddlebag. The colonel eyed the sun and said, "Would you have coffee with me in my quarters, Mister Ikard? Bit early for whiskey."

"Well, yes, sir."

"Can I have your animals watered and fed?"

"I'd be much obliged. Thank you, sir."

The colonel called to a black man with two stripes on his uniform sleeves; he arrived at a jog. "Tend to this man's horse and mule, Fletcher." Mackenzie asked Bose, "Do you want him to unsaddle your mule?"

"Yes, sir. When he eats and drinks he wants to roll and dust his back, and if the saddle's on he'll just crunch it."

Another nod. "I've noticed with the pack mules. Come with me."

The enlisted soldiers slept in tents, but the officers' quarters were finished enough to have roofs, windowpanes, and door. There was a desk between them. With his saucer balanced on his knee, Bose drank the sweetened black coffee and perched politely in a chair. Mackenzie drank with his left hand, and because it was not his natural hand, he was careful in its movements. He barely sipped his coffee before setting his cup in the saucer. "You may have noticed that most of the soldiers here are Negroes."

"Yes, sir."

"The 4th Cavalry and our infantry are almost all black, except for the officers. I asked for this command, and I'm honored to have it. My orders are to enforce the Treaty of Medicine Lodge," Mackenzie went on, revolving the cup in the saucer with his good hand.

"You probably aren't familiar with that. It says that the Indians on the plains south of the Arkansas River must henceforth reside on reservations in the Indian Territory. They are not to leave the reservations, except with permission for brief hunting forays. If they do, they are legal hostiles, and they can be shot on sight. I see you're tempted to smile."

"No, sir. Just that—"

Mackenzie raised the bad hand. "I know. They ignore the treaty. They laugh at the treaty. Even ones on the reservations. But we are going to seek out and crush these plains Indians and make all of them consent to the fact that the war against civilization is lost, and their way of life has come to an end."

Bose blinked his eyes and nodded.

"Kiowas and Kiowa Apaches," Mackenzie went on, "they're troublesome, but they're not very numerous. Southern Cheyennes still have fight, but they've been licked again and again, and defeat has a way of making an impression. Custer mauled them on the Washita, and now he's gone off to break the will of the Northern Cheyennes and the Sioux. I know Custer well. He was the class ahead of me at West Point. He struggled to finish, while I was at the top of my class. He doubtless has contempt for me, just for that. But never mind Custer. He's gone from this country, and Custer is going to be Custer."

Mackenzie gave the coffee cup another slow twirl. "My intention is to go after the so-called 'free' bands of Comanches. Whip them, the reservation renegades will wilt like tulips in this godawful sun. Are you with me, Mister Ikard?"

"Sitting here, I am."

The colonel laughed. "Now, along with this cavalry of Negroes, we have the attachment of infantry. I heard your remarks to Sergeant Hayes. They amused me. Foot soldiers in a war against the horse Indians are useless. But the army is high on its ways, and its budgets. I've worn out a forest's worth of paper and a goose farm of

166

quills trying to reason with my superiors. The army refuses to mount the infantry as a matter of tradition. But, Ikard, I have a bit of budget at my discretion, and I have found that saddle mules can be purchased in Texas for one hundred dollars a head. Much cheaper than horses. First thing I noticed about you is that you chose to come in here riding a big black mule, and trailing a fine horse. You've told me you're a muleteer. I don't need teamsters, got plenty of those. But can you teach troops to ride mules, in a hurry? And can you train shavetail mules to be ridden?"

Bose chuckled. "Easier to say yes to the first question than the second."

"Also, I need scouts that our troops will trust and follow. When I arrived here, the army's decree was that all scouts would be Osages or Delawares. Good fighting men, I suppose, but what the hell do they know about the country we're going into? Soon as I could, I ran off the Osage and Delaware scouts. The Tonkawas have a nasty habit, you may know. They believe it's proper to eat some flesh of the enemies they just killed. Makes them strong and holy, or something or another. They hate Comanches because Comanches have battered the Tonks for generations. The Comanches hate Tonks because they're cannibals. The Tonks are useful, but their hatred is such that it's hard to trust their judgment, if you're a soldier in the ranks."

"Yes, sir," Bose said. He raised the coffee cup to his mouth but returned it to the saucer. The refreshment had gone tepid.

"Ever been around black Seminoles?" Mackenzie asked.

"I knew one on a trail drive once. He was a cook. Had one hand, the other a two-pronged hook."

Bose wished he hadn't said that. Didn't want to imply anything about the colonel's mutilated hand, but the colonel ignored the remark. "I like them for scouts. They intermarried with runaway slaves in the Florida Everglades, and when that fight was lost, they had the good sense to run to Mexico. They know the Kickapoo, they know the Mescalero Apaches, they know the Comanches. There's only one thing wrong with black Seminoles as scouts in this campaign. You know what that is?"

"No, sir."

He banged his hand on the desk, making the cup jump and spill coffee in the saucer. "Because they're black, and they're Indians, my troops don't trust anything they say!"

Mackenzie went on, cracking the knuckles of his bad hand with excitement. "But imagine it, Ikard. An army of Negro cavalry and mounted infantry is about to crush the earth's most dreaded horse savages since Genghis Khan rode out of Mongolia. It's history, man, and you can be a part of it."

Bose had put the cup and saucer on Mackenzie's desk, after gaining a nod that it would be all right. "Now tell me again exactly . . ." he began.

"When we take the field against them, you will be one of our scouts. In the meantime—and I'm not talking about a long period of time—you will train our infantry to be a mounted force on mules."

He added, "I'll have to call in the bursar for exact numbers, but the pay might be better than you'd think."

Another beat. "But you have to enlist."

"Ah."

Mackenzie was up and walking now. "Two years, what's two years in a young man's life? All scouts are private in rank, but that doesn't mean anything. Army thinks it has to call you something."

"Do I have to wear a uniform?"

"Well, you might give it a try at first. But I'm of a mind that scouts who are riding out front ought not to advertise who they are."

"I couldn't wear one of those caps," said Bose, still rankled by his near-fight with that Sergeant Hayes.

"Oh, bosh," said Mackenzie. "We'll make a bonfire of those things before we set out. Everybody knows you have to wear a hat under a plains sun."

The man was an evangelist of the army. Bose felt like he was being called to go down to the river and be baptized. "All right, sir."

"Good for you! Fletcher, come in here. Bring a set of enlistment papers. We need you to bear witness."

Once more, the Corporal Jim Fletcher arrived at a breathless jog.

"Raise your right hand," Mackenzie said to Bose, raising the odd claw of his own. "Repeat after me."

⋛⋚

Mackenzie preferred the company of scouts to the officers in his command. He liked to stare at campfires, and sometimes he grew talkative. One night he was sitting in a field chair sipping whiskey, with Bose and two of the Seminoles seated on the ground. Mackenzie studied Bose and cracked his knuckles. "Ikard," he said, "you know the name Quanah Parker?"

Bose nodded. "Yes, sir."

"I talk a bit to these natives around here, you see. Hear it said you went up against him and came out pretty fair."

"Oh, that fight was a swirling thing. I'm lucky I'm still breathing. I didn't know who he was. Wasn't near the kind of fights you've been in, sir."

"Not long ago he killed two mounted and armed Texans with a lance. These white halfwits out here *brag* on him." Raising his cup of whiskey, the colonel reflected, "I had a brother who was killed by a heathen in a loincloth. Stuck him in the throat with a spear."

He went on with some amusement. "When I was two years old, my father went to sea in command of a navy two-master. Alexander Mackenzie was the name he was born to. He changed it to his mother's maiden name, Slidell, thinking it might help win him some inheritance from an uncle, and it did. The brig he commanded was named the *Somers*. They were ordered to the coast of Africa to help

169

the English blockade the slave runners. In a fit of temper Father hanged three members of his crew without trial, on ten minutes' notice, for what he judged to be mutiny and conspiracy to commit piracy. One of them, a midshipman, turned out to be the son of the Secretary of War, which put a considerable crimp on Father's naval career, though a court martial acquitted him of the charges. He went to Spain to write books about his travels. Had quite a following. He died a couple of years ago. I never was very close to the man."

Mackenzie kicked the coal of a mesquite root apart. "Now his brother, John Slidell, was a diplomat, and I did admire him. Uncle John was appointed commissioner to Mexico when I was a boy. Polk sent him down to Mexico City to set the Texas boundary and buy New Mexico and California, but the Mexicans wouldn't accept his credentials. He was highly insulted. When Lincoln was elected, Uncle John couldn't abide that, so he went Confederate, and Jefferson Davis appointed him ambassador to France. To get to Paris, he tried to run the blockade on a mail ship out of South Carolina that the Union navy captured. He was a prisoner for a while. The incident damn near sparked a war with the English, who were dickering with the Confederates for their cotton, so finally the Union let him go on his way. Uncle John idled out the war in Europe, still lives in England. I'd like to see him again."

Mackenzie gazed at Bose, who rested with an elbow on the ground, and the Seminoles, who sat cross-legged. "My Aunt Jane," he went on, "was the wife of Commodore Matthew Perry, who opened up Japan, made them accept the United States flag, by God. Big jowly fellow. I've got one brother who's an admiral in the navy now. The other, my baby brother, was the one who got speared in the throat on the Chinese island of Formosa. So what," he said with a bark of laughter, "am I doing out in this shit-hole of a prairie — with *you*?"

14

A YEAR HAD PASSED SINCE Quanah had come into the canyon country with a fine herd of horses stolen out of Mexico and a beautiful young wife on the best one, a thick-chested bay. Quanah thought the stars had at last lined up with favor in his sky. That fall's hunt had gone well. Parra-o-coom had approved of his bargaining with Old Wolf and had sent out young carriers and captive Mexican packers with one hundred buffalo robes for the Mescaleros in exchange for three hundred horses and mules that enriched his herd and those of his elder war chiefs. Quanah had added robes made from eight cows that he killed as a compliment to his father-in-law, a gift in gratitude for his daughter. Hides of cows were smaller than the bulls' but they made softer and warmer robes, and the best of all were the autumn hides, when the bison had put on the rich brown fur that protected them from the oncoming winter.

Quanah spent several weeks smoothing the bois d'arc sapling shaft and sharpening the head of his grandfather's lance. Iron Shirt had made the spearhead from the axle of a wagon, and even with its age it could still be honed as sharp as a knife. Quanah fashioned a decorative collar for the head with feathers of a cardinal and peregrine falcon. To-ha-yea took an interest in this; he watched her decorate the shaft with swirls and sparkles of beads that she tapped and glued in the hard wood. Quanah's lance was admired and envied. Her beadwork became a fashion of the craft.

Quanah could carry the lance because Parra-o-coom approved it on inspection, and he proved he could use it, too. They wintered on the Canadian that year, avoiding trouble with the bluecoats but eager to turn fury loose on buffalo hunters and a new enemy, the gangs of surveyors who walked the prairie with their sticks and spyglasses. In the spring he joined a raid of Quohada and Kotsoteka who set fire to houses within sight of the big Texas town San Antonio, a place with much bitter history between the two peoples. The raid stirred a long and furious pursuit by a company of rangers, who said to hell with the occupation army of the North. In the rough country out by the Devils River, Quanah circled back through a cedar brake and with some acrobatic riding he put his lance deep in two of them. It slipped in and out like a knife in a bowl of suet. Quanah was as thrilled with these kills in close fighting as he was raised to be, but he had lived twenty-three winters now and was mature enough to stop bragging. In his lodge hung just one scalp, that of the red-haired boy he put an arrow through the day the black cowboy gave him his whipping with a quirt.

He did not take peyote before a raid—it was too dangerous, he wanted his head clear—but he knew he had finally found his medicine. After he took down those rangers with his lance, the headman and fellow raiders came back bragging that his surprise solitary attack so turned the morale of the fight that the heavily armed Texans had to quit their horses and go scrambling through the thorn fields on foot. Parra-o-coom called a council of elders that included Yellow Bear and they came out of it with Quanah elevated to the rank of war leader. His True Friends the Little Horses honored him with a headdress of eagle feathers that almost reached the ground, even as tall as he stood. Possession of such a bonnet signified him as a war leader of great stature. And he had shown many of his brothers the power and way of the peyote road.

Yet not one of these True Friends would accept his wife. The humiliation of To-ha-yea had started as soon as their moccasins hit the ground. After coming out to thump his forearms on Quanah's shoulders and welcome him back, Parra-o-coom had given her a broad smile, yawped on in words she couldn't fathom, and called out his number one wife to thrust a bowl of spine soup in her hands.

But as the girl looked around in amazement the chief gave her new husband a wink and darted his tongue from side to side.

They acted as if Quanah had brought among them a captive wife who was a whore. What else, besides his own impure blood, could explain his bringing into their lives this Apache? One night he saw some old women coming toward their lodge with willow switches. They were coming to give her a whipping for nothing more than being what she was. Quanah's bellow sent the hags scuttling on their way. To-ha-yea loved him now with all her bones, Quanah was sure of that, but nothing in his power could overcome her homesickness and persuade her that these plains were where she belonged. They made love and they fought, and because Spanish was still the only language they could speak to each other with any confidence, they didn't always make their quarrels clearly understood. He thought that if they could just have a child her unhappiness might ease. But he couldn't give her even that.

He seemed able to make her happy only when they were inside his lodge. When the flap was closed, their groans of love were so rambunctious that jokes were made about them within the camp. It didn't bother him—in those instants there were just Quanah and To-ha-yea, on all the earth. One cool morning found her resting her forearms and elbows on the sleeping robe and glancing over her shoulder. He rose against her from behind, both of them breathing hard, holding her breasts then running his hands, one after another, over her stomach and ribs. She gathered her hair and pulled it away from the nape of her neck. The valley between her shoulder blades glistened with sweat. Quanah caught himself and drew back, then tossed her, turning her over, and she spread her arms to receive him, grinning. Her ass just fit his large cushioning hand. Under him she twisted and bucked and arched her back as the hornets' swarm of pleasure roiled out of him, then she cried out and flung her chest against him, gripping and yanking on his braids. As they lay panting and wet she drew her legs up around his hips and rested her soles on his calves. "Are you all right?" she murmured.

"All right?" he gasped and laughed. "Yes, believe I am."

They lay on their sides. To-ha-yea wriggled against his loins and held his hands to her chest. "I like the way you smell," she said.

They murmured and half-dozed until she felt him stirring again. She liked to ride him in these times when it was slower, pressing her palms against his chest and sawing back and forth against his root, her hair loose over her face until he raised his hands and held it back so he could see that moment when her eyes began to flutter and every feature softened, and she moaned again.

Later he said, "I bet this time we did it."

She shook her head. "You're hexed."

"What?"

"Hexed by a witch. It's a belief of our people: when there's this much heat and still no baby—"

"Tu gente," Quanah murmured. Your people. He rolled on his stomach and rested his chin on his wrists.

"Tahvoa," she said a moment later, playfulness in her voice.

"What?"

"Whiteass. Did you know your ass is white? Look at it."

His shoulder blades moved a shrug. "To-ha-yea, these are your people now. Our People. *I'm* your people."

"Quanah, I'm Apache. You can't just throw that off like we threw off our clothes. I'm proud of it."

His wife withdrew from him, rolled up in robe, and turned her back to him. He touched her shoulder but she resisted. "Let's don't fight," he said.

"One of us is always saying that." Then her voice went colder still. "I don't think I'll ever have your baby."

Quanah flinched. "And I'm to blame?"

"Blame?" She considered the word and yawned. "Maybe I'm to blame. Maybe I keep it from happening, because I'm afraid. What would I do with a child in a place and life like this, if something happened to you?"

⨯⨯

Trying to control himself, Quanah wrapped his breechclout between his legs and up over his belt, yanked on his leggings, slipped on his moccasins, and walked out where his footing was surer. The start of another fall hunting season found the Quohada camped in Blanco Canyon, along the Clear Fork of the Brazos. Horse races and games were part of the preparation for the hunt. Observing a crowd between the lodges and the river, Quanah decided to walk down and watch the young women play a match of double-ball. He had not gone far when To-ha-yea overtook him, grasped his arm to her chest, and whispered, "I'm sorry, I'm sorry. I don't know what makes me say those things." Just when their tension and frustration boiled and frothed out of the pot, she offered the touch that cooled the moment. He pulled her forehead against his shoulder and as they walked he eyed the wealth of horses and mules spread across the valley floor. If only he could make her see the world he saw.

The playing ground was marked by two stakes driven into the earth at the distance of about two arrow flights. Clad in hide dresses and moccasins, with their eyelids painted red and smears of black drawn across their cheeks, the twenty girls on the field were the fastest runners and quickest and surest sticks in the band. Half of them wore short blue shawls over their dresses. The players got ready by jigging up and down on their toes, twisting their hips and shoulders, bringing up their knees in prancing stretches. Each of them carried a crooked stick, natziminá, that had been stripped of bark and rubbed with a buffalo bone until it was gleaming and smooth. As the players ran to their positions they gave each other clacks with their sticks, which sounded like a host of bucks fighting, and stirred yells of support from husbands, brothers, sisters, children, old folks favoring one team or the other. Men paced about making bets.

Quanah watched Weckeah, who gripped her stick with hands spread at about the width of her body and wiggled her hips, waiting for the toss that began the match. The game was called double-ball because the thong was weighted at both ends by two smooth rocks sewn into the leather. A warrior walked out twirling the thong. The leaders of each team squared off, glaring with excitement and concentration, and then with a shout he flung the thong high. The players leaped and stabbed at the airborne thong, and when a girl managed to catch or scoop it up, she sprinted with it toward the goal. Opponents hurtled forward, trying to snatch the thong away. They lunged and left their feet, trying to knock the runner down. With shrieks the players charged and collided with their shoulders, not the sticks. They slashed at the runner's stick, trying to knock the thong loose, but if any player used the stick as a spear or club, she was jeered.

Braids flying, they were in no time sweat-soaked, knees and elbows skinned from their tumbles, but the game never stopped, not even when one of them went down and didn't get up. The blue shawls and the buckskins battled back and forth, hurling the thong at the goal when they hoped they might be close enough to score. It had to catch and lash around the stake; when a scoring throw missed, they trudged back to midfield, then the official flung it high, and they were off running again.

Weckeah wasn't the fastest runner on the field, but the blue shawls continually passed the thong to her. No others on her team caught and maneuvered so well. Using other runners for interference, she would skid to a halt, pivot, and yield ground, coming back around, then wheel again and jump forward with a burst of speed, flipping the thong to another blue shawl just as an opponent clipped her legs out from under her. But then she was up again, she caught another pass of the thong, and she ran straight at a buckskin. She sent that one stumbling with a feinted pass, then was pulling away from ones not possessed of the same endurance or resolve. As she ran past the stake she twisted in the air and lightly tossed it, and it looped around the goal and hung there as if it had throttled a sandhill crane.

The blue shawls were whooping and jumping up and down around her. Quanah yelled and leaped off the ground as Weckeah trotted out, her stick held high. Then he noticed how To-ha-yea stared at him. "Isn't she a little old to be doing that?" she asked.

"She's having a good time," Quanah said, once more deflated. "It's just a game."

"Why do you look at her like that?" said To-ha-yea.

Quanah sighed. "You imagine things. She's like a sister. Someone I grew up with."

"You always do."

Weckeah:

WHEN QUANAH CAME BACK from Mexico with the Apache, I was rattled and angry. I don't know why I thought I deserved to be. I was the one who ran him off when I still loved him. So I tried to act happy for them and help her learn our ways and language. But women have a sure instinct about who their rivals are, and To-ha-yea was no fool.

And I was floundering in my own quicksand. My sister's husband Tannap made it very clear he was not going to give up his claim on me. His father, Eckitacoap, kept sugaring the pot, offering my dad more horses. I could try to keep stalling, but without Dad's support the only way I could stop it was to run away.

Where to? And eat what?

Quanah and I had started talking again—it was almost like it was when we lived among the Nokoni, before the rangers came, the tragedies destroyed his family, and he had to go live among the Quohada. We found an odd kind of privacy out among the herds.

Despite all the tearing down and moving of camps, our band had over fifteen thousand horses and several hundred mules. Boy herders were out all the time, watching for thieves, wolves, lions, bears, and magpies. If a horse had sores, with a flash of those white wings and green tails magpies would swoop down and grab hold of a horse's back and tear at the scabbing until the horse went crazy. A flock of magpies could stampede a herd as fast as a grizzly. The boys knew Quanah was an important warrior, so they turned away in consideration, and people were out caring for their animals' galls and hooves and taking their turns moving them down to the river and drink. He and I could walk almost unseen.

One evening when twilight was turning the grassland purple, we were feeding his horses treats of young cottonwood bark. He said, "I'm afraid I'm going to lose her."

"The mare?" I said, nodding at the sorrel. He gave me the glance that I deserved. "I know," I said, smiling. "Your wife's unhappy. But where would she go?"

"Back to the band of her father. I always said I'll send her back anytime she wants. A moon ago I was deciding which boys to ask to take her."

"But she didn't go. She chooses to stay."

"So far."

"And you want her to."

"Yes, very much."

"Well," I said, annoyed that we were talking about this, "it would be better if she'd hurry up learning our language and ways."

"Why don't you marry me?" he said.

"What?"

"You could teach her all these things she needs to know."

I stared at him in disbelief. "You're asking me to be your *chore wife*?"

"No, no," he hurried to say, his cheeks and throat flushing. "Never. That's not what I mean. The two of you would be the same to me. Always."

"Oh, yes. Men say that. But one of us would wind up being the boss wife." I couldn't resist taunting him. "Which one would it be?"

After a moment he said, "All right. You know which one. You would."

I gave the mare's hip a slap. "Quanah, you're always making up worlds you wish were true. You've got your troubles and I've got mine. I can't put off Tannap or my father much longer. Every time I throw a fit and say I'll never be the wife of that man, Eckitoacup comes along to Dad and promises that Tannap will always keep my mother and him in meat, and think of all the grandsons. Then he ups the offer in horses. For my father it's become a matter of losing face. Can't he make his women do as he wants?"

"That's the old way," said Quanah.

"But it is the way."

Quanah's war and hunting horse was a young black stallion with a small white blaze from the point of his mane to an eyebrow. Quanah called him Arecatua, Deer's Son. It was unusual to have one that excelled at both battle and the hunt. He nudged at my arm for more bark. I fed him some shreds.

Quanah asked, "How many horses does Eckitoacup offer?"

"Fifty. Dad took got a lot of pleasure telling me that."

Quanah pursed his lips and contained his dismay. "Would you marry me," he persisted, "if some way I could match the offer?"

"Oh, stop it, Quanah. Dad would never consent to my marrying you. No matter how many horses you brought him, no matter what you did for him—not if you were war chief of all the people. You know why—it's because you're half-white."

Quanah was angered and stung, acted like it was a big surprise. "You don't feel that way, do you?" he said.

"No. But you know it's the truth."

"What if we just ran off and did it? Piss on his good wishes."

"He'd have the right to kill me."

"Oh, sure," Quanah scoffed. "Would you marry me, Weckeah? If I could change his mind some way?"

The man could be maddening. I yelled loud enough that Deer's Son snorted and whirled away and a fat herd tender rose up staring, like a bear. "Yes, Quanah! There! Does it make your heart jump to hear it? Yes! But you know we can't!"

179

15

WILLIAM TECUMSEH SHERMAN had distributed his command among officers who served with him and fought with valor in the War against the Southern Rabble, as he put it. He was not thrilled now by having to put down a guerrilla insurrection of horse thieves and nomads. "When they laugh at our credulity, rape our women, burn whole trains with their drivers to cinders, and send word that they never intended to keep their treaties, then we must submit or we must fight them," Sherman told an audience in Chicago. "Fighting Indians, I will take my code from soldiers and not civilians." The army, Sherman grumbled, had no business having to commit to such an inglorious campaign. "It's not apt to add much to our fame or personal comfort." Sherman really didn't care to get much closer to any Indian war than the shore of Lake Michigan. The whole business seemed undignified—beneath him.

Sherman frankly expected Phil Sheridan to take care of the situation on the Southern plains. The man was only forty. Sherman had spotted and boosted him as a young captain in Ohio. Sheridan was a hero at Booneville and Murfreesboro, and as a brevet major general he'd fought with Grant and Sherman at Chickamauga, and his cavalry took Missionary Ridge. From another victory at Lookout Mountain Sheridan led his troops on to the Shenandoah Valley, where they killed Jeb Stuart, the rebs' cavalry commander. After the war, Sheridan stepped on too many moneyed toes while running the Occupation of New Orleans. Sherman relieved him of that command, then ordered him, face-to-face, over dinner, brandy, and cigars, to whip the army's Department of Missouri back into fighting shape and put an end to all this Indian raiding. Sheridan was a beneficiary of the Treaty of Medicine Lodge, which hoodwinked some tribal chiefs into accepting reservations in the Indian Territory. The southern plains tribes believed, mistakenly, that the treaty obligated the army to keep white buffalo hunters from crossing the Arkansas River and extending their commerce south into the plains of Texas. To the contrary, the generals ordered their subordinates to stop any interference with the hide trade; if the hunters were willing to risk battles with enraged Indians and ask for no protection, then show their wagons to the best fords across the Arkansas. "It would be wise," Sherman quipped to Sheridan once, "to invite all the sportsmen of England and America for a grand buffalo hunt, and have one grand swipe of them all." Burning every cornfield, grain silo, and meat smokehouse had been Sherman's record of war in his march across the South, and he never lost sleep over it. As Sherman's surrogate, Sheridan explained the principle to the Texas legislature, where some save-the-varmints hokum had gained currency. By killing the buffalo herds, he testified, the hide hunters were destroying the Indian commissary.

The second part of Sheridan's strategy was to mount military campaigns against the hostiles during the winter months, when their horses were weakened from hunger. Sheridan proposed to go first after the Southern Cheyennnes. Sherman told him that would be fine, but then he learned Sheridan had given the assignment to that self-promoting fop, George Custer. Grant was elected president while the Cheyenne campaign was being carried out, and Custer, after touting the news of his great victory at "the Battle of the Washita," sent Grant a promise and possibly a smooch that he'd like to shoo the Sioux and Northern Cheyennes out of rumored gold fields in the Dakotas. Then the bombshell: Grant, of all people, turned over Indian policy and administration of the reservations to the *Quakers*. "Grant stood by me when I was crazy," Sherman sighed to friends, "and I stood by him when he was drunk; now we stand by each other." Sherman had accepted his appointment to Grant's Peace Commission with too much contempt to show up for any of its meetings, but he had to say it helped keep a lid on the pot until the Union Pacific railroad reached the Rockies at Cheyenne, Wyoming. With the plains cut in half, Sherman was confident the hostile tribes were finished. He foresaw two great reservations in which the tribal distinctions would soon dissolve. Comanches and Sioux would just be Indians, poor farmers.

But reports filtered up to Sherman about a Comanche half-breed, Quanah Parker, who was leading raids in Texas wearing an army coat and stripes; a loudmouth Kiowa named Satanta seized on every chance to tell army officers that if they wanted to stop the raids in Texas, they ought to *move* Texas someplace else; and in the north the Sioux Crazy Horse and Sitting Bull dared the soldiers to come. These were not reports from the field that Sherman was happy to review. At the same time Grant commenced his strange waltz with the Quakers, he made Sherman his General of the Army and promoted Sheridan to lieutenant general, giving him posh headquarters in Chicago. Sherman thought the general had grown too fond of the cushions of his walnut chair. In Chicago Sheridan hosted a party of artists, architects, and the like for Sherman, the night before he made his speech about the Indians. Sherman couldn't understand why such an able man had not put to rout a bunch of nomads living in hide tents. And in irritation told him so.

Having seen the east end of the Confederacy, Sherman had no desire to venture west and set foot in Texas, but politics required him to. The Texans raised a piteous howl about the punishment they were taking from the Indians, so Grant summoned and leaned on him with much whiskey breath to undertake a fact-finding tour of the place. Muttering all the way, Sherman traveled to New Orleans and caught a boat to the port of Indianola, and then bounced overland to San Antonio, where he commenced his inspection tour, working his way northward in an ambulance with an entourage that included two colonels, fifteen cavalry, two scouts, and the adventurous prairie traveler, Major General Randolph Marcy. Grant had thrown Marcy the job of inspector general as a sop. Viewing all things through the prism of the army, Sherman thought him a tragic figure. Marcy had gone up the Red River of the South to its source in fabulous canyons that to this day were unknown except for his reports and journals, which were so well-written and lacking in overt malice toward the Indians that the army allowed him to publish them commercially, and his book *The Prairie Traveler* made the career soldier a modest fortune. Marcy was a fine and accurate cartographer. But in the war between the states, Marcy had the excruciating curse of a son-in-law who was a superior officer. That son-in-law was George McClellan, Lincoln's choice to head the army until he froze up in cowardice and shame in the face of Lee's forces in Virginia. Lincoln relieved him of his command and eventually decided on Grant. Sherman had to sympathize with McClellan; in Kentucky he had been stuffed in a sanatorium himself after he was relieved of his first command. But, well, one could imagine the awkwardness that would flood the conversations of William Tecumseh Sherman and Randolph Marcy.

Before the war, a line of about twenty army forts and camps was strung north to south to protect the Texas frontier from the Indians. Now Congress budgeted them just half a dozen. Ignoring one near the border with Mexico, his party rolled to Fort Concho and then with new escort to Fort Belknap on the Salt Fork of the Brazos. Twenty years earlier, that post had been situated on the first wagon road through this part of the Indian country, a road that Marcy surveyed. But in drafting the map of that country, Sherman took note, Marcy gave the Red River another name, Ke-che-ah-quo-ho-no, and the Clear Fork of the Brazos was Tock-an-ho-no, and Paint Creek was Oua-qua-ho-no. Comanche names. Might sell books in Boston, but it was too conciliatory for Sherman's taste.

The generals had drawn an ambulance for the tour because the wheels and axles had springs, but the Butterfield Road surveyed by Marcy was still little more than a cow trail; the jolts and jostling were continuous. Sherman thought the terrain was handsome enough, with knee-deep stands of prairie, plenty of hardwood timber, and creeks running clear across beds of stone, but it bored him. As did Marcy.

One time that Sherman ceased yawning was when Marcy told him about encountering the white captive Cynthia Ann Parker in a Comanche camp during his exploration of the Red River. Marcy said she had a sullen lout of a husband who turned out to be the war chief Nocona, and a couple of small sons who ran around begrimed and naked. "What did you do about it?" Sherman asked.

"Why, nothing we could do. She was hanging buffalo meat out to dry like all the rest of them." Marcy leaned out and spat tobacco over the wagon side. "Lord, that camp stunk. She had a brother there, too, and he wasn't any captive. He was a turncoat, gone native. Told me he'd been ransomed home to his Texas kin and had come back on his own. Looked like smallpox had taken an ice pick to the man's face. Scary-looking little fellow."

Sherman's wizened and worried-looking visage puckered anew at the word turncoat and the thought of that infuriating report he had gotten about the half-breed Comanche who wore a soldier's tunic. "Would one of that woman's sons be the one the Texans prattle about, Quanah Parker?"

"Has to be," said Marcy, excited. "Has to be."

"Yahh!" scoffed Sherman. "I don't believe any of it."

"What do you mean?" said Marcy.

"I don't think there's any Indian war out here. I don't think there's anything."

"General, I've been all through this country. It's not half as settled as it was when I saw it twenty years ago."

"Look there, General," Sherman mocked him. He pointed to a couple of boys who sauntered toward the wagon in overalls, easy as you please. They had their thumbs hooked in their bibs like they were self-satisfied politicians, such as Grant. "Either they're not in any danger, or their mamas and papas don't have the sense to come in out of the rain. I believe it's both."

To scout for Sherman's escort, Colonel Mackenzie assigned Bose Ikard, two Seminoles, and a Tonkawa called Jim Pockmark. Lieutenant Robert Carter, a big sunburned red-haired man from Maine, called up the troop for review by Mackenzie and started to tell him about his plans to greet General Sherman with appropriate ceremony and a cannon salute. Bad Hand waved him off. "I know the general," he said, "and what you're going to find, Lieutenant, is an irascible coot who thinks he's bullet-proof. He doesn't think the fires of hell will raise a blister on him. I don't care what he says— these are your orders, Lieutenant. You'll pick up his party from the Belknap troop at Cotton Wood Spring. Harness his ambulance with a team of fresh mules and ask him to please stay at my quarters tonight. If you have to keep a hill between your men and the view of General Sherman's wagon to keep from raising his ire, do so, but get him and General Marcy from Belknap to this post. Scouts, you know the way. Each of you range out one to three miles from his wagon—Ikard on the point. When the general's here we'll arrange a brief audience a few civilians demand and then feed him a hearty breakfast and trot him on to Fort Sill. *But by God get him across the Salt Creek Prairie.* I don't have to remind you what happens there all the time—that grassland's killed more travelers and troops than any other place in this godforsaken land—and I'm not going to have the Commanding General of the United States Army murdered and butchered on my watch. Is that understood, Lieutenant?"

"Yes, sir!" Carter was always banging his hat-brim with his salute. Bose and the Tonkawa glanced at each other. Pot-bellied and gap-toothed, Jim Pockmark belonged to a small dying tribe, caught in a squeeze between the Mexican and white Texan settlers and the unrelenting hatred and power of the Comanches. But he had survived the pox and gone out with the rangers, and he had fired the shot that killed the Comanche war chief Iron Shirt in the rout on the Canadian River. Jim Pockmark had survived thirteen winters with a fervent Comanche price on his head, and until they relieved it from his shoulders he was not going to stop going out to fight them and cut them up. He loved the taste of Comanche liver.

As Bad Hand predicted, one of the generals beamed at their approach but the grizzled one did not. Except for the lieutenant, all the troops and scouts before them were black. Bose could see that the one called Sherman was not pleased to see them wearing the same uniform he did. The general, a tall thin man with a short salt-and-pepper beard that he did not bother to shave from his throat, stood up in the wagon seat and exploded in a rant as Carter tried to conduct his ceremony. "These mules are doing fine," Sherman growled, "and I appreciate Colonel Mackenzie's kind offer of his quarters. But haul that goddamn howitzer back where it belongs. If you fire that anywhere close to me I'll have your bars and your ass, do you hear me?"

"Yes, sir!" Carter shouted again, with another one of those salutes.

"And get those troops out of my sight. We don't need any god-damn escort. The general and I are having a little chat." Bose could see that the other general, Marcy, who had a well-barbered gray beard, did not share Sherman's sense of their total safety.

※

The Salt Creek Prairie extended between a cone-shaped sand-stone hill called Squaw's Tit and a thickly wooded mesa named Cox Mountain. Amid jumbles of boulders and the shadows of junipers and post oaks, the raiding party had spread their blankets and hobbled their horses around Squaw's Tit the prior night. Most of the raiders were Kiowas and Kiowa-Apaches, but some were Comanches. One of the Comanches had a thick neck, narrow shoulders, and an odd name—Isa-tai, Wolf Shit. A member of the Quohada band, Wolf Shit had a wife and babies, a small herd of horses, and a record of not much luck or valor on the warring trail. Wolf Shit seethed with jealousy when he saw young war leaders like Quanah and Cohayyah strutting through the camp. Adding to his annoyance, he had not done well in the recent hunt. Unless Isa-tai got off just the perfect shot, he didn't have enough strength in his arms and shoulders to pull a bowstring back and sink an arrow so deep in a buffalo's innards that the force knocked its knees to the ground, allowing him to claim it as his kill. Wearing his arrows like flags, they tended to keep on running, and someone else killed and claimed them. The other hunter might choose to share the kill, but Wolf Shit had no close friends—who would do that for him? He could appeal to the chief of the hunt for justice, but it was seldom granted. He envied the white hunters who knocked the bison down with their long guns. Wolf Shit could not feed his children or keep them warm just by killing buffalo calves. So he had drifted into the reservation of Horse Back's Nokoni band on the north end of the Wichita Mountains, where he collected on the monthly issue of beef and blankets by the Quakers. They didn't question whether he was of the Nokoni—to whiteasses, all Comanche people were the same.

Not much was going on among the peace Comanches, just a bunch of men stumbling and falling from a fresh batch of corn shine, poisabá. After trading the fresh beef for some pemmican and jerked meat that he loaded with wool army blankets in the hide panniers on his packhorse, Wolf Shit rode on through the small handsome Wichita range to the camp of the reservation Kiowas, which was near the soldiers' Fort Sill. The bluecoats were building it with maximum contempt right around a bend of Cache Creek from a Comanche holy place, the sheer black stone Medicine Bluff, where young men conjured visions and sick old men sang their songs then leaped off head-first. Wolf Shit was pleased to find among the Kiowas a great deal of mischief in the making. Satanta, Satank, and other war chiefs had been smoking pipes with young men and talking up a big raid in Texas; they believed they could groom young firebrands and come back with an abundance of horses and mules.

Wolf Shit knew the Kiowas to be exceptionally alert to omens.

They might call off a long-planned raid if one skunk crossed their path at twilight. Yet they forded the Red River at a malodorous place called Skunk Bend; they dreaded skunks, but they disliked quicksand more, and it was a reliable crossing. Kiowas had been known to start fights if Comanches wore white men's looking glasses. Kiowas were also incredibly afraid of owls.

The night they arrived at the overlook of the Salt Creek Prairie, they built no fires that might alert whites. Satanta stomped about wrapped in his red sash, brandishing his bugle and attended by one of the pretty boys he favored. Satank was an older and venerated Kiowa chief who was enraged that during the past winter Texans had killed his favorite son and pipe bearer. But the old war chiefs were not the ones that Wolf Shit studied. His eyes were on the shaman Mama'nte, Sky-Walker.

The Quohada's old Jaybird Pesters had recently dropped dead off a horse in Tule Canyon, and he had never been much respected as puhakut. Isa-tai had decided that the hole left by Jaybird Pesters could be his way to prestige and power. He was looking for the tricks of men who knew how to use their medicine. The war chief who had the devotion of the young Kiowa warriors was the Owl Prophet. A slim man who looked like he was always in the course of having a vision, Sky-Walker was not a braggart like Satanta, nor was he a member of the elite Koitsenko, the Real Dogs. Sky-Walker saw the future through owl medicine known only to him.

Kiowas were afraid even to look at the owl that Sky-Walker conversed with. The big owl rustled and muttered on his gloved right hand, and periodically it called out in the manner and voice of a great horned owl. But Wolf Shit watched Sky-Walker closely and determined that his owl was a well-skinned dead one. It had buckeyes in its eye sockets, and Sky-Walker made his owl rustle its wings by blowing against the hand on which it perched. Wolf Shit did not begrudge the Kiowa war chief his medicine or his tricks. But he saw that the Owl Prophet was a magician. His owl was a puppet.

When Sky-Walker crooned to his owl in the moonlight and it

raised its wings and answered, "Whoooooooooo whoooo," some of the young Kiowas moaned in fear. The shaman told his fellow war chiefs and the raiders what the owl medicine said. "Tomorrow two parties of white men will come this way. The first will be a small party. The owl says we must let them pass. The second party is the one we'll attack. There'll be coups and scalps and a great many horses and mules."

Wolf Shit had a few buttons of peyote he had carried away from the rituals that Quanah led among the Quohada. He chewed and spat the choke in privacy, his head hooded by one of the green wool blankets. With ease, Wolf Shit called up the person of power he knew he was becoming. He saw himself riding at a lope through the cottonwoods and broad valley of the Canadian River, except on looking closer, his shoulders and hams and thighs cast off bright gold reflections from the sun, and he was riding a giant wolf, not a horse. These were excellent omens, and except for the scratchy wool of the blanket, he slept well that night. The first time he woke up, he tossed off the blanket and saw Sky-Walker sitting by himself and gazing at the sheen of the Salt Creek Prairie. Wolf Shit started to go sit down and tell the Kiowa how much he admired his medicine and power, but he saw the Owl Prophet's lips moving and his shoulders heaving, and he decided not to intrude on the man's vision.

The morning unfolded the way the Owl Prophet said it would, except that he failed to mention that the first rider would *not* be white. It was a tuh-tahvoa on a Medicine Hat paint. A black man on that horse was an insult to the Kiowa raiders. Several of them raised a jeer at this dirty whiteass trying to scare them with Cheyenne horse medicine. To Kiowas, a paint of any pattern was a woman's horse; the warriors' favorites were bays or duns with black ears. Satanta was all puffed up to blast the signal of attack on his bugle, but Sky-Walker made a cutting motion with his hand. Satanta lowered the horn from his lips. The owl medicine had spoken. Young ones watched with frustration as the black rider and his paint gelding clopped out of the range of their breech-loaders and Spencer carbines, followed by the wagon occupied by two old soldiers and a driver. Some raiders jumped on their horses in their eagerness to attack the troop of cavalry, which they believed satisfied the owl medicine. "No, no," Mama'nte hissed. "These are not the ones. Be patient." The owl moved around on his hand and hooted. A couple of coyotes answered. Everyone knew that was a very good omen. Wolf Shit was impressed that the prophet's trickery was strong enough to call them up.

On a magician's whim, William Tecumseh Sherman and the lesser officer Randolph Marcy dodged their deaths that day in Texas. Bose Ikard, when he heard about the attacks of the next wagons that come down the trail, would go to his grave certain that he survived that scout of the Salt Creek Prairie because he rode a Medicine Hat paint.

The storm was dumping so much rain on them that Wolf Shit couldn't think straight. And he wished he could shut the women up. The women who had come with the raiders started screeching as soon as Satanta quit blowing his horn. They hurried the blood rush, all right, but there was plenty of that already. The Kiowas' first attack was a horse race, all of them trying to arrive there first and touch the plunder, claim it and count coup. A young warrior yelled out his claim of the first coup, the war chief Big Tree hollered out the second. But then a Kotsoteka Comanche called Ord-lee pitched off his horse and was dead when he hit the mud. Amid the explosions of thunder, tomoyaquet, and the guns and plumes of black powder smoke, a teamster ran out from behind a wagon, and Wolf Shit's carbine misfired. He cursed and swatted the fleeing teamster across the back, but he didn't want to break the stock, so he jammed the rifle in the sleeve beside his leg and thumped the horse's ribs, doing his best to trample the whiteass. As the man turned to face him

Wolf Shit swung with his war club and missed—and in the exertion lost his seat on the rain-slick horse. He jumped up and whacked the teamster several times but couldn't knock him down. Wolf Shit dropped the club and with a howl ran forward with his knife. He thought it would go in deep, but it ricocheted off the teamster's ribs. The whiteass grabbed the blade and held on, and down they went in the muck. This shouldn't be happening, thought Wolf Shit—it was his greatest feat as a warrior. Never before had he counted coup. But the teamster got the knife turned against him. Wolf Shit hollered for help then fought like a cornered badger when he realized that none was coming. He butted the man hard, leaving himself blind for a moment. Wolf Shit's teeth wound up clenched on the man's ear; he tasted its wax. The teamster bellowed and started shoving at the knife instead of trying to tear it from Isa-tai's hands. Wolf Shit had sound teeth and powerful jaws, and in no time he chewed the ear clean off. The teamster hurled him in a somersault and staggered off in the deluge, holding his side with one hand and his head with the other.

Wolf Shit sat winded in the mud for a moment, then realized the ear was still in his mouth. He dropped it in his hand and held it fiercely. There were two other members of the Quohada band in the raid, and they would have to support Wolf Shit's claim—he had the evidence in his fist. He had fought and bettered a Texan hand-to-hand; no one would be able to deny him as a warrior now.

No more fire was coming from the wagons. Bodies of teamsters were strewn about. The mules were either panicked or shell-shocked in their harnesses, but not one of them was down. In amazement Wolf Shit dashed forward to claim as many mules as he could. A Kiowa boy called Gun-Shot sprinted past on a better horse and threw Wolf Shit a grin. It turned out he had a prophetic name. With a whoop Gun-Shot reached a wagon and raised a canvas flap. "I claim this wagon," he exulted, "and all in it, as mine!" A teamster named Sam Elliott lay on his back in the wagon, shot in the kidney, praying he would either pass out or die. He rolled over with a long-barreled Remington pistol in his hand, stuck it in the boy's face, and blew it half off.

After that it was mayhem, rage. Some raiders were herding up the mules, others were taking scalps, others were hauling corn sacks out of the wagon, cutting them open, and dumping them in the mud. In their fury they chopped and tore up things that moments earlier they would have wanted to keep. The teamster Sam Elliott died hard for shooting that boy; the raiders got a fire blazing in all that rain, tied him upside down to a wagon tongue, and tipped him back and forth. Somehow the Kiowa boy survived being thrown on the back of a horse and floated across flooding rivers. He never spoke again nor seemed to recognize anyone, but he was quiet and patient almost until the end. The ones who carried him to his parents' lodge tried to keep the blowflies away, but the wound was just too big. The screwworms burrowed quickly. When the boy died, screaming, they were gorging and writhing in his brain.

The thing that most impressed Sherman that day was the mountain of blue and white clouds that rose across the prairie from the west. As it closed in on them he could see a violent shaft rising upward and spinning off funnels like children's tops. It was a furious and majestic cloud. The mules snorted and fought their driver as lightning struck in bolts that just stood there blazing; he hadn't heard such noise since the cannonades at Shiloh and Vicksburg. The storm arrived with dusty blasts of cold wind and then big splatters followed by diagonal sheets of rain. The wind blew so hard they couldn't hold onto their slickers and were drenched at once. There were pops of hail on the canvas of the wagon, and then rain that fell like it never meant to stop.

Mackenzie was an able officer, Sherman supposed. He knew

of Grant's high regard for the colonel, but anyone who got hit by gunfire as often as Mackenzie had was not someone the general cared to stand beside in a lightning storm. When they reached the fort, the colonel suggested they postpone inspection of the troops and the fort because of the downpour, a suggestion that Sherman gladly accepted. In a dry uniform but still in wet boots, after a mess of cornbread, venison, and greens the general longed for his bed but instead received a motley sampling of the politicians and farmers of Jacksboro. As one after another carried on about the depredations of the Comanches and Kiowas the general pulled his chin toward his chest and scowled with such incredulity and hostilty that the sparse hairs of his fuzzy pate stood straight up.

"This is a county of loyal Republicans," said a sniveling justice of the peace. "Before the war there were just thirty-seven slaves in Jack County, and thrice that number of free niggers. The vote in this county was seventy-six to fourteen in support of the Union and against secession—"

"Judge," Sherman snapped at the man, "I don't give a rotten fig about Republicans or Democrats. The carping and bickering of political factions in this nation remind me of seagulls quarreling over dead fish."

"Beg your pardon, General. I just meant—"

"'Before the war,' six hundred thousand men on both sides had not yet given their lives in the course of it."

Fort Richardson's headquarters fell so quiet that there was no sound but rain drumming its roof. The magistrate sat rigid in his chair, as did the other men and wives who had imposed on Sherman's good graces. "What became of all these Texas Rangers who were supposed to teach our horse soldiers how to fight with pistols? I've heard that bunk since the war with Mexico!"

Colonel Mackenzie and General Marcy peered at Sherman with growing alarm. "The legislature disbanded the ranger companies, sir," Mackenzie said.

"Well, call them back. Bang the drums and blow the flutes."

"The legislature acted on the orders of Congress and the army," the colonel continued. Marcy rested his chin in his palm and stayed out of it.

"Indeed, sir! I believe it was our noble purpose to disarm the rebel provinces. Yet here I've never seen so many gun barrels and kegs of cartridges in all my life. Settlers on the northern frontier of Indian country built their houses in clusters for security; the Mexicans do it, too. Out here people think nothing of building the houses miles apart. What Indian trouble you have is mostly confined to horse theft. If there are real brigands about, I suspect they're Confederate renegades. In any case these people are armed to the teeth. Have the rugged Texans lost the knack for defending themselves?"

Mackenzie stood and tugged nervously at the white glove he wore on the mangled hand. "I wish to thank you, ladies and gentlemen, for putting aside your suppers and joining us on such a stormy night. We've had a frank discussion here, and I'm sure we can—"

"Yes, yes," Sherman sighed, waving off the attempted diplomacy. "I hope you will all forgive me. It's been a long day, but that's no excuse for my foul temper and reproachable manners. Please commit your requests and complaints to writing. I will deliver them personally to the Secretary of War."

Sherman's sacrum was on fire from the constant banging of that wagon seat. Almost always he ordered his valet to put up his private tent, but in this weather he decided to accept the colonel's offer of his roof, fire, and bed. He sat for a moment considering the gray hair and small roll of fat around his waist, then raised his arms and accepted the valet's nightshirt.

The general was sunk deep in Mackenzie's feather mattress when he heard echoes of the colonel's voice. He shook his head and in the reflex of warring was immediately awake. "Yes, what?" he demanded. The colonel was fully dressed and wore riding boots and spurs. The glove was gone from his bad hand. Other people were in the room, some of them black. One of them was Bose Ikard.

"I'm sorry to have to wake you, General," Mackenzie said. "If you could please dress and come with me—there's a fellow here you need to see."

Sherman could tell from the colonel's voice that he was not being treated to some more local color. "Excuse me a moment then," he answered. Sherman grunted as the sleep-addled valet helped him wrestle out of the nightshirt. He pulled on his pants and boots, strapped his suspenders over his shoulders, and looked at his watch—four o'clock. He buttoned his coat, ran his hand back and forth over the stubble on his scalp, and poured himself a glass of water, which he gargled and spat in the chamber pot. He relieved his bladder, then yanked open the colonel's door, not meaning to bang it quite as hard as he did.

"Should we wake General Marcy?" Mackenzie asked.

"No, let him sleep," growled Sherman.

Mackenzie, Lieutenant Carter, Bose, and the Seminole scout Adam Payne led Sherman to the regimental sick bay. Attended by the post physician, a man named Thomas Brazeal lay on an examining table, shirtless and bandaged heavily around his waist. Highly agitated, he would try to lurch upright and the doctor would gently force him to lie back down. Brazeal clutched a blanket around him, though the air was muggy and warm, and he was bruised and abraded all over. The doctor had cleaned most of his wounds, but his beard and a tangled knot of hair on one side of his head were matted with red clay mud and blood. "What happened to you, sir?" Sherman asked.

Brazeal spoke barely loud enough to hear. "Gnawed me."

"Say again?" said Sherman.

"One of them bit my ear off. Stabbed me with a knife, but I got my hands on it and wouldn't let go." The man looked at the palms of his hands, which were wrapped in blood-soaked gauze.

Sherman flinched and said, "By God, I see that now. Who did this?"

"Indian. I expect Kiowa or Comanche. Forgot to ask."

Mackenzie was pacing, cracking his knuckles. "General Sherman, what time did that storm blow through on your detachment this afternoon?"

"A little past three. Why?"

"This man is a teamster. There were twelve of them, hauling wagons of corn from Weatherford to Fort Griffin. They were on the same road you traveled but were headed the opposite way. They started across Salt Creek Prairie less than two hours after you passed."

The injured man had the strangest blank look. "You were in a devil of a storm," Mackenzie coaxed him. "How did you know you were being attacked?"

"A bugle."

"What, sir?" said Sherman.

"One of them was blowing on a bugle."

"Ah," interjected Mackenzie. "The Kiowa chief Satanta is well-known for carrying an army bugle."

Sherman couldn't take his eyes off the white gristle showing in the man's ear. "How many were there?"

"In that rain . . ." Brazeal shook his head. "I don't know. Maybe a hundred. Wasn't no backing them up."

"A hundred!" said Sherman.

"Tell the general how it happened," said Mackenzie.

"The bugle started squawking and I thought, what the devil is that? Then we seen them riding down off Squaw's Tit, and we started trying to get the mules to circle up the wagons. They rode and shot faster than we handled our mules."

"What happened to your other men?" Sherman asked.

"I hate to think," the teamster replied. "There was a lot of shooting, and I made a run for it, didn't see it all. The Indian that got after me knocked me over with his horse, then he come after me with a war club, then he got me good with his knife." Brazeal shuddered. "I'd be dead if it wasn't raining so hard. He couldn't stand up either."

Sherman was reflecting on his own close call. A band of that size could have easily overrun his party. His gaze roved far away for a moment, then he stooped in front of the man and tried to gently touch his ear. "Get away from me!" the man cried.

"Sir, I have to ask you to calm down," Mackenzie rebuked him. "This is General William T. Sherman."

"Nasty thing bit me, I'm liable to get rabies or lockjaw," the man shuddered, pulling the blanket close around him. "I don't care if he's Robert E. Lee."

16

Unaware of General Sherman's existence, Quanah and his wife were camped with the other Quohada in upper Blanco Canyon. It was a gentler place than Palo Duro and Tule and other breaks in the escarpment. The Clear Fork of the Brazos meandered from headwater springs through a corridor of cottonwoods and willows, rolling swells of bunchgrass, sloping bluffs marked by clinging juniper and other brush, canyon rims of caliche and sandstone. The infant Brazos ran reasonably clear of mud and salt, and without much danger one could ride a horse up or down the cliffs at night. In their migrations the buffalo spilled off the llano twice a year and grazed down the canyon grass, which grew back taller and thicker when they were gone. On the poorer soil of the upland breaks the snakeweed was abloom now, tinting the whole canyon yellow.

In Quanah's lodge nothing much had changed with To-ha-yea. Late at night, sleepless, he would take stock of himself. The peyote road had shown him the way to powerful medicine and recognition of a name, Quanah Parker, that mocked, confused, and enraged the Texans. But he could never put out of his mind that his coup remained counted by the tuh-tahvoa. All he had to do was look at the scars on his chest and ribs left by the nigger's quirt. And this Apache girl in his arms was cutting his heart to pieces.

But he was a war leader now, one of Parra-o-coom's favorites. He couldn't just lie up in his tipi and brood. As he often did, one day when the sun was low Quanah strolled out among the horses, looking forward to talking to Weckeah. Deer's Son, his war and hunting horse, clopped over to him nodding and twitching his ears. Quanah played with the black, turning circles so that the horse followed and nosed after the treats of green cottonwood bark he smelled and expected. His other horses and mules came around; so did the pair of mares that Weckeah rode. A breeze picked up. Even amid the salty rankness of three thousand horses and mules, the musk of the buffalo permeated everything. When they migrated it was like the earth just offered them up. The dusk turned dark enough that Quanah could see the first stars. The horses observed him for a moment then moved off grazing. He saw Weckeah coming and walked to her with pleasure. But when she drew close he saw that she was crying.

"What is it?" he said. "Weckeah, what's happened?"

"No one died," she said, wiping her cheek with her palm.

"Is it more with Tannap?" he said.

Weckeah nodded. "I'm sorry. It's not your trouble."

Quanah tried to grasp her arms. "It is my trouble. You know it is."

She pushed him off. "It's like they were gambling, throwing bones," she said. "Eckitoacup ran his offer to seventy horses; that was enough for Yellow Bear. Done! Tannap comes for me at my mother's lodge in two mornings."

"Seventy horses," Quanah whispered, awed at the man's riches and extravagance, and how he would put them to force for a son who already had a wife and children. Quanah had gotten his wife for just six mules and a promise of kindness and trade with her Apache father. How many horses did a man like Yellow Bear need? Horses to them were getting to be like the white man's money. It was nothing but greed. But Weckeah was nami, the younger sister, and if the old man wanted the old ways to hold, then they held—she had no voice in the matter. Quanah swore and flung a fist at the air.

"I'm not asking you to do anything," she said. "There's nothing you can do. I just had to tell you before it happened." She stood close to a Quanah and for a moment her palm was cool against his jaw. After she was gone he sat with his back against a cottonwood beside the river and let the night close around him. He never watched a moonrise that made him feel sadder.

Parra-o-coom was nursing sore hips and knees and the suspicion he had gotten old. The war chief knew for certain he'd gotten fat. The Quohada band that he had led for years made war on Texans, Mexicans, Tonkawas, Utes, Pawnees, Navajos, white buffalo hunters, and a new enemy, the land surveyors. Though they were aloof and still went their own way, the Antelopes allied in varied ways with the Kiowas and Kiowa-Apaches, Cheyennes and Arapahoes, and lately those Mescalero Apaches who continued to fight the whites. Though Comanchería was half the size it had been when the Spaniards printed the name on a map, as long as the Quohada and Kotsoteka held out the fight, settlement was closed in a triangle from the Arkansas River in Kansas to one day's ride west of Fort Worth to the Pecos River in New Mexico Territory. The Kotsoteka's war chief was another old firebrand, Mow-way, or Shaking Hand. Parra-o-coom, Mow-way, Nocona, and Yellow Bear had all come of age together. Parra-o-coom and Yellow Bear would never let Mow-way forget that he shook the generals' hands and put his mark under his name on the treaty paper at Medicine Lodge. Mow-way just laughed and waved off their insults. So he lied to the bluecoats—they lied to him. But Parra-o-coom suspected that deep down Mow-way was ready to give up the fight.

Despite the Comanche bands' contempt for the soldiers and occasional bloodshed between them in the past, Parra-o-coom, Mow-way, and other elders urged the raiding parties to avoid conflict with the bluecoats. For one thing, the bluecoats had gone against the Texans in the war in which the white nation devoured its young, and they conquered the Texans. The other consideration, far more important, was the sheer number of the bluecoats and the quality and assortment of their guns. At the Medicine Lodge parley, the soldiers had shown off their new nightmare, the Gatling gun, which fired bullets so fast the pops of explosion couldn't keep up—Mow-way called it a stutter gun.

All the war chiefs were getting old, and young leaders were emerging. An odd one in Quanah's view was Isa-tai, Wolf Shit. Quanah could see his jealousy when he and other proven young warriors walked through the camp. *He* fancied himself Parra-o-coom's successor. After old Jaybird Pesters died, Wolf Shit's chosen route to power and glory was as puhakut. He closely studied the tricks of other shamans, and he put himself in trances and began to prophesy. He dreamed and predicted that a comet would appear, and that its passage would suck all the rain out of the sky. Sure enough, that summer a bright comet with a worm-like tail crawled across the southern horizon night after night, and since its departure, the plains had turned exceedingly dry. And Wolf Shit had a rare ability to cast spells on people's minds. If the bluecoats attacked them with a stutter gun, he would simply swallow the bullets out of the air and pass them through his bowels in good time. Quohada swore they had seen him do it.

Parra-o-coom saw in Wolf Shit a schemer of more ambition than promise. And the prophet failed to inform him that Bad Hand Mackenzie finally had the orders he'd been praying for. Insulated by their cherished solitude and preoccupied by the fall hunt, the Quohada had no inkling they were now at all-out war with the United States Army. On a morning that still felt like summer, four of the band's outriders arrived at the war chief's tent with their horses blowing and lathered. He had barely made it to his feet when the scouts were yammering that six hundred bluecoats were camped a day's ride away.

"Six hundred!" he exclaimed.

The scouts said most of them were the black ones, the buffalo soldiers. In ragged formation a number of other tuh-tahvoas rode mules. The buffalo soldiers were followed by fifty heavily loaded wagons and a long column of pack mules. The scouts were black Seminoles, the foul Tonks, and one black on a Medicine Hat paint who used the tack and wore the clothes and boots of a drover. The bluecoat chief was easy to pick out; he jogged back and forth along the columns, showing off a sleek gray horse with a snapping gait—Bad Hand's prized pacer.

They had been hearing about Mackenzie since the No-Finger Chief first came to the forts on the Concho River and the mesquite barren between the Brazos and the Red. At first his purpose seemed to be to keep the reservation peoples in the territory from attacking the Texans. Bad Hand's mutilation and reputed strangeness were objects of curiosity to the Quohada. Two nights earlier, the outriders said, Bad Hand and his followers had made fools of themselves. He had left most of the black mule-riders guarding the wagons, but under sky covered by dense cloud he tried to shove all his horse soldiers, some of the mule-riders, and half the pack mules through the badland breaks of Yellow House, the next canyon to the south. There were shouts of anger as the mules busted straps and led their teamsters on blind chases as fast as the skidding earth and rockslides carried them. The soldiers wound up in a cramped box canyon too steep to climb. They could only hunker and doze and cling to the reins of their horses, which they didn't unsaddle. All night, panniers and saddletrees could be heard cracking and spilling as pack mules kneeled and rolled like itching dogs. One outrider chortled to He Bear that Bad Hand hadn't known his jábi from his nejuhcutaen, his pocketknife from his collarbone. The scouts went on that it took the soldiers half the next day to right the wagons, repack the mules, and find their way out of Yellow House's maze of raw dirt and rock. But they were camped now at the mouth of Blanco Canyon.

The scouts' mirth vanished when Parra-o-coom tore into them for failing to ride hard as soon as they saw the soldiers. "We should have hit them when they were all tangled in the Yellow House," he erupted. "That No-Finger Chief would have given up on them as fighters and turned them back." The outriders slunk away, leaving

Parra-o-coom alarmed but exhilarated. He sent one of his sons for his war horse, put on his best leggings and badger-skin vest, and with a shove of assistance from his number one wife, he mounted with a celerity he hadn't felt in months. He galloped through the lodges bellowing. "Quohada! Tend to your weapons and horses! Every boy who's twelve or older get ready to fight! And every woman whose children aren't babies! If you're old or lame or have babies, help pack up all we have, get out the travoises, and strike the lodge poles! Herders, circle up the horses and mules! Bad Hand and his band of dirty whiteasses and cannibals are paying us a call!"

From the lodges rose a thunderous jeer. Mothers snatched their little ones out of the way of horses and riders tearing through the camp. The warriors were dividing into groups of those who had guns and those who fought with bows and arrows, running off the wild energy of their horses as they drilled for the fight. Unable to comprehend the shouts and gabble, To-ha-yea cried out, "Quanah, what's happening?"

"Buffalo soldiers are coming. A lot of them."

She put her hands on her forehead and groaned. Overcoming his urge to rush outside and join the pandemonium, Quanah sat down beside her and put his arm around her. "They're making a big mistake," he said. "These are our canyons. They're farm slaves who have been made into soldiers. They can't fight. When we're through with them, they'll never want to come out in this country again. They'll wish they'd never seen it."

"You don't know them," she replied. "You didn't see what they did to us in the Guadalupes. You haven't seen babies shot to pieces in their mothers' arms. You didn't see the fire they set to our ranchería."

"It won't be that way here, To-ha-yea. Not with Our People."

Quanah was still trying to reassure her, loading his Henry repeater and .44 Colt, when a breathless young runner called his name outside the lodge. "Parra-o-coom wants to see you," the runner said. "Now."

He dodged horses and saw that many lodge skins were already stripped and poles were coming down. He had to get help for To-ha-yea; she didn't know how to tear down their lodge and pack everything on the travois. Making himself gather his thoughts, he announced himself outside the war chief's lodge. "Come in," Parra-o-coom growled. Quanah stepped through the flap and found Yel-low Bear, Cohayyah, and others on the council seated with the war chief, handing around a pipe. Parra-o-coom motioned for Quanah to sit. Yellow Bear threw him a quick glare, then drew in on the pipe and passed it to him—a grudging sign of respect. Seated with the elders, to Quanah's displeasure, was Wolf Shit. So the odd duck re-ally was a power.

Parra-o-coom said, "The scouts tell us the bluecoats come with six hundred men. Even if they're buffalo soldiers, they have the Spencer carbines and pistols—and the stutter guns for all we know. We can answer with less than three hundred who are strong and able. We'll answer all right, the No-Finger Chief's not raising that ugly hand to spank us. He means to finish us all."

Quanah started in on some of his old bluster, but Parra-o-coom snapped, "Listen to me, Quanah, don't talk. We have to strike camp and move our horses and elders and children. The soldiers could catch up with us tomorrow even if they sleep long and come at a walk. I want you to go among the Little Horses, Big Horses, Crow Tassel Wearers, and those of you who go down the peyote road. Wolf Shit here will be one the riders. Everyone knows his medicine is strong. Call out sixty or seventy of our best, at your choosing. I want you to go after the soldiers and hit them hard. Scatter them, scare them, kill them if you can. But what you have to do is slow them down. When they gather their wits and come after you, they'll find themselves in a storm of Quohada. All along the way we'll be mak-ing them think there are more of us than we are. The farther you bring them up the canyon, the shorter the distance across its floor, and we'll be making rain of bullets and arrows from high ground. Unless they burrow in with the prairie dogs they'll have no cover."

Quanah went back to his lodge and told To-ha-yea about his great honor and opportunity. She had calmed down by then. "I know how my people fight the white eyes," she said. "I've just never been through this with yours."

That matter always—her people, his people. He sat with her for a while, though his mind raced with all he had to do. "You often talk about Lozen."

She nodded at his mention of the Warm Springs Apache who had prepared her for the initiation of the White Painted Woman. "In all but blood she's my sister."

"She's a beautiful woman like you, and she's one of the Apaches' great warriors. Old Wolf and all those men in Dog Canyon told me that. Think of Lozen during this time when I have to be gone, and you'll know what to do."

He gave her the carpenter's hammer that had been his war club since that standoff with the Leopard Coat Man and the whipman drover. "If a dirty whiteass gets close to you," Quanah said, "hit him on the head with this. He won't get up."

To-ha-yea took the hammer but seemed apprehensive of its form and weight. "I'd rather have a shotgun."

He held back an impulse to sigh. He was in such a hurry. "Do you know how to use it?"

"Of course. You set yourself and point it and pull the trigger. If one of them gets close enough to need shooting, you don't want to miss."

"You've done that before?"

"Yes," she said with a flash of anger. "I killed a man once, a buffalo soldier. In the Guadalupes."

Quanah looked at her in wonder. There were so many things he didn't know about her. "I'll get you one right now."

"I'm going to be all right," she swore to him. "Do what's been given you. Don't worry about me."

Quanah took his time preparing himself. He loosened his braids and for a while enjoyed going loose-haired like To-ha-yea. She helped him paint his face, throat, and entire upper body. He considered his reflection in a hand mirror, one of the last things his mother had given him. He made a point of turning his skin the same color as the black soldiers he was going out to meet. To-ha-yea re-braided his hair, intertwining strips of otter fur. He tied off the ends with ribbons of red flannel, put gleaming hoops of Mexican silver through the holes in his earlobes, and added his necklace of bear claws. He wore moccasins, deerskin leggings, and a loincloth that hung to his shins.

"Very good," his wife admired him.

He smiled and put on the headdress of eagle and red-tailed hawk feathers that his brothers in the Little Horses had given him. The bonnet hung down his back to his calves but was light and airy. This was the first time that wearing it seemed right. Quanah knew what some warriors thought and said of him—that he used to be a blowhard, that he was often selfish and unfair in awarding horses after a raid, that his heart was contaminated by its flushing of half-white blood. But no one he handed the pipe had refused to ride with him this time. He looped on his forearm the shield crafted by his Uncle John. He gave the shield's fringe a vigorous shake, then stepped out where his lance was propped against a rack, absorbing strength from the sun.

Many riders were painting their horses in wild patterns and colors. Some tied scalps to their horses' bridles. Quanah brushed Deer's Son's coat to a gleam and braided strips of red flannel and bits of shiny metal in the black's mane and tail. A fire at the center of the camp was already blazing. The Quohada made no attempt to hide their preparations. All over the camp, men were singing songs for the War Dance. Many were about power and glory, but there were also love songs. The celebration of the War Dance beheld the fact of dying, wives and mothers who'd be keening, and children who'd grow up forbidden to speak their fathers' names.

Quanah walked to the lodges of Yellow Bear and formally asked Nice Enough to Eat if he could speak to Weckeah. Her mother looked him over in his battle finery and sighed. "Quanah, you know your family was our family of best friends." As she turned away, tears rimmed her eyes.

Quanah and Weckeah walked out among the herd. Her cheeks were painted vermilion, her eyelids gold, and she had on the blue shirt she had worn that day Yellow Bear's followers arrived and they celebrated the feast of the Buffalo Tongue. She was one of the women Parra-o-coom had called out to fight. "You look wonderful," he said.

"So do you."

"I need your help, Weckeah. To-ha-yea's eager enough. She's just uncertain. Please help her tear down our lodge and load up. Look out for her and see that she gets back to the Mescaleros, if anything happens to me."

"All right."

"And something else," he said. "I want you to be my dancer tonight."

She laughed and shook her head—the nerve. "What about your wife? What about Tannap?"

"To-ha-yea doesn't know our War Dance," he said. "And what of Tannap? He's not one of our riders. He's a flute player, and there's nothing wrong with that. He'll get his chance to fight."

"He's not a rider because you didn't ask him to ride."

Quanah shrugged. "I'm sorry if his feelings are hurt."

"It would cause trouble with him, with his father, and with my father." She waved her arms. "Before we heard about the soldiers, he was coming to claim me in one more night!"

"Weckeah, *trouble* is at the far end of this canyon!"

She gave in with a grin and raised her arms, jangling bracelets. "All right, Quanah. He's not my husband yet. He can't come get me

207

at my mother's lodge as long as the camp is moving and every lodge pole's down."

"That's right."

She took his arm in hers and teased him with the tip of her breast. "You'd better not let him cut my nose off." In the old days it was the punishment for a woman's infidelity—and still a husband's legal right.

"He knows I'd kill him if he did."

17

B AD HAND MACKENZIE'S TROOPS moved up the canyon slowly, their progress impeded by hundreds of buffalo and the treacherous burrows of an endless prairie dog town. They passed a series of rag-tag adobes and lean-tos of brush, comanchero camps. The Tonks, who answered to names that included Lincoln, Grant, Old Henry, Job, and One Armed Charlie, took the lead among the scouts, having convinced the colonel that they could smell Comanches. The black Seminole scouts were led by David Bowlegs and Adam Paine. Sent out with the Seminoles to ride the ridges of Blanco Canyon, Bose stared at tawny plains that stretched without feature except for clusters of buffalo. He saw nothing else tall enough to cast a shadow. But hanging on the shallow soil and scattered down the cliffs below were sumac and shin oak that gave way on the floor to thick stands of tufted prairie, mixed groves of walnut and juniper, and the winding bottom of river, sand, cottonwood, and willow. The labyrinth of canyons Mackenzie had brought them to invade was an underworld of twists and turns the Comanches knew like the lines of their hands. On the canyon floor the soldiers turned up a parfleche bag filled with spoons carved from buffalo horn, a child's moccasin stitched from the hide of a skunk, and a great deal of bones gnawed recently enough that they still drew flies. The buffalo grass was spotted and worn by the manure piles and hoof wear of the big horse herd. Yet Bad Hand's soldiers and scouts rode all day without seeing one Quohada rider. Where were they?

The marchers still had a couple of hours of light when Mackenzie's officers relayed his order to pitch camp. The colonel was frank about not caring to fight with his bowels plugged up with cold hardtack. In addition to Bose's scouting and mule-riding training of the infantry, he had become the colonel's favored cook in the field. With the mess wagon left behind at the canyon's mouth, all the rations were packed in by mule. Bose hobbled the front hooves of Juneteen and Tricks in his customary manner, hitching those leather straps together and then tying them with short ropes to their halters. He left his horse saddled, having drawn the midnight watch. Helped by a private who built a fire and cut up potatoes and carrots, Bose withdrew from a mule's panniers a Dutch oven, a skillet, and the clamped jar of starter dough. The soldiers had been warned that even accidental discharge of a pistol or rifle was grounds for a court martial. The Seminole Adam Paine was a bowman, though, and he brought in the fresh carcass of a buffalo calf. Bose had learned to make son-of-a-bitch stew with beef, but with a little more salt and chili powder, the bison version was tasty. He cut up the brains, heart, liver, gonads, and glands and put them in the pot with the private's chopped vegetables and cuts of lean chops and loin. He tossed several handfuls of salt and chili on the meat, filled the pot with water to cover the stew, trimmed off the rich fat around kidneys, and stirred in that suet, but he threw the foul-tasting kidneys away. At once a pair of crows swooped and nabbed them and flapped off cawing with their accomplishment. Bose was fond of a fair number of birds, but they did not include crows. He pulled handfuls of starter out of the sourdough jar and mixed in enough flour and water to make biscuits for the officers' mess. He pressed them in the skillet, put a lid on, and started them baking on the coals when the stew smelled done.

While he cooked for the officers, the enlisted men built no fires, had suppers of cold biscuit and dried bacon, and were put to hard labor. Mackenzie ordered them to cross-sideline every horse and mule—an impossible task, for there were eight hundred of them. He obsessed about losing his stock to the Indians. The cavalry trick of cross-sidelining was supposed to hobble the animals securely while allowing them to graze their fill; wherever the grassland was sufficient, there was no need to buy and haul wagonloads of hay. Straps with thick brass rings double-stitched in the leather were buckled around the animals' right front and left rear hooves. Lengths of rope were pulled through the hobble rings and the welded eyes of long steel pickets that were hammered in the ground. "This way they can graze but they can't run," Mackenzie boasted to the big Yankee lieutenant Robert Carter, another of his favorites who would come out of the campaign with a Medal of Honor. Pouring stew on the officers' mess plates and crowning each with a fresh biscuit, Bose observed the hobbling with some alarm. Even if the Comanches somehow failed to see the smoke and fire, the clanging of all those hammers and pins had to have rung for miles.

Bose and the private scoured the pots and the officers' mess plates in river sand and repacked them in the mules' panniers, though they'd have to pull it all out again for breakfast at three in the morning, when he got through riding his watch. He found a soft spot of ground beside the river and dozed with the horses and mules sounding restless, coyotes yipping their cockeyed serenade. The Tonk One Armed Charlie kicked Bose's boot when it was time for him to take his watch. About two o'clock he was circling Tricks from the river bottom back through the main camp when the gates of hell opened and Comanches rode right out of the earth. At least that's how fast they seemed to burst upon the camp.

In light brightened by a three-quarters moon, Bose got as close and chilling a look at the Quohada raiders as a man could ever want, and he had no difficulty recognizing their leader. On a black horse Quanah Parker raced out front with his face, chest, shoulders, and arms painted black and a white-feathered bonnet billowing above the horse's croup. He raised a long-barreled Colt pistol in his right hand like it was a burning torch. Others in the mob wore the hats of buffalo horn and were shooting in the air and at the soldiers and waving blankets and banging cowbells. Soldiers came out of their sleep and blankets shooting blindly at muzzle flashes. "Get to your horses!" the officers were yelling. "Every man to his lariat!"

That was a difficult order to heed. The horses and mules were squalling, sunfishing, turning flips in their cross-sidelined hobbles. In terror they got all tangled up and fell over with legs and hooves flailing. They bucked the picket stakes out of the ground, snapped the lariats out of the hobble straps' brass rings. In the frenzy of shooting and yelling the broken ropes and iron stakes weighted at their ends lashed and popped like bullwhips. Bose saw one man after another laid out bleeding and knocked silly. The whooping and bell-clanging raiders made a broad turn back and stampeded close to a hundred head right through the camp. At the last glimpse of Quanah Parker, he was loping off on the black with a lead rope and hackamore on Bad Hand's sprightly and elegantly stepping pacer.

More of Mackenzie's men were down with broken shoulders and cracked jaws than gunshot wounds. Some were unable to pull their carbines out of their scabbards because rope burns from trying to hold their horses had torn meat off their hands. The officers and sergeants were bellowing at the troops to saddle up, which hardly restored the animals' calm. Corporal Jim Fletcher at last got a horse saddled and bridled for Mackenzie, who was in an almost cheerful fury, directed in even parts at himself and Quanah Parker. "So, men," he cracked, "this is what they mean by the fucking Staked Plains." The colonel had his boot in the stirrup and was pulling on the saddle horn when suddenly they heard a strange whisper, then a sound like the first big splatters of a rain. Mackenzie groaned and let go of the horn; he was lucky his spur didn't hang up in the stirrup or cinch and get him dragged. Cries of fear and hurt erupted in the night.

"Son of a bitch!" howled Mackenzie. A bunch of Indians had come right up to the edge of the camp and lofted a rain of arrows. Mackenzie rolled about on the ground with his hands clasped under his thigh, then got up and tried to hop before Fletcher and one of the

Seminole scouts persuaded him to sit back down. Bad Hand stopped cursing his battle luck and commenced taking very deep breaths. "Surgeon, get us a surgeon!" Lieutenant Robert Carter yelled. The arrow had struck Mackenzie in the front of his thigh, square between his hip and his knee. He threw a fit and started wrestling with the shaft like it was a pipe wrench; the feathered end broke off in his hands, and he fainted.

The arrowhead was barbed against the bone. The company had a new doctor from Baltimore named Rufus Choate, a captain in rank. When Mackenzie came back to himself he waved off the surgeon's offer of chloroform, clamped one of his riding gloves between his teeth, and raged, "Get it out of me, God damn you, sir! *Get it out.*"

The soldiers followed the shallow river and the tracks of the horses, which crossed the stream back and forth. If the Comanches had been trying to get away, they wouldn't have plunged them through all that river bottom sand. Mackenzie's officers had gotten four platoons organized enough to begin the chase — three cavalry and one mule-riding infantry. Bose rode in the platoon of Lieutenant Carter. The light was gray and dim where their horses trotted, but the sunrise behind a canyon rim was turning a bank of clouds pink. Carter sent Bose, Adam Paine, and the Tonk called Job angling up a loose bluff to see how close they were to Quanah's raiders and the stolen herd. With no time wasted, their horses came jumping, sliding, and galloping right back down. No more than a quarter mile away, the raiders were circling their mounts and letting them drink as others moved on the captured herd. The scouts had seen Indians all over the canyon floor, in the gullies and on ledges and silhouetted on the rims. "There's hundreds of them," Bose was telling Carter when a great shout echoed down the canyon.

Extravagantly painted Comanches raced toward them pounding

on their shields and raising a hellish cry of insults, promises, and taunts, but when they arrived they didn't close for battle at once. They loped their horses in disciplined circles and figure eights, drawing closer with each pass. Two riders paraded about the center of this horse show with staffs flying pennants that dragoons with good eyesight recognized in the dawn as scalps. One of the scalp-bearers rode bareback on Mackenzie's pacer.

"Look at those devils," said Carter. "They got squads, formations." At a distance and higher pitch they heard an almost melodic kind of screeching. Dozens of women swarmed toward the fight, many on horses, some on foot. And with the sun up over the canyon, they turned it back on the soldiers with mirrors. Blinding glints of light sparkled up and down the canyon walls.

Lieutenant Harold Heyl looked like he had swallowed a tarantula. Seeing Heyl's frozen confusion, Carter assumed command. "Don't circle up," he yelled. "Deploy on the run, and let them have your carbines!" As one set of dragoons jogged rearward with fists tight on the reins of two horses, another set would lie prone in the grass with their rifles. Though it was a slow way to retreat, the relays and the longer range of their carbines kept the Indians from swarming over them. Then Bose saw something that stirred the hair on the back of his neck. "Lieutenant, look!" he shouted at Carter. Lieutenant Heyl and his platoon had mounted up and were making a dash for it. Seeing this, some of Carter's men ran to their horses and took to flight as well. The infantry trained by Bose vaulted in their saddles and went bouncing off in the mules' ungainly canters, daylight showing between the cantles and the seats of their pants. The Comanches raised volleys of fire and hurrahs of laughter at the runaway soldiers.

"I don't believe it," Carter sputtered. "We're a legion of runaways." He told Bose and the remaining dozen, "Mount up, bunch your shots, and give your horses their heads. It's our only chance." At once they had to traverse a deep and sheer gully, which left two of the riders, who weren't born to such endeavor, hanging to their horses' necks, carbines fallen in the dust. Bose looked back and saw Quanah leading the race of their pursuers. It was like the running fight in the Palo Pinto country, and in the race between Quanah's black and Bose's paint, Bose was not riding the faster horse. The ravine they fled for now was filled with cedar brake, not cactus. They were closing in on the juniper's cover when the paint stumbled badly and almost went down. A front hoof had broken through a prairie dog tunnel, and Tricks came out of it limping. Bose threw a look back at the Comanche riders and brought his Colt around to use as best he could. The eyes in the big one's black-painted face narrowed. Quanah had recognized him.

Seconds later the horse of a white private named Seander Gregg took a shot in the spine. Thrown clear in a spray of sand, Gregg was a blacksmith's son from some village in the Arkansas Ozarks. Bending horseshoes was what he figured he'd be doing when he joined the army and was sent out west. He made no secret of his displeasure that he was both outnumbered and outranked by niggers in this outfit. But he wanted help now from anybody who'd give him a backward look. "Lieutenant, my god," he cried. Carter yelled at the others to stand their ground, but they were given pause as soon as they had their horses turned around. Amid the crowd of Comanches there was no mistaking Quanah—the feather headdress bobbed like a strutting barnyard turkey—but he kept the private and his horse between himself and the gunsights of the soldiers. "Use your carbine!" Carter shouted at Gregg. Trying to lever a shell in the chamber, he yanked too hard and jammed it. With a posture of disgust Quanah jogged the black up to the private, stuck a Colt barrel to his temple, and fired a blast that flung him on a yucca plant. Then Quanah arrogantly turned his back on Bose and the others who'd made it to the cedar brake.

The Quohada sent riders up the sides of the ravine and considered ways to come in and finish them. Two of them slid off their horses and huddled on the ground. They scooped up litter and kindling, dusted it with gunpowder, and struck sparks from their flints and steel. A puff and spiral of smoke soon rose, and they quickly had a fair blaze going. The unrelenting gunfire and ricochets caused their horses to break loose from the tree where they'd been tied. With a clatter of hooves the horses ran back down the ravine. The unhorsed Quohada danced out from behind a rock and hurled firebrands, trying to light the cedar. Bose knew if it caught, they'd be broiled in an instant. Close around them now he could hear the women's banshee ruckus, but then the screaming stopped. In amazement the soldiers and scout watched the riders wheel their horses and thump them into a run with their knees and heels. The trail of Quanah's headdress hung out behind him in the wind. All across the canyon the sight of Bad Hand's columns and the music of the bugles put the Comanches to flight.

The soldiers pulled up and reorganized because the colonel was in such pain. He refused to let a pair of them help him from the saddle. "You'd not get me back on," he said, mopping his face with a bandanna. A detail of soldiers reclaimed Seander Gregg's body, pulled a gunny sack over the head and torso, and lashed it to the pack saddle of an unhappy mule. The two Quohada who had set the fire were in desperate trouble. They tried to chase down their horses but found themselves cut off by Adam Paine and several leering Tonkawas. The Comanches sang death songs and snarled insults at the Tonks as Job and One Armed Charlie trotted from rock to rock. When the guns were quiet the usual row erupted with the officers and sergeants over what parts of their enemies the Tonks would be allowed to eat.

Glad enough to postpone the battle, troops crouched on their heels with their reins in hand and smoked. Leaving Mackenzie in the care of the assistant surgeon, Captain Choate set off through the cedar with a lieutenant named Tom Miller and two of the buffalo soldiers. The uproar with the Tonks subsided. After a while the doctor and his detail re-emerged from the junipers. The Tonks' voices rose again, this time in a grunting chant of a song. Among the uniformed soldiers, Bose had struck up a friendship with a sergeant named Hubertus Holland. They had in common a past of being house slaves. Hubertus had belonged to a Virginia tobacco planter whose house and barns had been set ablaze by General Sherman, and that was the end of that way of life, for all of them.

Listening to the Tonks singing, Bose asked Hubertus, "How come the Tonks and Comanches hate each other so?"

"They say the Tonks are ritual cannibals," Hubertus answered thoughtfully. "They believe that swallowing an enemy's flesh gives them magic and sends the enemy's soul to perdition, or whatever they'd call it. But I'll tell you—give 'em a chance, those Tonks don't just treat themselves to a little nibble. One time when Colonel Mackenzie was forming up the regiment at Fort Concho, I saw the Tonks hack a Comanche up and cook him with roots they scrub out of the ground. Wasn't taters or onions but something like that. This was before he started trying to put a stop to it. The Tonks were dancing 'round and 'round, and I saw one of 'em with human meat in his jaws, way more than he could swallow. That Tonk was shaking his head like a dog when it gets hold of a snake."

As Hubertus was telling that story, Captain Choate reappeared before them, glared at their failures to leap up and salute, but walked on, followed by Lieutenant Miller. Slung over the lieutenant's shoulder was another gunny sack.

"Heads," the sergeant muttered, tightening his horse's cinch. The sorrel grunted and raised a hoof. Bose noticed the horse was slipping a shoe.

Bose started to remark on the loose shoe to Hubertus, then asked, "What did you say?"

"Captain Choate done took the heads," Hubertus repeated. "Tonks and buzzards get the rest. Doctor's a scientist, you see. He's going to send those heads to the Smithsonian Institute, Washington, DC."

Every mile of the narrowing canyon they heard the shrill clamor of the Quohada women. The women knew those places where the curves of the canyon and composition of the cliffs created echoes, and the cries grew louder and would seem to come from all around them. Up in the rocks and ridges the Comanches had sharpshooters—good ones, too. The wounded had to be cared for and carried back; the sniping slowed the cavalry advance. Mackenzie sent his best marksmen ahead and up the canyon walls to silence them or force them back. The Spencers of the army sharpshooters had more accuracy at a distance than the Comanche carbines, and the exchanges of fire had the desired effect. The dragoons put their horses to the gallop and gained a few hundred yards on the Indians. The carbines fell quiet, and the women's trilling cries rose to a collective shriek. "Seagulls," exclaimed Mackenzie, who had been born to an oceangoing family and had lived much of his boyhood in varied ports. "It's like a flock of gulls someone has thrown a piece of bread."

But Mackenzie's soldiers were incapable of running the Co-manches down quickly because the Indians' mustang-looking horses had as much speed and more stamina than the big army horses. The Comanches pulled away, crossing back and forth over the canyon; for a while that afternoon, as Mackenzie sweated and growled, the Tonk and Seminole scouts were scratching their heads. But then Adam Paine gave out a whoop and pointed to a ravine where a swath of horse tracks marked the canyon rim. The soldiers had no maps and few reliable stories about the llano but were delighted that the Indians had taken to the treeless open country. The retreating Quo-hada and the attack party led by Quanah Parker had gotten all the good out of Blanco Canyon they could. Now they were running for it, headed almost due north. They were trying to haul their en-tire existence—their babies and elders and a winter's meat and a treasured herd of three thousand horses—to the pair of hills called

Quitaque that marked the next canyon cut from the escarpment, the Valley of Tears.

Mackenzie gripped the saddle horn with what was left of his right hand and wobbled from the pain but ignored the surgeons urging him to let his junior officers take command. The soldiers came upon debris where the Quohada had camped without fire a few hours the night before. "No chance they'll get away from us now!" Mackenzie yelled. Bose couldn't tell if the delirium in his voice was from his happiness or the fever of his wound. At a distance, riders tried to entice them into another chase. But the trail of the Quohada camp scarred the ground right before them. The horse tracks and travois gouges began to be littered with sooted kettles, untanned buffalo hides, splintered lodge poles, litters of puppies. "Look there!" Bad Hand yelled again. "You can see 'em now!" In the flatness of the horizon they hurried and strained, losing ground to their pursuers. The Quohada had to know they weren't going to make it. Mackenzie's 4th was going to extinguish the most dreaded band of Comanches in one bloody swoop.

But the sky had been changing all day. When the soldiers had set out that morning the weather was clear and still. Once they were up on the llano it began to get dusty and windy, and a thin overcast crept across the sky. Buzzards and hawks were flung about in wild loops by onrushing wind. The air pressure dropped so fast that the men's ears popped and their eyeballs felt like they were going to explode. The anvil cloud grew and spread over them like God's own hand. Lopped from the cloud's summit by high racing wind, the cloud far above them now was milk-white, but the horizon beyond the fleeing Indians and their horses and mules was a deep plum blue.

The norther hit so hard that horses screamed and reared up. Tarps tore loose from the mules' packs and popped at the ends of the lariats. One of the squares of canvas broke all the way free and wrapped around a mule, whose teamster couldn't hold him in the panic. Bucking and kicking free, the mule followed the tumbling tarp back toward Blanco Canyon. Lightning struck another mule and exploded her, spraying warm bits on men struck deaf by the thunder. The storm enveloped them in a squall of sleet, which soon changed to slants of hard, blinding rain; hailstones were bouncing high off the packsaddles and horse and mule skulls. Minutes later it changed back to more sleet, and then to more rain that froze the instant it splashed. Mackenzie raised the bad hand and pointed ahead as soldiers on foot rushed up to keep him from being thrown out of the saddle. For seconds they again saw the moving village of nomads clear before them, and then fog and sleet erased it all in the gloom.

The officers and sergeants were yelling at the teamsters to force the mules into the center, for their panniers contained the food and other supplies. At the outer ring the soldiers sat huddled and shivering, holding on their horses' reins. They tore tarps off the mules' packsaddles and spread them as best they could to cover their heads. The rain coated the animals and the miserable bivouac with an inch of ice. David Bowlegs dragged up a buffalo robe and tucked it around Mackenzie, whose teeth clattered so violently that Bose thought he was going to swallow his tongue. At last, it began to snow.

They couldn't see fifty feet around them in the wild swirl of it. On orders from Lieutenant Carter, soldiers broke out axes and began to chop apart packsaddle frames, and somehow they got a fire going. Supplies were strewn everywhere. The soldiers burned everything that they could break apart. As the wind died a little, the snow fell harder. Shaking within his slicker, Bose managed to get his horse and mule hobbled. He stayed near them, trying to absorb their heat. In the storm he watched figures throwing wood on the blaze; they hauled up a cast iron stewpot, and into it they emptied several rubber containers of water. Lieutenant Miller stirred whatever they were cooking with an axe handle. As the night wore on Bose watched them, and despite himself, the thought of having something hot to eat made his mouth water. The voices grew louder—voices charged by flasks of brandy and whiskey. Some Tonks stood around the fire with blankets and robes around their shoulders, but few of the Seminoles or black soldiers were going near that bunch. Bose conversed for a while with Tricks and Juneteen, promising he'd treat them better if they could make it through the night. He stomped and blew on his hands and finally walked toward the fire, taking his mess bowl in case they had a buffalo or pronghorn soup. On principle he'd thought he'd go hungry if it was horse or mule.

Captain Choate glimpsed Bose out in the shadows and called out to him. "Scout, you're a cook. Come over here, bring your seasoning and spoon. Tell us what this needs."

The lieutenant staggered and caught himself, drunk. Captain Choate wrestled the axe handle away and resumed stirring. Heat from the fire kept Bose coming, and within the swirl of snow the blaze cast a fairly strong light. Holding his tin bowl, he peeked over the rim of the kettle at the broth.

Rolling over and over in it were the heads of the two Comanches that the Tonks had killed in the cedar brake. The faces were still smeared with war paint; eyeballs jumped around loose in the boil like eggs. As Bose recoiled, Lieutenant Miller guffawed and slapped his hands on his thighs. The doctor smiled serenely and raised the axe handle ropy with strands of their hair. "So as to measure," he explained, raising his flask, "the capacity for reason of their evil skulls."

Bose lurched away and kneeled beside his animals for a while, and when he stood he slipped their hobbles in his saddlebag. He twisted the stirrups, breaking off the ice, but he failed to knock all of it off the horn and pommel. It was one time he wished his horse didn't have that glaring white splashed all over him; an unmarked bay stood a better chance of going unseen in the murk. He checked the cinches and balance of the mule's panniers and wrapped the lead rope around his gloved hand. Wishing Ranald Mackenzie better health, he gathered the slicker around him like a skirt, raised his boot to the stirrup, and with a very cold seat between his legs Bose quit the United States Army.

18

QUANAH COULDN'T REMEMBER taking so cold a bath. The pool he sat in now was the headwater of Acunacup Neovit, the river the Texans called the Pease. It was the second day after the norther and blizzard. The pool was stirred by the bubbling release of the springs and the thin waterfall pouring over the lip. The sky was cloudless and brilliant, melting icicles pattered on the translucent white rock that enclosed the pool, but the air was cold enough to pull up feathers of steam.

Quanah clamped his teeth to keep from shivering. It was the ritual bath of a headman whose riders had won a great victory. There was no weeping this day in the Valley of Tears. Waiting their turns in the pool were warriors whom he'd rewarded for special bravery in division of the captured army horses and mules. Parra-o-coom had, of course, expected to receive Bad Hand's prize gray horse, but in a show of independence that hinted at the coming changing of the guard, Quanah kept the pacer for himself.

Someone touched him on the shoulder, and he at last stood up. Two women quickly wrapped and patted him dry in a soft robe tanned from the hide of a young buffalo bull. As other warriors waded out into the water, Quanah sat back down on the bank. The women pulled the robe down and rubbed his shoulders, neck, and chest with the aromatic oils of juniper berries and musk from the glands of beaver and otter. He thought of the boys who used to taunt him. *Fragrant, Fragrant.* No one jeered him now.

The ritual baths were preliminary to the Dance of Joy. It was the victory of everyone in the band, not just the fighters in their prime.

There would be a Scalp Dance in which women formed a line and stepped out shaking the lances and war clubs of the heroes in their families and clans. The Quohada did not know of Bad Hand Mackenzie's reflection that the nearest resupplies for his army were four days' hard drive across the llano to forts in New Mexico Territory. Or that the No-Finger Chief had admitted to his junior officers that he'd pushed the men too far and hard. They didn't know that Bad Hand had been badly wounded and that his medicine men told him that if he persisted in this furious chase of Quanah Parker, he was either going to die or lose his leg.

The Quohada knew only that the bluecoats had gone back out of sight and left them with several scalps and more than a hundred horses and mules, including Bad Hand's fancy dappled gray. The Quohada attributed the victory to their bravery and medicine and the leadership of Quanah, not an opportune change in the weather.

Quanah walked back through the lodges reeking from the oils of juniper and musk. He had sat for the bath and rubs not just for the honor of it, but to catch the others off guard. The celebration would go on for days. He was not going to be near it.

Piled on the ground inside the tipi's flap were his weapons and tack, rolled-up buffalo robes, and enough pouches filled with enough food and supplies that it would be loaded on three pack-saddles. In the lodge he sat with his ankles crossed in front of To-ha-yea. She pulled her buffalo robe tight around her in the chill and said, "I don't understand. You've just beaten the soldiers. I hear your name on everyone's tongue. Why are we leaving now?"

He tried to phrase it in a way that would beguile her. "Think of how it was with your father's band. Why did they go off in the sierras? It wasn't because they never wanted to see their Mescalero kin again. They weren't turning their backs on their families and clans. They just wanted to go their own way. So they could carry on the fight and hunt and make love and go down the peyote road or any other path they chose anywhere on earth."

"No," To-ha-yea corrected him. "It happened because my father led us away when the elders spoke of giving up and going to live on a reservation, where we'd be fed out of army sacks like animals and disgrace the sight of our sacred mountains. That hasn't happened with your people, has it?"

"No. They'll never do that."

She watched him with a blend of fondness and suspicion. "What is it you're not telling me, Quanah?"

He took her wrists in his hands and drew a small breath, then moved his hand slowly down the slope of her ass. Not through yet, he spider-walked his fingers up her ribs and cradled her breast in his hand.

She flinched and laughed. "Your hand's cold."

"One of the first things we're going to do," he promised, "is go see Old Wolf and his band. This is a new start for us, To-ha-yea. Our lives are going to be different. They're going to be better. You'll see."

As drums pounded and male dancers crouched and hopped from side to side, hands on their hips, and yelled aww, aww, aww like crows preparing to fly, Weckeah brooded and packed in the lodge of Nice Enough to Eat. Upset but helpless to change the situation, Nice Enough to Eat had gone with Yellow Bear to the dances, giving her daughter some privacy. The next morning other unmarried young women would be dressing and painting themselves like they were the raiding warriors, and they would happily descend singing on the lodges of their favorite beaux in the Shakedown Dance. The warriors' fathers would be obliged to come out and give the girls a horse or two. But there would be no dance for Weckeah. Now that the battle against the bluecoats was over and the camp was built again, the bargain of the fathers was reinstated. On behalf of his son, who was no raider, Eckitoacup had delivered the seventy horses to Yellow Bear's herd. The next morning Tannap was coming to claim

Weckeah as his number two wife. Her sister Pasocopi would be para-ibo, the boss wife.

As Quanah slipped through the lodges, he smiled on thinking how puzzled Yellow Bear would be when he awoke and went for his morning constitutional to savor Eckitoacup's tribute and found that twenty additional horses with U. S. Army and Texas ranch brands had been run into his herd. Quanah had taken them to the Mexican herder and told him they were a special gift for Yellow Bear and that he'd better make sure none of them strayed, got stolen, or claimed by another Quohada. And the boy should tell him that Quanah would send more as soon as he stole them. The boy captive nodded, awed by the war leader.

Weckeah heard the scratching against the side of her mother's tipi and thought it must be a dog. She spoke sharply to scare it away. When the scratching continued she looked out through the flap and gasped on seeing Quanah. He held his index finger to his lips. "What are you doing?" she asked, looking Quanah up and down. He should have been wearing his grand headdress of hawk and eagle feathers and all his other finery. Instead he wore deer hides, a coat, riding boots.

Quanah said, "I've come for you."

"Come for me? Have you lost your mind?"

"No. But I will if you don't come with me."

"Do *what*?"

"Let's get out of here, Weckeah. Marry me, right now, this min-ute. Nineteen fighters are all ready to go. They all rode with me two nights ago, all of them have wives or sweethearts, a couple of them have children. More will be coming to join us. I just left a large gift of horses with your dad's herder." Her voice began to rise; he shushed her, cut her off. "I know it's the law," he said. "And I don't care, if that's what the law is. Your mother doesn't want you to be miserable. Your sister doesn't want this. And you don't want to be Tannap's wife. Yellow Bear's trapped by his greed, that's all. He'll be fine with us, once he cools down and thinks. You're his blood. Those

225

horse traders aren't. We've been waiting all our lives for this, Weckeah. I've brought up your horses. You're already packed. Let's go."

A month later, on a chilly spring day, Bose sat wearily with his back to the cut bank of the Concho River. Days of aimless riding and then weeks of hungry indecision had passed since he made a grown man's decision to quit the U. S. Army.

He had run south into barren country he knew, only to realize he had no wish to know it further. Out in that vastness there were Mexican settlers who'd ask no questions and give a drifting man a meal and work. But Bose found out real quick he was no goat shearer. The lanolin and parasites on the wool ate him up. Mexico was the easiest place to go, but that was no place he wanted to be. He had to be wary of patrols out of Fort Concho, he couldn't go anywhere near Fort Richardson, and he couldn't go back up the trail to Colorado and beg Charles Goodnight to get him out of a spot. Bose didn't mind being called a deserter; that campaign and outfit made him proud to quit. He had seen the floggings that Mackenzie was capable of when he punished a deserter. And those were just men trying to get away from the bad food, senseless orders, and boredom in the garrison dust of Fort Richardson. Desertion in the heat of battle, Bose had heard Mackenzie declare between yells of the ones being flogged, carried a sentence of a hangman's noose or a firing squad. Since the day when the solitary raider had ridden up and killed his half-sister Euphrasia for no reason at all, Bose would not have been surprised to open his eyes any morning to find it was his last one. But he had no interest in getting himself hanged. He never wore a uniform, for one thing. And men who did wear the blue uniforms were not popular in Texas. They were the occupiers of a beaten land.

As preoccupied as a man could be, Bose wrapped his arms around his legs and stared at a gar nosing through a couple of feet of green water along the bed of the creek. Behind him he heard the teeth and jaws of his hobbled horse and mule as they tore grass out of the roots and soil. He pulled his saddlebags up beside him and considered the fruits of his modest thievery: a windup alarm clock that had belonged to that maniac doctor and a dented bugle. He turned the bugle over in his hands and fingered the soiled Company D tassel. It was just two bends of burnished brass pipe; there were no wind valves to make it a real instrument.

He put the mouthpiece to his lips, aired up his lungs and cheeks, and blew "First Call." Anyone who'd ever been around a horse race track knew that simple tune. He'd taught himself two others that were imprinted in the brains of horse soldiers—"Stable Call" and "Water Call." The signal to let the animals drink was just seven quick notes, up and down. He hadn't mastered "Boots and Saddles," the call to tack up and prepare to ride. Bose played through the material again, trying to get some feeling into it. A couple of mourning doves took off. Though he did like the look and feel of it in his hands, he doubted anyone could coax real music out of a bugle.

He watched a hawk cruise and hunt the grass beyond the creek. It folded its wings and dropped downward in a spiral, came up flying with something in its talons. Bose returned the bugle to his bag and pulled out his harmonica. He wet it back and forth between his lips and played the high grieving chorus of "Rambler and Gambler," and played and sang some lines.

> *Lord, it's raining*
> *And the moon gives no light*
> *My pony won't travel*
> *This dark road at night*

Bose was pushing and sucking spit and air through the reeds, wobbling the sound with his hand, when Tricks and Juneteen snorted and jumped several hops to the ends of their ropes. He froze, staring at the Winchester and saddle sleeve that were propped on his bedroll just out of reach. He turned his head the other way and encountered the barrel of a .44 Henry repeater and an arched bois d'arc bow. Bose had managed to call up Quanah Parker and another Comanche.

"It's you," Bose offered in Spanish.

"Sure is," Quanah replied.

The other Comanche, whose name was Dog Hates Thunder, glared and pulled the bowstring farther back, a flick of two fingers from letting the arrow go. The head had been hammered and filed out of some piece of waste iron, and it was uglier than a coiled diamondback. Quanah, who wore a headband with two hawk feathers angled out behind his left ear, kept the Henry aimed at Bose, but he glanced at his companion and spoke to him. The other Comanche slid Quanah a look, shrugged, and put slack in the string.

Bose wagered all he had on something Goodnight had once told him about the strange customs and temperament of Comanches. "I'm real glad to see you," Bose said, "because I have no food. Tengo mucho hambre."

Quanah heaved an exasperated sigh and lowered his rifle slightly. Goodnight's information was correct. When travelers asked, they were supposed to be fed. It was tradition, a matter of honor with their people.

Which afforded Bose a little more time to go on breathing. He decided to get to the real point quickly. "What happened between you and me that time in the Palo Pinto country is what it is and can't be changed. But I was just a worker, a scout, for those soldiers in the Blanco Canyon. I left them when the Tonkawas killed two of your fighters that got separated from their horses. I'd tell you their names," he bluffed, for he knew them not at all, "except I know you don't like to hear spoken names of your dead." Quanah's grunt was not a sound of pleasure. "And then some crazy white man, not Mackenzie but a doctor, cut off their heads and started trying to cook the meat off the bones."

Quanah stared at Bose aghast.

"You saw these things?" he said.

"Yes, I'm afraid so."

Quanah had handed those fallen warriors his pipe and asked them to make the ride. One of them, his friend Breaks Something, had been with him when he went down the trail to Mexico, the time he found his Uncle John, discovered the peyote road, and brought back To-ha-yea. "Do you know what happens to spirits of people when they die that way?"

Bose shook his head.

"They become ghosts. You see and hear whole camps of them with herds one minute and then they're gone. Some come at you with long knives, shocking you with their terrible wounds. Or they slip into being the little men—the nenepi. They come at you in the night with tiny shields and bows and throw lances pointed with alligator spines." Quanah shrugged slightly. "So the old ones say."

Bose hurried on. "What those soldiers did was wrong, and I had no part of it. Neither did those black soldiers you choose to fight and kill."

Quanah studied him and thought on that awhile. "You were a scout for these people?"

"Yes."

"Were there Tonkawas among these scouts?"

"A few."

"You know those are bad people."

"They stayed off by themselves."

On Quanah's face was something like a smile. "How were you going to lead the soldiers to us?"

"We had no idea. We just rode around, trying to keep officers happy."

"Push your pistol over here. Despacio," Quanah told him.

Passing the harmonica from his right hand to his left, with the finger and thumb Bose pulled the Colt from his holster. He placed it carefully on the ground. Then shoved it with his boot. The other one put his arrow back in his quiver and collected the Colt and the

Winchester. Quanah advanced on Bose in a rolling swagger and snatched the harmonica out of his hand. He examined the tooling on the shiny tin coat and said something else to Dog Hates Thunder. It was the kind of German-made mouth organ that soldiers on the treaty grounds of Medicine Lodge, Kansas, had thrown to the tribes like candy.

Years earlier, some Comanche chiefs—none of them Quohada—had put marks on the piece of paper and promised to keep their bands on reservations in the Indian Territory, except when the soldier chiefs gave them permission to go off on hunts. In return, the soldiers promised that the buffalo hide hunters would never be allowed to come south of the Arkansas River. Parra-o-coom had sent Quanah to watch and tell him what happened. Both sides told big lies and tried to impress the other. The squawking noise from all the mouth organs had almost stampeded an immense herd of horses. Among the Comanches and Kiowas it was rare to see one of the keepsakes now.

The harmonica, not Bose's desperate claim that he was hungry, saved his life in those first moments of his capture. Quanah thrust the metal wafer back at Bose and said, "Play it some more."

19

THE SMELL OF COMANCHES standing close around was not a comforting aroma. As the audience in the camp glared and snickered and curs growled between their ankles, Quanah ordered Bose to strip everything off Tricks and Juneteen. When the saddle, packsaddle, panniers, blankets, bridle, halters, and ropes were dumped in a pile, a dog ran up and bit a stirrup like it was a living thing. Quanah approached Bose's nervous paint gelding and tall black mule. He coaxed them into standing still and in turn allowing him to cradle their chins in his large hands. He stood close to them, murmuring, and blew breath into their noses. Taking care not to touch their ears, he slipped loops of rope over their heads, flipped second loops around the noses, and with a hitch back under their jaws, tied simple hackamores. A boy took the catch ropes from Quanah and led them away. Another young Comanche knelt with a deerskin and carefully wrapped up the Winchester, holstered Colt, boot knife, bugle, harmonica, and alarm clock they'd relieved from Bose. Quanah gestured for him to come along. "Ahora podemos comer," he said. Now they could eat.

Bose glanced at the pile of tack. Deft brown hands would soon be ransacking the panniers and snatching his white wool Mexican saddle blanket; his horsehair and leather bridle and reins would be cut up for sinew and twine, its bit a handy scraper for some woman on her knees working a buffalo hide. Lost were the silver-studded saddlebags given him by his father and within them the papers from the doctor certifying his existence and discharging him from slavery. And the belts containing the gold that Goodnight gave him.

Quanah paused in mid-stride, as if hearing Bose. He turned and spoke to the others in a commanding voice, tapping his chest with his hand. That booty belonged to *him*. They cut their eyes and moved away.

With elaborate contempt, Quanah walked on with his back turned on Bose, whose gaze fell on the claw hammer hitched in his belt. It was just a dust-cloaked tool that day Quanah took it out of the drovers' wagon. Now it was his war club. The wood handle had been rubbed and oiled to a gloss, and the steel head was as bright and free of rust as a dime.

Bose knew this was not the Quohada band the soldiers had chased and lost in the ice storm above Blanco Canyon. The lodges were too few in number, there were no old people, and the river-bottom camp had a stripped-down look of recent occupation. Lodge poles were being straightened and the hides stretched and re-staked. But the horse and mule herd was at least the size of the 4th Cavalry's.

Quanah led Bose and the youth carrying the weapons toward two tipis and a fire. Attending it was a young woman with brown skin, round cheeks, and a broad forehead. Her hair was pushed back behind her ears and lay upon her collarbones with the look of having been cut with a knife, but nothing else about her was unkempt. She wore earrings and bracelets, beaded moccasins, leggings made from the stylish hide of a badger, a buckskin skirt cross-stitched up the sides of her legs with dark brown leather thongs, and a lighter buckskin blouse sewn with beadings and ornaments that had loose fringed sleeves. Over that she wore a poncho cut from the back and chest hide of a black bear; it signified her superior rank as a wife and the warring stature of her husband. A line of red marked the center part of her hair. Shadings of yellow had been lined across her eyelids, and daubs of red on her cheeks accentuated a small mouth that was provocative, whether she was angry or pleased. Weckeah wasn't happy now.

She fixed Bose with a hostile stare, then she and Quanah were arguing in sharp bursts of Comanche, and when she rolled her eyes at him, the dispute grew animated. The boy laid the deerskin and Bose's weapons on the ground and receded from the conflict. Beside the second tipi was a taller young woman with hair that splashed across her shoulders. She also wore clothes made of deerskin, but it had been tanned and worked finer and thinner until the garments had the look of blond velvet. A loose-fitting blouse decorated with fringe and tassels reached almost to her knees; under that was a skirt of more fringe and two circles of yellow trimming, and a pair of hide boots. To-ha-yea stood with a hip cocked, a pose full of spunk, but as she met Bose's gaze, the toe of one boot squirmed against the ground and her furry brows furrowed with unease. Her eyes looked as deep and dark as a well.

Quanah clearly had a taste for good-looking women and the capacity to claim them. Bose considered the white man's expression *squaw*.

Weckeah flung a remark at her husband and ducked through the flap of the first tipi. Quanah glowered past Bose at the gawkers who'd trailed along and spoke to To-ha-yea in Spanish. Among Comanches there were number-one wives and chore wives, and through broken promises and the headstrong nature of Weckeah, To-ha-yea had been relegated to the latter. "Make us something to eat," he said with an undertone of pleading. "Anything. Yesterday's stew." Bose thought she was of another tribe, perhaps a captive like him.

To-ha-yea stepped forward with a glance of resentment at the closed lodge flap. She slipped past Bose without looking at him and from a hide pouch slopped brown soup in a smoke-blackened pot. "Sit down," Quanah said, pointing at ground beside the fire. "Warm yourself."

Bose took a seat and locked his arms around his knees, but he thought that must make him look frightened and anxious, which he was, and he made himself relax. Looming over him, Quanah said, "What's your name?"

"Bose. Bose Ikard."

"Again?" he said.

"Bose," he repeated. "*Eye-card*. Bose Ikard."

"I've wondered," the big Indian said. "I'm called Quanah. Some white people call me Quanah Parker."

"Everybody knows your name."

"That true? Soldiers and Tejanos?"

"Claro. You're famous."

Quanah harrumphed with arrogant satisfaction and lowered himself to the ground. He watched To-ha-yea for a time, then extended his arm and laid back the fold of deerskin, inspecting the guns without great interest. He picked up the alarm clock. "What's this?" he asked.

Bose came up blank. "In Spanish I don't know the word."

"Tell me what it's for."

Bose thought a moment longer, then pointed at the sun, blurred by a layer of cloud, and with movement of his arm described its arc from sunrise to sundown. "It measures the where of the sun and passage of the night."

"How does it do that?"

"Can I have it?" Bose took the clock from Quanah and wound it enough to set it ticking loudly. The girl warming the soup gave them a glance.

"Oh, yes," said Quanah. "I know those. You find them in pants of people after a fight. You throw them away. Dead men shouldn't make noise."

Bose wished he could turn it off. "Why do you have one too big to put in your pants?" Quanah needled him.

Bose risked a smile and raised a forefinger. He checked the position of the hands of the clock, then gave the other knob a twist.

Quanah's ass cleared the ground when the alarm commenced its clanging. To-ha-yea also jumped, startled. Horses whinnied.

Bose got the bell turned off. Quanah's chin jutted and the ends of his mouth turned down when he was displeased. "Are you puha-kut, Bose Ikard?"

"What?"

Quanah used the Spanish word. "Un brujo."

"No, no," said Bose. He set the clock on the ground between them. "This is nothing. It has no power. It's a toy. I stole it."

The girl scooped the buffalo meat and broth into cracked china bowls that had likely been taken in a raid on some wagon train and served it with pieces of flat dried cake. With a flick of long eyelashes she satisfied some curiosity and took his measure.

"I see you like her," said Quanah.

Bose flinched. Keeping his eyes off her, he thanked his host for the food.

"Her name is To-ha-yea," Quanah went on proudly. "She's Mescalero Apache. She's learning the language of our people now. Isn't it so?"

"Jaa," she affirmed. She busied herself poking coals with a stick.

"The other's name is Weckeah. The sight of you soured her mood."

Bose's mouth and throat were as dry as chalk; he had no idea what was coming once they'd consumed this ritual meal of sharing with strangers and acknowledging hunger as the enemy of all people. He nibbled the spotted gray cake and was surprised by the tart flavor. Persimmon.

Quanah stretched one leg toward the fire and scooped stew into his mouth with his piece of cake. "Bose Ikard, do you have wives?"

Bose shook his head. Quanah sucked broth off his thumb and set the bowl aside. "None is not enough," he said. "Two may be too many. Go on, eat."

He dug in a pouch hung from his belt and produced what appeared to be a timepiece until he flipped back the lid. "I don't believe like some of Our People that whites make fine guns but everything else they turn out is a toy. I have an uncle who was born white but rode with us and lives in Mexico now. Strong-hearted man. He gave me this thing called a compass. It contains as much magic as anything I've ever seen." He leaned closer to Bose and showed him how the needle wavered but always sought the same direction no matter how he revolved the compass. "There's some force in the north that the point always seeks," Quanah said. "Nothing can throw it off. You know the North Star?"

"Yes, of course."

"Its true name is tatzniupi-puetuh-catutamiae. I believe the power to hold and direct this point of steel lies in that star. But the steel is shy and respectful and has a stubborn will of its own—it won't point directly at the star. When I witness power like this I try to put it to use. Some of our people say this gift from my uncle is just another trick—they don't want to have to think about it. But no matter how dark the sky or how covered up in weather, even when I'm on the llano, it always lets me know the direction I seek." Quanah smiled and put the compass away. "Which is not the same as knowing where to go. For that you need another kind of magic. Are you through eating?"

"Yes," said Bose, swallowing hard. He tentatively handed the bowl to the Apache wife. To-ha-yea took the bowls and carried them away from the fire. "I knew your mother," Bose blurted. "And your sister. She was just a baby then."

Quanah gaped at this man who'd put whip scars on his chest. "I ought to kill you just for speaking of them. What do you mean you *knew* them?"

"I was the slave of a doctor in a town called Weatherford. When they were captured, I was a boy. The rangers brought them to the doctor's house, and they stayed there several days. I cooked for them, brought wood to their stove. Then they were taken somewhere by their kin named Parker. I don't know what became of them. It makes no difference; I just thought I'd say it. Your mother was kind to me. Kinder than she had any reason to be."

A muscle flexed and twitched in Quanah's jaw. He blew out a huff of breath, got up, went inside the first tipi, and came out holding a battle lance that was longer than he was tall. The shaft was brightly and elaborately beaded. A ruff of red and black feathers had been worked into the sinew and glue that connected shaft and spearhead, which was as long as a horse's skull.

Brandishing this thing, Quanah started yelling. Men, women, children, and dogs came toward the fire and Bose. With a buffalo robe pulled around her shoulders, the Comanche wife came out of the tipi. The other wife, the Apache, kept her distance.

About twenty men carried bows and proceeded to notch arrows to their strings. The archers paired off in two rows beside the stream. They spread out about thirty yards from each other, all eyes on Bose.

Quanah's hand shot out and plucked a swatch of Bose's hair. He examined it and said with contempt, "Hair like this has no value. Sometimes warriors take the scalps of tuh-tahvoas, but they usually throw it away. In the long ago, there's a story about tuh-tahvoa captives—I think it may have come from the Tanima band, the Liver Eaters."

The bowman who had been eager to put an arrow in Bose interjected a remark. Quanah nodded and said, "Dog Hates Thunder is right. The story came from the band called Maggots on the Penis. It was their custom to fornicate with their mothers and make wives of their sisters. They were also called Wormy." As Quanah spoke, he paced and circled Bose, who stared straight ahead. "The story is told that people like you were traveling with the people called Seminoles. They had taken up the Seminole ways. The Wormy band had a battle with them in the brush country south of here, and several tuh-tahvoas were taken captive. Maggots on the Penis had never seen people with black skin—they believed it doubtful that they could be human beings. Their puhakut told them that the black's flesh was just as black as their skin, so they built a fire and got out their knives and investigated. They burned and scraped and were disappointed. But they weren't near as sorry as the tuh-tahvoas."

Several Comanches laughed. Quanah paused and considered his lance. "We don't have worms on our peckers, Bose Ikard. And that's not what we do with captives. Look there." He pointed the

237

lance at archers who were testing the tautness of their bowstrings. "If you're fast enough to make it to the river, you're free to go."

Bose stared at the gauntlet and had to laugh.

"You don't even want to try?" said Quanah.

"I may be what you call me, but I'm no fool."

"You don't trust your own medicine," he taunted Bose.

"I was born to a slave owner's medicine. It never was mine."

As Quanah puzzled over his answer, archers jeered Bose, who caught a glimpse of the Apache wife. She watched the game intently.

"Then you've made your choice," said Quanah, gesturing to the bowmen that it was over. "In this band, so it is with all captives. You'll live among us and do as you're asked. As long as you do that, no one's going to hurt you. But if you try to run away, I'll kill you myself. It will be my obligation for not doing it in the first place."

Quanah shoved the lance until it broke the skin of Bose's throat, just below the chin. It was razor-sharp. "Do you understand?"

"Easy as reading a compass."

Quanah gave the shaft another push. "Don't be smart with your tongue."

When he withdrew it Bose resisted the urge to touch the cut. "All right."

Quanah poked the lance at the contents of the deerskin carrier and gave the harmonica a nudge. "Now that is a toy. These people here would like to hear you make it toot." The archers had slung their bows on their shoulders and were putting arrows back in their quivers. Quanah motioned for everyone to come close around. Bose licked his lips and moved the harmonica back and forth until he had enough spit restored to have a chance to play it.

"Let them hear your singing, too," said Quanah. "You're a songbird."

Bose decided on a sappy Stephen Foster tune that was easy to play. As he moved his hands and breathed melody in and out through the reeds he watched bowmen curl their lips and wave him off. Women laughed and beat their palms on their thighs. Children jiggled up and down and clamped their hands over their ears. They didn't know how funny it was, "Jeanie with the Light Brown Hair." Bose played through the eight bars once and started over, and raising the harmonica like it was a piece of candy he sang lines that didn't belong to anything they were or anyplace around him.

> I dream of Jeanie with the light brown hair,
> Borne, like a vapor, on the sweet summer air;
> I see her tripping where the bright streams play,
> Happy as the daisies that dance on her way

Man wants me to be his jester, thought Bose. His clown. Yes, sir, Master, for all the while I need to see my way out of here, I can do your shuck and jive. His flutters of fingertips and palm quavered the sound and brought to the faces a few grudging smiles. One of those, he noticed, belonged to the pretty Mescalero.

20

NEVER LETTING BOSE FORGET his exhibition on the honey-colored horse, Quanah put him to work breaking stolen colts and outlaw brutes that did not care to be ridden. Bose had to learn their way of staying on a horse, doing it the hard way. The saddles they used were at best pads with a bit of support for the backside; there were no stirrups. Many just rode bareback. Bose was thrown so often that he was bruised all over, so sore he could barely walk. During the horse- and mule-breaking, men gathered and watched in a judgmental circle, pulling for the bucking, snorting beasts.

Bose's clothes were soon filthy and tattered. Weckeah gave him one of Quanah's worn buckskin shirts, which hung far off his shoulders; with help from the wives he managed to keep his three pairs of dungarees in patched repair, for he wanted nothing to do with any breechclout. Weckeah's attitude moved from hostility to indifference to occasional pleasantries; from the start she and To-ha-yea seemed to tolerate him with more ease than they tolerated each other. Quanah kept Bose's tack, guns, packsaddle, panniers, and everything else he owned hidden away in a cache somewhere. He gave Bose a bony line-backed mule to ride. Bose got to keep his boots and his weather-battered hat.

Late one day he was sitting bone-tired with the boots and hat off and his feet soaking in the river. A few strides away, To-ha-yea walked down to the bank carrying water bags made from bladders of buffalo and antelope. The day was warm enough that she was sleeveless under a light poncho. The descending sun and tree shadows were behind Bose, and in the glare and poles of shade she didn't notice him. She kneeled on the sand and lowered herself to the water like an animal, pooling handfuls to drink and then washing her face. He was intensely aware of the down on her bare arm.

"Hello," he spoke up.

Surprised and flustered, To-ha-yea answered, "Where have you been?"

It was a traditional greeting among her people; one did not comment on the quality of the morning or day like Mexicans or call another's name with the rudeness of the white eyes. Bose knew none of that about Apaches. Her choice of words gave his heart a quick thudding that was misinformed.

With a quick laugh she wiped her mouth and dried her hands on her skirt. She lowered one of the bladders in the water and began to fill it. "I didn't see you," she said.

"It's because you never look at me."

Her glance was wary. "Yes, I do."

"Never mind. I like looking at you." He leaned back on the heels of his hands. "I'm not supposed to say that. Forgive me."

After a while she said, "When you first came here you scared me. Because of something that happened once with someone like you."

"Like me?" he ventured lightly. "What did I ever do?"

In the face of her unhappy memory he said, "I know what you mean. Do you want to tell me what happened?"

She shook her head.

"Please. I'd like to know."

"I don't know you well enough."

Bose nodded and stared off. Whatever it was, it must have been bad.

She changed her mind. "The white eyes are always telling us where we have to live, and where we can't, and sending soldiers trying to make sure we do what they say. It can never be where we belong. There's a river in the west called Río Bonito. It looks out on four mountains that are sacred to us. When I was a little girl the white eyes sent soldiers and said we couldn't live there any longer. They made us go to a bad place on the Pecos called Bosque Redondo."

"I know Bosque Redondo. It is a bad place." He remembered when Goodnight's cattle drives approached the impoundment, policed by the soldiers of Fort Sumner and the famous Kit Carson. Cornfields the Navajos had been made to plant were parched sticks; a couple of hundred of them came out from their hogans and walked beside the herd, all but drooling. Comanches raided them constantly. Soldiers at the fort were accustomed to taking their brandy and ale while enjoying the racket and spark of Indian gunfights in the night.

"But I thought all the people there were Navajos," Bose said.

"Yes, they were made to leave their country, too. There were many thousands of them, just a few hundred of us. But Navajos and Apaches are enemies, they're fighting all the time! We couldn't live with them in a place where we were all going to starve or die of the plagues. And Apache bands don't want to be made to live all together, either. We call the Tonto and San Carlos bands Brainless People, and they've probably got some name like that for us. So one new moon in the season called Earth Is Reddish Brown our people gathered what little they could carry and pack and brought up the horses; my father, Old Wolf, and another chief took us to a place of hiding in the Sacramento Mountains. The bluecoats were very angry because they didn't know we were going to do it until the sun came up and they saw us gone. But they were busy making the Navajos starve, and they left us alone for a while. After a while they let the Navajos go back up in the mesas where they want to live and came with guns after us. We couldn't help noticing that the soldiers had changed—almost all of them were now people like you. But the soldier chiefs were still white eyes.

"While we'd been living at Bosque Redondo the Mexicans had built up a villita named Placitas and planted more fields and tree farms along the Río Bonito. Our raiders started coming out of the Sacramentos and killing all the Mexican men and boys they could get their hands on. Sometimes they brought them back to our ranchería so that women who'd lost husbands and sons could do the killing. They tied the Mexicans' hands behind their backs and then followed them around, chopping them apart with axes."

She glanced at Bose to see his response to that. He revealed none.

"My father said many times that the fighting was going to lead to big trouble," she went on, "and he was right. The soldier chiefs said we had to go live in another river valley, the Tularosa. The valley's too high in the mountains. If you try to winter up there, you'll freeze to death. So my father took a band of us many mountains away, to a range where no Mexicans or white eyes lived. It was a wintering place in the Guadalupe Mountains called Manzanillo Springs. The soldiers just stumbled on us, I think. In the time it took to take one breath my life went from quiet voices and sounds of birds to men yelling and shooting, horses screaming. Our fighters were outnumbered, trying to get to higher ground and cover, and soldiers began to start fires. I was by myself in a wickiup, which is made of brush. The one who ran in my hut looked too young to be among them. He had light skin, like you, though I know some call it black, and he had, como se dice, spots on his face."

"Scars?"

"No."

"Pecosos?" Freckles.

"Yes, those. The negro had a rifle strapped across his shoulder and was carrying a torch. Before he set the fire, he acted like he wanted to make sure no one was in there. He knocked off his hat when he didn't stoop low enough. He rubbed his head and said something angry and was reaching down for his hat when he saw me. I must have scared him as much as he scared me, because he dropped the torch. My father had given me an old shotgun. 'This is for rattlesnakes and white eyes,' Father told me. 'Anything bad that gets close enough to hurt you.'

"It was all smoky in there, and the soldier was standing between me and the one way out. If he'd just gotten out of the way, I would have run. His eyes were on the shotgun, and he started trying to get the carbine off his shoulder, but got his arm tangled in the strap. He hadn't started out wanting to hurt me, but he was in a hurry to do it now. So I pointed the gun like my father taught me, pulled it snug so it wouldn't break my shoulder, and I killed him."

With a frank look at him she pulled the water bag out of the river. Bose contemplated the torn knees of his britches and began to tug on his boots. "Can I help you with the water?" he said.

She frowned. "No, but thank you. Women here watch me all the time. I can't do enough work to suit them." She sat back on her calves and moccasins, palms on her thighs. "No one here has ever heard that story," she told him. "No one's ever asked."

"Why are you here?" asked Bose.

To-ha-yea shrugged again. "Quanah gave my father six mules and promised to replace the buffalo sleeping robes the soldiers set afire, and he did. I wanted to come with Quanah. I thought he was the Gray Ghost."

Bose had no idea what she meant. "I would have followed him anywhere," she said. She left it questionable whether she still would.

The Apache girl gave him another direct look. "You were a soldier?"

"Not in my mind I wasn't. I was with them for a while. I ran off from them." He shook his head at the folly of his life. "I killed a Comanche one time," he told her. "Both of us too young to be doing that. Like there's a proper time to start. But it just happened. It had to."

"Quanah told me."

Bose stared at her. "He told you that?"

"Yes. You killed his best friend."

244

Bose looked at the sundown and sighed. "So that's why it's so personal. It's a wonder he didn't shoot me on sight."

"He thinks if he did that, he'd be killing some part of himself."

He blinked and shook his head. "What?"

"He talks to them. Those scars you put on his chest."

⊰⊱

Weckeah didn't hesitate to exercise her rights as paraibo and load chores on Bose or To-ha-yea, leaving it to them to comprehend her bursts of temper. He began to recognize the odd sounds of their speech, though he stammered, trying to repeat them. Day after tomorrow was pinacuarenapuetzco. Crack her those pecans, naquehtábaene. Months of late winter, tochuetómo and tómoramarohcat. To him the trade language of the plains sounded like people with a bad cold, onibuecacát, trying to hawk up phlegm.

As more young men and their women came in from the bands of Quohada and Kotsoteka, supplies arrived with them strapped on packsaddles and dragged by travois. One day as Quanah directed and Bose did the heavy lifting, they put up three more lodges on the rise above the river. Behind Quanah's main lodge, Weckeah and To-ha-yea would now have their own tipis, so they could have privacy and there wouldn't be such tension. One of the new lodges was set aside for the sacraments and rites of the peyote road. And the other went up so that Bose would no longer have to sleep out in the weather.

If Quanah hadn't done that, Bose would have had to grab whatever horse he could and run to keep from freezing. The northers seldom lasted long, but that winter they came like they were piled up waiting their turns. Buried in his buffalo robes, Bose peeked out from his lodge and watched horses indistinct as ghosts, slinging hooves over and over at the drifts of snow, trying to get to the grass. Others stood on hind legs like they were trying to mount the cottonwoods, peeling the bark until it was beyond their reach.

But the bitter time of the year passed. On both sides of the river bottom stretched flats of sand and caliche, sotol stalks and scrawny mesquite; the bed of the Middle Concho was bone-dry half the time. But the tufts of bluestem prairie and the cottonwood and willow trees belied the surrounding appearance of hunger and thirst. The rain was spare, but when it came it fell in torrents. Gullies and draws poured storm water east down the Concho branches, and a rise of square-topped mesas broke it west down Centralia Draw, filling a broad shallow lake that seldom dried up, and the porous bedrock replenished one of the biggest springs on the trail to Mexico. Bose saw a herd of buffalo that must have stretched twenty miles across. Mule deer were plentiful and had more meat on them than the whitetails he grew up knowing, and they were easier to hunt than the Quohada band's namesake pronghorns. Turkeys gobbled and roosted in the river bottom cottonwoods as spiky hooves of javelinas clattered on the rocks below. Bose would watch the little wild pigs munch their favorite delicacy, the tunas of prickly pear, and he thought they must have very hard tongues.

Quanah had picked the spot with knowing. The whites' road stretched from Indianola on the Gulf of Mexico to San Francisco, but the army explorers and surveyors never knew about the nearby Big Lake and cold-water spring; they thought the raiders who sacked the mule trains and stagecoaches just spun out of the desert like whirlwinds. Quanah's band of runaways were the wild seeds of Comanchería. They had no interest in the formalities of picking a council and civil chief and pondering the days they'd be spending telling lies in a smoke lodge, if they lived. Their equivalent was the lodge put up for their peyote rituals, from which they stumbled at dawn every few days. They laughed and proclaimed their band Canauocueteka, Cactus Eaters.

One day Quanah, his wives, and Bose sat beside a supper fire. Quanah remarked to Bose, "You know, I didn't steal your Medicine Hat paint and tall black mule. I have horses and mules of my own that I like better. But they're good animals, so I won't take what I could get, trading them. I'll keep them for you. If I let you have them now, you'd run away the first chance you got. I wouldn't want to have to work too hard to run you down."

Bose wagged his head in a nod of sorts and glanced at To-ha-yea. Was he once more a slave? Neither the white doctor in the Palo Pinto country nor his son had ever laid out their arrangement in such a clear manner. "You can go out in my herd," Quanah offered, "and make sure their weight is good and their hooves are in good health."

"Thanks," muttered Bose.

"Come with me," said Quanah, standing up. "Enough of that big mule. You need a horse to ride."

Watching where he stepped—both for rattlers and the piles of shit—Bose trooped after Quanah among the hundreds of horses and mules, whose coats were still fuzzy and shaggy from the winter. The boy Black Rope had already caught the gelding and he led him forward. Bose gasped. With his hands on his hips, Quanah bent over and let go a hoot of laughter. Bose's new ride was Bad Hand Mackenzie's dappled gray pacer.

The colonel spent months at Fort Richardson nursing grudges and his old battle wounds as his surgeons tried to keep the festering new arrow wound from turning into gangrene. But in the middle of the next summer, 1872, he took five companies of cavalry and one of infantry back out on the plains. He would find the hostile bands, he decided, by forcefully enlisting and convincing comancheros they had damn sure better help. He drove his men for two weeks across the searing plains to Fort Sumner in New Mexico to pick up one Polonia Ortiz, a professed adobe brick maker whom Lucien Maxwell had thrown in jail for stealing from him. Relieved to be out of a stinking and sun-baked hole in the ground, blind as he could be in the glaring sun, and informed in blunt Spanish what was going to happen if his information proved wrong, the comanchero led Bad Hand and his troops across the llano to the sprawling camp of the Kotsoteka. Chief Mow-way and the Meat Eaters had fallen in the habit of putting up their lodges at Fort Sill and taking their rations from the Quakers during the winter. Come spring, with explanations that they were going on the buffalo hunt, they returned to their redoubts in the Texas Panhandle and raided as they wanted. Mow-way was at Fort Sill treating with the Indian agent and some English speculators in strange round hats when the comanchero Polonia Ortiz showed Mackenzie the two hundred sixty lodges amid sand hills along the North Fork of the Red.

So many Kotsoteka were killed in that half-hour fight that their women filled up a deep clear water hole with bodies and turned the water pink, trying to keep Bad Hand's Tonks from carving them up to eat. Mackenzie told the soldiers to burn every lodge and buffalo robe in sight. They rounded up two thousand horses and mules; Meat Eaters who had gotten away proceeded to steal them right back that night, along with the herd of the Tonks. But Mackenzie made hostages of a hundred thirty women and children, and in supply wagons he trundled them to Fort Concho. Several died along the way from childbirth and blistering heat. It was almost one year to the date of the freak ice storm and Mackenzie's calamity in Blanco Canyon.

Mow-way's heart and defiance were broken. He led remnants of the Kotsoteka back to Fort Sill, where he begged the Quakers to reason with this terrible man Bad Hand and make him let them have their wives and children back. As a defiant and cohesive band the Meat Eaters were finished, though many of their fighters soon joined the Quohada camps of Parra-o-coom and Quanah Parker.

Mackenzie couldn't follow up on his defeat of the Kotsoteka and find either of those bands, and the colonel read one preposterous claim that Quanah's renegades had run off fifteen thousand horses and mules that spring and summer. And there were rumors, which left him in a sputtering rage, of some nigger with them on his gray horse Prize!

The rumors were true, though Bose was unarmed and did none of the burning or shooting. Bose knew he was being used in a way that someday could get him stood up against a wall or prodded up a gallows, if the crossfire between the Comanches, cavalry, and vigilante rangers didn't kill him first. Bose rode with Quanah's band, helping herd the stolen stock, because Quanah assured him his bones would be bleaching on the plains if he didn't, and he hadn't found the opportune moment or the horse that would allow him to slip away.

He sure couldn't make a run on that brainless gray. The pacer was a smart-looking thing, snapping out his hooves before him with flash of knee and coronet, but he couldn't be kicked out of that gait. His right legs swung forward in unison, and then the left ones—pacing was just something he was born to. He could speed up faster with that gait than other horses could trot, but any of the Indians' horses could overtake him in a gallop. Bad Hand's gray rattled Bose up and down hard while simultaneously pitching him from side to side. Mackenzie used to say it was like riding a hard-charging camel.

Bose had learned enough Comanche that he began to follow some of what was said around him. When Weckeah's mood was good, she slowed down so that Bose and To-ha-yea could understand her. One day they were gathering buffalo meat that had been drying on racks in the fall sun. To-ha-yea had shouldered a load of the jerked meat and walked back toward the lodges. Weckeah blew a strand of hair out of her eyes and considered Bose. "You know you could get away from here any night you want," she said, which startled him. Bose laughed.

"Look at all those horses," she went on. "You know ones that can run and keep going without water. Get a dark one, ride with your shirt off. Or some moonless night catch that paint of your own you trust so much. Keep riding until it's night again. Nobody's going to chase you any farther than that." She chuckled. "No one lazy as Quanah."

Weckeah looked toward To-ha-yea, who had stopped and in a dance of weariness slung the yanks of meat to her other shoulder. "Why don't you take her?" Weckeah said with a conniving little smile. "Why don't you just ask? I bet you fifteen horses she'd go along."

Bose shook his head and laughed again. He muttered in English. "Thanks for the help."

21

Weckeah and her women friends and kin twittered like chickadees over her pregnancy, but like all mothers born Comanche she had fits of dread about losing the baby. She quit riding her horses and ordered To-ha-yea and Bose to fetch things for her that a child could have carried. Weckeah had a ravenous appetite for the plums, sumac berries, onions, and sunchokes that women in the band foraged in the Concho bottom, but she had trouble keeping food down and suffered wrenching cramps long after she felt the baby's nudges and kicks and morning sickness should have passed. Even as her belly swelled, she lost weight and her face turned gaunt. Apprentice midwives in the youthful band surmised the curse of sorcerers; Weckeah longed for the experience and consolation of her mother. She thought every twitch and pinch of her entrails was a miscarriage. Quanah didn't know how to reassure or comfort her, and in the lodges built above the stream the number-one wife exercised her full rights of tantrum and spite. "She used not to be a mean woman," Bose muttered to To-ha-yea after one of Weckeah's tirades. "I think she's just gone crazy."

"Huh," grunted To-ha-yea, who was snatching up empty parfleches and water bags. She stuffed them in shoulder packs and handed one to Bose. "Come walk," she said. Weckeah had collapsed in her lodge to rest, and Quanah was snoring in the main one, following a night of songs and hallucinations in the peyote lodge. As Bose followed To-ha-yea through the cottonwoods, past grazing horses that raised their heads and observed their passing, she griped,

"I've seen her step right over his arrows and guns. I've seen her pick up a poker and stick the left end of it in a fire."

She mystified him when she said these things. "So?" he replied.

"Taboo! She's pregnant!" She gave him a disgusted look. "You're just like them."

"Not exactly."

West of the Middle Concho's bottom a rise changed steadily from prairie to worn alkaline soil and a spiky barricade of rock, yucca, sotol, prickly pear, and lechuguilla. Bose was glad he still had his boots, but in moccasins To-ha-yea picked her way right through it. She filled up parfleches with juniper berries that covered the ground around a brake of the prickly evergreens. In camp she customarily boiled them soft, sweetened them with honey, and mashed them into a paste, which she shaped into balls and put on the ends of sticks, to be roasted lightly. But she wasn't collecting them now for food. "What she needs is a tea boiled down good," she said, tossing berries in the palm of her hand. "That'll move the rocks in her insides."

She filled other bags with mesquite beans that she would shell or drop whole in the stews or grind into rough flour for bread cakes cooked on rocks dragged up in the fire. From yuccas she cut flowers, buds, fruit, and chunks of root. They stooped and gathered such things for several hundred yards, rousing a pain in Bose's lower back, then she found what she was really looking for on shelves along an arroyo cut by eons of flash floods.

One of the mescal plants had put up a stalk of pale blooms that stood half again as tall as Bose and attracted a considerable swarm of bees. To-ha-yea crouched beside another one and with her knife carefully trimmed out the central leaf bud. "Mira," she told Bose. He skirted the bee swarm and looked over her shoulder. The round wall of the plant began to seep clear liquid that soon flowed like a small spring. She handed Bose a long hard reed and said, "Taste it." He knelt beside her and gingerly sucked out some of the clear sap.

"Very sweet," he said. Sweet and fragrant.

"It's aquamiel," she told him. "Honey water."

With the drinking tube she sucked mouthfuls of fluid from the maguey and patiently transferred the honey water to buffalo bladders sealed with resin. "We can come back twice a day," she said, "and find it filled back up." She trimmed the buds out of several plants and extracted more aquamiel, and while she was at it, she sliced off tips of leaves that were as hard and sharp as a snake's fang and gave them a yank; they broke off attached to fibers that she peeled away from the edges of the leaves. She snipped them off and harvested several more of these notions of mescal, her people's needles and thread.

When they got back to the camp they found Weckeah seated on the ground outside her lodge, thoughtfully holding the mound of her stomach with one hand and gnawing a hank of jerky in the other. She looked half-inclined to apologize to them, but overcame the urge. To-ha-yea offered her one of the water bags and said, "Drink this."

"What is it?"

"Honey water. It's stored inside a special plant. It'll make you feel better. It's good for your baby."

Whatever its effect on her digestion, Weckeah liked the aquamiel's flavor a great deal. So Bose and To-ha-yea hiked back and forth through the thorns and spines to the arroyo of magueys and drained off the reservoirs of honey water. Bose lay awake at night thinking of the ridges and parting of To-ha-yea's collarbones and the way angled sunlight collected in the hollows of her eyes and turned her cheeks amber. But after several of those hikes he started wishing Quanah would round up another colt to break.

"Can I make a suggestion?" he said, leaning against an arroyo ledge.

She looked up and paused, stopping the reed with the tip of her tongue. He said, "Why don't we bring a mule and packsaddle and a bunch of water bags to fill up? We could keep them cool in one of the springs. That way we wouldn't have to walk so much."

She grinned and spoke around the reed. "Sometime I'll show you why."

⧓

Bose found it difficult to sleep when Quanah and his bunch carried on inside the peyote lodge—singing, confessing, tooting eagle whistles, beating on drums. Quanah sang more than the others and usually led the chorus when they joined in. He had a big loud baritone voice. He wasn't too bad a singer, Bose thought, considering the songs were tuneless.

Though Quanah once invited Bose to join them, he hadn't poked his head or set foot inside that tipi. He believed the peyote road was some kind of strange religion, and he was godless, always had been. His father, Doctor Ikard, used to claim proudly that he didn't believe in any god, which made Lady Isabella wail with alarm, but she never went to church either. The noise and wafts of sage and cedar smoke coming out of the peyote lodge left Bose fascinated and confused. He would roll out of his sleeping robe and watch through the flap of his tipi, though there was little to spy on. Someone might emerge, stumble off muttering to himself, and retch himself dry in the brush. It would have been no different out back of some Jacksboro saloon. Bose would doze off and jerk himself awake hearing a storyteller ramble on and on. But one such night he raised his chin and saw To-ha-yea duck in the tipi carrying a water pitcher and dipper and wearing a bright red shawl. That girl was a peyote eater? He didn't know up from down or sideways with these people.

The next time Quanah and his bunch embarked on their peyote road, a pack of coyotes answered their singing with their own serenade. The camp dogs were in an uproar. The coyotes' yips and cackles sounded like there were dozens of them in the pack—probably there were four or five. Bose liked the sound of coyotes; he drifted off to sleep.

Then he came awake and would have sat up with a knife to the

254

intruder's throat if he hadn't realized the pressure on his bare chest came from To-ha-yea's hand. "To-ha-yea!" he gasped. "What is it?"

She left her hand there and his heart slowed down. When he sat up he reached for his shirt but she stayed him, put her hand on his arm. She handed him a water bag. "Taste this," she said.

He took an incautious swallow and choked from the raw fire in the back of his throat. She suppressed a laugh with the palm of her hand. "Honey water starts fermenting the first day. Mexicans call it pulque."

"You tricked me," he said, taking another sip. "It tastes like sotol."

"Yes, they're similar. Except with sotol you roast the crown of the plant and mash it to get out the water. Desert liquor's not so good for mothers and babies. Or people who are trying not to fall down."

An eruption of singing and drums carried across from the other lodge. "You eat the cactus, too," Bose ventured.

"Not much," she answered. "They borrowed the ritual from my people but most of them can't accept having a woman in their ceremonies now."

"What does the cactus do to you?"

She jabbed him in the ribs. "It makes you scream like a mountain lion. Charge like a bear." She went on, smiling. "For most of those men it's all about war power and medicine. Not Quanah, though. He learned it right from my father and the Mescaleros. He knows there's more in the world."

They finished off the pulque and sat with their shoulders touching. "Whoo," Bose said. She agreed, fingering the tip of her nose.

"What are you doing?" he said.

"It's numb," she answered, then laughed and gave him a bump of her shoulder. "You thought I was afraid somebody was going to cut it off."

"No, I do not know anybody would do that."

Their voices had slowed down and seemed to ring with echoes.

"Not to anybody as pretty as you."

"What difference does that make? It's all right to cut off the nose of someone who's not? But it's true about my people. I've seen women cut and scarred like that since I was a little girl. And you know what's crazy? After a man's done that to her, she goes on living with him."

She tucked hair behind her ear and gave Bose an arch look. He swooped to kiss the back of her neck but lost his balance and had to catch himself with the heel of his hand. She pushed him upright, then ran her fingers through the coils of hair on his chest. "I've been wanting to do that."

"I think I don't know where to start."

"Don't think."

It got a little frantic after that. She was on her back on the sleeping robe, the sheer weight of him a pleasure, his hand exploring with a lightness of touch that pleased her, the driving of their hips insistent, her foot perched on the back of his calf. "Let's slow down," she said, running her hands through curls on his head that had not been barbered in a year.

Bose rolled and crushed her shoulders in his arms, her ribs in his hands. Lord, she smelled good. "Oh, thank you, brother," he sighed.

She said, "What?"

"Nothing," he said, desiring to kiss her more. Swallow her whole.

"No. What did you mean by that?"

"Girl, I did not mean nothing. No thing. Come here. Come right here."

But with heels of her hands she shoved him away. "What did you mean?" she demanded.

Dizzied by the pulque and the bewildering change in her mood, Bose gaped at her and stammered. "I didn't mean anything! Just . . ."

"Just what?"

He spoke up for himself in exasperation. "What do I know? This way of living, they say men share."

Her voice turned icy. "If you believe Quanah thinks you're *brothers* . . ." Bose glanced with alarm toward the drums and the singing. "And if you think he *sent* me. And if you think I'm something to *share* . . ."

When she was gone he lay there desolate with his head propped in his hands. As she lurched through the flap and trotted off through the trees a tall young man happened to be leaning against a cottonwood and looking that way. Quanah had come out of the peyote lodge to get a breath of air.

22

THE RIDERS WHO CAME OVER the rise above the camp weren't Bad Hand's soldiers. Their faces and horses were war-painted and they wore hats of buffalo scalp and horns; they were Eckitoacup, his son Tannap, and young Quohada who envied Quanah and his bunch and all the horses they had and were spoiling for a fight that would decree the band's future. But in passing the pipe, Eckitoacup said his purpose was to reclaim his honor and avenge Quanah's eloping with his son Tannap's rightfully claimed bride.

Quanah laughed grimly and watched them walk and prance their horses forward. "Come to make war on us," he remarked to Cohayyah, who had joined the band in the fall. When Mackenzie's soldiers overwhelmed the Kotsoteka on the North Fork of the Red, the young war leader Cohayyah had led the Meat Eaters who fought back with distinction and escaped. Though word spread among the soldiers and Texans that it was Quanah who stole back the twenty-five hundred Kotsoteka horses and mules from the soldiers, plus the herd of the Tonkawa scouts, he was actually many rivers away from the Red's North Fork at the time; that honor and feat belonged to Cohayyah. When the once-great warrior Mow-way proclaimed himself a peace chief and promised to keep his young men on the reservation at Fort Sill if Bad Hand would bring back the hostage wives and children, Cohayyah led belligerent Kotsoteka not to Parra-o-coom's camp, but rather to join Quanah's hellions on the Middle Concho.

The party of Eckitoacup and Tannap had not bothered to scout too well in going out for battle—they were outnumbered three to one. "They want a fight, let's give them one," said Cohayyah.

"No," Quanah growled. "No bloodshed over this. I'll take care of it."

He stomped through the bottom yelling at Black Rope to bring up Deer's Son, his warhorse. Weckeah came out to Quanah rigid with fear and blaming herself. "I knew they were coming," Weckeah said. "I knew they would."

"Don't get excited," he cut her off. "Nothing's going to happen. Nobody's going to get hurt. Those people are just confused."

Quanah didn't take time to paint his face or put on any battle finery except to fling on his headdress of hawk and eagle feathers that the Little Horses had given him. He wanted to remind Eckitoacup, his son, and their followers that he enjoyed the greater esteem as a warrior in their own camp. "Bose," he shouted. "Get your horse and bring your mouth pipe. Come with me."

Bose saddled and bridled Mackenzie's gray, and they rode out toward the oncoming party. "Play something," Quanah told him. "And sing as loud as you can." Quanah kicked the black into a lope, and the pacer bowed his fool neck and in his prissy gait stepped out to keep up, left legs swinging forward in tandem as the right ones came back. Reining with one hand, Bose stood up in the stirrups to keep from getting bounced sideward, and advanced on the intruders playing his mouth harp and singing. He had no idea what the conflict was about. He just recognized the buffalo horn hats and war paint on fifty or so faces. Under these conditions, on such short notice, the tune about town-trash cowboys would have to do.

> *While you're all so frisky I'll sing a little song*
> *Think a little horn of whiskey will help me along?*
> *It's all about the top hand who busted flat*
> *Bumming round town in his Mexican hat*

See him in town with a crowd that he knows
Rolling cigarettes and smoking through his nose

As they drew near the riders Quanah said, "Wish you could play a flute."

"How do you know I can't?"

Tannap had mirrors hanging from his earlobes, braids, and the bridle of his sorrel horse. He commenced beating his rifle against his war shield and booted the horse into a dance. Bose couldn't follow his rant except when he flung his hand and spat the words goineroibo tuh-tahvoa, nigger musician.

Quanah ignored Tannap and formally addressed his father as "Ta'pave," brother of all, then greeted the others, "Marúawekwai." Tell me all about it.

Eckitoacup inquired into his health.

"All right, and yours?" Quanah replied in kind.

Quanah turned his horse toward Tannap and with a smile addressed him. "Mirror man, did you bring your flute? Here's a man with another kind of wind-noise pipe. I thought the two of you might want to play and sing together. I can use your shield there for a drum."

"You'll find out what I do with my shield," Tannap growled.

Quanah's smile brightened. He turned to the old man and said he was certain they had not come to do evil, eit-ma-han'it.

"You are an arrogant man who continually insults us," Eckitoacup lashed out. "You come out here with no one but this songbird. One more warble out of him and I'll put an arrow in his gizzard."

"Oh, I hope not. He pipes and sings just in hopes of pleasing you. I have greeted you in courtesy, Ta'pave. My wife Weckeah respects you as father-in-law of her sister. She sends her good words to you and her sister."

"Weckeah is by rights *my* wife," Tannap yelled at Quanah. "She belongs to me. You stole and soiled her."

"Well, now. Soiled her." With his heels Quanah moved the black horse toward Tannap's smaller sorrel. Bose thought he was a gifted bully.

"This matter is the law of Our People," Eckitoacup said. "To make this wrong thing right, you have to give the woman back. Otherwise we fight."

"You're the one who's got it wrong," Quanah replied. "Weckeah is not mine to give or your son's to own. What you ask is never going to happen. She's carrying our child."

Tannap gave his shield a furious shake.

"You don't want to fight us," Quanah told Eckitoacup. "We are all Our People. What kind of bad medicine would make us fight each other? And look there," he said, pointing toward the camp. "All those men on horses, and there are those among them who are as hot-tempered and dangerous as your son. I pleaded with Cohayyah. I told him, 'Cohayyah, please don't get our men all riled up to fight. Let me ride out and talk to those people. It's my trouble; give me a chance to resolve it.'"

Unaware that Cohayyah and his followers had joined Quanah's band, Eckitoacup, Tannap, and the others gazed at the riders and horses emerging from the river bottom. Bose could see them counting.

"Let us hear your solution," said the old man, beginning to back down.

"You told my father-in-law you'd give him fifty horses if Weckeah would marry your son. When she married me instead, did Yellow Bear give them back?"

"No," he answered huffily.

"Of course not. But do you remember I also left you a gift of twenty more army horses the night we left?"

"Eckitoacup, go out in my herd and cut yourself out seventy horses or mules. And then cut out twenty more because this bothered you enough to come here. And then if you would—because

Yellow Bear is angry at me, and I don't know where the Quohada camp is—cut out fifty more and drive and give them to Yellow Bear. And then all these riders who came with you can pick out twenty more for themselves. My herder will show you which ones are mine. Some animals are favorites of mine and my wives and my friend here; the herder will move those aside. But there are plenty more excellent ones that you can choose from. When you're done, then come smoke and eat and tell us how it is with Our People and the camp of Parra-o-coom. If you believe I've wronged you, let these who came with you bear witness that I made it right."

Several riders in war paint and buffalo hats remarked on his generosity and wealth. Any prospect of a battle had evaporated. "And me?" fumed Tannap. "You think twenty head is going to satisfy me?"

Quanah squinted as if to give it great thought. "No, flute player. For hurting my eyes with glare off those mirrors, I'm going to give you ten."

Four days later, a solitary rider approached the camp. Yellow Bear rode through the lodges, past the stares, until he reached the four tipis built higher in the trees. He gave his horse to Bose to lead away, after first studying from head to toe this captive of foul complexion and surprising reputation. He put his arms around his daughter and held her for a long time. "Don't cry," he told her. He asked her to forgive him for being a stubborn old fool. Then he walked forward and gripped the arms of Quanah and said, "My son."

Yellow Bear beckoned everyone in the band to come close around. "Your raids, horses, and victories are the talk of Our People," he told them. "We Quohada are the leaders, and we must know we are all one band now. The attacks of the Texans and Bad Hand's soldiers have made us hard nuts, thick-shelled and small like the pecans shaken from trees on the Little Wichita. Parra-o-coom and the council have watched and heard you well. You have a fine camp here, but ours in Mulberry Canyon is better. We need your numbers and your courage and your ability, and you could stand some of the caution and wisdom that comes from having a camp with old men and a smoke lodge." People laughed. "It's time for you to come back."

On the occasion of their rejoining Para-o-coom's band, Quanah gave Bose back his mule and the Medicine Hat paint. Bose cut Mackenzie's gray back into the herd, compliments to anyone who wished to claim the fop. In the camp in Mulberry Canyon, people called out, "Naoquit!"—Rejoice! Quanah and his band were received like conquerors fresh home from the wars, but in the larger band hostility and suspicion once more outmatched the acceptance that had come Bose's way on the Middle Concho; now more than ever, he was Quanah's man. The adventure with To-ha-yea and the pulque couldn't be repeated, though he could scarcely breathe from the closeness when they were putting up the lodge poles and stretching the hides. They were outsiders, people of other tribes, and Quanah was not the only one watching them. "First chance I get, I'm going," Bose swore to himself the third night he slept on the new ground. In the large camp lodges were put up close together. He promised himself that while enduring the crescendo of cries and moans of her making love to Quanah. Weckeah must have heard them, too.

A few days later the midwives built a birth lodge out of brush. Only the midwives and Weckeah's mother, Nice Enough to Eat, were allowed inside when her water broke and the labor began. Mothers in Comanche childbirth stood, hanging to a strong frame of wood. Quanah fretted and cringed hearing her cries until at last the midwives called for the grandfather. Yellow Bear listened, nodded, and contained his disappointment. If it had been a grandson he would have exulted to Quanah, "Ehaitsma"—it's your closest friend. But he celebrated the birth of any healthy child and said, "Esamop'ma"—it's a girl. They named her Nahnacuh.

Quanah and Cohayyah had been plotting to sack Fort Concho and rescue the Kotsoteka hostages, but they waited too long. Even Parra-o-coom sent a Mexican boy he loved like a son to beg the Quakers at Fort Sill to no avail; the soldiers said that surrendering to reservation life was the only way the Kotsoteka would get their hostage families back. One day as a line of spring storms moved in, the Kotsoteka women and children were loaded in bluecoat wagons and under heavy guard hauled across what became two weeks of mud and floods toward the reservation in the Indian Territory. A horde of Texans of the breed inclined to live in Jacksboro got drunk and set out to lynch them, but with guns at the ready a captain and buffalo soldiers under Mackenzie's command ushered them across Red River. The reunions were made amid scenes of reported joy. An optimistic Quaker informed a correspondent from the *Daily National Republican* that the white road to Washington town was all built now; the wars on the southern plains were over.

Meanwhile, the Quohada firebrands in Mulberry Canyon prepared for battles that would chase the Texans into the Gulf of Mexico as the great chief Buffalo Hump had once done. Quanah found that Parra-o-coom's lungs were rapidly failing him, and during Quanah's months on the Middle Concho, the odd-looking shaman, Wolf Shit, had become the Quohada's rising young man. Isa-tai predicted that a comet, tatzinupecahpi, would blaze across the sky, and then correctly told them how many nights it would burn. He stated now that his medicine was so strong that no bullets could harm him, that he could breathe life into the dead. A lot of people believed him.

In the ravine of Mulberry Creek, Quanah watched Isa-tai with interest and amusement. No doubt about it, the shaman was a force and a rival. One day when Wolf Shit was making these claims to a crowd, Quanah called Bose aside and handed him his small hide bag that contained the alarm clock stolen from the army surgeon. "Can you still make this speak?"

"Claro," said Bose. "Where and when do you want?"

Quanah pointed with his chin at Wolf Shit and his crowd. "Put it back in the little sack, go over there, and set it on the ground near the prophet. Don't make a show of it. Just move on through."

Bose set the clock for an imminent time and did as he was told. The shaman was telling the crowd about how the world looked from the other side of sunrise when the bell erupted: BRAAANG.

He jumped high and far as his audience scattered.

Wolf Shit glared at the laughter of Quanah and Bose—took special note of Bose—and tried to recapture his crowd. "I did that," he assured them. "Make it happen all the time."

Before the season of raids began they had to turn to the work of making sure they'd not go hungry the next winter. The big hunt occurred in early summer when the buffalo had finished molting and their coats were prime. The night before it began they had a Buffalo Dance, and it was one in which women danced with the men. The drummers were beating on the skins, and the best singers were singing; the women formed a line and then sashayed across the dancing ground and picked out the ones they wanted to dance with. Quanah saw To-ha-yea hanging back in the shadows, as she always did. Weckeah approached her and made To-ha-yea take her hand. The two of them came across the ground together—several dancers gave them a curious look. Weckeah stretched out her other hand to Quanah and beckoned for him to come. At first Quanah was puzzled, but before he knew it, he was out there in the firelight dancing with both of them. Some of the hunters and lovers were charmed by their inclusion of the Apache. Others were incensed.

The Comanches never hunted buffalo with guns. It was disrespectful to the prey and impractical. Rifle explosions at close range would have panicked and scattered them; the riders wanted to keep them hazed in a running circle. The hunters rode only in their breechclouts because it was ritual and they wanted nothing between their horses' shoulders and their knees. All commands were passed on with pressure from their legs, for their hands were occupied. The bowmen raced their horses right up on the hips of the heaving bison. A good horse veered away as soon as he heard the bowstring snap. The buffalo might run some distance, but if the bowman's aim was good, it would begin to stagger wildly and fall.

Bose was surprised that Quanah subjected his black war horse to such peril. Quanah could ride and he was strong, but he had found he had little gift or patience for a bow and arrow. He preferred to hunt with the lance that only warriors of his stature possessed. The black had to run even closer to the buffalo than the horses ridden by hunters with bows. If the bison made one feint with its head the black leaped away; the horse had to leave it up to Quanah to remain astride, for he could easily get flipped upside-down or gored. Riding only with his knees, Quanah gripped the lance with both hands. As they plunged over a knoll he raised the long spear in one relaxed motion and then plunged it with the practiced ease of a man chopping wood. As they thundered on, Quanah kept the horse close, moving the lance around and then pulling it out, taking care not to break the shaft. The bison ran several more strides, but Quanah's thrust had pierced the heart and arteries, and it abruptly pitched to its knees, a fount of red spewing on the short mesquite grass.

Bose:

I SAW IT HAPPEN; we were in camp after their first big hunt. The hunters had quartered up their kills so the women could get started on the hides. They'd eaten themselves full of raw meat, starting with the liver and glands. I told them that since I hadn't hunted, in good conscience I had to wait. The women were slicing the winter's stock in thin strips that they hung on drying racks, which stood like a field of crosses all around the camp. The drying racks were so crowded it was hard to walk between them, but they had to put them up that close to keep the meat from trotting off in the jaws of coyotes and wolves. Fresh hides were stretched out and staked to the ground. While the women labored, the hunters lay about and snored. Quanah's peyote bunch had been up all night, and he had dragged out a robe and was sprawled in shade with the long fingers of his hands interlocked on his belly.

I was sitting on the ground with my back against the trunk of a walnut tree, reading part of a book. You didn't get much choice of books, because raiders just grabbed them and dumped them in sacks for later use packing their shields. Often as not they tore off the backs and ripped them up before they got back to the main camp. And there was some risk in showing I was able to read. But Quanah was all right with it, and the doctor and his wife had brought me up reading—I have to give them credit for that. The coverless book I'd picked out of the pile that day was written by an army officer named Randolph Marcy; it was called *An Exploration of the Red River of Louisiana in the Year 1852.*

Our camp along Mulberry Creek was a long way from Louisiana, but the stream was a tributary of the Red, and I flipped through the pages with interest. A heading caught my eye: "Hostility to Negroes." Marcy wrote that "upon inquiring of them the cause of their hostility to the blacks," the Comanches told him "it was because they were slaves to the whites; they felt sorry for them. I suspect, however, that they were actuated by other motivations than they cared about acknowledging, and that instead of wishing to better their condition by sending them to another world, where they would be released from the fetters of bondage, they were apprehensive . . ."

And he believed that they didn't want any new rivals interfering with their raiding. I read on about the Comanches' approach to slavery, which the soldier confused with captivity. No question I was fortunate because of Quanah's feelings on that score. Marcy had strong opinions about the subject, though: "These people, who are so extremely jealous of their own freedom that they will often commit suicide rather than be taken prisoners, are the more prone to enslave others, and this dominant principle is carried to the greatest extreme so far as regards their women. A beast of burden and a slave to the will of her brutal master, yet, strange as it may appear, the Comanche woman seems contented with her lot, and submits to her fate without a murmur. The hardships imposed upon the females are most severe and cruel. The distance of rank and consideration which exists between the black slave and his master is not greater than between the Comanche warrior and his wife. Every degrading office that is imposed upon the black by the most tyrannical master falls, among the Comanches, to the lot of the wretched female. They, in common with other Indians, are not a prolific race; indeed, it is seldom that a woman has more than three or four children. Many of these, owing to unavoidable exposure, die young; the boys, however, are nurtured with care and treated with great kindness by their mothers, while the girls are frequently beaten and abused unmercifully. I have never seen an idiot, or one that was naturally deformed, among them."

No, sir, because deformed infants were killed. I'd lived through the gloom and bad medicine when one of these murders was carried out. They also killed one of the babies if a mother produced the extreme bad medicine of twins. Strange taboo, I'd say. I looked at the women out in the heat on their hands and knees and could see how a learned white man visiting a Comanche camp might find the men sorry and the women wretched, but his coo-cooing of sympathy about nego slavery wasn't worth a rat's ass to me.

I skimmed on and—be damn!—found myself reading this: "There is at this time a white woman among the Middle Comanches, by the name of Parker, who, with her brother, was captured while they were young children, from their father's house in the western part of Texas." He got that wrong, thought Bose; the Navasota was an east Texas stream. Still: "This woman has adopted all the habits and peculiarities of the Comanches, has an Indian husband and children, and cannot be persuaded to leave them. The brother of the woman, who had been ransomed by a trader and brought home to his relatives, was sent back by his mother for the purpose of endeavoring to prevail upon his sister to leave the Indians and return to her family; but he stated to me that on his arrival she refused to listen to the proposition, saying that her husband, children, and all that she held most dear, were with the Indians, and there she should remain."

Right there on page 103 this man was writing about Quanah when he was about five years old, and his mother, his father, his brother, his sister, and his mysterious uncle. What this would mean to him, I didn't know, but I had to tell him. I looked over and he was still snoring, sleeping off the peyote.

On their knees, the women had scraped the hides clean of bits of meat, and were working them soft and pliant. Some toothless old women champed on them with their gums, acting like it wasn't an unpleasant way to pass the time. Others, who included Weckeah and To-ha-yea, were rubbing brains of the fresh kills into the hides with the heels of their hands. It was supposed to help the tanning in some way. Weckeah's mother was fanning flies away from the little girl's cradleboard in the shade of a lodge.

I marked the book's place with a wildflower and watched To-ha-yea. She had on one of those pretty fringed blouses that I guess she brought with her when she and Quanah married. All at once she jumped up, staring at the mess on her hands and arms and moccasin boots, and like it was poison she started trying to wipe the gore off her fine buckskin. She started screaming at Quanah, who jerked awake and leapt to his feet like an arrow had landed beside his ear. It was no conversation: the only one taking part in that ass-chewing was an Apache girl who'd had enough.

"No puedo hacerlo!" she raged. "No más! Llégueme a mi casa en las montañas, a donde puedo respirar." I can't do it anymore. Take me home to the mountains, where I can breathe.

269

23

QUANAH HAD NEVER BEFORE asked permission to come inside Bose's lodge—courtesy wasn't part of his nature—but he had also never before come through the flap pointing a .44 Colt. "She's doing this because of you!" he yelled.

"Bullshit, Quanah!"

"Otra vez?" he said, frowning.

As Bose had gained a loose grasp on the Comanches' dialect, the Spanish he and Quanah spoke also took on some English. Though the sound of it made Quanah wince, he was bewitched by the language his mother spoke as a child and doubtless in the last lost years of her life. "So many words that sound the same but mean something else," he once complained to Bose. "These have to be people with a lot to hide."

But there was nothing reflective about this exchange—Quanah jammed the gun barrel hard against his forehead. "Es una palabra de inglés," Bose tried to calm him down. "It's an expression of disbelief."

"Are you calling me a liar?" demanded Quanah.

"No, I'm not. I'm just saying you're wrong."

"Do you think I'm blind?"

"I don't know what you see. From the first day it was like you were running a choice filly in with an ugly jackass—like you were amused by the little *mule* that might pop out. But look at me, Quanah. Listen to me. It didn't happen. It never did. You do what you have to do, but don't blame me for this. You did it without any help from me. It's no one's fault but your own."

After some ragged breathing on both their parts Quanah sighed and said, "You're right." Hugely distracted, he plopped on the ground with the gun still cocked. Bose flinched and raised a hand toward the muzzle, as if that were any protection. "Sorry," said Quanah, letting the hammer down.

He sat disconsolate with his forearms propped on his knees, the grip of the Colt now loose in his hand. "There'll never be another one like her," he said. "But I couldn't stand not to marry Weckeah. I had to try to have them both."

"I'm sorry she's leaving, too. Sorry for us all."

Quanah squeezed his temples with the fingers of his left hand. He had the most graceful hands. "You have to take her," Quanah said.

"What?"

With another sigh Quanah pitched the gun on Bose's sleeping robe. "Her people live way across the llano. Her father's ranchería could be in one of a half dozen mountain ranges. They could be raiding towns and dodging rurales in Mexico. Who knows if she'll want to stay around him once she finds him? I just know what she's yelling at me now, and I can't be the one to take her. Even if I could be away from here that long, she wouldn't tolerate the company. There's no one I trust to get her there safe but you."

After a moment Quanah went on. "You've got a good horse and mule. The mare she rides is sound enough. You can have any others you want. You'll need back your guns, packsaddle, and saddlebags. And your sack of money." Quanah smiled. "The look on your face. You thought I stole it? Pissed it away buying guns and smoke from comancheros? You think your gold was anything to me but loose weight to haul around?"

Quanah dug his uncle's compass out of his pouch and flicked open the lid. "The Mescaleros' homeland is a valley of a New Mexico stream called Río Bonito. A trader told me the Big Whiteass Grant carved off most of their country but gave them a reservation there. Unless Old Wolf, To-ha-yea's father, has changed, he'd rather be dead than living on a reservation, but she can find people there who speak her language and tell her where to look." He indicated the compass and its needle quivering at the north. "You can find your way with this."

"No." Bose waved off the compass. "That's your uncle's gift. You need to keep that. Anyway I'm not taking her across the llano. I'm afraid of it."

"Well, you'll have to cross some of it," Quanah argued, "and better riders than you have gotten lost out there. I'm going to send you down one of the comanchero trails. You know those red and white cliffs yonder are Palo Duro Canyon, which Mulberry Canyon opens into. In the bottom of Palo Duro you'll follow the headwater of Red River. The water is clear and deep in some places but you won't much like the taste of its salt. No matter—if you just keep following the stream-bed, choosing the creek that flows the strongest when two of them run together, you won't get lost. You'll find the greatest of the canyons is like the others. It's eventually eaten by the llano. The red rock buckles in the ground and then the chalk rock is swallowed up, too. You come out on the sameness, the mesquite and prairie—and you think, what happened to the canyon?"

Quanah pressed the compass in Bose's hand with a look that was naked, holding not much back. "I'm worried about her making it, not you. Give it back to me sometime, if you have a chance. Now, when there's no more canyon and the tributaries of the Red are all dry creeks, you'll use it to cross the plains northwest for two or three days. You'll need to carry water, but unless you wander in a circle you'll come on the valley of the Canadian. Follow the Canadian west to the source, which you'll know by a big landmark mountain that used to explode and run rivers of fire. So the grandfathers say. Capulin Mountain's near the source of the Pecos, country you know through your travels and your friend the Leopard Coat Man. Follow the Pecos south, staying away from all the towns—they're comanchero towns. The whites have changed the name of Bosque Redondo to Fort Sumner. South of that one, you'll go west along a tributary stream called Río Hondo, toward mountains that by then could have snow. At the foot of those mountains you'll find the valley of the Río Bonito—and you'll have carried her home to the Mescaleros." There was a catch in his Quanah's throat. "It's many days ride, and it's dangerous. But you'll have her."

From Quanah's herd, Bose picked out two horses. One was a Roman-nosed little Indian mare that had a reputation of being able to run. Bose would ride the black mule and trail the paint, saddled and ready to go. To-ha-yea would do the same with the two brown mares. For a pack animal he chose a big gelding stolen from the army. The horse had a yellow coat with a black mane and tail, the color pattern that Comanches called dunnia. The buckskin gelding stood seventeen hands tall and was very broad; he had some European plow horse in his line. He was no fast runner, but he did what you asked him to, and didn't seem to mind being loaded with packsaddle and panniers. Someone had botched the job of altering the big letters U. S. on the gelding's hip, which was unfortunate, but it was a good sound work horse.

Bose spent most of a day trimming hooves until they were glossy and free of scales and cracks. The hooves of To-ha-yea's unshod sorrel actually looked the best. Indian horses were like mustangs—for the most part their hooves took care of themselves. Comanches pried the iron shoes off a stolen horse, if they could do it without injuring the hooves. They didn't like the noise, and the shoes made the horses less sure-footed.

The shoes of Tricks and Juneteen were worn but they still fit tightly—Goodnight always employed a first-rate farrier. One of the front shoes of the big army horse alarmed him a little. He tightened it down as best he could, using Quanah's hammer and a pouch of nails he'd scavenged. Quanah listened to the ticking and with amused curiosity watched him put the hammer to the use it was designed for. But the morning they rode out of the camp in Mulberry Canyon, Quanah just removed himself. Bose knew he was feeling low; still he thought it was cowardly to send Weckeah up with the cradleboard and their baby and give To-ha-yea her only parting words and embrace. No one else in the band said a word to her. Bose could tell from the clench of To-ha-yea's jaws and the glistening of her eyes that her mind and heart were in wild disorder. Bose clicked his tongue at Juneteen and gave the lead ropes of the paint and heavily loaded dun gelding a yank. In his haste he wasn't just trying to spare To-ha-yea's feelings. Quanah's absence also weighed on Bose. It was the second time in his life that some man had presumed to set him free.

During the past months Bose had come to know the twists, turns, and junctions of the canyonlands as well as any man not born to them. The rush and drip of water was the canyons' architect; the sheerest and deepest ones were nothing but erosion gullies cut for thousands of years in a rocky and crumble-soiled plateau that marked the south end of the high plains. Bose, To-ha-yea, and the five animals made progress slowly, crossing Mulberry Creek back and forth. They rode all day and after a cold supper in violet dusk they rolled into their bedrolls with hardly any words said. But the next morning dawned clean-aired and bright, with little wind and dust as the sun climbed higher, and the Palo Duro ravine coaxed them out of their introspection and gloom. If they had approached it on the llano they wouldn't have seen the precipice until they were right on top of it. Etched with white streaks of gypsum, the cliffs and broken peaks and mesas rose up with the same successions of shale, clay, and caliche, sandstone overlain by limestone, all of it painted shades of maroon, yellow, lavender, cream. Gnarled junipers, blooming clumps of primrose, and loco-weed found root in seams of rock five hundred feet above the canyon floor. Island prairies found purchase on shelves of cliff. Divided on the floor by the winding river, pink sand bed, and corridor of willows and cottonwoods, Palo Duro was a netherworld of buffalo grass, sunflowers, shin oak, mountain mahogany, red cedars that stood as tall and broad as magnolias in some southern town yard.

"Bizan," To-ha-yea remarked.

"What?" said Bose.

"It means Woman without Husband. Widowed or divorced."

"Oh."

She leaned forward and stroked the neck of the mare. "Do not say you're sorry. I'm not."

"Wasn't about to." But a few moments later, "You heal so fast?"

"No, and doubt I ever will, in all my heart. But I like being with you—and not having to look over our shoulders all the time." She bumped the sorrel with her heels and jogged on ahead.

There was not much wildlife, just some buzzards lazing over the chasm, but all around they saw beings in the columns and perches of stone: a head of a bear, a camel kneeling on a cliff, a tall man standing with a tilt of his hat. As the river snaked around, the figures of stone would go away and reappear as mysteriously as settings and risings of the moon. They rode until the backs and blankets of the horses and mule were soaked. They rounded a bend of the river and fractured wall of stone and encountered a waterfall that spilled off a ledge and filled a deep green pool about fifty yards across. "We could rest them and let them drink," said Bose. "Ride on in a while if you want."

"I'm tired, and it's pretty," she said. "Let's stop here for the night."

They let the animals wade out in the shallows and slurp their fills, then Bose unsaddled Juneteen and hung on the lead rope as the mule took his requisite roll in the dirt. He wriggled on his back and flailed his hooves like a big puppy, then huffed and rolled the other way and stood back up, giving himself a good shake. He laid back his ears, bared his long teeth, and honked and wheezed them a fond serenade. "We're laughing at you," said Bose. "Yeah, you." He tied the mule to a cedar, laid out his saddle and blanket to air, relieved the army horse of the packsaddles and panniers, then hobbled them all out to graze. When Bose finished his tasks and looked around, To-ha-yea was gone, and for a moment it unnerved him.

"In here," she called.

He walked to the bank and encountered her clothes and moccasin boots, then saw her treading water in the shade of the rock ledge. She raised her arms and sent herself plunging down, then burst up splashing and grinning. "Feels good," she said, swimming for a moment on her back. Her breasts and thighs gleamed as she came back out in the sun.

"Come in," she said. "Don't you want?"

He sat down and wrestled with a boot. "I'm not much of a swimmer."

"I won't let you drown."

Her arms were slick with soap as he drifted near. She washed her hair and went under again. "Where on earth did you get soap?" he asked when she bobbed back up.

"Remember when we went to find the honey water?"

"Hard to forget."

"And I was cutting up roots of cactus? That short spiky kind that can hurt horses' hooves?"

On her stomach she made a frog kick with her legs and cruised toward him. He looked down the slope of her shoulders and back, her ass and legs.

"Lechuguilla," he said.

"Si, eso." To-ha-yea raised her hand and showed him the pale chunk. As he swam toward her she leaned back, keeping herself buoyant with the waving movement of her arms. The line of water on her breasts and shoulders made a fine blouse. "Let me wash you," she said.

Soon they were all over each other. Before he lost the opportunity and what remained of his control he located a place where the rock ledge was smooth and he could keep his footing on the bottom. She enfolded him with her legs and kissed him with her tongue and gasped as he came into her.

"Lord, lord," he said.

"What?"

"Nothing. You cured me trying to talk."

She leaned away from him and put her hands on the back of his neck. "Are you being smart?"

His hands roamed her back and gave the soft points of her hips a gentle readjusting shove. "No. I was just, hoo, looking for something."

"Well, you found it. Yes you did." She raised her thighs against his sides and pulled herself up, the globes of her bottom resting in his hands. A gush of bubbles rose from the delicate shiver and gripping of their flesh. "Bose Ikard," she whispered, nipping him on the cheek. "I have wanted this so long."

24

CAPULIN MOUNTAIN LOOKED LIKE half the summit had been blown off, and lava cinders were indeed strewn all over northeast New Mexico Territory. White men claimed the volcano was dead now, but people who knew and lived around the mountain were certain it could erupt anytime, because sleet and snow would not stick to the rocks and ground. Bose and To-ha-yea let the horses and mule gulp their bellies full of water that seeped out through the bunchgrass springs called vegas, but he said, "It wouldn't be wise to camp here."

Though they'd encountered no comanchero riders or wagons, that luck could change. The Cimarron Cutoff of the Santa Fe Trail came around the other side of the mountain; the wagons of teamsters, freighters, and settlers were a magnet for parties of raiders of many tribes. Named for those marshes in the middle of a dry plain, Las Vegas, New Mexico, was close by and known for the enthusiasm of its vigilantes. The Canadian headwater's army post, Fort Bascom, was staffed with quartermasters who bought beef stolen off Texas ranches by Comanches and Kiowas and bartered it on to the comancheros. The butchers incinerated the branded hides in a furnace, and officers took their cut professing ignorance of all that. But however corrupt, no army post felt hospitable to a scout who might have a price on his head for desertion and consorting with the enemy.

Bose thought of going back over the Ratón Pass and presenting To-ha-yea to Goodnight at his ranch in the Greenhorn Mountains, then considered the line of bars and bordellos and the piss-smelling mud streets they'd have to negotiate on the periphery of Fort Union, the big supply post at the junction of the two branches of the trail; then he thought of the dour eyes and pinched mouth of Mary Goodnight, and the urge to call on Mister Charlie faded.

As the horses and mule sucked marsh water through their teeth and raised their dripping chins, Bose slipped one boot out of the stirrup and sat back on Juneteen with his leg propped across the saddle horn. "We could go west straight from here," he proposed, "on to California. The gold rushers and Mormons have already cut and marked roads that way. I heard of a place out there on the Pacific called Point Reyes. Or we could go to San Francisco and find out what a city's like. Or a place called the Russian River where there's redwood forest and government grazing leases that they're all but giving away. A man gave me a little sack of gold, and it's enough to start and stock a ranch. We could get one going and then come find your father. I wouldn't ask you to marry me, To-ha-yea. Just go somewhere and live with me, as long as you can stand it. I'm a good man, and with you I'd make a better one."

It was the most heartfelt speech Bose had ever made. She answered with deflection, as was her habit. "The man who gave you gold was the white father, the doctor who made you a slave?"

"No, that man's dead and gone. I'm talking about the one who hired me to go up the trails with his cattle."

"He calls you a friend then sends you away and tries to relieve his guilt with gold."

"Fair enough . . ."

"Gold seekers are the worst kind of white eyes," she said. "They'll eat dirt and drink slime trying to get their hands on it. But they're cursed by the Mountain Gods, because gold is the sun, Ussen Himself, a part of the sun that Apache people can touch. We don't have to go to California. We know where it lies in these mountains, and we keep it secret. My father and his riders would rob the stages and mail trains but especially the caravans of miners; they took the white eyes' gold, pried it out of their teeth with knives, and threw it off cliffs, sank it in the caves of springs. I don't want anything to do with white eyes' gold, Bose Ikard."

But god damn it, Bose had just offered her all of himself he had, and she flung it back at him like she was throwing out dishwater. His love was not the easiest woman in the world to get along with. He took his leg off the pommel and gave his hat brim a downward yank. "You won't see me trying to pan rocks out of a creek or carrying a pick into some mine," he tried to explain, instead of just roaring the hurt and anger in his head. "Gold's nothing but a word, the way I use it. It's money, it's rocks, and some people use rocks to reckon the worth of what they have and want. It's just like a Comanche's horses, a Kiowa's mules. And I've seen you wearing silver."

She gave him a strange look. "Silver's not the same as gold."

"I like you best wearing nothing. Maybe a necklace."

Her cheeks and throat colored with pleasure. "Yes, you and I do have that. Who would give that up for gold? But people do it all the time." She moved her horse and put her hand on his arm. "I have to go make sure that my father's all right. I can take care of myself, if you want to go to California. I hope you won't. I'm asking you not to. Come with me. And in good time we'll see what you're going to do with your ranchería, and with me."

So they hewed to the plan and turned southwest, toward the foothills of the Sangre de Cristos, and amid rainy, sweet-smelling pinewoods and meadows they found the old pueblo and the rowdy mountain stream that became the languid and silted Pecos. Covering about fifteen miles a day, they built low fires to cook and keep gnats and horseflies at bay. They made love in his bedroll with his rifle and her shotgun in bare arms' reach. They gave wide berth to the comanchero villages of Anton Chico, Santa Rosa, and Puerto de Luna. Below those towns the Pecos advanced its eastward meander onto the llano. Wind swept along the stands of cottonwood and willow and from the riverbed raised clouds of sand that looked like smoke.

In chancing on the book of frontier travels by the soldier Randolph Marcy, Bose had noticed that he included expert drawings of maps. Before they left the Quohada camp, Bose tore out the page on New Mexico Territory and western Texas. He studied how the Pecos and its parent stream the Río Grande shared the water of New Mexico on almost parallel paths before parting and finally finding each other below the Texas wilderness of Big Bend. To-ha-yea watched with curiosity as Bose eyed the sun then positioned the piece of paper on the ground, just so. The Pecos was making an eastward bend but would come back around well north of the mouth of the Río Hondo. He thought that by using Quanah's compass they could strike almost due south and miss Fort Sumner by miles, sure to find the Pecos again by the landmarks Marcy called La Espía Peak—the spy—and Haystack Mountain.

But they'd barely broken camp the next morning when the big dun packhorse started limping. He was throwing that army shoe off his front right hoof. Bose thought of just abandoning the horse, but that would just be feeding him to wolves or a mountain lion. They had to go into town and locate a farrier. He moved the packsaddle and panniers to the back of Juneteen, cinched his riding saddle loosely on the dun, and let him come slowly along the soft ground of the river bottom; by the time they approached Fort Sumner, the sun was nearly down. He would have to put up their animals in a livery and hope the stableman would allow a black man and an Apache woman to bed down in the stalls. He didn't mention his fear to To-ha-yea. He didn't have to. She had more history in this place, the old Bosque Redondo, than he did.

The Swede farrier was not hard to find. Pieces of scavenged iron were scattered all over his yard. He demanded a tidy sum for his service, but said he'd bend a shoe to fit the big hoof the next morning. Bose told him to put a new one on the left hoof as well. He didn't want to tarry in this town jerry-built out of an abandoned army post, but he didn't want the packhorse throwing another shoe either. The farrier directed them to the livery, where a square-headed Pole agreed to stable the animals. He said he charged the same sleeping rates as the hotel, which this time of day, he cheerfully allowed, was already booked up for the whoring. Bose and To-ha-yea began watering, feeding, and brushing the horses and mule, but they hadn't come into town unobserved. A young fellow with a toothy and insolent grin slouched in the stable and said, "Is your name Ikard?"

Bose gave him a glance and acknowledged it was. The first thing that struck him about the boy was that he wore lace-up shoes, not boots. Then Bose placed him. His legs had shot up under him, and he had pimples on his cheeks and peach-fuzz on his chin, but it was the boy he parried with in Santa Fe.

Billy the Kid smirked. "Don Lucien Maxwell and Pat Garrett would like to invite you and the lady to join them for refreshments at Beaver Smith's Saloon."

Bose tried to beg off. "Oh, we're much obliged. But we're dusty and saddle-sore. Had a packhorse throw a shoe —"

"I said Lucien Maxwell. The Don."

To-ha-yea watched Bose with quiet alarm. "Está bien," he told her. "Two men here kind of know me. They want us to come see them in a while."

"I could have told her that and more," said the boy. "Tú eres," he launched on a mission of sweet-talking, "la flora más bonita que este camino viejo y fatigado ha te visto." The prettiest flower this tired old road has seen . . . He was grinning, joking, trying to get a smile out of her.

"I met you once," Bose set out to nip that in the bud.

"That right?" said the boy, tilting his head again.

"Sure is. Your name's Henry."

"Nope. Must have been somebody else. My name's Billy."

"Yeah, that too. We talked about your name many names. It was another stable, in Santa Fe. I watched you bravely murder a cat."

The boy's eyes and slack-jawed mouth gained a trace of recognition. "Well, come on, the gentlemen are waiting, and they'll be tickled to see you."

Bose rented lockboxes from the stableman, not caring much for the look of their sturdiness, and followed the boy across a barren patch that had been the fort's parade ground. Staring at the place where as a little girl she'd been made to go hungry amid several thousand Navajos, To-ha-yea clung to his arm.

The saloon hadn't changed. Keno, monte, and draw poker tables were starting to fill up with a rough crowd of drifters, drunks, and comancheros who smelled of sheep lanolin. The bar's centerpiece was still the big jar of pulque poured over the coiled remains of the rattlesnake. But tall Pat Garrett now manned the drink-pouring side. He'd trimmed his black moustache and had a roughly scissored haircut. "Come in, come in," he greeted them.

"Mister Garrett," said Bose, reaching across the bar to shake his hand. He indicated To-ha-yea. "This is my friend."

"Pretty thing," said Garrett.

"I'll say," the boy put in.

"Shut up, Billy," said a broad-shouldered man with his forearms on the bar. Lucien Maxwell wore his signature black whipcords, a red silk scarf tied under his shirt collar, and a low-crowned hat pulled toward his nose and an unlit cigar he was chewing. He looked to have rallied since the last time Bose saw him, in his nightshirt and spurs. Maxwell looked Bose up and down and said, "Yes, I recall you now. Goodnight's man. Used to call on us up on the Cimarron. Stingy and stiff-assed little man, Goodnight was, but I liked him. We told some raring good lies and did some business together. Where is he now?"

"Outside Pueblo, Colorado."

The Don nodded and gave To-ha-yea a longer look. "She a Navajo?"

"No, sir. Mescalero Apache."

"Ah."

"What can I get you?" said Garrett, giving the bar a slap.

"Just a beer," said Bose. She was staring at the scales of rattle-snake afloat in the pulque. "Some kind of soda water for her."

"I've got a good dandelion and licorice root beer," said Garrett.

"That'll be fine." Bose watched her blink at the strange taste and then take a second sip. His beer was flat. "What happened to Beaver?" he asked.

"What did you say?" Maxwell all but snarled.

Bose was startled by his tone of voice. "I was just surprised to find Mister Garrett the barman. Sign outside still says Beaver Smith's Saloon."

"Oh. I thought you meant the trapping trade. There was a lot of money to be made for a while." The Don pointed at a man sleeping with his head on his arms at one of the tables. "That's what hap-pened to Beaver."

"I'm just helping out the Don's son Pete," Garrett explained. "He manages the place."

"Truth is," said the Don, "I'm helping Patrick here out. He's hav-ing a little trouble walking. I'd like to have seen a man six-foot-five get taken down and chewed on by a three hundred fifty pound sow."

Lucien Maxwell might have married in a way once that made him the biggest landowner in the country, but who appointed this spiteful man *the Don*? In this shambling wreck of a place where gov-ernment once tried to imprison two tribes of enemies, maybe he'd bought and gotten what he deserved.

Garrett was pouring whiskeys. "What brings you to Sumner, Ikard?"

Just then Bose overheard a snatch of conversation from one of the tables that seized the muscles between his shoulder blades and spine: "*Who let that Indian in here?*" Knowing better than to look around, Bose said, "Oh, we had a packhorse throw a shoe. Be here for the night. But it's good seeing you again. What came of your surveying and buffalo hunting, Mister Garrett?"

"Hah!" the Don exulted. "Can I tell that story, too?"

Garrett smiled his consent.

"Comanches put him out of business real quick. Burned every one of his hides and stole his horses. But while Patrick and his partner were still trying to make a go of it, a hard cold rain set in; all they could do was watch the cook try to get buffalo chips to burn. Had a boy with 'em named Joey Briscoe. He'd found a little creek running, and he was trying to do his laundry. Boy was carrying on about how much his fingers hurt from the cold, and Patrick remarked that it would take a Catholic Irishman to be stupid enough to try to wash clothes in mud."

"Just funning him," said Garrett, blushing slightly.

"Joey was a little fellow, but he jumped up trying to fight him. Patrick knocked him down . . . how many times?"

"Eight, nine," Garrett replied with modesty and regret.

"And the boy wouldn't quit," the Don went on.

"I kept telling him."

"Next thing you know, the boy starts bawling, grabs an axe, and commences trying to kill Patrick, who's running around the cook's wagon, and the boy's winging that blade at his back and head. Patrick gets tired of that and on the run snatches up his Winchester. Next thing the boy knows he's on his back in the fire, shot bad in his brisket. Amazed at what he's done, Patrick saddles his horse and gallops him in circles. Look out, the skinners are yelling, here he comes again! As best we know, the killing of Joey Briscoe transpired over the line in Texas, but Patrick collects his wits and rides all the way here to turn himself in. Grand jury hears his testimony and declares a no-bill—clear case of self-defense." The Don looked at his barman. "Did I do it justice, Patrick?"

"Near enough," said Garrett.

"Reckon so," Maxwell cackled. "I was the jury foreman."

The boy who called himself Billy Bonney was employed as a fetchit for the Don and his barman. He was barely sixteen, but he was on the run from an indictment and two warrants that could get him hanged. He had been a schoolboy running with a gang of urchins people in Silver City called "street Arabs" when his mother, who owned a boarding house, went to her final bed with consumption. The stepfather William Antrim was trying to eke a living out of card games in the mining camps and elected to cut Henry and his brother Joe loose. Henry first got caught stealing clothes from a Chinese laundryman. A sheriff locked him in a jail that was a little stone house with an iron door and bars on the windows, but a homesteader had sensibly built it with a fireplace. The prisoner skinned up the chimney and took off on foot, covered in soot. He stole a horse with enough Mexicans watching for him to be charged with that major crime. And as it often happened to Henry, who was a poor rider, he got thrown by the horse.

The name on his arrest warrant for the horse theft was Kid Antrim alias Henry McCarty alias Henry Antrim. Still using a combination of those names, he found livery work at Camp Union, Arizona, a dreary post in the remote desert north of Tucson. During his residence in the motley town built around Camp Union, a band of Aravaipa Apaches set up a ranchería in a nearby canyon in hopes of calling off their war with local sheepherders and gaining protection from the army. Before dawn one morning, a gang of herders and San Xavier Papago Indians crept in the camp and butchered a hundred eighteen Aravaipas in half an hour. They also carried off children too young to remember, or at least testify, with plans to sell them in the child slave trade that flourished in the Mexican border country. The Kid was aware of his many faults but believed that was rotten behavior. The months at Camp Union stirred in Henry a great deal of sympathy and affinity for Apaches—especially young girls. The hard life made them leather-faced crones if they lived to forty, but when they were coming out as White Painted Woman they were famous for their looks.

Henry got crosswise at Camp Union with a burly farrier named Frank Cahill, who pummeled him twice then called him a son of a bitch in a dice game. The kid pulled a gun from his vest and shot the bully. Cahill lived long enough to make a statement to a marshal in which he identified the boy as his killer and asked that his body be sent to his sister for burial. The Arizona indictment named Kid Antrim and his aliases for first degree murder of Cahill. Some witnesses claimed that a fair grand jury would have judged it manslaughter, at worst. That was when he arrived in Fort Sumner, and on ranches close around he became Billy Bonney, alias Kid Bonney and, eventually, Billy the Kid.

Though To-ha-yea was three or four years older than Billy, that didn't stop him from trying to court her in Beaver Smith's Saloon. He slathered her with Spanish lines he'd picked up in the songs of mariachis and tried to keep her drinking root beer, which was also sold as cough syrup and contained some alcohol. He asked her to run off with him to Chihuahua City. Billy gave no thought to Bose as a rival—he was a nigger. Billy thought, I'm going to get her away from him and then steal his horse.

Billy sidled next to him and propped his elbows on the bar. "What are you drinking there?" he pleasantly inquired.

"Sotol." Bose felt the need for something with a little more punch than the flat warm beer. The kid turned to Garrett and raised two fingers. "Pulque for me, another sotol for our guest."

"You're too young to drink in here," said Garrett, who was wincing from the hog bites' wear and tear on his legs. It was hard for him to be on his feet.

"That's what they always say," Billy told Bose, grinning.

Garrett ladled pulque from the pickled rattlesnake jar and poured it in a glass, then refilled Bose's from the sotol bottle. The kid raised his glass and proposed a toast. "To good-looking women, don't matter what shade or what they speak." Bose shrugged and ticked Billy's glass.

Billy watched To-ha-yea, who was fending off the hustle of a couple of comancheros. "I do admire them beauties, tell the world I do," Billy announced, tossing down the last of his pulque and popping his glass on the bar.

"Tell you what I heard about Apaches," he said, turning to Bose. "When their men go off warring and make it back, girls who ain't virgins or already claimed, they take off all their clothes and paint themselves up like their favorite warriors, and they dance till the fire goes out. Then go off in the dark and reward them fighters good. Who needs virgins?" Watching her, he mused, "Darling, darling, would you dance for me? I'd go to war for you. I'd lick off all your paint."

Bose was debating whether to slap the punk when Maxwell, who was drinking gin and bitters, leaned close for a private word. "Don't mind Billy's bullshit. Knock him down if he gets to bothering you. Garrett, now, he's a different caliber of person. I'm encouraging him to run for sheriff when we get to be a county. Ikard, you may recall from your nights on the Cimarron that I like to provide my guests first-class housekeepers. How much would you take for her?"

Take for her?

Bose had his hand on her sleeve when the heavy swinging doors banged open, and a platoon of buffalo soldiers came in stomping dust off their boots. An unambiguous grumble rose from the card tables, and Garrett called out sarcastically, "Come in, fellows. First drinks on the house, in our gratitude. And come meet one of the *blazers* of the Goodnight-Loving Trail."

Bose's heart went cold.

They were on patrol out of Fort Stanton, an old post that the army had built on the Río Bonito trying to make it safe for Mexican homesteaders and ranchers to take over the river valley and mountains that the Mescaleros considered their holy place on earth. The Union garrison ran off when they saw the approach of John Baylor's Texas Confederates early in that war. Kit Carson regained the partly burned and thoroughly looted post for the Union a year later, was awarded the rank of colonel, and launched campaigns to bring the Apaches and Navajos to heel. But Carson elected to resign his commission and move on when all the troops ordered to Stanton began to be former slaves.

Several dragoons seemed to be fond of Billy. They cried, "Hey, Kid," and bleated like goats. He grinned, took off his hat, and swept it in front of him like a man taking his bow in a theater drama, but Bose could see from his eyes that he didn't like it. The boy's eyes were always darting, never still.

The platoon sergeant walked over at Garrett's summons and said his name was Rawlings. He was a large, thick-jawed man with very black skin. Where he'd shaved that morning, the bumps of hair root looked like a thousand small warts. He looked Bose up and down and took note of To-ha-yea. "One of those Texas cattle drovers, are you?"

"No, sir. Not anymore. The drives are pretty well played out. Country's a lot more connected with railroads, you know."

Rawlings gave To-ha-yea another look of appraisal. "Where do you hang your hat now?" he asked Bose, with his eyes still on her.

"Oh, I stayed a while in Colorado," Bose said. "Worked for one of my trail bosses on a ranch up there." A bead of sweat slid down his spine.

The sergeant gave him a close look. "You and this squaw together?"

Bose bristled. "I think that word usually means a married woman, sergeant. She's my friend, and I'm helping her get down through the territory, join back up with her father and her people."

"Happen to know her father's name?"

To-ha-yea, who'd given Bose no hint she knew more than a few words of English, answered sharply and proudly, "Old Wolf."

Rawlings fixed Bose with an unfriendly stare. "This woman is a renegade. And you are facilitating her transport."

"This woman hasn't done anything. She's been married to a man in another tribe. Which is why she's been away from her people."

Outside, a thunderstorm had formed above the sparse prairie. There were sharp cracks of thunder, a whoosh of arriving wind, and splats of rain on the roof. The sergeant harrumphed with an air of more to come, and raised his voice above the sounds of the storm and the din inside the saloon. "Mister Garrett, Don Maxwell!" the sergeant boomed. "Do you know who belongs to a big yellow horse stabled at the livery?"

Garrett and Maxwell looked at each other and shook their heads. Toweling a glass dry, Garrett said, "Can't say I do, horse or the owner. Why?"

Rawlings' eyes swept the crowd. "It's wearing a very interesting brand."

A hard gust of wind shook the saloon. A tumbleweed wedged itself between the swinging doors, and abruptly it popped inside, to the cheers of the gamblers. Billy Bonney had been closely watching Bose, the army sergeant, and To-ha-yea. He winked at Bose and said, "Patrick, Don Maxwell, we've got a bunch of hard-riding and thirsty fellows in here who want to *throw some bones*. The weather outside is a little rambunctious. Would it be all right if we had our game inside, just this once?"

Garrett looked at Maxwell, who indicated he didn't care, and the barman pointed to a wall beyond the monte tables. "Have at it," he said. "Just be courteous to your neighbors. Don't be knocking over any card games."

With another wink at Bose, the Kid strode off rattling dice in a cup, followed by buffalo soldiers still razzing him with that billy goat's bleat. "Mexican Liars!" Billy announced the game. The sergeant's troopers raised a whoop and several comancheros wanted in on it. Maxwell didn't give a shit, as long as Garrett didn't let it get out of hand; one good game of that would sell a couple of nights' worth of liquor. The players took turns shaking three dice in a cup and bouncing them off the wall. It was a game of bluff, winner-take-all, and a roller whose bluff had been called had to swallow two drinks to roll again. If the challenger bet wrong, then *he* had to down two drinks. Within an hour, players who stayed in the game were going to be falling-down and throwing-up drunk. That sergeant was going to be too busy trying to stop fistfights and stabbings in the ranks to investigate that packhorse's brand.

Billy had seen the packhorse and the crudely doctored brand when Garrett and the Don sent him to the stable to deliver the invitation. He'd just done Bose a huge favor. They could ride out, leave that livery an unclaimed horse, and be far downriver while the sergeant's men still moaned from their hangovers. Also, Billy was feeling lucky. Three of a kind was the usual winner in Mexican Liars, with a tray of sixes, which were called devils, the ultimate roll. "Pane, Half-Schmitty, Train," someone called a four-high straight. But soon Billy was doing almost all the calling. You could see how much he fancied himself a dancer. He carried on a running conversation with the cup in his bony left hand, palmed the other hand over the dice, raised it high, shook and kissed it, then flung the dice at the wall, flipping them back on the floor. "Devil, Titty, Titty," he yelped on winning a game with a six and two fives. "Devil with a *pair of Tits*," he crowed. With a snap of his fingers he spun a circle on the ball of his foot.

Bose was considering ways to thank the Kid for getting them out of a frightful spot when he glanced at To-ha-yea. The way she watched Billy strut reminded Bose of her smile when Quanah had him blowing his harmonica, that first day on the Middle Concho River.

25

I NTO HIS ADOBE, in that time and place where he clung to hopes and illusions, came the joy of children singing.

The Americans had changed the name of the cluster of riverside hamlets to Lincoln, but the Mexicans continued to call them Placitas del Río Bonito. Small plazas of the pretty river. Sweet smoke of the piñon breakfast fires, silver darts of trout in the pine green brook.

Slow waking up, Bose pulled his blanket to his chin and smiled. The singing voices were shrill and off-key with laughter—a sound of hands joined, brown knees prancing, dancing around the maypole. "Muerte al perro . . . muerte al perro . . . muerte al perro . . ."

Death, it came to him. Death to the dog.

Death to the dog?

"Muerte al perro . . ."

Death to *what* dog?

Shoving buttons at his fly, he shuffled barefoot through the corn husks that passed for a floor. Alert fleas jumped on his ankles and pants. He ducked his head to lurch through the rag of mosquito netting and crudely squared opening that passed for a door. The sunlight was fierce; he almost fainted.

The villagers scorned Bose because he shared his food with his dog. He plucked strings of mutton from his rolled tortillas and dangled treats over the mongrel, teasing him, making him jump, and then allowed the cur to lick the grease from his fingers. The peasants rolled their eyes when they saw him do it and relegated him to the barbarians del norte. The dog was the common yellow variety, longer of leg and ear than most, given to orgies of scratching that unsheathed his slick carmine pecker, and arrogant now that Bose had elevated his diet from offal shared with buzzards. Bose had named the dog Ferguson, after a drover who had been his friend on one of Goodnight's cattle drives. Trotting through the village in his company, the dog would glance at the brown women scrubbing clothes against the creek rocks, the naked children seated in the mud, and ease away from them, through the legs, under the belly of the tolerant paint gelding. He maintained more distance when Bose rode the mule. He would pause and sniff a columbine, ignoring people who would have gladly drowned him as a puppy. An uppity Mexican dog.

Now he pivoted and kicked at the end of a lariat strung over the limb of a bearing peach tree and wrapped around a fat woman's hip. With a word to the children, who moved back and gave her more room, the woman took a long sideward step and hoisted the victim higher. Ripe peaches fell to the ground.

Bose broke into a run. From the weeds of a corn and squash patch, he flushed a white duck with ugly red wattles on its beak. Squawking, dragging a leg, and flapping its better wing, the duck veered off through the crowd of children, who shrieked and leapt away from it. The duck's other wing was badly mangled; red meat and sheared cartilage glared from the joint. Bose reached the woman and got the rope away from her—had to give her a rude shove—and heard the bone pop. He gasped and let the rope go. Ferguson hit the ground like a feed sack.

Bose sank to his knees and stroked the creature's skull. A shiver passed under his hide. Blood and feathers were stuck to his muzzle.

"Godamighty, woman," he said. "Look what you done."

They all raised a cry then, a gabble that came so fast it swamped his understanding. The woman placed her fists on her hips and laughed at the heavens, at the silliness of this foreign stranger, this extranjero, and then tongue-lashed Bose, jabbing her finger at his face. One of the children came forward with the duck.

All right. Caught in the act—conceded. "Pero, ah, ah, pero no cree usted que eso es muy extremo?"

"No, Señor Negro con la corazón y la cabeza del Apaches," she mocked Bose. No, you black gringo with the heart and brains of the savages, this is my plaza and should still be my country. Lincoln, bah! A name that honors murder. Abolition of slavery was the very first measure undertaken by Mexico's revolutionary constitution. You do not belong here. You have set these things in motion. The responsibility is yours. And the mutilation of that cherished and blooded fowl, sir, *that* is extreme!

Bose carried the dog back to the adobe that he rented for a few cents a week and wrapped him in the blanket that was still warm from his sleep. Ferguson was a casualty of a conflict that greatly exceeded a maimed duck. People in America talked about the war between the states, or the other things they called it, and the punitive Reconstruction that followed in the rebellious states. Cross one state line to the west of the Confederacy, and the war of grudging reference was not that one, but another that had ended twenty-five years ago. More than a third of Mexico's territory had been gobbled by the gringo conquest and humiliating march through Mexico City. Powerless to change the outcome, campesinos like these settled into the sullen day-to-day life of people in a military occupation.

They resisted by burgling an armory and selling the guns to comancheros, whose trade was an outcome and symptom of the shattering defeat. They were indifferent about the schools—the only teachers were gringos—and that matter was better entrusted to priests. They ignored administrative notices and requests in English on matters like census and taxation. They held the black slaves sent in uniform to police the area in particular contempt. They lost land that Spaniards had with the authority of the Crown granted their families generations ago; it happened because they scorned the judicial system imposed by the occupiers. The campesinos resisted in small ways. They poisoned the rootstocks of a newcomer's orchard. They hanged Bose Ikard's dog.

He sat in front of the adobe wondering what he was going to do with Ferguson. He had no shovel, and he was not going to ask these people to borrow one. He supposed he would carry him up a dry arroyo and bury him under a pile of stones. He looked across the broad green valley from the snow-covered peak of Sierra Blanca to juniper-dotted foothills to the immense pan of llano to the east. Two stores and factions of merchants and enforcers contested with growing bitterness for the government contracts to provide food and supplies to the Mescalero Reservation. Fort Stanton was built up as a reinforced barricade between the Apaches and Lincoln and the farms, ranches, and other villitas that had taken root. The Río Bonito, which ran right behind Lincoln, was just one of the streams and strips of fertile bottomland in Lincoln County. Ranchers and farmers were shuffling quitclaim deeds and building homesteads on the Hondo, Ruidoso, Feliz, Peñasco, Nogal, Tularosa, and the Pecos. Old-timers, newcomers, and soldiers at Fort Stanton quarreled over water rights, and were tearing up dams and gouging diversion gates in irrigation ditches built by others. The prime suspects for these crimes were always the Mescaleros.

The Apaches were sequestered southwest of Fort Stanton on valley lands bordered by the Ruidoso and Nogal rivers and the Sacramento and White Mountains. They had half a million acres of rich grazing land, two hundred thousand more of pine forest and "sleepy grass" in the canyons of Apache Peak and other uplands, and the holy mountain, Sierra Blanca, towered twelve thousand feet and greeted their eyes everywhere on the preserve. The Quakers and colonels wondered, "How could they complain?" But that place inhabited by the Mountain Spirits and Dog Canyon and San Mateo Peak and Salinas Peak, all of them sacred to the Apaches, was now the property of the American government, for use and distribution as it saw fit. Cattle grazed the long valley grass but they belonged to white men, and the Apaches were forbidden to kill and eat them.

Bose and To-ha-yea had arrived at the reservation on a Saturday—issue day. Her people were standing in long lines waiting to be issued ration cards and meat, flour, sugar, and coffee that would have to last them all month. Many of them, new arrivals, were erecting their wickiups. To Bose the brush arbors looked like bird-nests turned upside down. Though he rode all that way to deliver her to her kin and clan, he was not made to feel welcome. They took one look at Bose and grouped him with the oppressors, the buffalo soldiers at the fort. She was looked down upon for arriving and talking freely with him.

Two days after they finished their long journey that began in the Quohada's Mulberry Canyon camp, she knew where her father was. "Old Wolf is in the Blue Mountains," she told him, "with others who refuse to live like this."

Bose had a good idea what the Blue Mountains were. Arranged on the southern horizon like some painter's palette, they were the northernmost range of the Sierra Madres. "He's in Mexico," Bose said.

She nodded with excitement.

"To-ha-yea, do you remember that wagon road that Quanah's band raided all the time when we were on the Middle Blanco?"

"Of course," she said.

"That road passes within two days' ride of here. There are Apache rancherías scattered along it all the way to the sierras in California. The road goes all the way to San Francisco."

"You're asking me again to leave my father and my people and go out there with you?"

"Yes, I am, until they figure out what they're doing. What chance do they have, dodging soldiers on this side that kill them on sight or lock them up as renegades, and rurales on the other who put bounties on their heads? And put the heads up like Christmas lamps?"

"My love, you know I have to see him."

The first of those words set his ears tingling. "To-ha-yea, we've come all this way. But I'm not going to Mexico. I can't."

"I'm so sorry to hear that."

She hadn't come to his adobe outside Lincoln in ten or twelve nights. Bose sighed and carried Ferguson to the little feed corral and laid him beside his saddle and other tack. He walked out where his horse and mule were grazing and absorbed another shock—one worse than the dog. Tricks was gone, stolen. He found the hobbles cut by a sharp knife and tossed on the ground.

Juneteen pricked his long ears forward and watched him. Bose sat on the ground and wept into his hands. After a while he mopped his cheek with his palm and thought, Well, I have to bury him, and I've got to go see her. He saddled and bridled the mule but got into a rodeo when he asked him to carry a dead dog laid across the saddle horn and pommel. Calling the mule every epithet and curse word he could think of, he dismounted, tied and knotted the lead rope so that a thief would have to use an axe to steal him, then walked up-river carrying the dog. He found a gully that became a small ravine, covered Ferguson's head with the blanket, and began to carry and set rocks on him, one by one, until it was a large tight mound. Some fox or badger would likely get to him, but he'd done all for that friend he could.

He walked back to the corral and adobe, observed by the woman and children in the peach orchard. She was aglow with her triumph of justice, telling the story to other women who had joined them. One of the kids threw a rock.

He rode Juneteen past the fort and a mill that marked the entrance to the reservation. The agency and the wickiups were spread across the end of a valley, beside the Río Tularosa. Pine-covered slopes came near the bank on the other side. Mescaleros stared at the black man on the black mule but made no effort to stop or approach him. I just have to tell her, he was thinking. Be with her a minute or two.

He peered as he drew close and stopped the mule. "Whoa, June-teen, whoa." Bose sat with his eyes closed and his hands crossed on the saddle horn, then bumped him with his heels and reached in his saddlebag, though it was unlawful to go armed on the reservation. Carrying a strange saddle, the Medicine Hat paint was tied up outside her brush arbor. Bose got down and tied up the mule at a distance, before he got to honking his greetings at Tricks. He approached his horse quietly and put a hand on his rump. Tricks turned his head and made a sound with his nostrils, clearly glad to see him. Bose unbuckled the cinch, put the stirrup on the horn, and pulled the saddle and blanket off toward him. He carried the saddle and blanket forward, then with a hop and heave and crash he slung them as far into her wickiup as he could.

Mindful of her shotgun, he stood well to the side and yelled, "To-ha-yea, are you in there? Are you all right?"

Her silence told him everything he didn't want to know.

Billy came running out barefoot, wearing only a pair of jeans. He had a gun in his left hand, but the hard end of Bose's gun thumped him on the head, between his eyebrow and ear.

"I'd put that down if I was you," said Bose. "There you go. Use that big toe and scoot it over toward me. That's good. Now you'd better get back inside to what you was doing. If I ever see you again, I'll kill you."

PART III

The Blood-Stained Grass

1874-1875

26

QUANAH THOUGHT the Cheyennes were haughty and vain. Their presence always made him edgy. All peoples thought spring grass and flowers sprouted anywhere they left a footprint, but the Cheyennes were arrogant to an extreme. They would go around shirtless with an inch of ice on the water in order to show off their Sun Dance scars. Quanah had several times been a guest at these affairs, when the Cheyennes made their camps on the Canadian and the Washita. Some warrior would come running through the lodges with leather straps punched and pulled through the skin between his neck and shoulder blades—two buffalo skulls bouncing and clattering behind in the dirt. This was how they found vision and power? Cheyenne stew was a bit too rich for Quanah's taste. He thought of them as pretty boys.

But they were strong and important allies now. As the Quohada band came into the lush cottonwood bottoms where Elk Creek emptied into the North Fork of the Red, Quanah was thrown off a bit to see they'd have to ride past the tall and elegant tipis of the Cheyennes on the way in. Beyond them more than three hundred lodges fanned out through the valley. The purpose of the council was war, but the occasion was the biggest Sun Dance the Comanche bands had ever attempted. Unlike their Cheyenne, Kiowa, Kiowa-Apache, and Arapaho guests, they had scant tradition of it.

The Comanches were going down this road at the insistence of Isa-tai, who rode beside Quanah at the head of the incoming band. To a man the Comanches indicated they were not going to hang by leather thongs in their chests from any lodge pole. Wolf Shit, who was not eager to do that himself, decreed that it wasn't a proper part of their Sun Dance. Quanah rode Deer's Son, his black war horse. Riding Bad Hand Mackenzie's gray pacer, which Bose had surrendered to his appropriation without regret, Wolf Shit extended his arms level with the ground and raised his jaws theatrically to the sky. Quanah turned and called up Bose on his paint gelding. It ruined the moment for Wolf Shit, who shot a glare at both of them. "I don't want you," Quanah joshed Bose. "Just your horse. For those ahead."

Bose returned the Cheyennes' stares. "Are they going to eat him?"

Quanah laughed. "No. They're the ones who believe in him. Gray eagles and white buffalo and Medicine Hat paints. They got so much help in the spirit world I don't know how they turn around. You'll like their cooking, though. Roast puppy stuffed with chokecherries—not bad."

That summer of 1874 Quanah and Bose were twenty-nine years old. Bose was no captive anymore; he had chosen to come back and rejoin the Quohada. Bose leaned forward and rubbed Tricks' spotted white neck. Looped to his saddle horn was his army bugle. He'd been showing the alliance how cavalry used the bugle to overcome distance, differences in language, and difficulty hearing. "Are you going to get them organized?" Quanah asked.

"We'll see about the Cheyennes," Bose answered. "But the Kiowas love it. You know Pago-to-goodle?"

"Sure, the one with the scar on his face. Eighteen winters old yesterday and means to be war chief day after tomorrow."

"He tells me he's going to take Satanta's bugle away from the old fart, and I'm going to teach him how to play it properly."

A group of Cheyennes were walking out to pay their respects and examine their animals. "Make yourself presentable," said Quanah.

"Who are you, my mother?" said Bose.

In the council Wolf Shit listened with a look of stony patience to all the nominations before announcing that Quanah's wife Weckeah would select the tree for the Sun Dance lodge pole. The shaman naturally thought his wife, She Invites Her Relatives, was the more fitting choice—one that enhanced his stature. But she was afraid of his power and medicine to the point of it giving her the shakes, and Wolf Shit needed Quanah just as much as Quanah needed him; this concession was an easy one for the shaman to make.

Late that day Weckeah walked through the grassy bottom accompanied by her husband, Wolf Shit, and chiefs, war leaders, and shamans of the guest tribes and bands. Hundreds of people pressed close around to the rear. Weckeah held her skirts and looked upward. She stopped in front of a cottonwood that raised an especially noisy leaf clatter; balls of its downy seed were alight in the breeze. She circled the tree, then pointed her finger at its strong young heart.

The next morning men chopped the chosen lodge pole down and trimmed it to the nook of branches that had caught her eye. For three days the people cut and dragged up timber for the lodge's twelve outlying posts, gathered brush to fill in the walls, and wove hide and vine streamers that would bind it all to the central pole. A party of hunters and women rode out and came back with the gold-tinged hide of a buffalo bull skinned out with great care; the skull, hooves, and lower leg bones were still in it. The women packed the hide with prairie grass, sewed it shut, and combed and brushed out the wool until the bull almost looked alive. Then they lashed it to the fork on top of the lodge pole. A crew of warriors slipped lariat knots around the pole and pulled and heaved it until on the fourth try the lodge pole and the buffalo totem stood upright. The cheering was so loud birds fled the trees.

On the fourth day the Mud Men were out in the creek early. They smeared handfuls of red clay on their horses and themselves, heaping it on their noses, sculpting one layer after another and letting it dry, until finally the ridges of crusted mud stood out like beaks of eagles. On their heads they wore hats of willow foliage that lashed back and forth as they made frightful noises at children. All day they galloped through the camps, riding backwards, chasing dogs. They were the clowns.

The other tribes had been standoffish till then, but their warriors began to preen and strut. Kiowas came out with their hair done up in the way of their grandfathers—long on the left side of their heads and shorn close on the right, showing off their earrings. They were loaded up with necklaces and ankle jingles. They walked around shaking their arms, making chimes of all the bracelets. These were the Black Legs and Skunkberry People and Koitsenko, the highest order, Real Dogs.

Unimpressed, the Cheyennes' Dog Soldiers and Kit Fox Men cruised around in light skin breeches with their bare chests thrust out, showing off the scars where they had hung and swiveled from their Sun Dance poles. Every society of the Cheyennes counted in its members at least one girl soldier. She was always a beauty, and the brothers dared rivals to give her a look or pat on the ass.

Taking it all in, Quanah and Bose sat on the ground beside Weckeah's lodge, scooping meat out of bowls with their fingers. "What is this, turtle?" said Bose.

"Beaver, I think. Maybe otter."

"Hmm."

"You can taste the mud."

"No, it's good."

Quanah looked out at the festivities. "What do you think?"

"I think somebody's liable to get killed having all this fun. And I bet some of them are thinking, Why not that dark-skinned fellow?"

Quanah studied him. "You're acting kind of moody today."

"Ah." Bose moved his hand like he was shooing a fly.

"Why'd you come back here?"

"I couldn't think of any other place to go," said Bose. "Also I know what it's like to have people trying to tell you where you have to be, what you have to be, and what you have to do. And then they say, 'Oh, here's a little food and a scrap of shelter, for doing what you're told.'"

Quanah:

THE BITTERNESS OF what Bose said that day was the most he ever revealed to me about being a slave. His mood and remarks spoiled what enthusiasm I had for Wolf Shit's Sun Dance. And as I watched the airs put on by the Cheyenne Dog Soldiers and Kiowa Real Dogs, Bose's words had me taking stock of the society I belonged to, the Little Horses, and the cheapness with which we called the brethren True Friends. I walked to the lodge of my other good friend, the whipman.

"Come in, Quanah," said Parra-o-coom. As I entered I had to duck under a bundle of crow feathers hung from the flap to ward off ghosts. It wasn't ghost sickness; he'd go out easier than that. He was going down from walking around drowning, what the whites call pneumonia.

In the lodge with him were two wives and Memory Woman, an eagle doctor. "They've got the air ripe," He Bear warned me. A small bed of coals filled the place with the pungent smoke of red cedar sprigs, which Memory Woman wafted toward him with her medicine feather from an eagle's wing. She wore the black kerchief that qualified her as a doctor, and had some peyote buttons seeping in hot water. She crumbled bits of half-dried iris flowers in the tea. "Leave us a while," He Bear told the women.

"You cannot smoke," said Tawaka, his number-one wife.

"Watch me," he grumbled.

He stuffed fresh tobacco in his pipe and lit it. "All but a few of the Honey Eaters have gone back to the reservation," I told him.

"I'm not surprised. At least they got to see this. At least they came."

"All the war talk must have scared them."

"They're proud people, Quanah. Their grandfathers were up to their necks in whiteasses when Quohada had hardly seen one. They fought hard and as long as they could. They just got tired."

"The Arapahoes aren't sure they want to fight either. They're telling the Cheyennes they may just watch."

"So? Has it come to us needing Arapahoes? Clear your mind, son. Look at all the horses and people you do have."

"Are they enough?"

"Might be. If you can keep them all together."

"We need the Cheyennes."

Parra-o-coom grinned at my worries. "Did I ever tell you how Our People made peace with the Cheyennes?"

He had told me that story many times, but telling it was a pleasure to a man in need of some. I smoked and listened like it was entirely new.

"Some Cheyennes ran off the horses and mules of a Yamparika hunting party who were camped on the River of Cranes, and they killed a couple of Yamparika. Then the Cheyennes in the company of some Arapahoes came down on a party of Kiowas who were trading horses to Crows for ermine robes and those elk teeth they like to wear in their necklaces. The Cheyennes swelled up with all this glory. One of their Dog Soldiers had a vision of them burning a winter camp of Quohada, Kotsoteka, Yamparika, and Kiowas on the North Canadian, and taking all our horses.

"I was a little boy when the Cheyennes started that fight. Got into the thick of it, they looked around and couldn't find one Arapaho." Parra-o-coom raised a hand before me and opened it like a blooming flower. "Feeling bad about running off, the Arapahoes later got them and us together at a place called Treaty Grounds. To make the peace, the Cheyennes offered us our pick of any of their horses and mules. We properly replied that Cheyennes didn't have many horses or mules we'd much care to have, but we would give every Cheyenne and Arapaho warrior two hundred horses. All these

Cheyenne eyes get to rolling, then our warriors came on the parley camp yelling and singing and driving four thousand head. Them peoples thought the sky was raining horses and mules."

I laughed on cue and said, "Have you ever seen them courting?"

"Courting women? Nah, tell me. I thought there was just one way."

I handed back the pipe and said, "I'd been hearing that some of their habits are not to be believed. So one night after I got through talking to their elders and war council I went out for a walk. Out of the trees these white figures were weaving around like fireflies. But they were people, not spirits, wrapped from head to moccasin in some kind of bleached cloth, with a slit across the eyes so they could see. And they were men, young men! You could tell from their height and the size of their feet. But they were singing in these high, high voices. And then flitting through the shadows you could see and hear the girls, singing back. It was one of the most curious things I've ever seen."

The old man tapped the pipe's bowl in his palm. "Listen, Quanah. It's an amazing thing you've done, bringing all of these people together."

"Wolf Shit helped."

"I know he did."

My habit of boastfulness erupted. "We're going to whip Bad Hand and his bluecoats once and for all. Then we're going to run the Texans out of the Brazos country. And once we've got them running, we're going to chase them all the way to the great salt water. See if they like drinking that."

As he'd done a thousand times, Parra-o-coom cautioned me. "You're a good young fighter, Quanah. But don't try to get it done all at once. Go get those buffalo hunters. Whet the appetite. Get the first blood first."

Outside we heard a great commotion. The crier rode through the lodges, telling everyone to get ready. Parra-o-coom asked me to stay and help him put on his battle finery; he wanted to see it and to be seen standing. Others of Our People retired to their lodges and came back with faces painted and hair done up. But I stayed with this man who'd been as good to me as a father, closer than the one I had. Just at twilight the drums began. The people moved as one toward the brush lodge with the buffalo positioned in the sky. The dance went: right stomp . . . pause . . . another step. Right stomp. Pause. Their feet became the loudest drum. I looked at Parra-o-coom, who was tottery and exhausted. It was too late for him. He had tears in his eyes.

⋛⋚

For the next three days the painted men danced. Half a dozen kept up pounding on a drum so large the women needed three buffalo hides to sew and stretch the skin. It wasn't a dance of leaping and whirling. The dancers shuffled, hopped, and blew eagle-bone whistles at the lodge pole, but they took no food or water, and they kept it up so long they lurched off and swooned on sage pallets. Magic was performed; Kiowa appeared to swallow a coachwhip snake. The Sun Dance was also a time of gift-giving. Young boys were brought forward to shoot an arrow into the pole, on which they hung the family's presents to their kin. Their aim and sense of distance were not always certain. A snoring Yamparika jumped awake with an arrow in his leg.

Wolf Shit didn't join the dancers, nor did Quanah, but they maintained a presence. While the shaman attended to spiritual affairs, Quanah, the acting war chief, called in favors, asked the advice of elders, flattered the warriors of the other peoples. One afternoon in his tipi he began sewing together a charm of hawk feathers for his lance. Outside, Weckeah was surrounded by Nahnacuh and other little girls. Some of them were older and understood more about what was happening. Quanah had been day-dreaming lustfully about a good looker named Chony, but he got a lump in his throat listening to his wife and mother of his child.

"In the long ago, Róco, Grandfather, was always telling Our People where to camp. He had the power to turn himself into anything, but he couldn't find them enough to eat. In shame Róco turned himself into a puppy. This little girl came up and tried to grab him, but he snapped at her because he was afraid. But then he rolled over and showed her his belly, the way they do. 'Don't be afraid,' the little girl told the puppy. She grabbed him in her arms and took him inside her lodge. 'Look,' she said. There was a hole in the ground, and inside it were thousands and thousands of buffalo. The little girl's father came in and said, 'Get that dog out of here.' When her father went away, she grabbed the puppy again, and this time she wrapped him in a fox fur, to hide him. Back inside the lodge, the hole opened up, and there were all those buffalo. Róco jumped out of her arms and started running around, howling, and he stampeded the herd right out of that hole. They tore down her father's tipi, so she picked up a club, meaning to kill him. He jumped up and bit one of those buffalo in the long hair, around the throat, and off the buffalo ran, with the puppy hanging on.

"Wasn't long before Róco came limping back. 'What happened, old man?' Our People said, thinking that really nothing ever happened, not with him. Róco pointed at some hills and said, 'Come sunrise tomorrow, they'll make the ground black there'll be so many of them coming to our arrows and stewpots, and we'll never, ever go hungry again.' For once, that old man was right. And it was all because of a little girl's love of her dog."

For the council Quanah wore a single eagle feather in his hair. He pulled on leggings, a white man's suitcoat vest, and a long yellow silk scarf, knotted at the throat, that he had traded a horse for in Taos.

He walked alone through the tipis, trying to quiet the voices in his head. People filled up the clearing around the lodge, hoping to hear a word and catch a glimpse through the brush walls. Fires burned all around. They cast a strange light on the buffalo in the sky.

He drew a breath and walked inside, where the most respected men of each people stood on the sage pallets. He exchanged greetings with a few, then took the center place on the ground, with Wolf Shit on his right. The prophet was unpainted and naked except for moccasins and a red sash wrapped around his waist. He had two hawk quills in his hair, and snake rattles were hooked in his ears. On the ground with them were Big Bow and Cohayyah of other Comanche bands, Stone Calf and Red Moon of the Cheyennes, and Satanta and Lone Wolf of the Kiowas. Seated just behind them were war leaders of the Kiowa-Apaches, who followed the Kiowa chiefs, and the Arapaho war leaders, who might or might not join the Cheyennes in battle. Three signers were poised to make the orations into the flowing language of palms, fingers, and wrists. Smoke from a ceremonial fire poured up the lodge pole toward the hole in the roof.

Quanah lit the tobacco pipe and blew the first puff up the pole, toward the sun. He offered more smoke to the earth and the four winds of direction, and then sent the pipe around. "Parra-o-coom is ill, as you all know," he told them. "He regrets he can't greet you personally. But he's here, and it makes him glad to see you." There were formal murmurs of respect.

He called on Stone Calf of the Cheyennes first. Stone Calf was as tall as Quanah, and had the kind looks and melancholy smile that made women in all the peoples sigh. "Our people were happy and rich in the country of the Arkansas," he began. "There was no hunger in the winter, and we were at peace with all of you here. But the whites were like the snowmelt in the mountains. There was no stopping them; every year a new flood came. They proposed a truce and asked our people to gather at a place called Sand Creek. You know that story. They put cannon on our lodges and ran their long knives through three hundred women and children. The whites talked about it like it was the greatest victory they ever had.

"And so we moved south into this country of the Red and Canadian and Washita. You know that story, too. The dandy soldier who calls himself Custer shot seven hundred of our horses and burned all we had. And so we moved on their reservation. Now their preachers pester us, and the wagons of the whites never stop coming from the east. Just once I would like to see one going toward the morning sun. They give us flour brown with weevils and bacon that tastes like carrion packed in salt."

The Cheyenne touched his chest. "You have heard me in these councils speaking of peace. I'm not ashamed. Last year, the whites put me on a train and took me to their big town Washington. Their president, who calls himself Grant, gave six of us his hand and once wrote his word that the buffalo hunters would never be allowed south of the Arkansas River. Yet here they are. This man Grant is a liar; what can we expect from the rest of them? We have gained nothing from trying to please them. So let me die as I want, with their blood on my hands and a stomach full of buffalo haunch."

Two of the Kiowas wanted to speak. Lone Wolf's eyes appeared soft and wary, but his voice was strong and bitter. "You say it right," he told Stone Calf. "We too have known Custer. Five winters ago he got Satanta and myself to come to the soldier camp under a white flag of peace. He wouldn't shake our hands, and then he took us hostage. When our hands were chained, the soldiers spat on us. He said he was going to hang us up by rope. We sat and panted like dogs in their jail until night was day and day was night, and I had all but forgotten who I was." He paused a moment. "Custer is gone from us now. They say he's gone north, where the Sioux and our other brethren Cheyennes are eager to meet him."

In many tongues there were yells for Custer's scalp.

"But let me tell you what is within my reach," Lone Wolf resumed. "This winter past I had to go to Mexico and bury two of my sons. Texans chased them down there and killed them. Com-

311

ing back through Texas I hated everything I saw. Horses and barns and cattle, everything and everyone. I want them all dead. But we have also made the mistake of going on the white man's reservation. We asked for guns and bullets for hunting when the buffalo herds come south. They gave us seeds and plows. I'm not going to stoop for my food like a woman! We are hunters, and the time for blood is on us."

The Kiowa Satanta wore a sweeping red robe and carried his bugle. He always had a young boy with him. Satanta could be a very long-winded speaker, and Quanah was braced for that, but he spoke up simply with a broad-faced grin. "The only part of the white man's road I'm going to take hold of is a repeating rifle. That corn they got, it hurts my teeth."

Laughter erupted and moved outside through the crowd. Satanta looked at Quanah and the other Comanches around the fire. "Young man, I don't know you well," he said. "But I knew and rode with your father. You have come with respect to each of our camps, and we appreciate it. Your words bring to mind that time of our fathers when all the peoples here ceased being enemies. That time when Comanches proposed the peace among us and sealed it with gifts of thousands of horses. The first time that all of us were one. You give us hope it can be that way again."

Quanah kept his own speech short. "All my life," he began, "I've been losing kindred and friends. My father, my mother, my sister and brother. All gone because of the whites. I want to call their names, but I can't, they're gone." In the pause a woman made a sound of grief.

"Two years have passed since the soldiers rode through the Kotsoteka lodges and carried away women and children. They said if we didn't send back all our captives those people would never see their families again. A lot of Our People sent them away, even though many were wives and adopted children and had no wish to go. Too many of us have gone begging on their reservation. We've seen the buffalo numbers fall like sufferers of pox. At Medicine Lodge the soldiers got some legendary chiefs to put marks on a treaty. They showered us with candy and trinkets and, like Stone Calf says, they told us the buffalo hunters would never be allowed to come south of the Arkansas River. Now they say that country belongs to Texas, and there's nothing they can do about it. Now buffalo hunters are all around us. But they won't be for long."

At Wolf Shit's signal someone started beating on a drum. "We have the warriors we need now," said Quanah, raising his voice, "and by this Sun Dance we have the medicine. And this man. Hear this man. He is Isa-tai."

Wolf Shit stood and paced lightly. Leaning over the fire, he dropped a handful of cedar twigs, which crackled and threw sparks. Using a feather fan, he pushed its smoke toward members of the council. He washed his hands in the smoke, bathed his face and hands in it. He danced around the fire, throwing his knees high and flinging his elbows, then began to chant.

Oh, Great Spirit, have mercy on us
Oh, Great Spirit, make us strong
Oh, brother Wolf Shit, show us what to do

The fire blazed up roaring in response to his medicine. Quanah swore he saw him grow a foot. "Behold me, chiefs and brothers," the shaman said. "Behold the son of a wolf. You have seen me in your camps. You have seen me blow out wagonloads of bullets and breathe them back in like fresh air. Deny me if it isn't true."

No one spoke. He walked before them, extending an arm.

"I have foreseen events of the future. My spirit left my body and flew beyond the moon and stars. Our Sure Enough Father told me that true peoples must never break the skin of the earth with plows. The Caddos and Wichitas were brave fighters, too. But they violated the earth and now they have passed away. Only warriors and hunters grow numerous and strong. When we have proven ourselves warriors again the buffalo will return for all time. Behold me, chiefs and brothers. My medicine is like no other. It possesses me with magic paint that turns bullets away. Other days, it allows them to pass through without harm or trace. My medicine is strong. Behold me, chiefs and brothers." He howled like a wolf.

The drummer bore down on his rhythm. Wolf Shit laid more cedar on the fire, which blazed higher, and his arms began to shake. Then he anchored his feet and slowly raised his hands. The right hand sprouted an arrow. Gasps of astonishment as he slowly turned it round. Then his left hand blossomed an arrow. And another. The shaman howled again. Under the lodge pole and the hole in the roof, one by one he let go of his magic arrows, and they vanished in the rising coil of smoke.

That moment the alliance was joined. They all chose to fight, and when the question was posed, they made Quanah the war chief. Afterward the bands feasted and sang late into the night. Lovers woke up in the tipis and heard it raining. In the morning people surrounded the lodge, staring at the stuffed buffalo. The arrows of the prophet were lodged in its throat.

27

THE HUNTERS CALLED THEMSELVES hide men. On the boardwalks of Dodge City they advertised their profession by never cutting their hair. They styled around in dungarees and knee boots, the grime and stench of themselves made acceptable by the money they lavished on the whores and whiskey and faro games. The busiest and most efficient of them were making a hundred and fifty dollars a day.

In dramshops back east, the market for bison had once consisted of a wooden vat filled with tongues and brine. Barroom food. Then tanners in England and Prussia discovered a trade secret that with time and commercial bribery jumped back across the ocean to Philadelphia, Queens, New Bedford. If the hides were shipped dry and soaked in just the right evil-smelling bath, they could be made into industrial leather. The hum of machines drove the price up to three dollars and six bits a hide; flatcars of the Atchison, Topeka and Santa Fe Railway rolled out of Dodge each morning loaded with a thousand hides, and at the fort, soldiers who were old enough were taken back in jitters and anxious dreams to Shiloh and Antietam by the incessant boom of the hide men's guns.

But an immense no-man's land separated Dodge City and Adobe Walls, and on the slope above the Canadian River, only coyote jabber and owl hoots carried in from the plains to Hanrahan's Saloon. Even the smartest hide men were half-crazy, or else they wouldn't have put themselves in such a situation, and the countryside seemed so empty that they could easily get caught up in the toil and greed and forget where they were. But in the long flat and lovely dusk the isolation began to weigh on them, and after supper they raised their voices and took to bitters and gin.

Playing a few early hands of poker, Billy Dixon was a short and swarthy twenty-four-year-old from West Virginia. Billy had the longest hair of any of the hide men; it was black and stringy and hung loose to the small of his back. Aside from liking the look of it and the looks of whores it drew, Billy never thought too much about his hair in Kansas. But hell, up there they had enough men and long-range gunnery to hold off a charge by Napoleon. In the Panhandle of Texas, they were begging to lose their scalps.

The saloon was constructed of prairie sod, not adobe. In fact, the only adobe anywhere close around was a ruin a mile away that gave their trade post its name. All that was known for certain about the five-foot walls, worn smooth by time and blizzards and sun, was that ten years earlier they had been put to emergency use as an infirmary by Kit Carson. His soldiers and an allied band of Utes had come down the Canadian from New Mexico to punish the plains Indians for attacking settlers' wagons on the Santa Fe Trail. The soldiers and Utes routed and burned the first village they came across, then shortly were made to understand they were surrounded by twenty Kiowas to their one. Soon the prairie was afire around them, and if the soldiers hadn't insisted on bringing along a couple of howitzers, the famed Carson would have had to sprout wings to get back to New Mexico alive.

Billy Dixon picked up his last card—a disappointment, it left him with no better a hand than three jacks—and looked across the table at Pat Garrett, who for reasons of discretion was calling himself John Long, an adaptation of the nickname Juan Largo that Mexicans had given him at Fort Sumner. Garrett had come onto the Texas Panhandle with Billy Bonney, the sixteen-year-old fugitive. Garrett had taken up with the boy because he liked his bravado and luck at the gambling tables in the saloons of Sumner, but as a cowhand on the Jinglebob Ranch of John Chisum, he'd just gotten run off for general laziness, for getting thrown by far too many horses that had to be overtaken and caught, and for nosing after Chisum's daughter Sallie like she was a bitch in heat. Billy Bonney was saddle trash, but Garrett figured it was always best to have someone watching his back.

Garrett proposed to Billy that they go off to St. Louis, adventuring and prospering along the way. Introducing Billy as his skinner—at which the boy blinked—at a camp Garrett had talked his way into partnership with one of the hunting parties from Dodge. Their partners were an Englishman who styled himself Cheyenne Jack and a German skinner called Blue. Garrett hunted with a Winchester, not the Sharps that the hide hunters favored, but he was a fast and efficient shot. But he soon got in a heated disagreement with the Englishman over division of the hides, in part because Billy was appalled by the foul skinning work and couldn't or wouldn't keep up. Garrett satisfied his resentment by leaving Cheyenne Jack and his German the skins and relieving them of their saddle horses, planning to sell them when they reached Kansas. But then they started seeing fresh signs of an extraordinary number of Indians. Garrett and Billy cut the horses loose and put their own to a high lope toward Adobe Walls, where Cheyenne Jack and Blue were well known. Just being careful, he announced his temporary name change and told the kid he should add another alias, Billy Ogg, to his growing list. "Agghhh," gargled Billy, who was trying to relieve a dusty throat with a swig from his canteen. Garrett snickered and told him that sounded just fine.

Soon after they arrived at the Walls, Garrett alias Long was relieved when word spread that Cheyenne Jack and his German skinner had gone missing. A search party found evidence of bloodshed at the camp on the Salt Fork of the Red, but it appeared a flash flood had washed the bodies away.

Others in the hand of stud poker that night were Dutch Henry Born, said to be a failed dairy farmer but an able horse thief himself, and a Scot named Charley Armitage. Born was speaking his Wisconsin German to Ike and Shorty Scheidler, teamsters who were drinking beer at the next table. The immigrant brothers had come out west because Ike had caught consumption in a sweatshop on Lake Erie, and they thought the plains might improve his health. The Scheidlers used oxen, not mules, and worked with a hunter camped on Palo Duro Creek, a few miles from the Walls. Ike had come in just that day from Dodge with a load of supplies. Their vast dog Hans, a Newfoundland retriever, was sprawled on his side between the tables, ignoring Billy's spotted setter pup Fannie, which circled and yapped, trying to get him to play. Garrett raised a boot and kicked the pup to shut him up, which irked Billy Dixon. Everyone's temper was on a short fuse.

"Gustav," said Garrett, who was annoyed the men were speaking German. "*Wilhelm*. You still in this game?"

Dutch Born looked at him closely and said, "It's your bet."

"So it is. Raise you two," said Garrett.

Armitage pitched in his cards, and for the hell of it Billy Dixon raised the bet back to the tall newcomer, pitching four bottle caps on the table. Each was worth a buffalo hide—the medium of exchange at the Walls, since there was a shortage of cash and bankers. Garrett had no hides to lose, but he did not like to while away hours doing nothing. If the cards failed him, they could take his note or kiss his ass.

Dutch was a powerfully built man with receding hair and, like Garrett, he sported a dark moustache. Holding his cards in his left hand, he had the right one clamped palm down over an open can of peaches. He'd take a pull from his beer bottle, set it down, slurp out a piece of peach and some syrup, then cover up the can again.

The saloon had thick wood doors at each end and one proper window with a pane of thick grease paper. A large crow had adopted the settlement, attracted by the buffalo carrion. The crow, which the hide men named Clyde, sat on the roof of the saloon observing the end of the day and the flow of human activity with dismissive caws and chatty squawks. Periodically Clyde would shoot through the doors and fly the length of the place like a swallow—cawing as hunters tried to bat it down with hats or the barkeep's broom. The chunks of sod in the saloon's walls were a yard thick and stacked in such a way as to leave holes where a man could either stand or kneel and see to aim a gun out. Kerosene lamps illuminated a rough bar, and on the tables candles were set in halved pans of old army canteens. Two dried buffalo hides were laid out on the dirt floor for entertainment time. Bugs poured through the gunports in the walls, and the slap of hands on cheeks and mosquitoes was constant. This night another element added to the atmosphere—falling dirt.

The roof was supported by a cottonwood ridge pole laid lengthwise across the walls. Cross-ties of brush and scrap lumber were set across the pole, and about a foot of dirt had been thrown on top of them. But the roof had been leaking when it rained, so late in the day some of the boys had been up there with Jim Hanrahan, shoveling more dirt. As Dutch considered his cards, there was another cave-in.

He looked at the mud clods in his peaches, then abruptly jumped up yelling and in a frantic dance peeled off his shirt, revealing hairy shoulders and a couple of bullet scars. A scorpion landed on the table, froze for an instant, and then made a dash for survival as Dutch whammed after it with his beer bottle. It had plunked down his collar and scorched him good.

Laughter erupted all around, but Dutch singled out the high voice of one of Billy Dixon's skinners—a twenty-year-old named Bat Masterson, who sat at a nearby table writing in a bound book with a pencil. Billy Bonney alias Ogg sat beside him drinking beer. They were the youngest ones in the Walls.

"Find that funny?" said Dutch, looming over Masterson's chair.

Though his adam's apple bobbed, Bat talked back to him freshly. "Time it happened, I thought it was." In Dodge, Masterson had tried to cut the swath of a cavalier, but he hadn't been able to convince hide buyers he was a marksman. He could only get hired as a skinner. On a busy day, by the time he reached the last carcasses they were bloated, fly-ridden, and foul. Skinners couldn't wash the stench out of their clothes or bathe it off their skin.

Dutch lifted a cigar out of Shorty Scheidler's hand. "What the scorpion feels like," he said, "is having a hot ash put to you."

"Don't do that," said Bat, watching the cigar stuck close to his ear.

"Sit down, Dutch," said Billy Dixon, running his hands through his hair. "Put your shirt on. Nobody wants to look at your belly."

Holding the cigar with his forefinger and thumb, Dutch put his little finger to the tip of Bat's nose. Bat pushed the hand away.

"I don't think I'm liking you much," said Dutch.

"I can't help it," said Bat, grinning. "Or make myself care."

⋙⋘

Billy Dixon lost the bet to Garrett's piddling straight and decided he could use some air. He finished his glass of gin and whistled at the setter pup, which galloped into a table leg, following him out. As Billy walked he made a cigarette and smoked it. Nighthawks dipped and whistled in the darkening sky. Adobe Walls consisted of a single row of buildings, all facing east, in which the saloon and a blacksmith shop were flanked by the stores of Meyers & Leonard and Rath & Company. The competing merchandisers sold produce and hard goods at a handsome markup, offered the hide men meals in a mess hall, and in most cases bought the skins and hired wagons for transport back to Dodge.

First on the scene, the Meyers & Leonard outfit was larger and more elaborate. Holding up an earthen pitched roof, the walls of the store and mess hall were made of logs set upright in a trench. Its corrals and hide yard were enclosed by a stockade of eight-foot cottonwood poles hewn to a point. At the corners were crude turrets where men could crawl up on a ladder and maintain a lookout, or just admire the stars. All the other buildings at Adobe Walls were built of prairie sod. The merchandisers and hide men had chosen this spot because a hay meadow filled with sweetwater springs channeled two creeks down into the brackish Canadian, and the banks were level enough and the riverbed firm enough for the teamsters to get their mules and wagons across. Wagons were parked all around— some behind the town on the flats, more down in the cottonwoods, where a nice breeze had the waxy leaves clattering. No more than a dozen people actually lived in the Walls, but tonight more than thirty would throw their bedrolls there.

With the sun down, most of the Walls' inhabitants came walking toward the saloon—even Hannah Olds, who had a shawl on her shoulders and a hand on the arm of her stooped husband William, a Rath & Company clerk. Trailing after them was her pet foal Inez, covered with a blanket made of flour sacks. Some hunters had found the mustang abandoned and brought her into camp. She was so weak she could barely stand, and the ants had stung her so badly that she had bare patches on her hide, and she shivered all the time. Mrs. Olds bottle-fed her until she could eat grain and sewed the blanket to keep her warm. Now she was as frisky and troublesome as a goat.

Mrs. Olds normally avoided the rowdiness of the saloon, but sometimes the want of social company overwhelmed her, and the nights when she came over, the men watched their language and minded their manners. Mrs. Olds was a nervous soul, and for good reason. Except for captives of the Indian bands, she was the only white woman south of the Arkansas River. The couple had come to the Walls after their boarding house in Dodge burned down. Some boys dug the trading post's one sod outhouse for her, and all the privacy she had was a sheet drawn across a corner of the store. She cooked meals for the stinking and dirty men who came through Rath & Company, but she served them all on white ironstone, and she always had a smile for Billy Dixon. He touched his hat as they approached him. "Mrs. Olds," he said, "I sure enjoyed your dumplings tonight."

"Why, thank you, Billy. It's all in the lard," she said.

Billy's insides were in fact quite roiled by the jackrabbit meat and turkey gizzards she plunked into her dumplings. Some of the hide men said Olds had once been a fur trapper and Indian fighter up in the cold high country, but was reduced by decrepitude now to cooking pan bread she put out with her meals. As Mrs. Olds breezed on about her secrets of making dumplings, Billy picked up his pup to stop her from brawling after the filly's feet. Billy found that amusing and curious in women—compliment them on a mudpie, and they'd answer with a saga.

With Fannie roaming and sniffing ahead, Billy circled the buildings and hide yards and approached his horses and mules, hobbled and tethered around his wagon, which was loaded to pull out the next morning. In the failing light the ricks of hides in the yards looked like loaves of black bread. Someone hailed him, and he turned to see Jim Hanrahan coming. A tall man with sandy hair and a gray goatee, Hanrahan had a more serious and forceful presence than most of the men at the Walls. In Dodge he had gotten himself elected to the first term of the Kansas legislature. Any enterprise that was fervid and unregulated, he aimed to be in it. He struck Billy as the sort of man who lay awake all night thinking about money.

"How's it going, Billy?" he said.

"All right. You?"

"Mood in the place seems a little down tonight."

Billy answered, "Why wouldn't it be?" For the first three months of the Walls' existence there hadn't been any Indian trouble. But then came the incident at Chicken Creek. Teamsters from Dodge, who used to come in singing to their mules, had severely changed their tune. "I hear Dudley and Wallace finally got buried," said Billy.

"Yeah, the boys that drew the beans got their brave up. Some land office surveyors came along and helped them. Now there's people with a damn fool job." Hanrahan fell silent and reflective for a minute. "Boys said Dudley and Wallace were both carved to a filigree. Couldn't really tell if they'd been scalped."

Hanrahan suddenly brightened. "Say, Billy, I've been wanting to talk to you. I've got teamsters and seven skinners and a sorry-ass drunkard who can't or won't kill enough animals to keep them busy. I'd like to run the drunkard off and go partners with you. Fifty-fifty."

"You're going to fire Dutch Henry?"

"I'm not looking forward to it, but I will."

"He might shoot you."

Hanrahan scoffed. "The boys would lynch him. Who else would pay the freight on their whiskey? Dutch don't like it here. He'll be glad to go on back to Dodge, once he's paid out."

"I'd want to keep my own skinners," said Billy, who employed five of them and a cook. "I could keep twenty busy."

Hanrahan ran figures through his head. "I just hired that new kid, Billy Ogg. Says he's a skinner. I don't much care for your boy Masterson."

"Oh, I'd have to keep Bat."

"He's a smart aleck, Billy, and I hear he's slow."

"He gets his work done, and he can laugh with an ear full of maggots. I've seen him do it. I just like to have him around. Makes a man feel lucky."

Hanrahan shrugged. "All right. Whatever keeps the shooter happy. The rest of us are just help."

Billy said, "I'd better tell you, I'm under-gunned."

"I thought you had a good .50 caliber."

"I did, but we had a mishap in the river. Got in water too deep, and the wagon started floating and wobbling. I was afraid I was gonna drown the mules, so I cut the harnesses. The wagon turned over. That .50 is full up with sand somewhere in the Canadian. Wasn't the best day I ever had."

Hanrahan squatted on his heels for a minute, playing with the pup. "Tell you what," he said, looking back at the buildings. "Go back up there to Rath's store and tell James Langton I sent you. He's got a new .44 Sharps he's been holding aside; a fellow offered him eighty dollars for it, but that fellow's not here. Tell James I'll give him ninety dollars cash, and half of it can come out of your share when we settle up."

As they started back Billy was exhilarated by the turn of events. Fannie half-whined and howled, and all at once instinct had her frozen in a point, raised foot trembling. She looked back at Billy to see if she was doing it right. "Good dog," he praised her; a covey of quail broke out of the buffalo grass, which sent the pup leaping and barking after them.

Billy turned and watched the birds' curving flight—and took a quick step back, rattled. Beyond a motte of trees were a number of mesas, about a mile away, and while they had been talking a full moon had jumped up in the sky above them. The last few nights, while it had been building, the sky had been overcast. Now the moon looked as big and juicy as a fresh orange cut in half. The sight of it raised the hairs on the back of Billy's neck.

"How's that for a Comanche night lamp?" he said.

"June moon in Texas, God help Mexico," Hanrahan stated the proverb.

"I wonder," said Billy, "if you ever go back to putting that in mind with sweethearts and valentines."

28

THROUGH THE NIGHT the warriors of the five peoples strung out smoking and waiting in a long grove of cottonwoods in the Canadian bottom, with their leaders and Bose gathered at the rear. After seeing what Quanah's signals and Bose's bugle could do with their horsemen in practice maneuvers away from the Walls—it turned into a game, of course—the war leaders generally if grudgingly consented that his bugle was the best way to bridge the languages and maintain communication. None of them had any experience with such a large war party. Quanah had made Satanta swear he wouldn't start blowing his horn, too. Despite all the promises, only about a hundred Kiowas had come in with Satanta and Lone Wolf. But many of the Kiowas who had come were Koitsenko, and the Real Dogs were riled and eager to bite. It all made Bose very nervous; he never really knew where he stood. A dark-skinned young Kiowa named Gets Around Quiet watched and followed him all the time. The youth envied and wanted that dented curl of brass. With that bugle, a vision had told him, he could soar unseen to far ends of earth and sky.

There were no huddles of strategic discussion in the cottonwoods. The warriors painted their faces, arms, and chests, and brooded intently on their individual medicine. Tobacco smoke lay heavy in the air. A great number of Comanches were putting on buffalo scalp bonnets adorned with hawk and eagle plumage and topknots of magpie. Stories of church and Bible always slid off Bose like melting sleet. Still it was eerie, watching them move around in the darkness with black curled horns on their heads. Quanah asked him if he would consider wearing one of those helmets. Bose replied carefully that he was honored but it didn't seem right. Quanah nodded and said it was a shame; on that Medicine Hat paint he'd make a sight. Bose did consent to shed his split-out shirt and battered hat, and he wore a bear-claw charm and necklace, a gift from Quanah. Bear medicine, Quanah told him, could heal wounds before they were inflicted.

Sitting on the ground, the war chief pulled diagonal smears of black paint across his own face with his fingers, then reached across and daubed some on Bose's cheek. "Already black," he said.

"Change the man's name. Call him Pays Attention."

Quanah grinned and said, "It's the color of death. Why people are scared of you." Bose was pondering the value of this new information when Wolf Shit walked into the grove of trees glowing like a firefly. In the moonlight he was again stark naked except for a bouquet of sage leaves on top of his head, and now he was painted daisy pollen yellow from his toes to hairline. He gave Bose a fright.

"Cheyennes," Wolf Shit hissed at Quanah.

The war chief sighed. "What about them?"

"I just saw two of them eating a skunk."

"They're funny people. They like the flavor."

"Killing a skunk on the war trail can ruin the medicine!"

"I know." Quanah sighed again and thought it through. "Were they eating it raw?" he finally asked.

"No," Wolf Shit said.

"Then they must have killed it and cooked it before we were on the trail. There haven't been any fires."

"Ruin!" Wolf Shit raged.

"What do you want me to do?" said Quanah. "Send them home?"

Bose had been watching him grow vexed with the wear and tear of maintaining a medicine man. He didn't know how much of Wolf Shit's hocus-pocus Quanah believed. But he was certain that hard practicality was one element of his alliance with the shaman.

If magic tricks were capable of holding all this force together, Isa-tai could pull buzzards out of his ear, for all Quanah cared.

As the moon rose there was a stir of horses being brought up and saddled. A young woman came through the trees holding a shield and leading Quanah's war horse, Deer's Son. The girl was not Weck-eah; she and Quanah seemed to be having themselves a little slip-away. It was none of Bose's business.

Even in summertime Quanah always wore leggings. You never knew, he said, how long you'd have to stay on a horse. Above the breechclout he was bare-chested except for a blue scarf with a star-shaped silver clasp. Still visible were the thin scar lines Bose had laid on him with a quirt. Bose was still baffled by the finer points of counting coup. The girl pushed the loop of Quanah's black shield snug to his bicep. She squeezed his hand in parting, and walking away, she cast back over her shoulder a long simmering look.

When she was gone Quanah turned to his horse. Bose watched him weave the mane and then fix the braids and bridle with hawk and jay feathers, pieces of tin cans, shreds of calico cloth. He knelt and unrolled the hide of a buffalo calf, took out and put on his eagle-feather war bonnet, and standing up, flipped the long trail of it over his head. "I wish I didn't have to wear this," he muttered. "It's going to be hot." He picked up his lance, then took out something long and tubular and held it like a scepter.

"What's that?" asked Bose.

"Smoking pipe," Quanah said, showing it to him. "War chiefs are the only ones supposed to carry it into a fight, but Wolf Shit will have one, count on that. Leader's got the hardest road; the pipe keeps it straight and located, people coming along behind. I'll put it in my arrow quiver when the fighting starts. Carry it again, soon as it's over."

Bose gave a nod, as he often did, that contained no under-standing. He couldn't see what was going on behind all that black paint on Quanah's face. Bose had saddled and bridled Tricks, leaving cinches loose so he'd sleep. The saddle leather still showed the leather patching from the rebuilt horn, required all those years ago by this man's attempt to kill him. In the saddle sleeve was Bose's .30 caliber Winchester, and looped around the saddle horn was the army bugle. Quanah inspected the business end of his lance and said, "We're bound to get separated, lose each other. But try to keep me in sight, for whenever we need the horn. If we need it. Prophet says we're going to kill them like old women in their sleep."

"Nice of him to put it that way."

"If something happens to me, don't stay around here."

"Don't worry."

After a moment Bose said, "I'm not going to shoot."

"Oh, I'd shoot," said Quanah, with a slight frown. "I'm not saying you have to hit anything. But people are going to be watching you."

"All right," said Bose.

"Hear me now."

"I said all right."

⋈

Bat Masterson was an aspiring scrivener. In another century and life he would come to the end of his days as the sporting page editor of a New York City tabloid called the *Morning Telegraph*, railing in his column against the bum white heavyweights paraded forth against the nigger champion Jack Johnson. But burning in the bound journal of lined paper now was a grimy and tattered envelope that contained a note signed by one Ina Coolbrith. That a woman could possess such a name intoxicated Bat; her breath must be like perfume; the fancy of it stirring on his cheek raised a lump in his britches. Miss Coolbrith was an editor for the *Overland Monthly* in San Francisco, and she had written Bat: "Though the narrative you have penned is fast-paced and splendid, it is, dare I say, a bit too brutal. If the chase for Bison on the Great Emptiness cannot be made to seem more sporting, perhaps you should redirect your attention to the eccentricity and flair of the men and women drawn to those Desperate Parts. Try us again."

Bat stared at the hunters, skinners, and teamsters in the saloon as if they might be paintings on a wall. He arranged the candle just so, sipped from his bottle of Brandon and Kirmeyer beer, and touched his pencil lead to his tongue. "The Cheyennes had broken out," he wrote, then drank again and rested. His gaze narrowed on Hannah Olds, who sat with her husband and poured Jamaica Ginger into a glass. "In the houses of prairie sod," Bat resumed, "hearts of loyal wives and mothers fluttered from the Dismal River to the Cimarron. How far they were from comfort and the hearths of their fond girlhoods!" He thought for a moment of Ina Coolbrith and her note, then changed the first sentence to read: "In Desperate Houses of prairie sod . . ."

Bat was elaborating on a story he had heard told many times by his friend and boss Billy Dixon. "Malvern McShan and the other freighters could not spare more than a wave of greeting to the children who came out from the farms to watch the long train pass," he wrote. "They had driven one hundred wagons of barely dried timber to the borough a-building at rail's end in Denver, but now these brave teamsters had to make their safe return to Fort Hays, and for the Indians the sight of them would have made a mighty inviting target. Whilst Malvern and the rest had been promised well-broken teams, the mules they got were big, wild aberrations of hot Spanish blood and temper. The hard trundle west had not improved their disposition, nor made them easier to handle. Dear reader, a wild mule team with an empty load is like a wasp-stung finger on a finely-shaven pistol trigger. 'Decamp yourselves, ye balky buggers!' said Malvern, just as Jeb Doran pushed his mules and wagon alongside, desiring conversation. Two teams, not one, heeded Malvern's command, and that is how the great six hundred mule stampede of 1868, which destroyed the town of Inspiration, Kansas, began."

Sitting in a chair beside Bat Masterson was Billy the Kid. Both were about as formed as egg whites just cracked on a skillet, though neither lacked certain kinds of ambition. Bat wasn't sure he wanted the other tagging along after him like a little brother. He didn't like the way his eyes flicked around, though maybe it was just a nervous habit. "Let me see it, I read the last one," Billy pestered, looking over his shoulder. "Made some good suggestions."

Bat closed the journal and put it in his knapsack. "It's rough," he said. "I'll buy you a beer if you'll go get them."

While he was gone Billy Dixon walked in holding a .44 Sharps as dearly as an infant son. "Look here, Bat," said the hunter and boss.

"Whose is it?"

"Mine! Hanrahan bought it for us."

"Hanrahan? Us?"

Billy Dixon looked around to see where Dutch Henry was seated, and lowered his voice. "He's backing us, Bat! Dawn tomorrow! He's got seven more skinners, and he's hired your drinking buddy there."

"Really," murmured Bat. "This boy? I didn't know that."

"This ain't like that country around Dodge, that's been hunted out. The big herd hasn't really started migrating yet. In two weeks this place will look like a mud sea of buffalo. Soon as we find you a proper gun, you're my next shooter. We're gonna get rich."

"You'll let me shoot? Why, bless your heart. I'll be damned."

It was just as well Bat had put up his journal, because Shorty Scheidler was rosining his bow. Shorty played the fiddle and his brother Ike blew the French harp, though his consumption had cut into his wind. Other harmonica players were always eager to join in. Soon the place was rollicking: Hanrahan had to help his barman Oscar Shepherd keep up with pouring the liquor and beer, and on the hard skins in the center of the place, the blacksmith Thomas O'Keefe danced a turn with Andy the Swede, who managed the hide yard for Rath & Company.

Pat Garrett watched the scene, brooding, and sipped his mix of

London Swan Gin and Hostetter's Stomach Bitters. He wasn't happy that Hanrahan had hired away his New Mexico fugitive Billy, who'd explained that being stuck here was giving him the willies, and he'd like to have a little money to scare up a real card game. Hanrahan's shooter would soon find the boy was no skinner. Garrett was beginning to think he was asking for trouble, taking him to Dodge City, St. Louis, or anywhere else. He had a constitutional objection to doing anything he was told. Look at him out there. You'd think it was a room full of whores he was trying to please. With hands on his hips, Billy the Kid was dancing an Irish jig.

When the ridge pole cracked, it sounded like a rifle shot. Hanrahan, who had thrown a bedroll on the ground a few yards behind the saloon, lurched and sat up with his pistol unsteady in his hand. He looked at it and thought he couldn't have hit a bear dining on his kneecap. "Injuns!" his bartender, Oscar Shepherd, exclaimed. Hanrahan calmed down as he woke up, and he couldn't see anything outside but horses, the outlines of the buildings, and the pale white moon. Hanrahan pulled on his boots and walked around the saloon, in the darkness holding his palm up. What had been an occasional sifting of dirt was now a light but steady rain. "Oscar," he said.

"Yes, sir." Holding a shotgun, Oscar crouched behind the bar.

"The roof's about to fall in."

A silence. "No, it ain't."

"Yeah, it is. The ridge pole's broke."

"Nah."

"You heard it!"

"I heard a gun. I come awake scared and thought it was Indians. Somebody probably just killed a snake. Or rolled over in his sleep and blew a foot off."

"Get out of here, damn you, or you're gonna choke and die in the thick of your burying." There was a sound of snoring. Hanrahan walked quickly through the place, disturbing chairs and tables. "Who all's in here?"

Oscar came around the bar. "Beats me."

Hanrahan found a man and kicked his boot. The snoring stopped.

"Who is that?" said Hanrahan.

Pat Garrett said, "Never, ever do that to me again. It's John Long."

Hanrahan rousted them all outside, and, sure enough, moonlight revealed that the thick cottonwood log that held the roof up was bowed and sagging. Hanrahan walked around the saloon in a frenzy. "Overloaded the ridge pole, we sure did. Throwed dirt on that roof all afternoon."

"What time is it?" said one of his veteran skinners, Mike Welsh.

Hanrahan pulled his watch out of his pocket and read it in the moonlight. "Two in the morning."

"I just passed out," said the skinner.

Hanrahan clapped the watch shut. "Grab some shovels but be careful. Send some men with axes down in the bottom and log us a good thick tree; we'll need a sturdy prop for the ridge pole."

Garrett yawned, adjusted his coat and hat, and strolled off. Oscar and Welsh looked at each other. "Can't it wait till light?" said Oscar.

Hanrahan waved his hands wildly. "No, it can't wait! If I lose that liquor inventory, by god, you'll walk back to Kansas."

By the time he got to Billy Dixon, who was sleeping under his wagon with the setter pup and his new .44 close beside him, Hanrahan had ascertained the need to modify his style of entreaty. Cranky Mike McCabe, a skinner on Billy's crew, had arisen from his slumber beside a hide rick in the Rath & Company by throwing a punch at him. One could see how he came by that nickname. "Billy," said Hanrahan. "Wake up. I need your help."

The young hunter listened to his new backer and partner and wondered through a gin headache if he had any choice. Guess not, he decided, and after drinking water and pouring some over his head, he ambled to the saloon with an axe and shovel and the pup. "Civic duty!" he hollered at the louts. "Save the saloon!" About half the men bedded down around the Walls in time got up to help. Bat Masterson wandered over and walked inside the saloon. "It don't look broke to me," he said, and went back to his bedroll in the Meyers & Leonard corral. Andy the Swede bossed the job because he had dug the sod blocks and built the place from ground up. Billy, the blacksmith Tom O'Keefe, and a pair of skinners took turns chopping down and trimming an elm tree with a low fork; they went from still drunk to hungover to sweated out and recovered, if a shade delicate, in less than an hour. The Scheidlers harnessed a well-trained ox that, once tables were cleared out of the way, pulled the log through the saloon and, when the men braced and shoved it upright, inched the prop creaking into place under the ridge pole. "Drinks on the house!" Hanrahan exulted. A good number of men took him up on it. They were up on the roof shoveling dirt, passing a rum bottle, and singing.

> *Bill Jones had two daughters and a song*
> *One went to Denver, the other went wrong*

The moon was finally down. Billy Dixon stood near the saloon smoking with Hanrahan, Andy the Swede, and others who hadn't already gone back to their bedrolls. "What time is it now?" said Billy.

"Four," said his partner, reading his watch.

"Don't make no sense to go back to sleep," said Billy.

"Time to be up anyway," said Hanrahan. "Bring in stock."

Billy nodded. "Get in a day of shooting before it gets too hot. Early bird gets the worm."

"Yeah, all that merry shit," said Andy the Swede. They watched him march to Rath & Company and bar the door shut behind him, before the sentiment spread.

Billy wasn't in a hurry; he just liked the look of that time of day. He sent Frenchy, his half-breed Choctaw cook, to rouse Bat, Cranky Mike, and his other skinners, and got the Choctaw to start a coffee and breakfast fire. He checked the readiness of his wagon again and with the setter pup walked out across the flats. The new skinner, who called himself Billy Ogg, was out there. He was not a bad-looking boy but he had an unfortunate pair of front teeth. The dew was thick on the buffalo grass, and the sky in the east was losing stars and softening into gray.

"I'm your hunter," said Dixon.

"I know," said the other Billy.

"You ready to go to work?" asked Dixon.

"If it'll get me out of Adobe Walls. No offense."

"None taken. We'll be tearing up Dodge in no time."

"How far is it to Dodge City?" asked the Kid. He rued the day he let Garrett talk him into coming out here on these plains. They should have gone to Old Mexico, Billy told him all along.

"Hundred twenty miles," answered Dixon, who started to fire him now and let him get some sleep. He wondered what Hanrahan was thinking—the boy could dance a jig, but whoever he was, he was no buffalo skinner.

"Damn," said the kid. He picked up a rock and sailed it. "I got a kink in my legs, way I slept. I think I'll try and jog it out. See you in a while."

Watching him cross the pasture in a slow trot, Billy could tell by the lightness of his step and the looseness of his hands that the boy was an athlete. He threw that rock like a baseball player.

⋗⋚

Quanah rode out front, the others coming along single file, until they reached the broad sand bed of the Canadian, which was just beginning to change from night's charcoal to its dawn of pink. Crossing the riverbed in ground fog, the riders divided into four columns, except for Wolf Shit, who reined off to the right. For the battle he had exchanged Mackenzie's gray pacer for his white horse, which like his skin was painted bright yellow. Far ahead, they could see horses, mules, and oxen; some of the hunters' animals raised their heads and stared. Beyond the livestock were wagons and the squat sod structures and ricks of buffalo hides, as tall as buildings themselves. Vultures huddled darkly on the ground; already the sky was full of them. The place gave off a powerful stink. War leaders with some years on them, men who this day would stay back and manage the spare horses, kept up a steady crooning to the young ones, trying to keep them calm, until finally riders were spread out and walking their horses forward in one long straight line.

Dixon recognized his remuda by the long dark neck of his favorite saddle horse, Slowpoke. As daylight kindled, the grassland turned blue. He had closed half the distance to his horses when he saw something curious about the ground fog. It wasn't acting right. It stretched all across the horizon and took on vague pieces, depth. The first thing he was certain he saw was the front of a paint horse with a bonnet mark on its head. "Oh, Jesus," he said. Just then the first fire rim of sun appeared behind them, and more Indians than Billy Dixon had ever seen yelled, "WaaoooOOOOOOO!" and kicked eight hundred horses into a thundering run.

Their faces and chests were painted red, black, and yellow, some with slashes of combination across, or eyes and mouths set off by the color, and the horses were daubed up bright as candy wrappers, too. Billy saw shields, lances, a long feather headdress, and domed helmets made from the skulls and horns of buffalo. And mixed in with the shrieks and horse uproar was something exceedingly strange. Billy swore he heard a trumpet.

It was bedlam, the Book of Revelations, and in the face of it Slowpoke went berserk. He was lunging and bucking and about to break his neck or rip out a stake driven deep in the ground. Billy found himself running toward the Indians to try and save his horse. He got a hand on the rope and yanked the halter off. The horse took off bucking and then ran flat out. Billy raised his new .44 Sharps and fired one shot into the rose-colored dawn.

The riders were close enough now that bullets were thudding and skipping all around him. The bugle sounded again, and a column of the Indians veered left toward the hide men's tethered and hobbled horses. Billy watched this in a stupefied daze. His setter pup Fannie cowered under the wagon, and Billy wondered what he could do for him. He finally realized that he was not acting on his best mental behavior. At last he fled.

He looked back and saw Billy Ogg a hundred yards or more to his rear. The Indians were close enough to him that some were drawing back bowstrings. That boy, Billy Dixon thought, isn't going to be playing any more baseball or dancing any jigs, not in this life-time. But Dixon looked back again and saw a sight that amazed him. The other Billy was running a world championship quarter mile. He just made himself relax and lean into his stride, elbows pumping to his ears, and the horses weren't gaining on him very fast.

"Indians! Demons!" yelled Billy Dixon, slamming the stock of his new gun against the thick barred door. "God damn it, let us in there!" Someone threw the door open at last and Billy jumped inside. With an Indian right behind him and leaning down from a freckled horse with a war club, the other Billy ran through the closing crack of door headlong into Hiram Watson, who was stand-ing barefoot in his cotton drawers, and knocked him all the way to the bar.

29

THE HORSES HAD BEEN snorting and sidestepping, anxious to go. Quanah aimed his black forward, then banged his heels against its ribs and raised the lance. The war whoop erupted at the center of the column and as thousands of hooves thudded it billowed upward and out and reached full cry. Prairie dogs skedaddled; meadowlarks and a covey of quail blew upward, followed by the ungainly flapping of the buzzards. Bose had licked his lips constantly and squeezed the bugle in his hand. His heart was beating so hard he thought he was going to fall off the paint.

Quanah threw a look back in the direction of Bose, raised his left hand, and swept his arm in an arc. Bose blew a squadron call, then the four-note "Left Oblique," and watched amazed and proud as, on the flank, riders he'd been drilling peeled off neatly to round the hunters' horses and mules back toward the old-timers coming along to herd them. At the gallop he put the horn to his mouth and blew the sixteen-note cavalry charge. Out before them a hobbled mule spun a circle in panic, going down with hooves flailing. From a wagon, he saw the starburst of a lone muzzle flash.

Bose saw white men jumping up and running all over the compound. Caught far out in the open, two of them almost didn't make it to the nearest door. Three buildings were set in line about fifty yards from each other, and in no time the crowd of horses around them was ten deep and jostling, the tiny windows shot and broken out. Warriors swung up and ran screaming across the roofs, and from what Bose could see and hear, almost all the gunfire was going in, not out. As he followed Quanah in a circle of the compound he saw the shaman maintaining a distance on his yellow-painted horse. Wolf Shit pointed here and there, dispensing his magic, like a man conducting an orchestra. Behind him the sunrise looked cool and flameless, a ball balanced on a plate.

⊰⊱

Near the building with the picket walls, some Comanches moved their horses around a wagon with a white canvas tarp. Inside it, the German teamsters Ike and Shorty Scheidler were hiding under a pile of buffalo robes. They had awakened too late to run. They had their arms tight around Hans, their black Newfoundland retriever, trying to keep him quiet. A Nokoni reservation runaway named Cheyenne swung off his horse to the wagon ledge and with a knife slashed the tarp to see what loot awaited them. Shorty panicked, threw off the robes, and rewarded the warrior with a pistol blast. The force of it forced Cheyenne backward and dumped him on the ground. The gunshot didn't kill him but it sealed the immigrants' fate.

Quanah kicked the black and rode through the cries and swirling bullets. Ike Scheidler fell back riddled, sock feet kicking. Quanah drove his lance deep in the brother's belly, then he made the man waltz with him, turned his horse's head around, and slowly set him down on the ground beside Cheyenne, who found his knife and buried it in the teamster's throat. Then the real fight began. This scene would be played out again and again, painted on Comanche shields and the walls of tipis, long after the fighters of that morning were unsteady getting up on a horse.

The Indians had never seen a dog that big. The Newfoundland's head was the size of a buffalo calf's, and in one roaring leap it was all over them. Hans' teeth looked as big as a mountain lion's. Quanah backed his horse up, trying to free the lance from Shorty, and almost lost his seat trying to get away. A Quohada named Yellowfish was up in the wagon. The dog vaulted on the ledge, then they disappeared—heavy thumps against the canvas, cries of terror, until at last the warrior dove out the back, chewed up good. Soon a dozen Comanches were riding around the dog, which was tiring and roaming like a bull, but then it would rally and charge the horses, trying to knock them down. The horses weren't thrilled with the game. At last Cohayyah shot the Newfoundland three times with a pistol, and its massive loyal shoulder ploughed to a halt near the body of Shorty Scheidler. The Kotsoteka got off his horse and, in honor of the dog's bravery and ferocity, he trimmed off a piece of his scalp.

The stores and saloon were separate islands under siege. None of the men inside the buildings had any idea what was going on elsewhere. The Indians made short work of the gate into the picket stockade of the Meyers & Leonard store. Afoot and mounted, soon they were all around the store, the structure of which proved to be a disaster. Bullets sang through the sand-calked logs, and there was enough space between them that Indians set bows against them and set arrows flying in the murky space. Pots, chairs, and store merchandise flew into shards and splinters; it was a miracle none of the eleven men inside had yet been hit. Shouting orders were the horse thief Dutch Henry Born and the skinner Cranky Mike McCabe. But none could get close enough to the battle ports to return much fire. Pat Garrett, alias John Long, clenched his teeth, ran forward, began to throw corn and flour sacks against the walls, and bellowed at others to help.

The situation inside Rath & Company was no less desperate, though the store's sod walls provided more protection. There were only six people in there, and not one of them was a hide hunter. James Langton, the store manager, tossed his supper of rabbit and gizzard dumplings. Hannah Olds fainted, and when Andy the Swede and the blacksmith Tom O'Keefe splashed her face with water and brought her around, she made them sorry. Mrs. Olds took stock of her special predicament and lost her mind. With strength and quickness that stunned them, she fought off their hands and grabbed her husband William's pistol from his belt, forced it toward her temple, and through the wrestling got off one suicidal shot that missed her but stung the ear of George Eddy, a pot-bellied man who kept track of the store's accounts.

Eddy was a preacher's son from Old Home, Alabama. He stood with two hands on the pistol they'd torn away from Mrs. Olds and stared at the mayhem. His ear was bleeding, and his lips moved in prayerful gibberish. Just then a hand and arm painted with orange circles reached through the small window and roved the room, firing shots methodically from a Colt .44. The hand and arm belonged to a Cheyenne Dog Soldier named Horse Chief. Ears ringing from the blasts, George raised William Olds' gun and pointed it at the limb in the window. He never saw a face—only the hand and arm and a shoulder. The gun's kick almost jostled it out of his hand, but he heard a groan. The long-barreled Colt fell out of the hand. Fingers clawed at the hard sod block, then the hand fell away. The first Indian killed at Adobe Walls was shot by a bookkeeper.

Because of the pre-dawn construction work, most of the men in Hanrahan's saloon had never gone back to their bedrolls, or at least fully back to sleep, so the defense they put up was a little more prompt and spirited. Bat Masterson had made his dash from his bedroll spread near a salt lick in the Meyers & Leonard corral. Masterson, Billy Dixon, and Billy the Kid manned gunports and fired with their pistols because the Indians were right on top of them. Their eyes and mouths were full of dirt jolted loose by bullets thudding into the sod. The ceiling rained soil again as Indians ran across the roof. At both ends of the place, horses were being whipped and driven against the heavy doors braced by an iron bar. If the hinges came loose, it was all over. The squall of wounded horses was awful.

"You hear that bugle?" yelled Bat.

"I hear it," Billy Dixon replied.

"Who the hell is that?"

"Don't know. I done give up hope for the army."

Abruptly the Indians pulled back a distance from the saloon, beyond the range of the hide men's revolvers. They should have maintained the swarm, for the men inside quickly brought up their rifles. Soon the big guns were booming all around and filling the place with smoke. But Billy Dixon could only curse and fling off shots from his pistol—the case of bullets for his new .44 Sharps was over in the Rath & Company store.

Adding to everyone's agitation, Hanrahan's pet crow Clyde kept flying through the place cawing. The poor thing was trapped, and they weren't about to unbar the door and shoo it out, but it did sound exceedingly amused and critical. Billy the Kid got so annoyed that he fired a shot, trying to kill it. This unnerved them all, and soon everyone was screaming at each other. Undone by his run, the snapping bullets, and now all these men raging at him, the boy killer vaulted over the bar and hit the floor, covering his head with his hands.

Billy Dixon saw that Oscar Shepherd, the bartender, had one of Hanrahan's .50 calibers pointed out a port with a view toward the river, but he was so bothered by the recoil that he either jerked the trigger or bucked the stock with his shoulder, endangering nothing but birds and earthworms. Sweat poured off his face, and his hands shook terribly. "Here go, Shep," said Dixon, with a hand on his shoulder. "Let me try."

The bartender shoved the buffalo gun at Dixon like it was burning blisters on his hands. Billy rested the long barrel on the sod and reloaded, watching Indians horses run past the saloon. He heard the bugle again and squinted—his jaw dropped. "Bat, look yonder. Paint horse, three o'clock."

"Yeah."

"There's our bugler. Nigger on a white man's saddle."

Bat hastened off a shot that missed. The paint moved out of their view. "There's a nigger needs killing," said Bat.

"We'll get him next time around," said Billy.

Dixon took his time with the shot he had. He picked out an Indian who had cut off one side of his hair and was coming around on a pale dun. The Kiowa had a leather strap around the horse's neck. He performed an agile and showy stunt of hooking his arm in the strap, his heel on the back of his saddle, and firing a rifle from under the horse's neck. Billy laid the .50's sight just under the horse's withers. The powder blew the bullet through the horse and out the back of the Indian, killing them both, and sometimes a horse will die like a chicken that had its neck wrung, and this one ran on a way, stiff-legged and ghostly, before it fell.

The warriors began to ignore the bugle and resume their traditional form of a circling siege. Quanah was on foot taking care of Yellow Bear, his father-in-law. A horse had fallen and broken his leg. "Go on, go on," said Weckeah's dad, sour with disgust. "Somebody else can carry me out."

The warriors found that the tall ricks of hides behind the stores created sanctuaries in the lanes of fire, and farther back, switchgrass had grown up high around the hillside brooks and springs. But the sun was well up now, and the hunters hadn't exactly lain down like slumbering grandmas. Trying to shore up morale and halt the rearward drift, a Kiowa called Crippled Mule unfurled the dog rope of the Koitsenko. The dog rope of the Real Dogs was a long strip of buffalo hide ornamented with feathers and porcupine quills; tied to it was a painted wood stake. Crippled Mule walked out in the open, hammered the stake in the ground, draped the dog rope across his shoulder, and stood with his arms folded over his chest. The expectation, of course, was that his courage and medicine would draw and hold the line. Crippled Mule had just begun to relax when a bullet from Pat Garrett's Winchester smacked through his chest and rolled him up in his ceremonial leather. Fellow Real Dogs dragged him off in the tall grass for a proper dying, but none of them stepped out to help another man lying open in the sun. He was a Cheyenne and well enough to holler. "Daddy, help!"

"Hold on," his father called. "We'll get to you."

"I can't move my legs!"

Inside the Meyers & Leonard store, the shooters were organized now, and every time a Cheyenne made a dash for Soft Foot, the walls erupted with puffs of rifle smoke and drove him back. Stone Calf started three times, couldn't do it, and took out his anger and shame on his horse. He whipped him and bore down on the shaman Wolf Shit. The prophet sat perspiring calmly under his hat of sage.

"Can you hear that?" Stone Calf yelled at the prophet in Comanche.

"I see and hear all. I look through the dark at occurrences three sunrises to come. I'm aware of all things," said Wolf Shit, haughtily.

"Well, go help my son," the Cheyenne bellowed. "If bullets don't bother you."

Quanah swore and kicked his black into a gallop. Brandishing the lance, he turned his face toward the walls and bellowed insults at the booming rifles and the faces inside. A lanky young teamster from St. Louis named William Tyler gaped as the tall Indian with the lance and long feather bonnet sailed past. "What kind of Indian is that?" said Tyler.

"Comanche," said Cranky Mike. "Tell by the black face."

"That son of a bitch is crazy."

"Yeah, and listen to them yelling," said Dutch Henry. The uproar sobered them all. "He's got their ire back up. Here they come again."

"Well, there's one we can put a muzzle on," said Tyler. "I'm gonna go out there and kill the one that's down and make 'em watch me do it."

Cranky Mike laughed. "Bullshit, don't go out there."

"Watch me." Tyler pulled his pistol from his belt, and they unbarred the door for him. Stooped over, he ran to the Scheidlers' wagon and peeked around it through a wheel. The Cheyenne boy saw him and started singing his death song. Tyler put an end to that with a bullet through his head, and was about to run for the hide yard when a horse came around from somewhere and kicked him in the ribs. Tyler sat still for a minute, trying to breathe, and looked around for the damn horse. Then he saw the mess under his arm and realized he was shot.

Tyler's best friend in the compound was Bat Masterson, who was staring out a port in the saloon and saw the whole stupid thing transpire. Bat turned away in anguish, then told Dixon, "Billy, I gotta go."

"Where'd you have in mind?"

"Outside Meyers' store. Tyler just got hit through the lungs. I saw it."

There was no changing Bat's mind, and Billy couldn't stop thinking about his new rifle that was silent because he'd left the cartridge box in the other store. Following a brief discussion with Hanrahan, both doors of the saloon flew open, and while Bat ran one way, Billy dashed the other. For the next half hour, Bat was preoccupied in the Meyers & Leonard store, helping his friend William Tyler die. They talked about a whore in Dodge City named Marla. Meanwhile, in the Rath & Company store, Billy Dixon was greeted like a regiment of the United States Army. Hannah Olds was huddled under a blanket with her husband's arms around her. "Billy, you've got to stay and help," pleaded James Langton, as Billy prepared to run back to the saloon with the cartridge box under his arm. "Look at us. Nobody in here can shoot."

They were indeed a downcast lot. Above Mrs. Olds' kitchen, Langton had built a transom to let the heat and smoke out, and sacks of flour and grain were stacked on an attic shelf. He never got around to putting a window in. Billy took his new .44 caliber and climbed the ladder. Beyond one of the hide ricks, he saw an Indian crawling in the tall grass, about five hundred yards away. Billy sat on one flour sack, crossed his legs, and laid the gun on another. He let

the sight move with the Indian and took great care with his breathing and slow squeeze of the trigger. He should have thought to brace
himself, though, because the kick skidded his ass right through the
dust on the flour sack, and he came off the ledge with his arms and
legs flailing, dislodging a metal wash pan and landing with terrific
breakage on a shelf of her ironstone china. The other end of that
board contained a tray of her utensils—knives and forks and spoons
went flying in the air.

"Oh, no, they killed Billy," shrieked Mrs. Olds.

"No, they didn't," he announced, staring at his boots and dungarees. "They just stood him on his head, and like to broke his neck."

Shielded from the hunters' view by one of the hide ricks, Quanah shared the water in Bose's canteen. His feathered bonnet was
sweat-bedraggled; the sun was now straight overhead. Bose could see
Wolf Shit moving his yellow horse back and forth about two hundred yards away, and truth be said, he wasn't seeking any cover—he
just wasn't fighting.

"It wasn't supposed to be this hard," said Quanah.

"Maybe you had poor advice."

"What I need," said Quanah, irritated by the quip, "is half our
people on the ground. Horses are giving those hunters too much
target. We've got to get closer. I don't care how big and loud those
guns are; we've got ten, twenty to their one. Keep the ones inside two
of the buildings pinned down and ducking, the rest of us can go over
the top. Take those buildings apart with our hands, if we have to."

"All right," said Bose, though his look around was skeptical.
In effect, the great alliance was breaking up into dozens of raiding
parties.

"Can you make your horn say all that?" Quanah asked.

Bose blew the bugle until his lips and windpipe hurt and he

was sick of the melody, but finally they began to form back up in squadrons. He got them roughly positioned where Quanah wanted, though some were none too eager to quit their horses. He played "Fight on Foot," "Lie Down," "Commence Firing." A surprising number of them did.

But the minute Quanah raised his lance again and charged, they leaped back on their horses and came pouring in behind him helter-skelter. Some horses tumbled in face of the volleys, but again they swarmed around each structure. Quanah bore down on the saloon, whose occupants seemed to enrage him most. He drove his horse chest-first into the barred doors, again and again, and when the black began to flinch, he pulled him around backward to bang them with his haunches. Kiowas on the roof were trying to get the sod to burn. It barely smoked, and bullets through the roof had them dancing.

Frustrated, Quanah moved his horse around the saloon. Inside, Billy the Kid had been jeered so much for his cowardice that he suddenly regained his composure and brass. Through the small window in back, he popped shots at the big Indian and taunted him. "Piss on you, bare ass!" Quanah jammed the lance through the hole at the skinny boy, who ducked the spear just in time. Bose saw the shooting and jousting. Concerned about the risks Quanah was taking, he tied Tricks to the axle of an overturned wagon and brought the sights of his Winchester to bear. The youth bobbed up again and flung a shot at Quanah, who reined around and came after him again with the lance.

Bose's one-eyed squint guided by the gunsight produced a clarity that astounded him. The youth trying to kill his friend Quanah was that lunatic Billy—To-ha-yea's lover-boy. He waited for the head shot, and just like the Winchester's sight was a magnet, it was offered. At the last instant Bose thought about those soldiers at Fort Sumner and the dun packhorse with the botched army brand, and he fired a shot that clipped the window's edge, knocking Billy down with the blast of debris. Peace be with you, fucker.

The warriors were astounded by Quanah's performance, but he couldn't break open the doors, and the pile of horses, some of them screaming, forced them back. The snap, hiss, and skip-sing of bullets overwhelmed the senses, but Bose found himself moving in an ether of strange calm. Horses in shock were paired up and standing noses to tails, shifting weight on their hooves, as if none of this were possible. Maybe, thought Bose, the spotted gelding Tricks really was a magic horse. How else could its rider not be hurt or dead?

Bose lost sight of Quanah for a while, and couldn't say with certainty how long the fight went on. At some point that afternoon he found himself sitting on the ground with his back to the Scheidlers' wagon, which the warriors had roped and pulled over on its side. Bose had Tricks' reins wrapped around his fists and his Winchester's stock planted in the ground, leaning wearily on the rifle, when he felt a gun barrel put to his head. Bose cut his eyes around at the young Kiowa, Gets Around Quiet. As best he could, with the paint trying to shy away, Bose conveyed his message.

What do you want? It's yours.

Keeping the gun hard against Bose's temple, the dark-skinned youth broke the leather thong around his wrist and seized the bugle, then snatched the reins of Tricks. He was one Kiowa who believed in Medicine that paints. Gets Around Quiet leaped in Bose's saddle, gave out a screech, and galloped out to save the day, brandishing the bugle. He rode fifty yards before a rifle slug entered one side of his head and turned the other into semblance of a busted watermelon.

That good horse had endured enough—he just kept running, and in the peso-trimmed saddlebags he carried Bose's identification papers and his sack of gold. "I got the damn nigger, boys," Dutch Henry Born was crowing. "Put an end to his music."

Garrett shook his head. "I'm not sure that's what I just saw."

"What?" yelled Born. "Who shot him if I didn't? *You?*"

"Gentlemen!" the Scot Charley Armitage intervened. "What does it matter who killed him? Let us all proceed to kill the others!"

It took Bose a long time to understand what the Medicine Hat paint and its Kiowa thief had done for him. They left behind an unidentifiable dark-skinned body, multiple eyewitnesses, and physical evidence in the form of a dented curl of brass. They made the bugler at Adobe Walls an almost innocent man.

30

QUANAH'S HORSE COUGHED, staggered, and fell. There was no chance to mourn the black, for it couldn't have happened in a worse place. They were out in the open, far from any wagons or hide ricks, and the eagle-feathered bonnet clearly marked Quanah for who he was. The hunters' bullets chewed up ground and grass everywhere around him. Toward the creeks there was a little grove of plum trees, but it was a quarter mile away, and the only cover between him and the trees was the carcass of a skinned-out buffalo. Quanah retrieved his lance and pulled his rifle and the quiver with his pipe out from under the black, whose breathing was ragged. He put his hand on Deer's Son's face, saying his goodbyes, then ran to the foul bulk of carrion, which had been worked to the bones by buzzards and crows and teemed with ants, beetles, and maggots. But the cover was sufficient that he could look around and plot his next move, which he sure hoped was soon. He could smell the sweet poison bait plugged in the carcass for wolves. He was looking for somewhere to run when the wallop landed between his shoulder and spine.

The pain was immense. Quanah blacked out for some period of time, and when he came back to himself his right side was useless—he couldn't move or feel his arm. He could think of few times when he'd been more discouraged. Then out of a lake of heat mirage, he saw a wobbly rider bearing down upon him. Quanah pulled a hand across the sweat and smeared paint and gore, and peered again. The rider bounced all over the back of a galloping brown mule, trying to stay on. It was Bose.

Quanah apologized for the sorry state he was in. "Tis'che-woon'ie," he said. Looks ugly.

"I can't do that pretty trick of yours," Bose yelled down at him, wrestling the mule's hackamore and head as the bullets skipped and sighed. "You're going to have to help me."

Quanah shoved at the ground with his good arm and staggered to his feet. Bose fought the mule close, reached down and grabbed Quanah by his buttocks, and unceremoniously dumped him across the hornless Indian pommel. "I know you people don't like bridle bits," said Bose, fighting reins and banging his boot heels as the mule rolled its eyes and strolled a circle. "But now and then you need to abuse a mule."

"Estoy en su deuda," said Quanah in formal Spanish. I am in your debt.

"Not yet, you aren't," Bose replied.

Quanah stared at the moving ground and tried not to faint. "What happened to your horse?" he asked.

"Kiowa stole him. This mule was all I could get. Minute you was down, I lost all my popularity."

The brown mule finally gained a trot. Bose kept a hand pressed on Quanah's back to keep him from bouncing off. Quanah clung to Bose's leg with his good hand and watched the trail of his eagle feather headdress drag the dirt. He started laughing. "Look at us. They're going to paint us on shields. Walls of lodges."

"*Run*, you bastard," Bose hollered at the mule.

⧓

By late afternoon Quanah could sit up. Sensation tingled again in his arm. He had been moved back into a cottonwood grove over a little rise, out of sight of the buildings, where Bose helped a medicine woman dress the wound. Stone Calf and Red Moon of the Cheyennes and Lone Wolf, Satanta, and Woman's Heart of the Kiowas had demanded a leadership council. Big Bow and Cohayyah, who were leading the fight now, came in to listen. The Cheyennes and Kiowas wanted to know how the Comanches' war chief had been shot in the back when every white man they knew about was hunkered down in front of them. A signer was on hand to make sure everyone understood what was said. Wolf Shit attended but refused to sit. It had not been a good day for his prophecies. He looked like he wanted to go down to the river and take a bath.

"It was the tuh-tahvoa," Wolf Shit declared.

Suddenly everyone was yelling. "He's going to shoot me and then risk his life coming to get me?" snapped Quanah, trying to stand up. "Man seems to know his mind a little better than that."

"You were shot by the dirty whiteass you brought into our camps," insisted Wolf Shit. Satanta blew a toot on his bugle to stop the arguing.

"Somebody shot you," said the Kiowa Woman's Heart. "One of *us*," he added conspiratorially, moving his gaze from one to another.

Quanah didn't need a prophet to see where all this was headed. "It was a ricochet," he tried to talk sense to them. "Or just a shot gone wild. Forget it."

Tabby-suna was a vain and ambitious young warrior from the remnants of the Kotsoteka band. He had gone into this battle with a mule's tail wrapped around his neck, signifying his great skill at stealing horses, and a blond woman's scalp woven into the nap between the horns of his buffalo skullcap. He made quite a show on a running horse. Tabby-suna was ambitious, and for months he'd been muttering and projecting himself as Quanah's rival. "Tell me this," he challenged Wolf Shit. "Do the whites now have bullets they can fire in circles?"

Though Tabby-suna said it to mock the shaman and Quanah, a number of men in the cottonwood grove gasped fearfully at the thought. Wolf Shit threw up his arms in indignation. He never got a word out, though, because just then they heard a loud *smack* and a horse's grunt. Wolf Shit's matching yellow horse stood blinking with blood running down his face, then his knees unlocked and he raised dust landing on his side, struck square between the eyes by a .50 caliber Sharps bullet that had carried over the rise. So much for magic paint.

⋝⋜

On one of the few horses the hide men still possessed, Dutch Henry Born rode out the first night with the explanation that somebody had to warn other hunters imperiled in the region. He must not have found many, for he was drinking whiskey at breakfast in Dodge City thirty hours later. "Three whites, about two hundred Indians, and one nigger," he would estimate the death toll.

The actual count of warriors killed was nearer forty, but by the time Born made his boast, another man had perished. Hannah Olds was unhinged by her near-suicide and the killing of her pet mustang foal in a barrage of arrows; unable to comfort or distract her, William Olds had taken his pistol and posted a somber lookout from the attic window of the Rath & Company Store. On the horizon he saw some Indian riders, yelled out warning of another attack, and came scooting down the ladder. Mr. Olds' shoe leather shot out from under him, and as he tumbled, the Colt went off and made a mess of his old bald head.

Billy Bonney, alias Ogg, dosed his hurt feelings and sore throat with a bottle of Merchant's Gargling Oil, which was eighty proof alcohol and contained two grams of opium in a two-ounce bottle. Billy and his tall friend Pat Garrett, alias John Long, who would be recalled for his vile temper and coolness under fire, commandeered a captured pair of Cheyenne horses and the second night they skinned out for New Mexico Territory. "You better stay on that horse, boy," Garrett was heard ragging him. "I'll not come back for you."

Beside the walls of the saloon, Billy Dixon was in a fine mood the third morning. During the night his setter pup Fannie had wriggled up against his bedroll, whining and licking his face. Billy had thought for certain the dog was dead. In the Meyers & Leonard store, Old Man Keeler made them all breakfast of coffee, biscuits, and fried buffalo steak. Around the compound, men were looking for souvenirs and used poles unearthed from the picket walls to roll horse carcasses on sleds of dried buffalo hide, so they could be pulled and skidded farther away and set on fire. William Tyler, the Scheidlers, and William Olds were buried. The hide men could still see Indians, but there hadn't been anything worse than sniping since the prior afternoon. Billy watched a number of them silhouetted, some on foot, some on horses, on the flat of a mesa a thousand yards away. He was confident they were out of range. With nothing else to do, he positioned a rock on the ground, laid the .44 caliber on top of it, and gauged the wind. The pup lay panting at his side.

The shoving and shouting on the mesa concerned the display of human heads that the hide men had staked on the pickets of the Meyers & Leonard walls, condemning the spirits of those warriors to wander in that sad condition for all time to come. One of the heads had belonged to Soft Foot, the son of Stone Calf. As the distant muzzle puffed and a bullet the size of a cheroot flew and spiraled, Stone Calf raged at Wolf Shit, who had washed himself clean of yellow paint but was taking none of the blame.

"You're the ones who ruined the medicine," he yelled at Stone Calf. "Can't go one night without eating skunk!"

"*Pole cat* medicine," bellowed a Cheyenne named Hippy, trying to get at him with a horse whip. Several Comanche and Cheyenne men held him off. The shot that made Billy Dixon famous drifted with all the velocity of a wounded bird. It didn't even kill the Comanche it struck, an old Tanima named Sun Goes Down. It just knocked the wind out of him and tumbled him off his horse.

Hardly giving up, raiders swirled across Texas like smoked-out hornets, but the great alliance led by Quanah collapsed. Every night

353

of the Adobe Walls siege, fewer fires smoldered in the cottonwood bottoms.

"Guess it's time for me to go," Bose told Quanah the third night.

Quanah nodded, staring moodily at the coals. His injured arm was bound to his side. Chony, the girl who'd come with him to share in his glory, and one of his future wives, sat glumly with her chin in her hands. "Where will you go?" Quanah said.

"I don't know. Leopard Coat Man told me once I ought to find some big town that suits me. I doubt I have the nature for that."

Quanah tugged at the girl's earring, trying to cheer her up. "I hope you haven't waited too long."

Bose said, "Are we all right? You and me?"

Quanah grinned and poked around like he was trying to find the quirt scars on his chest. "All right and more. Go get a good horse and mule."

Bose sighed. "I shouldn't have ever lost the ones I brought here."

Quanah shrugged. "Well, it happens. Find somebody that didn't lose a horse or mule."

Quanah brooded a moment, then said, "One thing I never understood."

"What's that?" said Bose

"Why didn't you just stay with To-ha-yea? I would have."

"Man, she quit me just like she quit you."

Quanah shook his head. "That kind, they don't leave nothing but the grief."

⊰⊱

Just as it had been when the rangers rode down and snatched his mother and sister and killed his stepmother at the Nokoni camp on the Pease River, when the end of it all came, Quanah was nowhere close around.

In the wake of Wolf Shit's disgrace, the Kiowa shaman Sky-Walker emerged as the most trusted seer. With no taste for big alliance, raiders listened to the Kiowa, who carried an owl that shifted around and rustled when the prophet put his lips close and carried on their conversations. Sky-Walker assured the holdouts that they would never be found if they put up their lodges beneath the towering cliffs along the juncture of Palo Duro and Tule canyons. There were about three hundred lodges of Kiowas, Kiowa-Apaches, Comanches, Cheyennes, and Arapahoes. The emerging Comanche war chiefs were named Red Warbonnet and Poor Buffalo. Most of the ones who followed Quanah had been with him on the Middle Concho.

One month after the battle of Adobe Walls, the daytime sky turned black in a way that had never been seen before. From the Black Hills of the Sioux to the railyards of Denver and to the camps of the holdouts in the Red River's great remote canyons, a plague of Rocky Mountain locusts consumed stands of tall-grass prairie in seconds, ate the wool off sheep, the leather off saddles, blocked and derailed trains with their massive crunch and a flood of brown drool. Quanah decided he'd better lead his wives, daughter, and followers on a journey south to brush country along the Río Grande, and there make a harvest of peyote, before the grasshoppers ate that, too.

Meanwhile, from a base camp on a Pease tributary called Catfish Creek, the obsessed Bad Hand Ranald Mackenzie punished his thirteen companies and Tonkawa scouts with futile searching of one canyon after another. In the heat mirage they saw a wagon that turned out to be driven by the notorious comanchero, José Tafoya. Mackenzie ordered him tied to a wagon tongue and a fire was built under his head. With pole levers, interrogators lowered him howling to the blaze. In no time Tafoya told Mackenzie exactly where to look.

At dawn his troops gaped at what they were about to do and went skidding, running, some of them somersaulting down a cliff of Palo Duro, trying to hold onto their carbines and reins of their horses. One of the Tonks killed Red Warbonnet, the first to shout an alarm and run out to fight. There was a great deal of shooting but few on either side got hit. Mackenzie's troops went from village to village, setting fire to every lodge and sleeping robe, and they captured fourteen hundred horses. Mackenzie had learned his lesson in the battles of Blanco Canyon and the North Fork of the Red. He had the horses driven into Tule Canyon then pushed up a trail and out on the plains. The herd was guarded by more sentries than the tents of his own men. After sunrise and breakfast, Mackenzie told the Tonks to pick out the ones they wanted, and then the horse and mule screams began. The dust from their milling turned the sky brown, the sun copper. The soldiers were killing two a minute, but it took eight hours to shoot them all. All that remained of Comanchería was the legend of a ghost herd led by a Medicine Hat paint.

That fall it rained and flooded for weeks on end. In the canyons tarantulas came swarming out of their red dirt holes. Kiowas were so scared by all this bad medicine that they spent nights on their horses, trying to sleep with blankets on their heads. Quanah and his band wintered in the sand dune hills west of the Pecos, where they left no tracks and could dig a hole to find water but shivered through the cold and had little to eat. The following spring of 1875, with reservation policy taken back from the Quakers by the army, Mackenzie sent out scouts and security with a Methodist preacher, physician, and interpreter named Jacob Sturm. Wolf Shit, whose powers were resilient, drank sugared coffee and smoked with the preacher and called him po'ah-rivo, road-teller. "Our People," he said, "are ready for Jesus and the white man's road."

Quanah's band was camped in Blanco Canyon, where he'd known his greatest glory. As generations of his family would tell it, he went up by himself on a mesa. A lobo wolf came close and howled at him, then trotted off east in the direction of his birthplace in the

Wichita Mountains, in the land that would be called Oklahoma. Some time later a low-soaring eagle brushed Quanah with shadow and flew after the wolf. Quanah and the others who ran off to the Middle Concho had raided and stolen horses with a fury the Texans had never seen, having the time of their lives. Now they accepted the signs of Quanah's wolf and eagle; the women took down their lodges and loaded their travoises and they overtook the moving village of Isa-tai's followers and Jacob Sturm. They hunted along the way and one night had a dance. William Tecumseh Sherman had by then signed orders that, if they survived, seventy Comanche leaders should be chained and shipped in freight cars to prison in a dank stone fort built by Spaniards in Fort Marion, Florida. One of those was supposed to have been Quanah Parker. But Mackenzie was still esteemed as the brightest junior officer in the army by Ulysses S. Grant. The president countermanded that order; the prison train never left the station. Bad Hand, the No Finger Chief, rode out to meet Quanah with the formality of Grant accepting the sword of Lee.

Within a few months Mackenzie wrote the old patriarch Isaac Parker, who had tried and failed to tame and reclaim Cynthia Ann, that her son was "a man whom it is worth trying to do something with." The Texan never wrote back. Bad Hand appointed Quanah the reservation chief and issued him documents that guaranteed him free travel, even to Mexico. But the followers who had come in with him were herded in a rock corral at Fort Sill, and there they stayed for many weeks. Soldiers laughed and threw them slabs of raw meat.

PART IV

Peyote
Road

1909

31

AN OLD MAN DOZED in the front porch shade. Two legs of the cane-bottomed chair, and both of his, were poised in the air. A dark hand rose and brushed off a fly that scrabbled in coils of white beard. Actually a bee, judging from the thump against his hatbrim. A bead of sweat caught a rib and slid all the way to his spine. Annoyances.

The light was dusty and pale, drained by the heat. Time of year when plants wilted and people yearned for the first norther. One past noon, judging from the shadow. A tall, bone-thin white man was paying him close attention.

He had a black moustache and a very sharp chin. He stood with one boot on the porch and rested his arms on a thigh that looked like a drainpipe wrapped in khaki. He wore a long businessman's coat and a hat with a ring of sweat around the crown. To his rear, a chestnut horse hitched to a buggy moved flies with its tail in the shade of the bois d'arc trees.

Got to get me a barking dog. People going to sneak up on you.

"Bose Ikard," said the one on his feet. "Your kinfolks claim you're dead. No doubt wish it."

Bose set the chair legs down. "Pat Garrett. How you been? Drunk?"

Garrett smiled. "I walked up on you asleep," he said. "That used to be impossible. Used to be the source of your fame."

"Man comes by fame all sorts of ways. Buffalo hunters. Killers. Strikebreakers." He bit the words like they were cloves of garlic.

With long fingers, Garrett flicked a ladybug off his knee. He feigned a sad brow. "Bose, I'm sorry. I've been asked to bring you in."

Bose flinched, just barely.

"Not far," Garrett offered. "Mineral Wells."

"Asked by who?"

Garrett stepped up on the porch. He reached in his coat pocket, produced a leather wallet, opened it, and thrust it twelve inches from Bose's face. The badge looked genuine, but no eyes their age could read that close. When Bose tried to move the badge back out to focus, Garrett clapped the wallet shut and returned it to his coat.

"Seem like I heard a story, not long ago," said Bose. "President Roosevelt was down to a Rough Riders reunion in San Antonio. The El Paso customs inspector came to town for the occasion. The customs inspector got the president of the United States to stand for photographs with a friend of his from El Paso. Irishman. Gambler fellow. Those pictures turned out to be a discomfort to President Roosevelt. And Inspector Garrett lost his appointment. I heard." Bose scratched the stubble on his jaw. "Show me that badge again. Show me your jurisdiction."

"Your hand's shaking, Bose. Am I making you nervous?"

"Shit. Never come the day."

"There's no statute of limitations on murder. Or treason."

"Lord, help." Bose laughed, though his heart was pounding. "You're the one made a medicine show of killing a man. That boy passed twenty-five years ago. You wrote yourself a book. Got rich, got famous. How long you gonna roll around in that grave? Can't you keep him down? Don't you mind the stink?"

Garrett stepped back from the porch with both hands in his coat pockets. He turned his back on Bose and watched a buzzard make a low wobbling pass.

"You ought to try and get along with me," he said. "You're wanted for your fine company and your smart conversation, just now. It is hoped," he said, "that you will sleep without worry or waking in your own bed tonight. You're better than sixty years old."

The screech of cicadas rose and sawed and rasped. With a flash of salmon rouge, a scissortail ascended from the fence-row brush, chasing a fly. The elegant little bird rolled its long tailfeathers like a woman kicking sheets away with young bare legs. He shrugged. "All right. Nothing shaking here."

Garrett looked relieved. He walked on the porch, peered through the door, and assessed the meager contents of a tenant shack with holes in the floor. "You might want to shave and wash," he sniffed. "Put on clean clothes."

✕✕

Garrett let the horse take his time. Bose wore his good white shirt, khaki dungarees, a pair of knee-high riding boots that laced up the front, and a light brown hat with a sharp low crown. With his razor, he had left a line of white whiskers under his lower lip. He wasn't going to shuffle into town in no sharecrop overalls. His stomach was flat. He had all the teeth that showed. He still had some style.

The highway west out of Fort Worth and Weatherford was rolled and packed with sandstone grit. The cotton fields gave way to sun-bleached pastures as the buggy clicked on. Garrett broke the silence. "For the record, I had to go to Santa Fe and court the legislature six months before they'd honor that fool governor's five hundred dollar reward. The hotel bills and card games cost me more than that. Fortunately, the common people took me to their hearts. When they heard how the politicians were behaving, they mailed me twelve hundred and fifty dollars, most of it in worn bills and silver. That's all the money I ever made off Billy Kid Bonney. Billy the Kid." He spoke the names with severe distaste. "I wrote that book with two newspapermen. One was an old drunkard who couldn't hit the type-

363

writer keys, and the other didn't have the first idea how to sell it. I haven't done too well with partners, in my time."

"I'm sorry to hear it," said Bose.

"My conscience is clear."

"Glad to hear that."

"Have you left your wife for good?"

Bose stared straight ahead, stonily.

Garrett clucked his tongue and flicked the reins at the chestnut rump, smiling. "I fear I have quit mine," he said.

"I take special assignments," he went on, "in my former line of work. Did you know that in Old Mexico I am licensed to practice law? I arrange opportunities for American investors who wish to take advantage of the copper, silver, and mercury mines. I'm an expert on irrigation, Bose. I can *make water flow uphill*. I own a ranch in Doña Ana County, New Mexico. I breed the finest Steeldust and Cleveland Bay horses in the territory. I maintain a stable of Peruvian thoroughbreds. My son Poe is the trainer and jockey. You recall my wife, Apolinaria?"

"Oh yes. Cooked you chicken soup when that pig liked to have ate your skinny ass." Bose wagged his knees and clapped his hands lightly at the thought.

A roiling column of dust moved down the long hillside before them. The chestnut pricked his ears, and Garrett pulled the reins tight, braced his legs, and controlled the horse as the motorcycle passed. "By all rights," he continued, "I'm a happy and fulfilled man. So why is it that I'm living in El Paso with a thirty-eight year-old trollop? Look here, Bose." He stretched his lower lip with his finger and displayed the dark stub of a fractured bicuspid. "I've had more fistfights in six months than in the last twenty years. Frank Amador did this to me. A stoop laborer who stands five feet seven inches."

Garrett was at least six-five, though his posture, never good, had worsened with age. "I awake in the mornings with the riled beast of a lad in my Turk's pajamas," he said. "It seeks the trollop and side-winds under her tent flap. I fear for myself, sometimes. Where's my tranquility? My peace of mind. What the hell is going on?"

In a second-floor room of the Hexagon Hotel in Mineral Wells, Quanah Parker stood before a mirror and attached a silver starburst pin to the knot of his red silk cravat. Theodore Roosevelt's bally-hooed wolf hunt on the reservation prairie called the Big Pasture and their resulting friendship had made him the most celebrated Indian in the United States. Most of the canines taken on that hunt were coyotes and a few wolf-dog mixes, but it didn't matter. They rode behind greyhounds and rough-haired staghounds that could cruise up beside a wolf or coyote and flip it by the nape of the neck. Quanah thought Roosevelt was an odd man, forever cleaning his glasses and spewing opinions and questions like a Gatling gun. He danced around in a bramble on the hunt and popped the head off a coiled rattlesnake with his quirt. For the president's speech in the little town of Frederick, Oklahoma, Quanah and the Texans delivered him down the main street at a full gallop, elbows flapping.

Quanah worked sleeves of beaver over his braids. Crescent moons swung at the ends of fine silver chains that were hooked in his earlobes. Under his black Homburg, pinstriped blue serge suit, and boots sewn from the pink, yellow, and purple hides of gila monsters, he was also the most powdered Indian in the United States. Every day after his bath he flung handfuls of talcum powder on his back, his buttocks, his balls. At home, his wives took turns cleaning up the floor. He was not a favorite of hotel maids.

Under the sun no man could help but sweat. His people deified sweat; it flushed affliction from their veins, clarified their wits, and honed their reflexes. Sweat was good medicine. But more and more, Quanah took exceptional pains not to smell. Despite his robust size, despite his many wives and ex-wives, despite virility evidenced by his twenty-two sons and daughters, counting the ones that died, Quanah ached all the time. His spirit was riven, and obsessions stewed in the wound.

Quanah buttoned his lapels and dropped his room key in his pocket. He was expected at this hour at the cattle growers' and trail drivers' baths. Steam would fog the mirrors, and water would drip from gurgling overhead pipes. In the baths, the old cowboys looked like bleached stewed prunes. Told the same old stories. The invitation letter had come addressed to "Capt. Quanah Parker, Big Chief Comanches." Their patronage made him tired.

Memories the old men shared were like jiggers of horseradish tonic. But enterprise was the heart of it. The ranchers coveted the sheen of rich Indian grass in Oklahoma. Quanah had made his people good money leasing grazing to ranchers in north Texas. Near the Medicine Mounds, in gratitude they named a town Quanah in his honor. Burk Burnett had fifteen wagonloads of lumber trundled from Wichita Falls across Red River so they could build Quanah's Star House on the prairie at Cache. They told the story that Quanah was commissioning himself a general, like the soldier chiefs at Fort Sill, when he had his blue roof shingled with white stars. They told it like fathers passing on the fanciful yarns of their little boys. Truth of it was, Quanah just liked stars.

His hand was on the doorknob when he stopped. He swung about and paced. He rested his arm on the chest of drawers and gazed blankly at the flowered wallpaper. It was not yet Saturday, and he did not like to violate ritual. But he pulled out the top drawer and removed a pouch made from the pelt of a black fox. He emptied it carefully and scattered dark cactus buttons across the top of the chest. He arranged the small ones in the shape of a crescent moon.

One was as large as the gonad of a yearling calf. In the long ago, he had picked it green in a dry gorge in the rough country of Mexico, then rode eight days north to lay it on the bare stomach of the Mescalero who broke his heart. Quanah's herb was known and honored now by the Kiowas, who called their road the Church of

366

the First Born and were just as evangelical as the last Comanche war chief; and by Caddos, Cheyennes, Wichitas, Pawnees, Arapahoes, Poncas, Osages, and Otos, whose lodges Quanah had initiated and served as road chief, tribe by tribe. The fetish herb passed from hand to hand around their midnight fires and would be prized by his survivors until it turned to dust. He held the herb in his palm now and listened closely. After an exasperated silence, Father Peyote sighed.

Quanah selected four buttons—a fraction of his usual dose— and returned the rest to the fox-hide pouch. He carried the nubs to the window, pulled back the lace curtain, and with a clockwise movement of his hands offered them to the sun blazing over the town's tin roofs. Ignoring the bitter taste, he chewed the buttons one at a time, patiently, working the woolly centers loose and forward, against his teeth. He hawked the fibers on the carpet. He swallowed each of the buttons with two stern gulps, then walked to a pitcher of water and poured himself a glass. He drank it smiling at the sun.

Quanah let the feebles pass before he ventured out. On the stairs he encountered a well-dressed white man and woman. "Good afternoon," he greeted them. "Isn't it warm?" The man curtly nodded, but the woman slipped him a curious look. From a seam of buttons over her tightly girded waist, the flat yellow and orange head of a corn snake began to emerge. It became a honda knot of a lariat, braided in gold. The rope poured blazing from her middle like a thing possessed, looped and writhed, re-entered her stomach with a sly flick of a serpent's tail. On the street a little girl with braids and petticoats ran out of an ice cream parlor and collided with him; when she looked up, her eyes leaked jets of blue flame. Quanah raised an orange hand that was grotesquely scaled and placed it on top of her head, guiding her on her way. The herb was feeling fast and playful. His heart was soaring.

32

As Garrett's buggy came into the outskirts of Mineral Wells, they were overtaken by a jackass party in a merry hurry. Concessionaires had taken to renting donkeys to health faddists for scenic outings up in the hills. The women in this bunch jiggled on sidesaddles; their hats were laden with paper flowers and waxed fruit. The suited men whacked their burros into a trot with riding crops. Garrett steered the chestnut to the right, stood up, greeted the ladies with a forefinger to his brim, and tried to offer any of the gentlemen a business card. With a derby on his head and a cigar clenched between his teeth, the last one laughed at Garrett. He stared after them blackly and sat back down.

The resort of Mineral Wells now rivaled Galveston. In an old mustang canyon, a homesteader swore that his well water healed his rheumatism, and a few dippers a day restored the wits of a crazy woman, his wife. She lost her mind one day when renegade Comanches were still a peril, and a hard crossing of the Brazos killed one of their oxen from exhaustion, still in the traces. It just went to its knees on the bank. Then a lightning bolt struck and killed the other ox. The homesteader was deaf for several days. He hired some men from Weatherford to help him build a double-log cabin on their claim, and then he got a water well dug, and the blather of his wife cleared right up. Well, there was money and market in that story. Hotels and conventions, bathtubs and clarinets. Fixed with porticoes for sidewalk shade, the buildings were built of sandstone or brick. Sign-painters had covered up the sides with offerings of bottled-water cures for sore throats and inflamed eyeballs. "Takes the temper out of Red Heads," promised one brand. "Puts ginger into ginks and pepper into plodders."

Garrett pulled into a livery and left the horse and buggy with a boy. They walked past the long open drinking pavilion next to the Crazy Well. Under chandeliers and tooled bronze ceiling, fops and ladies fanned themselves and held glasses of water like they were goblets of champagne. Crazy water. To Bose it tasted like the same old gypsum brine that cramped bowels all over the plains. Local hawkers of the stuff proposed that these particular ground salts contained a trace of the fad lithium, endorsed by New York doctors as a cure for all manias. Maybe Bad Hand Mackenzie gulped too much out of his canteens.

Mackenzie had gotten his precious general's star fighting on against the Sioux and northern Cheyennes after Custer's miscalculation on the Little Big Horn. Mackenzie twice invaded Mexico, scattering the Kickapoo in the Sierra Madres, and bluffed the last hostile Utes out west into surrender. Sometime in the eighties he'd come back to San Antonio to command the army in Texas—which made Bose nervous—and the Indian fighter was in all the social pages with a sweetheart and fiancée. Then shocking word spread even to cotton farms in Parker County that Mackenzie had been relieved of his command, suffering "paralysis of the insane." Syphilis was the most common slander. He died in an asylum on Staten Island, New York, the year before the turn of the century. Hardly anyone but old Indians attended his funeral. Bose admired and enjoyed his acquaintance with the man but couldn't rightly say he mourned him. He'd spent fifteen years in dread of Bad Hand testifying against him.

"You're awful quiet," said Garrett. "Are your nerves steady? I'd hate to have to shackle you."

"Take your hand off my arm."

They climbed a hillside that boosters called Welcome Mountain. On its summit was the Chatauqua Theater. Garrett walked up on the columned porch and opened doors of beveled glass. Bose removed his hat and followed him up stairs carpeted in blue. On the second floor there was a door elaborately painted 5¢. Garrett turned the brass doorknob and found it locked. He knocked several times politely. Then he kicked it with his boot.

A bald white man with pink suspenders and jittery countenance opened the door. "You're Garrett?"

"I am."

The man looked at Bose and turned pale. "My god, man. You can't bring him in here."

Thing is, Bose was thinking, you don't ever hear that said in regard to a nigger bound for jail. He threw Garrett's hand off his sleeve, brushed past the man in the suspenders, and entered an anteroom with red carpet and walls, except for the one in front, which was black. He began to see that a couple of dozen chairs were lined up in rows, facing a curtain. "You're shining," the woman said. "The light behind you. The silver in your hair."

She was wearing a dark blouse with yellow flowered patterns, several necklaces of silver, coral, and turquoise, and long earrings of white pearl. Her hair was put up with a silver comb on the back of her head.

"Do you know me?" she said.

"I see it's you."

To-ha-yea smiled and looked past him. "You impress me, Mr. Garrett. I had booked the whole day. And prepared for your apologies."

"You had prepared to pay for my train ticket. And my Dallas recreation."

"I thought of that, yes."

"But a man can't live on retainers," he said.

"Fully paid, can a man keep his word?"

"Begging your pardon, señora. None of this puts any color in my tea."

With a nod she opened a clasp purse in her lap and withdrew a white envelope. She made Garrett edge between the chairs to reach it. She made a proud man stretch.

Garrett touched his finger to his hatbrim and glared at Bose. And then he plunged down the stairs and banged the lobby doors against the hinges. He took the front steps two at a time, coattails billowing. He descended the slope as far as the first post oak shade. He sat down with his back against the tree and took his hat off. His thin black hair was wet and matted against his skull. Garrett the manslayer. Garrett the whore.

He reached inside his coat and raised a pint flask filled with sweet Canadian whiskey, his adam's apple juggling like a carburetor's float. In time he drew the back of his hand across his moustache; the breeze felt good against his face. Garrett pulled the envelope from his other coat pocket and held it to his nose, breathing her perfume. A man does what he has to do. He cut the flap with a penknife and began to count the twenty-dollar bills.

In the steaming bathhouse of the Crazy Well Quanah lay on a sheeted table with his arms hanging off the sides and a towel stuffed between his legs, like a breechclout. He grunted in tremors and kept his eyes shut. Otherwise, he had found the shoves and whacks and probing thumbs of the masseur set off crashing waves and vortexes of color that were a discomfort to him, just now. His stomach and the herb were punishing him for violating the ritual.

On the table next to him lay Charles Goodnight, the Leopard Coat Man. Quanah had spent a third of his days hoping to catch and kill him. But the year of Adobe Walls, Goodnight had lost his Colorado ranch and his money in a national panic that caused the failure of his bank in Pueblo. Leaving his orchards and alfalfa fields to his creditors, he drove a herd of salvaged longhorns into Palo Duro Canyon, where he built a dugout and started over with a ranch that soon spread far out on the plains. The enormous pile of Indian horse bones ordered by Ranald Mackenzie littered the prairie. He allowed the Comanches and Kiowas to come over and hunt deer and what remained of the buffalo with an escort of Fort Sill cavalry. On the first of those hunts Quanah shook the hand of a grimy little long-haired army scout who said he was Billy Dixon, the man who fired the impossible shot at Adobe Walls. And then he met the rancher who made a point of wearing a tattered vest cut from the hide of an ocelot. Goodnight was a brave old coot. He told Quanah more than he'd ever known about what happened to his family on the Pease, and said he was sorry.

Quanah worked hard at purging all hate from his spirit, and in the years since then the old rancher had doted on him like an adopted son. Goodnight was a saddle-gnarled man with small feet and a very large head. He had a craggy brow, eyes set deep and close together, and a beard that turned white years before his hair. As another masseur kneaded his wrinkled flesh, he was trying to interest Quanah in his cross-breeding of cattle and buffalo. "You start a buffalo bull and just a fair Angus cow," the old man carried on, "because birthing a bull calf will always kill her. But she's got an even-money chance of delivering a heifer. When that cattalo's four, now you can go either way, but I like to breed her back to a buffalo. Her bull calves won't be fertile, but the cow calves will. When you get them heifers grown, you put Angus bulls on them, and you got yourself a cattalo herd. Good meat, and they don't wander. Won't tear up fences like a buffalo will."

The heat, damp, and smell of perspiration made it hard for Quanah to breathe. And the herb suddenly launched him to his heart's deepest shame. Ten years after Quanah and his last holdout band gave up, some Texas cattlemen had paid Quanah and three other Quohada men to come to a convention in Fort Worth, a place of train yards and slaughter houses, the reek of much cow manure. One of the men who rode the train with Quanah was his father-in-law, Yellow Bear. Near the sprawling stockyards they followed the old cowboys from saloon to saloon. None of the Quohada drank more than a ceremonial taste of the whiskey; they weren't going to give the Texans the satisfaction of seeing them drunk.

On the cheap, the ranchers had put them all up in one hotel room. Quanah deferred to the others and took the floor. Horned Frog and Cotopak Birdsong soon snored side by side in the feather bed. Quanah and Yellow Bear talked long into the night about children, grandchildren, and what the ranchers ought to be paying the people for leasing their good reservation grass. Despite all the battles they'd fought, Quanah respected no man more.

It was a wintry night, and the room was not heated with the chortling and clanking steam radiators they were used to finding in hotels. It was a new kind of stove with an open blue flame. Restless in any structure of the whites, Yellow Bear opened the window and leaned out for a moment, then laughed. "I'm cold and old, Quanah." The elder arranged his blankets on the floor, then blew out the kerosene lamps and studied the stove on his hands and knees. In the remaining light, Quanah thought, he indeed resembled a big-bellied bear. Like he was deciding whether to break in a barn. Yellow Bear took a deep breath and huffed out the blaze.

Quanah came awake with his cheek on the hardwood. He heard the men pounding on the door and calling his name, but he couldn't move or answer. When the Waggoner Ranch foreman, the hotel manager, and a deputy sheriff broke the lock and burst through the door, they almost broke Quanah's neck. He lived and breathed because of the air that got in the crack between the door and the floor. The others died inhaling the poison heating gas. On the reservation some claimed murder, negligence at best. Isa-tai used the tragedy and discord over the grazing leases to challenge Quanah in the next election for reservation chief. Quanah narrowly defeated Wolf Shit in the tribal election, but Weckeah never stopped blaming him for the loss of her dad.

"Plus I have found," Goodnight was saying, "that it cuts way down on your salt costs." Quanah looked at him and gaped. The old scout and ranger had turned into a buffalo bull—a rare white one, the kind worshipped by Cheyennes. Hunters had sprawled him on his belly with the legs stretched out. They'd knifed the hide around the throat and rolled the brisket down so they could cut through the shoulder joints, but they'd taken care to peel the hide back from the hump without getting it bloody.

The bison chewed his cud and returned Quanah's gaze.

Quanah clamped his eyes shut and begged the herb's forgiveness. He made himself concentrate. "How long you been breeding them cattalo?"

"Thirty years."

"How many head you got now?"

A dour pause. "Forty."

"Have to save a lot of salt to make that into money."

Then Quanah was riding his best horse of the war and chase, Arecatua, Deer's Son, and was using the light saddle pad without stirrups, in the old way. But the great black horse was dead, killed at Adobe Walls. But sometimes the herb took them at a lope into the valley beyond the sundown. He was glad that he arrived so well-mounted; it meant he had lived a good life. The broad river valley had dunes of white sand beside the clear-running stream, and its rustling cottonwoods were the tallest he had ever seen. He arrived during the migration of the sandhill cranes. There were thousands of them. The sky was cloudless, and it struck him that he had never lived in a place that had no wind. He saw hunters running a herd of buffalo, then the vast herd of horses, and then the lodges beside the stream. The riders who came toward him were the greatest Comanche chiefs who ever rode—Iron Shirt, Buffalo Hump, Nocona, Ten Bears, Parra-o-coom, Mow-way, Cohayyah, Voice of the Sunrise. They beckoned for him to follow. He saw his mother on the gray horse she was riding when the rangers took her and Prairie Flower away. Naduah jogged her horse out to greet him, and she stretched out her arm and said, "I have something for you." It was a peach, pivaronab. In those days the fruit was exotic to them—they called it a Mexican persimmon. But there was no alum to pucker the roof of his mouth and tongue; it was all sweetness. He took the ripe peach from her and saluted her with it, seeing and laughing with her at last. The rich juice ran down his chin.

⋈

The white buffalo spoke again. "I've been working hard on getting your mother back to you."

Quanah opened his eyes and was relieved to find a man. "I appreciate that," he said sincerely.

He wanted his mother's remains to lie among people who knew and loved her. But her white kin in Texas, a numerous, stubborn, and powerful clan, were dead-set against the one they called Cynthia Ann being dug up and moved to an Indian grave in Cache, Oklahoma.

"I've got people greasing the legislature now," Goodnight said.

Greasing it. "I hope that helps," said Quanah.

"It would have helped," the old man yelled, "if you hadn't stood for pictures leading a 'Peyote Delegation' to the constitutional convention in god damn Oklahoma!"

Quanah set his jaw. "Law they're trying to pass up there is wrong."

"You've got powerful friends in Texas, Quanah. Burk Burnett, Dan Waggoner, Sul Ross—"

"Sul Ross!" Quanah exclaimed. "He's no friend of mine. Got himself elected governor on grounds of killing my father, which he never did. I bit my tongue, but that man's a liar."

"Well, I never liked that one either," Goodnight allowed. "But you've got to help people who can help you."

Quanah made a sound of distaste. "You ever hear from Bose?"

"Now and then. I write him letters and send him money."

Quanah raised a hand to stop the masseur from kneading his backstrap. His thumb was digging right in the scar tissue where he'd been shot at Adobe Walls.

"Son of a bitch has stayed mad at me for nearly thirty years," Goodnight went on. "But he'll write me a letter now and then. And, oh yes, he'll take my money."

33

Bose sat with his forearms on his knees, facing the black curtain. "Don't be angry," To-ha-yea said gaily. "Bose my rose. I just wanted to see you again."

"You're taking chances with an old man's heart."

"Come sit closer."

They always spoke Spanish before. He remained where he was.

"You were so angry at me. I wrote you letters and you never wrote back. You're such a hermit, they say. Mr. Garrett said he didn't think I'd ever get you to come to town."

"I'm not mad at you anymore. Haven't been for ages, and I never got any letters. I sure would have written back."

"Oh, that's a shame." She stood and with a rustle of her skirt moved between chairs toward him. He remembered a hoyden grabbing a fistful of buckskin and with a show of young bare legs leaping on a horse with a blanket for a saddle. She lifted his hat from his hands, placed it aside, and took the chair next to him.

Bose looked around at the man with the suspenders. He fiddled with a large box set up on a table with a contraption of wheels attached. The man's mortification was apparent. Bose said to her, "Garrett called you señora."

"I've had three husbands," she said. "The next one after Quanah, Jim Kanseah, was just like my father, Old Wolf. We had four years together. He hated the reservation and loved Chihuahua, the City of Mules. He went down there, and like my father, he fell in with the band of Victorio. You were wise that time you refused

377

to take me to the Blue Mountains. That boy Billy didn't take me down there either; he had every reason to go and nothing to lose by disappearing himself in Mexico. Both Old Wolf and my husband Jim Kanseah were killed by Mexican soldiers in the ambush at Tres Castillos, in the Blue Mountains. Later I married a good man named Armando Chavez. He had a ranch in the Mogollon Mountains. Much land, and they found some silver. He died of a cancer three years ago."

"I'm sorry," responded Bose. "My wife's named Angelina. She and I, oh, we got our ways."

The man with the suspenders cleared his throat. "We're ready, madam," he said. To-ha-yea turned and nodded; the bump of her knee sent a tremor through Bose. It had been a long time since anyone had given him the delectable chills. A whirring racket began. Bose clamped his hands on his knees and turned stiffly in his chair. "What is this, To-ha-yea?"

"It's a motion picture." She touched his hand. "Watch."

THE BANK ROBBERY
Frank Canton
Al Jennings
Quanah Parker
Heck Thomas

Some people had trouble seeing the things at first, they got distracted by the mites dancing in a cone of pale light. But Bose saw the images of it right away. In a block of light on the black curtain, men in tall hats rode up to a log house. They wore gun belts and bandannas. One raised a hand in greeting. When they were inside a horse stood swishing its tail.

Next appeared a squat building in some barren town. Men in boots and derbies and a woman in a long dress with a sunbonnet thrown back from her hair strolled in and out. A spotted dog nosed around. Eventually one saw a sign painted across the building that read Bank of Cache. Suddenly three men jumped out of the window. Men were running; long plumes of smoke shot from their pistols. Two of them were down in the street, and they continued to point their guns and shoot each other.

"Isn't it silly and grand?" said To-ha-yea. "Every day thousands of people sit in the dark for hours and do nothing but this."

"Quanah had something to do with it?"

"He made it with a bunch of his cowboy friends in Oklahoma."

A man galloped a horse down a street where an automobile sat parked. Another man ran into the street with a shotgun, it appeared, and fired another blank of black powder smoke. The portly robber jumped out of his saddle and hit the ground trying to run. He rolled about holding his knee.

Bose laughed. "Old fool, I'll bet that did hurt."

Riding a light-colored horse, Quanah led the posse out of a side street in the town. He wore a long-sleeved white shirt, a vest from a suit of clothes, and a high-crowned hat. He looked and dressed like the others, except his face was darker, and as the horse jogged, one could see the braids flopping on his collar. Wherever they went, the following of dogs grew. Accompanied by a young blond woman who gave her horse a continual whacking with a quirt, the bank robbers put their horses across a creek; abruptly they pulled up and one dumped a man, apparently wounded. It took a while for the body to float.

"I've seen it a couple of times before," To-ha-yea said. "The girl's the best rider of them all, and she's pretty, isn't she? Wonder why she didn't get her name on the screen."

A man was talking to the bank robbers at a house in the country. As a gelded horse was led around them, he raised his tail and let fall a great deal of digested oats and hay. The posse ambushed the robbers in a river bottom. After the gunsmoke cleared, Quanah jogged around minding the horses and looking very agitated that the girl was so upset. Coming out of the bottom she rode unhappily behind a man whose head was thickly bandaged, though he still wore his hat. A mule-dawn wagon hauled the bodies. Quanah looked a little paunchier, but when he touched the horse with his heels he bounced easily and long-armed in the saddle, leading them out under a sign that said Wichita National Forest & Game Preserve. Bose grinned. "An actor, what do you know. Reckon somebody paid him to do that?"

"I think he paid them."

Bose let himself touch her skirt with his thumb and forefinger. "Don't believe for a minute I don't like seeing you, girl."

To-ha-yea watched Bose's hand until he grew self-conscious. When he started to move it, she caught it, turned it palm up, and worked her fingers between his own. In front of the Bank of Cache, Quanah was slyly circling his horse through the happy milling crowd, making sure he was the first and last rider in the posse captured on camera. The señora smelled like Paris, France. They held hands in the dark and watched the moving picture.

The old half-breed climbed the long hill overlooking Mineral Wells, clutching the handrail of the log switchbacks, dismayed by how often he had to stop and blow. Below him, the town that the whites built for their madmen glimmered and surged like a band of foot warriors with torches. An orchestra struck up a tune on a hotel roof. Geysers of yellow, pink, and sapphire rose and fell with the tones of brass and drum. The sound machine they called a trombone brayed loud and crudely. Its spurt was the green of melting copper.

As Quanah stalked the hillside, he heard scrapes of movement in the brush and caught a glimpse that made his neck hairs stand on end. He had seen a painted shield of the little people, who stood no higher than his calf. So be it, then. Amid the whippoorwills and singing clouds of gnats, from time to time he heard the *hsst* of a small and deadly stone arrow, aimed at him. Moonlight danced on the foliage of the post oaks and set off sprays of glints in the sandstone. At last he reached the crest of the mesa. As he walked across it, the noise of the town receded. A big fine moon was up. Long pale grass shimmered in the clearings, and he could see wooded ridges half a day's ride away.

Quanah:

OUR SURE ENOUGH FATHER: In the long ago, this here mesa was a place of power. The buffalo wallowed and calved here and bunched up horns against the cold north wind until the grass greened up again, behind me on the plains. People could know the spirits, here on this mesa. You could look out there and see.

That river out yonder, Tock-An-Ho-No, was a magic stream. Clear, sweet river. Banks of red soft sand, and the bluish grass stood high as a horse's withers. Turkeys busted out flying like coveys of quail. Never seen the like of wild horses, along that stream. Catching them was harder work than horses that you stole. Push them back up in the canyons, bound to rope a few. Used to eat the poor ones. Put those heads on a deep bed of coals, listen to the sweet brains hiss and stew.

I rode here. Rode lots of places in my time. Rode so far in Mexico I heard green parrots talk like people and saw monkeys flipping by their hands and tails in trees. Shipped a horse on a train and rode it down a slick brick road in Roosevelt's inauguration parade. Pennsylvania Avenue, he sent me a picture signed. But I belong in the canyonlands and on the plains.

Quanah sang part of a song, one of many that he wrote.

> *Dawn is coming*
> *Sun Eagle, arise*
> *Fog's on the river*
> *Coyote's singing*
> *Beaver, it's dawn*

People, arise
Strike the lodges
Haul the poles
The horses are eager
Blowing cold steam

Daylight, red flower
Dawn I'm bringing
Peyote I'm bringing
It has a power
It moves along

I've got to go back up there and make another speech in that white town Oklahoma City. They're all in council now. First they got the grass, then the land that grows it. Now they're trying to get up a law that takes away our herb. The last power and seeing we have. I got to convince them not to do it. They won't hear unless I give them Jesus.

Lies we got to live with, to go on living at all.

White man gets prayers out of books. Don't even have to think about it. Say it out loud and it does him good. Walk right in that church, sit down, say somebody else's prayer, and get away with it. Our People don't have books. All we've got is what's right here before us. That's all we've got. It's hard for us to pray. Nobody gives us a prayer to say. It's got to come out of our minds. And if it doesn't come out right, it can kick back on you like a mule. You're liable to get your ass torn asunder. Peyote's not easy on you like that Bible is.

For a number of months, Quanah had suffered a series of small strokes. Now, as he pondered his address to the newborn Oklahoma legislature, he had another. The flameouts weren't all that painful.

He seldom even lost his feet. Things went black for a time, and he jabbered as he surfaced from the murk. Later, faint bruises might appear under his jaws. For a few days the left side of his face was frozen and numb.

But facial paralysis was a sure sign of ghost sickness. He'd seen what it did to his father, and he feared the disease like no other. As presence came back to Quanah, he saw the moonlit fingers of the Brazos valley. And in the dark ravine below, people were climbing slowly, looking up, clutching at rocks and branches to keep from falling. They wore suits, high stiff collars, watch fobs, and vests, but none wore hats. The tops of their heads gleamed like plowed fields in a blackland prairie. Terrible enemies, doomed to wander forever on earth. They'd been scalped.

"Here now," someone said. "Let that go. Come sit down. Here. Lean against this rock."

Quanah felt two pairs of hands on him, then the lichened slab. It was a black man, kind they used to call a dirty whiteass, and an Apache woman, both of them handsome still.

"I know you," said Quanah, sorting things out.

"Sure you do," the other replied. "You're already feeling better. You'll be all right. Just sit there and rest. You'll be fine."

Quanah mopped his face with his hand. "Why, you're Bose," he said.

"Sure am. And here's To-ha-yea, it's a miracle, come to see us again."

She walked to Quanah, put her arms around him, and kissed his shirt and chin. His thinking was clearer now but he found his arms were very weak. "Your singing was lovely," she told him. "It always was."

"I sang?"

"Do you recognize this canyon?" said Bose. "Before they built the town?" Quanah thought about it and had to shake his head. "It was the mustang canyon," said Bose, "where you chased me and those others. That first time."

"Bunch of hairbrains," said Quanah. "Now we're old ones, not half as dangerous." The memories stirred up habits of tuibitsi, the young braggart he used to be. "How many children you got, Bose?"

"Fifteen. You?"

"Eighteen."

To-ha-yea, who had no children, gaped at them in amazement. "Just that one wife?" said Quanah.

"None else would have me. And she rues the day."

"I got me seven. This one's Monday, that one's Thursday."

To-ha-yea shook her head and watched them carry on. They were becoming the ancients before her eyes. Then she said, "Look what's happened to the moon."

A cloud was passing over it, turning it brown—except the sky around it held nothing but stars. "It's an eclipse," she said. The moon was filling up the sky, even as it dimmed.

"We saw that once," Quanah recalled. "In that place where I found you, Dog Canyon, above White Sands. Your people knew the sky was trying to put out the moon. Before it even began they went to the foot of a hill, babies, old ones and all, and stood in a circle singing until they made the darkness let the moon go. Your people made me feel like an ignorant man."

But the light of this moon was going out, and the dogs in the town and countryside raised a terrible cry. Far out in the Brazos valley, in all his numbers Brother Coyote chose to speak. The yips, barks, and howls spoke to people of power. It surprised and flattered Quanah that he could still hear. He wished he could share it with these ones who knew him in his prime.

But the message was no good. Quanah foresaw the manner of his passing. The ill would come on him far from his home. He would make himself board the train, endure the ride, and in the language of signs tell his deaf mute driver Dummy to hurry him to his house with white stars on the roof and sleeping porches he had built for each of his wives. So he could go out saying all their good names. Weckeah, Chony, and Tonarcy whom he called Too Nicey, and Coby, To-pay, A-er-wuth-tak-um, Mah-cheet-to-wooky. Ah, but they had no room in Star House or his legacy for the first one. They just called her the Apache. Their keening would scare the daylights out of the grandchildren. White men would come from all around and make speeches. Thanks to the Leopard Coat Man, he would be put down in the fresh earth next to his mother. But not deep enough. Coyotes would dig up his grave and scatter his bones.

Afterword

I GREW UP in country along the Texas side of the Red River that was not peaceably settled until the Comanches and Kiowas gave up their resistance in the 1870s. Nearby small towns named Quanah and Nocona honored our history with the names and steadily percolating lore, but not with statues. One day a friend and I clambered across the eerie Medicine Mounds and explored the bend of the Pease River where the rangers of Sul Ross and Charles Goodnight captured the Comanche woman who turned out to be Cynthia Ann Parker. Another day, in Oklahoma's Wichita Mountains, I watched soldiers at Fort Sill practice rappelling on the black stone face of Medicine Bluff, another place of spiritual importance to the Comanches. In nearby Cache I found Quanah's famed Star House still standing and looking pretty sound. The pasture around it was littered with odd junk of some dormant carnival.

Early on, as this interest began to take form as a book, a friend suggested that I write a biography of Quanah Parker. It seemed like an easier climb to him. I thought about it and decided that even with someone as chronicled and lionized as Quanah, that book would leave me with too much mystery. Quanah's last speech, at the State Fair in Dallas in 1910, was quoted in the press in the condescending herky-jerky Indian dialect of the day. On the battle of the Blanco Canyon: "No ride me in like horse or cow. Had big war. I fought General Mackenzie. He had 2,000 men. I had 450 men. I use this knife. I see little further, perhaps eight miles, lots soldiers coming. I say hold on—no go over there. Maybe we go at night. Maybe stampede soldiers' horses first. I gathered maybe 350 United States horses that night. You see how bad me was at that time?" Who knows, maybe he really spoke English that way. Yet I found letters he wrote to Charles Goodnight and other rancher friends in a big graceful hand, and his phrasing was formal and concise but articulate. His life was torn in two and the world of his birth and rearing was destroyed when he was thirty years old. Only in fiction could I begin to conceive what may have gone on in such a man's mind.

Quanah Parker and Bose Ikard are known to have encountered each other once in a furious running fight between young cowboys and Comanche raiders that occurred in the Palo Pinto country west of Weatherford on April 24, 1869. I found a brief but vivid description of the battle in *History of Parker County and the Double Log Cabin* by G. A. Holland (1937). My fictionalization of that event, in which young Quanah was noted for wearing a blue U.S. Army coat, was the point of departure. These characters are fictional, but their evolution in my imagination and on the page was informed and bolstered by twenty years of research and a lifetime of intense curiosity. My test of historical fiction is what's plausible — I was after what *could* have occurred.

Quanah and Bose were about the same age, and they were in many of the same places at the same times. In history Bose is known for that one Indian fight, in which he rode as a freed slave with his white half-brother, and J. Evetts Haley relayed praise of him in *Charles Goodnight: Cowman and Plainsman* (1936). Larry McMurtry fictionalized him memorably in his 1985 masterpiece, *Lonesome Dove*. Bose was an Indian fighter and drover on cattle drives led by Goodnight and Oliver Loving for three or four years in the late 1860s. After being freed from slavery to his father, he wound up employed as Goodnight's trusted "detective and banker" on the perilous trail they blazed across West Texas and New Mexico Territory. Prospering on a ranch in southern Colorado, the trail boss then told him to go back to the Palo Pinto country and learn how to farm, because there were other black people there. Bose's adventures while making that solitary trek are unknown. He gained a large family and lived in and around Weatherford until 1929. A school there is named for him. Like Quanah, Bose must have developed a unique outlook on life.

Weckeah was one of the first of Quanah's several Comanche wives. She ran away with Quanah and his wild bunch to the Middle Concho River in defiance of her powerful father, who had promised her to another man in observance of tribal tradition, and in exchange for a herd of horses. Very little more is known about her. Quanah's first wife, To-ha-yea, was a Mescalero Apache. On the way back from one of his Mexico travels he gave her father a few mules in tribute, and took her out to his band of nomads on the buffalo plains, where the Comanches' very different way of life made her miserable. After a year or so she went back to her people in New Mexico. Of that woman's life and marriage to Quanah, history yields scarcely more than a name.

For dramatic reasons I compressed and shifted the chronology of some events, such as the time Quanah rode into Mexico to find his uncle John and got stomped and battered by one of his bulls. In the Panhandle-Plains Historical Museum, I learned a great deal from the materials Bill Neely compiled and donated to the museum after writing *The Last Comanche Chief: The Life and Times of Quanah Parker*, first published under another title in 1986. Other vital research and insight can be found in Jo Ella Powell Exley's *Frontier Blood: The Saga of the Parker Family* (2001). A notable short history is Margaret Schmidt Hacker's 1990 *Cynthia Ann Parker: The Life and Legend*. Those historians part company in the continuing dispute of whether the future Texas governor and revered Texas A&M president Sul Ross killed Quanah's father Nocona, or Peta Nocona, in the assault on the Pease River camp. I believe the evidence supports Quanah's contention that while Ross killed another man with a similar name that day, Quanah and his father and brother were away from the camp when Cynthia Ann and her baby Prairie Flower were captured, and that Nocona later died after a day of picking plums in the Canadian River bottom. Coho Smith's tale about an encounter with Cynthia Ann and her Texan cousin was published posthumously in *Cohographs* in 1976. In the Dolph Briscoe Center for American History at the University of Texas, I found John T. Baylor's longing fictional rhapsody for the then-captive Cynthia Ann in a November 1860 issue of his otherwise rabid newspaper *The White Man*. W. S. Nye's *Carbine and Lance: The Story of Old Fort Sill* (1937) is a cavalry captain's riveting, bitter account of the campaign that Colonel Ranald Mackenzie led against the Comanches and their Kiowa and Cheyenne allies. It angered Nye to see Quanah cheered by Texans in a parade.

For an authoritative overview of the Comanche way of life, the best source remains *The Comanches: Lords of the South Plains* by Ernest Wallace and E. Adamson Hoebel (1952). Some of the best writing about their far-flung raiding is in Paul Horgan's *Great River: The Rio Grande in North American History* (1955) and T. R. Fehrenbach's *Comanches: The Destruction of a People* (1974). The Comanches' dialect of Shoshone is now almost extinct. I found some convincing short glossaries from Comanches who lived through the last of the wars, but I stayed close to *Comanche Vocabulary*, first compiled in Spanish in 1866 by a Mexican attorney, politician, and historian named Manuel García Rejón, edited and translated to English by Daniel J. Gelo. On the matter of the shaman Isa-tai's name, some old-timers suggested drolly that history's customary translation, Coyote Droppings, entered the record because white people were skittish about saying the words Wolf Shit. Isa-tai redeemed his reputation after his fiasco at Adobe Walls and was a political rival of Quanah in the reservation years; the men who offered that interpretation may not have been in Isa-tai's camp.

Mildred P. Mayhall's *The Kiowas* (1962), Donald J. Berthrong's *The Southern Cheyennes* (1963), and Morris Edward Opler's *Apache Life-Way* (1941) are sources full of good scholarship and are pleasures to read. Leon G. Metz's *Pat Garrett: The Story of a Western Lawman* (1973) lays out a telling portrait of a rough and violent man in the nearly lawless sprawl of New Mexico Territory. The WPA arts project during the 1930s commissioned writers to interview people who had known Billy the Kid. Reviled as an orphaned "street Arab" in an Arizona mining town, he became a skilled horse and cattle thief and a merciless killer who had a way with women—and was notorious for getting thrown off a horse. *Adobe Walls: The History and Archaeology of the 1874 Trading Post* by T. Lindsay Baker and Billy R. Harrison (1986) contains a fascinating account of the decisive battle between the alliance of plains tribes led by Quanah and the outnumbered but well-armed buffalo hunters who included the young Bat Masterson.

I first learned of Quanah's evangelistic role in the plains tribes' peyote cult and prominence as a ritual songster in the library of the U. S. Department of the Interior in Washington. An excellent source on the ritual and language of the faith is the haunting *Straight with the Medicine: Narratives of Washoe Followers of the Tipi Way*, as told to Warren L. d'Azvedo (1978). Gene Fowler's *Crazy Water* (1990) tells the story of Mineral Wells' heyday as Texas' wackiest health resort. When Quanah was the Comanches' reservation chief, he acted with some cowboy pals in a highly regarded 1908 movie, *A Bank Robbery*, that was directed by a former U. S. deputy marshal and filmed on location near Quanah's home in Cache, Oklahoma.

In this book's long gestation I've been entertained and inspired by many fine novels set on the American frontier and points beyond, among them Thomas Berger's *Little Big Man*, Larry McMurtry's *Lonesome Dove*, Cormac McCarthy's *Blood Meridian* and *All the Pretty Horses*, Pete Dexter's *Deadwood*, E. L. Doctorow's *Welcome to Hard Times*, Bryan Woolley's *Sam Bass*, Elmer Kelton's *The Wolf and the Buffalo*, James Carlos Blake's *In the Rogue Blood*, Ron Hansen's *Desperadoes*, David Marion Wilkinson's *Not Between Brothers* and *Oblivion's Altar*, C. W. Smith's *Buffalo Nickel*, Stephen Harrigan's *The Gates of the Alamo*, Elizabeth Crook's *Promised Lands*, Robert Flynn's *North to Yesterday*, Bud Shrake's *Blessed McGill* and *Borderland*, and John Graves' *The Last Running*.

In addition to friends and colleagues mentioned above and on the dedication page, I want to thank Roy Hamric, James Hoggard, David Lindsey, Jim Hornfischer, Jim Anderson, Kip Stratton, Jesse Sublett, Christopher Cook, Beverly Lowry, Billy Bob Hill, and Gary Cartwright; my TCU Press editors Judy Alter and Susan Petty; and my wife Dorothy Browne, who remarked with a laugh not long ago, "The most exotic book title I've ever seen on my dinner table is *Comanche Vocabulary, The Trilingual Edition.*"

Jan Reid
Austin, Texas
March 2010